RELATIVE

JUSTICE

ALSO BY ROBERT WHITLOW

Trial and Error

A Time to Stand

The Witnesses

A House Divided

The Confession

The Living Room

The Choice

Water's Edge

Mountain Top

Jimmy

The Sacrifice

The Trial

The List

THE CHOSEN PEOPLE NOVELS

Chosen People

Promised Land

THE TIDES OF TRUTH NOVELS

Deeper Water

Higher Hope

Greater Love

THE ALEXIA LINDALE NOVELS

Life Support

Life Everlasting

RELATIVE
JUSTICE

ROBERT
WHITLOW

THOMAS NELSON
Since 1798

Relative Justice

Published in Nashville, Tennessee, by Thomas Nelson. Thomas Nelson is a registered trademark of HarperCollins Christian Publishing, Inc.

Thomas Nelson titles may be purchased in bulk for educational, business, fund-raising, or sales promotional use. For information, please email SpecialMarkets@ThomasNelson.com.

Scripture quotations are taken from the King James Version and the Holy Bible, New International Version®, NIV®. Copyright © 1973, 1978, 1984, 2011 by Biblica, Inc.® Used by permission of Zondervan. All rights reserved worldwide. www.zondervan.com. The "NIV" and "New International Version" are trademarks registered in the United States Patent and Trademark Office by Biblica, Inc.®

Publisher's Note: This novel is a work of fiction. Names, characters, places, and incidents are either products of the author's imagination or used fictitiously. All characters are fictional, and any similarity to people living or dead is purely coincidental.

Library of Congress Cataloging-in-Publication Data

Names: Whitlow, Robert, 1954- author.
Title: Relative justice / Robert Whitlow.
Description: Nashville, Tennessee : Thomas Nelson, [2022] | Summary: "A powerful legal drama novel that explores what happens when in-laws with vastly divergent backgrounds end up practicing law together and find themselves in the midst of a complicated lawsuit against a huge drug manufacturer"-- Provided by publisher.
Identifiers: LCCN 2021055877 (print) | LCCN 2021055878 (ebook) | ISBN 9780785234692 (paperback) | ISBN 9780785234708 (library binding) | ISBN 9780785234715 (epub) | ISBN 9780785234722 (downloadable audio)
Classification: LCC PS3573.H49837 R45 2022 (print) | LCC PS3573.H49837 (ebook) | DDC 813/.54--dc23
LC record available at https://lccn.loc.gov/2021055877
LC ebook record available at https://lccn.loc.gov/2021055878

Printed in the United States of America

22 23 24 25 26 LSC 5 4 3 2 1

To those who are willing to look beneath the surface in the search for truth. Your perseverance will be rewarded.

It is the glory of God to conceal a matter;
to search out a matter is the glory of kings.

Proverbs 25:2 NIV

PROLOGUE

EMERSON CHAPPELLE, PHD, REMOVED HIS GLASSES and rubbed his eyes. He'd been grading papers for the chemistry class he was teaching as an adjunct professor at a local community college. Emerson didn't like teaching. Research was his passion. But money was tight, especially now that his wife had moved out and taken her significant income as a real estate broker with her. Emerson had put off getting a haircut, and his thinning brown hair was careening off in rebellious directions. His thin legs poked out of the shorts he'd been wearing all week, and his new polo shirt was stained with spaghetti sauce. Well-worn brown sandals sat beside the door.

The cell phone resting against the stack of papers on his desk vibrated. When the number popped into view, Emerson's heart started pounding. The phone calls were more frequent, and the voice mails, which began seven days ago, had become threatening. It was mid-August in Durham, North Carolina, and even though the air conditioner for his home office was set at sixty-eight, Emerson broke into a sweat.

"Hello," he said tentatively.

"Where have you been?" the voice demanded. "You were supposed to meet me two days ago in the parking lot for the Kingfisher. I waited over an hour for you to show up."

The Kingfisher was a bar on East Chapel Hill Street. Emerson and the bookie often rendezvoused there but never went inside. The caller was a burly young man in his mid-thirties with dark hair. Emerson knew him as Nick, but he never was sure that was his real name.

"I didn't have the money."

"That's not an answer," Nick replied.

"I know, I know, but there's a problem with the loan. My wife moved out and hired a lawyer who's filed papers in court that froze our home equity line. I'm financially hurting right now."

The phone was silent for a moment. Emerson checked to make sure they were still connected.

"There are other ways to hurt," Nick said.

Emerson swallowed. "There's no need to talk like that. You've made a lot of money on my account. If you give me time, I'll pay you back and lay down a deposit to hold in case I have a loss in the future. I was on a hot streak before this happened."

"And now you owe $278,000."

"Wait. I thought it was $272,000."

"Interest. If you want a lower rate, borrow from a bank."

A high-stakes gambler, Emerson had experienced exhilarating highs and devastating lows. This, however, was the worst situation he'd ever been in.

"What about your retirement account?" Nick continued. "You told me it was worth over half a million."

Emerson bit his lower lip. That, too, had been frozen by his wife's attorney.

"It is," he said. "But after I pay taxes and the penalty due for early withdrawal, that will wipe me out."

"Not my problem."

Emerson glanced at a letter he'd received several days earlier from a major pharmaceutical company. It was the fulfillment of a lifelong dream. His wife knew nothing about the contents.

"I just received an offer from a drug company that wants to license a medication I patented. What if I give you a percentage? When the company sells the new drug, I'll receive royalties. This is going to be huge."

"No way, Doc. You're the gambler, not me. I'll give you a week to cash in the retirement account. If you pay me in full by next Friday, I'll reduce the payoff to $280,000."

"Ask Lance about the drug company deal," Emerson said desperately. "He'll appreciate the opportunity."

"Ask him yourself," the bookie replied. "He's listening to this call."

Lance Tompkins oversaw Emerson's gambling account. Over the past ten years, the chemist had gone through numerous runners and local contacts. Lance, who lived in Houston, remained constant. Emerson suspected the former MMA fighter had links to an organized crime syndicate. He had steadily increased Emerson's credit line, the big advantage of using an illegal bookie over betting through Las Vegas.

The first time Emerson met Lance was at a big bash in Texas for high-stakes clients. Since then, they'd gone fishing in the Bahamas and to a couple of Super Bowls. Their best junket was to the Masters Tournament. Emerson picked the top three finishers in the correct order and parlayed a modest bet into an upper-six-figure recovery. It was the one time he considered cashing in and quitting. But the lure of the next big score was too great. Eighteen months later, he was back in the red.

"Lance, sorry about the delay," Emerson said in a subdued voice. "I got overextended, not that I'm blaming you."

"I totally understand," Lance said in his Texas drawl. "But Nick has a job to do. I have a job to do. We all do. And your job is to get your account level. You and I've gotten along fine for a long time. I'd hate to see it end badly."

"I don't want that to happen."

"Tell me about this drug patent."

Relieved, Emerson switched to teaching mode. "It's a nausea suppressor that works directly on the sympathetic nerves instead of having to—"

"Plain and simple," Lance interrupted.

"It will help people taking chemo from getting sick to their stomachs. I've been interested in that type of problem ever since my mother suffered terribly from nausea when she went through chemotherapy for esophageal cancer."

"There's already a bunch of stuff that does that," Lance replied. "My aunt took something when she had breast cancer. It kept her from throwing up. She said it was a miracle drug."

"But every drug doesn't help all patients. And there can be side effects."

"Yeah, whatever my aunt took made her feel dopey."

"Correct. This one is based on natural compounds and has fewer potential adverse reactions than anything else on the market."

"Natural compounds?"

"It's plant-based. Compare it to penicillin, which came from a plant fungus. But my drug isn't something you can buy at a health-food store. It will only be available with a doctor's prescription. The market for this is huge."

Emerson knew he was exaggerating the economic potential of the antinausea drug, but penicillin was the most well-known comparison that came to mind.

Nick spoke. "Lance, are you sure you want to listen to this? The doc has been dodging me, and this sounds like just another stalling tactic."

"Shut up!" Lance said in a tone of voice that sent a chill down Emerson's spine. "If I wasn't interested, I wouldn't ask. What's the name of the pharmaceutical company?"

"Brigham-Neal. Their home office is in Connecticut."

"Yeah, I've heard of them. Are they offering you any up-front money?"

The letter mentioned $100,000 as consideration for the agreement, but the real return would be paid upon successful marketing of the medication. Emerson was past due on several high-limit credit cards, and he'd earmarked the advance to pay off those debts.

"It's a back-loaded deal. They don't want to risk up-front capital—" Emerson stopped. He was arguing against himself.

"I'm risk-averse too," Lance said. "But you've been a longtime client. Are you the sole owner of the patent?"

"Yes. I don't have any collaborators. I transferred ownership of the rights to a little company I set up to keep everything clean, neat, and confidential."

Emerson had filed the patent in the name of First Flight Research and Development, a corporation he set up to hide his involvement from prying eyes, such as creditors or his soon-to-be ex-wife.

"What's the drug called?"

"Relacan is the trade name the company is going to use. It sounds kind of like 'relief' and 'can.'"

"Has this Relacan gone through all the tests and trials the feds require? I know that can take years."

"Brigham-Neal did that as part of their due diligence. Because the components are known to be safe, it was an expedited process.

Everything came back good, and this week they notified me that they wanted to move forward."

Lance grunted. "Sounds like the real deal."

"Oh, believe me, it is."

"What percentage ownership are you offering me?"

Emerson had brought up the possibility in desperation without thinking it through. "Uh, twenty-five percent in the company that owns the patent."

"Don't insult me," Lance said in the same voice he'd used to shut down Nick.

"How about forty percent?"

"I don't do minority shares in anything," Lance replied crisply. "Because I like you and think this will be a fun deal, I'll take fifty-one percent and leave you with forty-nine percent. Otherwise, Nick will have my full consent to move forward and take any action necessary to collect on your debt."

As Lance spoke, Emerson felt the crushing weight of his life collapsing around him.

"Okay," he said.

"Fifty-one percent," Lance repeated.

"Yes, fifty-one percent."

"My lawyer will be in touch with you. If the paperwork doesn't back up what you're telling me, then we'll have a much shorter, less friendly conversation."

Now Emerson was fearful about being caught in a lie about the advance being paid for the contract.

"I may be able to get a small amount up front to sign the deal," he added.

"You just said that wasn't possible," Lance replied with the sharp edge returning to his voice.

"I'm working on it, but I can't be sure."

"How much are you shooting for?"

"Around $100,000," Emerson sighed.

"An extra $51,000," Lance replied in a more relaxed tone. "That will be a nice down payment."

ONE

IT WAS A COLD, RAINY MORNING IN LATE MARCH. Closing her umbrella that was sprinkled with damp cherry blossoms, Katelyn Martin-Cobb followed Lynwood Bancroft and Suzanne Nixon into the US District Courthouse for the District of Columbia. Wearing a gray suit, white blouse, and black shoes with medium heels, Katelyn ran her fingers through her short, dark hair. Petite at five feet three inches tall, she was physically fit from years of outdoor activity that included hiking, swimming, and skiing. She still loved the outdoors, but getting a chance to enjoy it was tougher given she usually worked sixty to seventy hours a week at the law firm.

The E. Barrett Prettyman building on Constitution Avenue in Washington, DC, was named in honor of a former federal appellate judge appointed by President Harry Truman. A muscular security guard with a military crew cut addressed the group of five lawyers and two paralegals.

"You'll need to leave your umbrellas over there," the young man said as he pointed to a row of round brass urns.

The guard's instructions were unnecessary. The litigation team from Morgan and Monroe knew the drill. The courthouse was like a second home. Katelyn placed her black umbrella beside the aqua-blue one used by Suzanne Nixon. A special order from the trial judge allowed the lawyers to bring their cell phones into the court-house as long as they didn't record or video any of the proceedings.

Katelyn owned twelve conservative courtroom outfits and kept up with when she wore each one on a spreadsheet. The blue, gray, and black ensembles were her litigation armor.

LASIK surgery had enabled her to stop wearing contact lenses, and her brown eyes missed nothing. It was Katelyn's ability to spot important details and remember what she'd seen and read that convinced Suzanne to bring the twenty-nine-year-old associate into the senior partner's inner circle at the law firm. Otherwise, Katelyn would still be spending most of her days in front of a computer monitor, crunching out thirty-page legal memos. If Mr. Bancroft had his way, that's exactly what she'd be doing. Large law firms weren't homogeneous kingdoms. They consisted of many fiefdoms.

Katelyn returned her Virginia driver's license to her purse after showing it to a security guard. She'd had a sense all morning that this might be the day when the lawyers would find out if the $32 million their client had spent litigating the case over the past three years would turn out to be a good investment. According to an expert who'd testified at the trial, every commercial airplane and private jet manufactured for the next ten to fifteen years would incorporate navigational components based on the disputed patent. The projected revenue for Morgan and Monroe's client over the life of the patent would be at least $2 billion.

Inside the courtroom, the lawyers and paralegals took out their laptops and powered up. The boxes of evidence and stacks of exhibits presented by both sides of the case were in the jury room where the group of seven women and five men had been deliberating for three days. While the attorneys waited, they had nothing to do. There had been halfhearted settlement discussions after the jury retired to begin their discussion of the evidence, but both sides believed victory was at hand, and their positions were hardened by the lengthy battle.

The corporate representative for Katelyn's client was a distinguished-looking older gentleman who was a mid-tier manager, not a top executive. He was there more for show than substance and didn't have the authority to make a decision. It didn't matter. Now, as they waited for the jury, the top lawyers from both firms passed the time talking about vacation homes and upcoming trips to Europe, Africa, and Asia. Katelyn and her husband, Robbie, were still paying off student loan debt and usually went to the beach near Wilmington, North Carolina, where Robbie's family lived, or to the mountains of Vermont where Katelyn grew up.

This morning, Katelyn heard Mr. Bancroft and Mr. Stanfield greet each other and begin discussing the pluses and minuses of sixty- versus eighty-foot yachts. Apparently, the eighty-foot length was a booming category. Sitting beside each other, they pulled up yacht photos on their laptops.

Katelyn glanced across the courtroom at Phoebe Jacobs, a lawyer on the other side of the case. Phoebe was a five-year associate attorney who was now eight and a half months pregnant. Even though they were on opposite sides of the lawsuit, Katelyn and Phoebe had developed a friendship. The two women didn't talk about yachts or exotic vacations. Instead, they focused on Phoebe's life as a mother with a three-year-old daughter and a son on the way. After four years of marriage, Katelyn and Robbie had begun seriously discussing starting a family.

"You just have to go for it," Phoebe told her during lunch a couple of weeks earlier.

"How do you handle your workload at the firm?"

"With a thick skin." Phoebe patted her growing abdomen. "I'm not afraid to use my sick days, and we hired a live-in nanny to avoid the germs Aaron would pick up at day care. I work hard at the office so I can afford the nanny and unplug when I walk out the door to go home."

The idea of a live-in nanny was a stretch for Katelyn, who'd always been a do-it-yourself person.

"What's it like at your firm for female attorneys with kids?" she asked. "Most of the ones who stay at ours end up off the partnership track and become permanent associates."

"It's the same with us. Tell me about Suzanne Nixon. I saw a big diamond on her ring finger. Does she have kids? I assume they're older by now."

"She had a lot of help from nannies and private schools. She has a daughter in college at Brown and a teenage son who goes to a prep school in Virginia. She's on her third husband."

"Except for going through multiple husbands, becoming a partner is what I'm aiming for," Phoebe replied. "But if the partnership track doesn't work out, we're committed to our children. My father was CEO of a small company in Upstate New York. He was very successful in business but left raising my siblings and me to my mother. We even took vacations without him. Philip and I aren't going to make that mistake."

"My father abandoned my mother and me and moved with his girlfriend to Oregon," Katelyn said. "After that, he never sent a birthday card, gifts at Christmas, anything."

"How old were you when he took off?"

"Eight."

"Your mother must be a remarkable woman."

"Yes." Katelyn hesitated. "She died in an auto accident when I was a senior in college. Hit by a drunk driver. My world collapsed."

Phoebe stared at Katelyn for a few seconds as her eyes filled with tears. Katelyn's reservoir of tears had filled and emptied many times during the seven years since she'd received the call from the police about the fatal accident. Today, the tank was dry. Phoebe took out a tissue and touched her eyes.

"That's terrible. Looking at a person, you can't tell what they've been through. How did you make it?"

"Threw myself into college and then law school. I've had my moments, but I kept pressing on. That's what she taught me to do."

"I'll bet your mom would be proud of you now."

"I hope so. She knew I wanted to go to law school."

Phoebe took a drink of water. "Did your mother get to meet your husband?"

"No, but his mom died around the same time as mine from breast cancer. Robbie and I met at a ski resort in Vermont during my third year of law school. He was a ski instructor."

"And gave you a lesson?"

"No, I've been on skis since I was little," Katelyn said and smiled. "He was teaching a beginners' class. Robbie has always liked kids and I'm sure he'll be all in with children. If we can't afford a nanny, he told me that he'd adjust his career so I would be able to keep my job."

"That's cool. What does he do?"

"He's a case manager for a nonprofit that places troubled teens in alternate living situations. Basically, they get them off the streets."

13

Phoebe stopped eating. "Aaron just gave me a big kick," she said. "That's his way of saying you're going to be a good mom."

———

Katelyn looked across the courtroom and saw Phoebe shifting uncomfortably in her chair. They made eye contact. Phoebe pointed to her stomach and counted from three to zero with her fingers, then made a motion of rocking a baby in her arms. Baby arrival imminent. Katelyn smiled and silently clapped her hands. She'd already bought a baby gift. A few minutes later, Phoebe left the courtroom. Judge Belhaven entered and everyone rose to their feet.

"Be seated," the judge said and cleared his throat. "The jury has reached a verdict. If both sides are ready, I'll ask the bailiff to bring them in."

"Yes, Your Honor," Mr. Bancroft and Mr. Stanfield both replied.

Katelyn's heart started pounding. She glanced at Suzanne. The litigator was staring ahead with a steely look in her eyes.

———

The law firm of Cobb and Cobb, Attorneys at Law, occupied the main floor of a hundred-year-old house two blocks from the New Hanover County Courthouse. David Cobb, the junior partner, leaned back in his chair. Slightly under six feet tall, David weighed only ten pounds more than when he was offered a baseball scholarship to Wake Forest. A third baseman, he relished the opportunity to snag balls that screamed down the foul line from home plate. Early in his freshman season, though, he ripped apart several tendons and ligaments in his right shoulder in a collision at second base, ending his athletic career.

David's dark brown hair was neatly trimmed, and he was wearing gray slacks, a white shirt, and a yellow tie. Carter Cobb, his father, always wore a suit and a tie to work. David did so only when meeting with a client or on the rare occasions when he went to court. The two men shared similar facial features, including brown eyes and a square chin. The main differences were Carter's size, as he was a robust six feet three inches tall, and in contrast to David's calm communication and reserved style, Carter had a booming voice and oversized personality to match. The elder Carter handled almost all litigation and was the primary business generator for the law firm he'd started almost forty years earlier.

The walnut desk in David's office had been passed down from his great-grandfather Cobb, who was a cotton and rice merchant, and the desk had survived from his ancestor's era. In the early 1900s, the Cobb family fortunes collapsed along with the prices of rice and cotton.

There was a knock on David's door, and his father entered. Sixty-three years old, Carter had made a remarkable recovery from a serious heart attack that struck him down five years earlier. His brown hair was making the transition to white.

"Lunch?" Carter asked. "It's chicken casserole day at Lupie's."

David checked the calendar on his computer screen. "I have to be back at one thirty for a meeting with the Jordan family."

"Don't tell them where you ate lunch."

The two Jordan brothers and their sister owned a competing restaurant where David and his father often ate.

"You drive," Carter said as they stepped across the porch and down three steps.

David's car was a four-year-old Audi that he'd bought from one of their clients who owned a dealership. It was a ten-minute drive to the restaurant located in a concrete-block building with a large mural of an underwater seascape spray-painted on one side of the structure. A slender, brown-haired waitress named Lindsay, whose sassy personality they were familiar with, pointed to an open table. She knew what they wanted to drink and soon reappeared with a sweet tea with three lemons on the edge of the glass for Carter and unsweet tea for David.

"The usual?" Lindsay asked David.

"Yep."

David always ordered the chicken casserole special with a bowl of Italian vegetable soup and corn bread.

"What about you, sweetie?" she asked Carter.

"Casserole, carrots, and green peas."

David and his father often ran into someone they knew at the restaurant. Today, though, it was a roomful of strangers.

"Zeke Caldwell called me this morning," Carter said after the waitress left. "Do you remember when I helped him get a drug patent for one of his home remedies?"

"Yes. I considered calling our malpractice insurance company to let them know a claim might be coming their way."

"Hey, it worked."

"True." David smiled. "It was an impressive piece of legal work. Does he have another one?"

"No, but he thinks someone has infringed the patent we filed. When he comes in, I want you to meet with him too."

"Why me?"

"You have a better eye for detail than I do. And it's been a shorter time since you took chemistry in high school."

David laughed. "I think the statute of limitations has run out on any expertise either of us had with chemical compounds, but I'll be glad to join the meeting. I've liked Zeke ever since he spoke to us at Camp Seacrest. Anyone who can hold the attention of ten- to fourteen-year-old boys has skills."

"Recently, he's been selling so much stuff at craft fairs and out of the back of his truck that he's cutting back on his hours at work."

"Is he still at Hester's Pharmacy?"

"Yep. Maybe Ralph Hester can keep going until both Ralph and Zeke retire."

The locally owned drugstore had managed to stay in business due to intense client loyalty and a delivery service. Zeke worked as a pharmacy assistant and delivered medications.

The waitress arrived with their food. David bowed his head. Carter prayed. Out loud. Even without peeking, David knew customers three or four tables over would look in their direction.

"And all God's people said, 'Amen!'" Carter finished with enthusiasm.

"Amen!" said a man at a nearby table.

The voice of agreement was from a man in his fifties wearing jeans and a faded T-shirt. He grinned and pointed skyward with his right index finger.

"Feels like church to me," he said to Carter.

"Because church happens whenever and wherever God's people show up," Carter replied. "It's not limited to Sunday morning."

David didn't mind his father's boldness. It was who he was. They started eating.

"I talked to Robbie early this morning too," Carter said after a few moments passed. "This time, I believe he's really made the turn toward the Lord."

Younger than David by four years, Robbie grew up with a mischievous streak that in his late teens turned into open rebellion. His personal life and faith crashed and burned after two years of college at the local branch of UNC in Wilmington. Taking off in a pickup truck, Robbie roamed the country for several years, working mostly as a fishing and hunting guide with spells of unemployment when he drank too much. Part of the time he lived in the back of the truck. Eventually, he settled down and returned to school at a community college in New Hampshire where he earned a degree in social work. When he met Katelyn Martin, news of their engagement sent shock waves through the rest of the Cobb family. So far, the marriage had lasted. David respected his sister-in-law as a very smart attorney who practiced law in a stratosphere far beyond anything David and his father knew. But what Katelyn saw in his brother remained a bit of a mystery. The family got together only a couple of times a year.

"I don't want to react like the older brother in the prodigal son story," David replied. "But Robbie's had spiritual spasms before."

"You're right. But I think it would be good for you to reach out to him."

"I can do that."

"And I think it would be great for all of us to spend more time together."

Puzzled, David asked, "What are you talking about?"

"To cross-pollinate. Especially to encourage Robbie and Katelyn."

"Okay," David responded slowly. "Is Katelyn positive about the changes in Robbie? She's never seemed interested in faith. They never go to church with us when they visit."

"I'm not sure what he's told her, or what she thinks. And he didn't ask me to bring this up with you. It's my idea, but I think it's a good one. I'm going to invite them to come and stay longer than a weekend."

David shrugged. "Fine with me."

Carter placed his fork beside his plate. "And we need to tell

Robbie that we forgive him for what happened with the boatbuilding business."

During his prodigal years, Robbie had started building fiberglass float boats to sell to river fishing guides. Carter and David each lost $40,000 backing the venture in hopes it would succeed and help Robbie settle down.

"I haven't asked him for that money in years."

"But you've never released him from the debt."

"For all practical purposes, I have. And $40,000 is a lot of money."

"So is $80,000."

David looked at his father with wide eyes. "You loaned him $80,000?"

"Yeah. Not all of it for the boat business."

David shook his head. "Wouldn't it be right for him to pay some of it back now that both he and Katelyn are working? I know he had some student loan debt, and there's no telling how much she borrowed to go to Cornell Law School. But they've both been working steadily for several years, and they're able to pay the rent on a nice townhome in Arlington."

"Just pray about it," Carter said. "That's been on my heart for a while, and I wanted to talk to you about it."

"Yes, sir," David said. "The son who stayed at home obeyed his father."

"And when I move on, you're going to step into my shoes and go places with the Lord I've never seen. You have a gift of helping people in trouble that goes beyond the practice of law. And you'll be better glue to hold this family together than I've ever been."

"Don't talk like that," David replied. "Eat your peas."

TWO

KATELYN WATCHED THE JURORS FILE INTO THE COURT-
room. Their faces revealed nothing.

"It's my understanding that you've reached a verdict," Judge
Belhaven said.

A middle-aged woman on the front row stood. A former high
school teacher, she'd been Katelyn's pick as the most likely fore-
person of the jury. Both Suzanne and Mr. Bancroft predicted an
executive with an investment banking firm would be the foreman.
They were wrong. Katelyn zeroed in on the teacher because of the
way the other jurors interacted with her during breaks in the proceedings. And the woman took notes.

"We have," the woman said.

"Have you answered all the questions given to you?"

"Yes, sir."

The forewoman handed the verdict form to the bailiff. Katelyn
had been part of a team of three lawyers who billed over two hundred hours formulating the thirty-seven questions given to the jury.
The bailiff transferred the verdict to the judge. All the attorneys for
both sides stood in expectant attention. Few things in life rivaled
the drama of waiting to hear a verdict.

It took Judge Belhaven several minutes to silently read the responses to the questions before announcing them in open court. His face remained inscrutable. The wait was excruciating. Finally, the judge began to read. The jury's response to the first, nontechnical question would chart the course for what followed.

"We find by a preponderance of the evidence that the defendant has infringed plaintiff's patent," the judge read.

In major corporate litigation, outbursts of emotion in the courtroom are rare. Judges frown on spontaneous reactions and professional decorum prevails. Katelyn stole a glance at Suzanne, but her face remained emotionless as stone. As the judge moved through the verdict, it became increasingly clear that Morgan and Monroe's client would be the only company able to offer the new technology. They'd won the future. The big issue left was the amount of damages owed for the defendant's violations of the patent in the past.

"We find that as a result of defendant's actions, plaintiff is entitled to compensation of $222 million."

Katelyn stifled a gasp. Privately, the litigation group had told their client that an award of $100 million would be a win. The main return on investment would be in the future sales. Again, Katelyn glanced at Suzanne. This time, the senior partner didn't try to stifle a satisfied smile. The faces of the other attorneys across the aisle revealed shock. The judge kept reading.

"We find that plaintiff is not entitled to any punitive damages."

This wasn't a surprise. The evidence of egregious conduct necessary to support a punitive damage award was weak.

The judge finished and turned to the jury. "Is that the decision of the jury?"

"Yes, it is," the woman replied.

The judge thanked the jurors and dismissed them. The court-room cleared.

"Any postverdict arguments?" the judge asked.

A middle-aged attorney for the defendant, whose job was to object to an adverse verdict, began to speak. A junior partner who worked closely with Mr. Bancroft had been assigned to handle the response by Morgan and Monroe. Later, there would be a posttrial motion to reduce the verdict and a notice of appeal. Katelyn made notes on her laptop. She would be called on to research some of the issues raised. An hour later when they left the courtroom, Phoebe was still absent. As the contingent from Morgan and Monroe exited, Katelyn stayed behind and approached a paralegal who worked with Phoebe.

"I was wondering about Phoebe," Katelyn began in a low voice. "I saw her walk out before the judge read the verdict, and she didn't return. Is she okay?"

"Oh, she was having contractions. They started right before we arrived at the courthouse and were getting stronger and closer together."

Katelyn caught up with the Morgan and Monroe group that was buzzing with excitement.

"Great result," Katelyn said to Suzanne as soon as they were in the hallway.

"In every way," Suzanne replied with a grin. "Come see me this afternoon after I return to the office."

The sun was peeking through the clouds when they stepped outside. Mr. Bancroft announced there would be a celebration after work for everyone who worked on the case. As soon as Katelyn was alone in her car, she called Robbie and told him about the verdict.

"That's awesome," he replied. "I knew you were awake for a

while during the night, tossing and turning, but I didn't want to say anything because I thought I might make it worse."

"Oh, that had to do with another case. I've been working so much on the trial that I was worried I'd overlooked something in a memo I sent Suzanne last week. I checked on it before I came to the courthouse, and everything was okay."

"Are you taking the rest of the day off?"

"No, Suzanne wants to talk to me this afternoon. You know her. She's always moving on to the next project."

"Will the firm do something to celebrate the verdict?"

"Mr. Bancroft said there will be cocktails and hors d'oeuvres late this afternoon off-site."

"Are you going?"

"Of course. I worked over two thousand hours on this case."

"What about us celebrating on our own?"

Katelyn paid to exit the parking garage.

"I hadn't thought about that," she said. "Do you mean tonight?"

"Or any other time you can fit on your calendar."

The high number of hours Katelyn had to work was a constant source of tension. Robbie understood, but that didn't mean it wasn't a strain on both of them.

"No, I'd like to do something with you. I just have to put in an appearance at the firm event, then I can slip out."

"We've been talking about trying that new seafood place on the river."

"I'd love that. I'll call you as soon as I get away."

Katelyn wove her way through traffic. In her mind, she was already transitioning to the posttrial issues the firm would have to address. Ever since graduating in the top ten percent of her law school class, Katelyn had wanted to work in a world with the highest level of intellectual stimulation. Morgan and Monroe was that place. She was being trained by some of the top legal minds in the country, and as Suzanne Nixon's protégée, she'd linked her career to a powerful mentor who could potentially propel her upward through the law firm hierarchy. Katelyn had already jumped over lawyers who'd been at the firm longer and attended law school at Harvard or Yale. The only thing missing was the chance to be in charge of cases. Katelyn always felt like a cog. Someone else operated the controls.

She pulled into her reserved space on the parking deck for the law firm. The fact that Katelyn had a specific space was a sign of validation by the management team. She'd been shocked when she received the news. She maneuvered her small, imported sedan between a Jaguar and a Mercedes. Robbie, who needed a vehicle for hauling camping and hiking gear, still drove an older-model gray pickup truck he bought shortly before their marriage. He preferred spending money to fix the old truck to buying a new one.

There was a glass-covered walkway between the parking deck and the office building. Ahead of her, Katelyn saw Franklin Deming, one of the law firm's best paralegals. The lanky young Black man with dark-rimmed glasses waited for her.

"Did you hear about the verdict?" she asked.

"No," he said. "But from the look on your face, it was good."

"Very."

She summarized what happened as they made their way into the building. Morgan and Monroe occupied two floors. There were twice as many lawyers at the headquarters in New York City, and a roughly equal number spread across Washington, Chicago, Atlanta, and L.A. Smaller branches existed in several foreign countries.

"Do you think the verdict will hold up?" Franklin asked.

"It should, given the deference Judge Belhaven gave the other side in drafting the questions for the jury. It would have been better for them posttrial and on appeal if the judge had leaned our way."

"Now that it's over, maybe we'll end up working together."

"That will be up to Suzanne."

"Yeah, she's the queen bee."

"And we're the worker bees."

The phone on David's desk buzzed.

"The Jordan family is here for their appointment," said Candy Palmer, the young receptionist. "They know they're fifteen minutes early. And Zeke Caldwell called again about scheduling an appointment."

"My father couldn't talk to him?"

"No, he's on a long conference call with Marvin Stancill."

"Okay, we're both going to meet with Zeke. I'll call him later."

David reached for the Jordan corporate file that lay on the credenza behind him. The family pronounced their last name as if the "o" were a "u." The purpose of the meeting was to discuss who would take over the family business now that their father, who started the restaurant, had passed away.

Bruce Jordan was sitting several chairs away from his brother, Morris, and his sister, Fran, who had their heads close together as they talked quietly. All three of them stood when David entered and shook Bruce's hand.

"How's your dad doing?" asked Bruce. "I've not seen him at the restaurant recently."

"Busy, but we were in a couple of weeks ago for lunch."

"I saw them," Fran said, cutting her eyes toward her older brother. "You probably weren't working that day."

"Come back to the office," David said.

There were three side chairs in front of David's desk. He preferred meeting in his office if possible. Bruce scooted his chair farther away from his siblings'.

"I reviewed the notes when you contacted me last year after your father's death," David said when he was behind his desk. "It looks straightforward. Each of you would own a one-third interest in the restaurant."

"No," Bruce said before anyone else could speak. "That's not going to work."

"And whose fault is that?" Fran asked sharply.

"I'm looking at her," Bruce retorted.

Fran picked up her purse and pulled out a small, ragged-looking notepad that she held up in front of her.

"And I'm ready to answer that question," she said. "Since January, I've recorded every day you showed up late or didn't come in at all. And the times you came in and caused a problem with the employees, I've written that down too."

While Fran talked, David glanced at Morris, who was the quietest member of the trio.

"Did you list the employees who've quit because you worked them so hard that you ran them off?" Bruce shot back. "And if you'd had a knee replacement and surgery on your elbow in the past nine months, you'd have missed more days than I did. There's no use in me being there if I can't contribute."

"Contribute?" Fran scoffed. "I didn't run anybody off who wanted to do an honest day's work. You cause way more problems playing favorites than Morris and I do. We treat everyone fairly."

"What about Kenny Robinson?" Bruce replied. "Want to tell David why he's no longer baking the best biscuits in the county for us and went down the street to work for John Holcomb?"

Fran's face grew red, and she took a deep breath.

"Hold on," David said, raising his hand. "Can we hit the pause button for a minute?"

"You need to know the truth!" Fran exclaimed.

"He sure won't get it from you," Bruce shot back.

"Okay, one at a time," David said. "Everyone will get a chance."

David leaned back in his chair and waited. Both Bruce and Fran started to speak but then stopped in midsentence as they talked over each other. They made a second effort with the same result.

"Go ahead," Bruce said to his sister. "I'll wait my turn."

"No, you first. I'll need to straighten out your lies."

David winced at the older sibling's choice of words. As he continued to listen, the acrimony was worse than he could have imagined. Finally, Bruce and Fran were silent and sat back in their chairs.

"Go ahead," Bruce said gruffly to Morris.

"No," the youngest sibling said and shook his head. "I have nothing to add. I want to hear what David has to say."

Morris's words hung in the air for a moment. Looking at the Jordan family, David felt a deep compassion for them well up inside. Along with compassion, a tiny seed of an idea emerged. Instantly, the idea was challenged by fear. He waited a few seconds longer before speaking. David was about to step out of the boat of his comfort level onto waters of uncertainty.

"You've been through a lot together," he said, clearing his throat. "And learned a lot about getting along when you were kids."

David knew his words made no sense.

"I don't know what you're talking about," Bruce said. "What does anything that happened when we were kids have to do with us now?"

David held up his cell phone. "This morning I was reading Proverbs 22:6: 'Train up a child in the way he should go: and when he is old, he will not depart from it.' I thought about that verse in relation to my own two children. But listening to you, I wanted to share it with you now . . ." His voice trailed off.

Then Fran made a sniffling noise. David turned toward her. Fran Jordan had never struck him as the kind of woman who would easily cry.

"I know exactly what you're talking about," she said. "Driving down here, I was thinking about how Mama used to make us stand in front of her in the kitchen when we'd get in a nasty fuss. Remember? She wouldn't let us move until we told her the truth about what happened and admit how we were wrong."

David's heart beat a little bit faster.

"Yeah, Mama was a foot-washing Baptist," Bruce said. "One of her favorite sayings was, 'If you ain't humble, you ain't right.'"

"I haven't thought about that in a long time," Morris added. "She sure tried to train us in the way we should go. That verse could have been put on her gravestone."

"Mama's gone," Fran said, taking a tissue from her purse.

And in that moment, David knew exactly what to say next. "But she still lives in each one of you."

THREE

FOR THE NEXT HOUR, DAVID WAS MORE SPECTATOR than participant. Fran took the lead, perhaps because as a woman she was more in touch with her mother's legacy than her brothers. She addressed Bruce and confessed that she had judged him in her heart, spoken negatively about him to other people in and outside the family, and expended her energy on what was wrong with him, ignoring what was right. Several times he tried to stop her, but Fran was strong-willed in every aspect of her character.

"No," she said when he attempted to interrupt. "I don't want it to stop until I'm cleaned out."

When Fran brought up some harsh words that she'd spoken at a family gathering shortly after Bruce's marriage, her brother wiped away a tear.

"Please, just a second," he said, holding up his meaty right hand. Fran stopped.

"May I tell Lisa about that? It will mean the world to her."

"I should do it," Fran answered.

"Not until she's had a chance to work it out with me."

"Okay."

When Fran finally reached a stopping point, Bruce responded.

He wasn't as eloquent as his sister, but the large man's words were like blows from a sledgehammer that broke down walls of offense and unforgiveness.

"I think your mama would be proud of you," David said when Bruce finally finished speaking.

"It's like what she put in us all those years ago suddenly came to life," Fran said. "She never let us off the hook until she got to the root of the problem."

They sat in silence for a few moments. David was waiting for Morris to take a turn, but the youngest member of the family remained quiet.

"Morris, do you want to say anything?" David asked.

"Oh, he's always tried to be the peacemaker," Bruce said before his brother could speak. "And we all know he's been praying for us. If it wasn't for Morris, we'd have blown up the family years ago."

"Is that right?" David asked.

"Pretty much," Morris replied modestly. "But there are a few things I need to say."

Morris confessed how he'd contributed to disunity in the family, but he also brought up times they'd hurt him. The fact that they'd wounded their younger brother affected both Fran and Bruce. To them, Morris would always be the baby brother they were supposed to look after.

"I'm sorry," Bruce said. "About all of that."

"Me too," Fran added. "I was way out of line in that situation with Liz. I'll speak to her too."

They sat quietly for a moment. The atmosphere in the room seemed lighter and fresher to David.

"What do you think needs to happen now?" he asked.

"We've confessed," Morris said. "Now we need to forgive one another and pray. Mama always made us do it from the heart."

"And there was no fooling her," Fran said. "She knew if we were faking."

"Would it be okay if I prayed first?" Morris asked David. "Then we can ask for forgiveness."

"Of course. It's pretty clear that I'm not in charge of this meeting."

They bowed their heads, and Morris offered a short prayer asking God to heal their relationships. The siblings then stood in a circle, asked one another for forgiveness, and granted it in return. Any remaining emotional reserve in the room evaporated. Tears ran down David's cheeks as he watched the Jordan family hug one another. Still sniffling, they resumed their seats.

"This is one of the best things that's ever happened in my law practice," David said, wiping his eyes with a tissue. "Thank you for letting me be a part of it."

"Go ahead with the paperwork making us equal partners in the business," Bruce said.

"Yes," Fran and Morris said and nodded in unison.

"And maybe we could come in to see you in a month or so for a checkup," Morris added.

"Checkup?" David asked.

"To help us stay on track," Morris replied.

"He's right," Fran said. "Knowing we have to come back to see you will help me. I need accountability."

"I'm a lawyer, not a preacher," David protested.

"Which means you should charge us for every minute of your time today," Fran said. "You can't put a price on what's happened here. And you're getting a free slice of pecan pie next time you come to the restaurant."

"I love the pecan pie, but the coconut cream is my favorite," David replied with a smile.

"You're getting a slice of each," Bruce said.

"Would you mind if I shared what the Lord did for you with my wife? She prays that I'll be more of a counselor at law and less of an attorney at law."

The Jordans all nodded.

"Thanks," David said. "Anything else?"

"No," Morris answered. "This turned out much different and way better than I expected."

Everyone stood. Bruce spoke.

"Oh, I guess you heard Chris Brammer resigned as head of Camp Seacrest," he said. "That's a sad situation."

The boys' camp near the mouth of the Cape Fear River offered ocean-based summer programs for boys between the ages of eight and fourteen. Founded by a group of local men who served in the Navy in World War II, the nonprofit camp hosted more than two hundred boys every summer during two- to four-week terms. Both David and Robbie attended multiple years and then served as counselors when they aged out of the youth programs.

"No," David replied in surprise.

"I thought your father would be in the know," Bruce said.

"He rotated off the board of directors last year. It's the first time in over ten years neither one of us is serving."

"Roger Wiggins mentioned it to me earlier today at the restaurant," Bruce said.

The Wiggins family were generous financial supporters of the camp.

"Did he tell you why?" David asked. "I thought Chris was doing a good job. Applications had been up, and the programs were the best I've seen in years. Day camp participation has been setting records."

"Maybe we shouldn't mention anything else," Morris said, cutting his eyes toward his brother. "We don't know the truth."

"You talked to Roger too?" David asked.

"Bruce and I stopped by the table to say hey. It had been a while since he'd come in to eat. Maybe you should call Roger yourself."

"I will," David replied.

"Thanks again for all you did today," Fran said, shaking David's hand.

David escorted them to the reception area. As they left, Bruce held the door open for Fran and Morris. It was a beautiful sight. He turned to Candy.

"The Jordans looked a lot happier when they left than they did when they got here," she said.

"It went well," David replied. "Very well. Is my dad busy?"

Candy glanced down at the phone. "He's on the phone with Marie Hampton. That woman can talk the paint off a wall."

"I had to deal with her when he was on vacation last month. Let me know when he's finished. I need to talk to him about Zeke Caldwell and Camp Seacrest."

———

Katelyn arrived for her meeting with Suzanne Nixon.

"You'll need to wait a minute," said Lisa Carver, the senior partner's administrative assistant. "She's meeting with Valerie Pinson."

"I didn't know Valerie was in town."

"Just arrived an hour ago."

After a career as an attorney with the Justice Department, Valerie Pinson left government service and joined the Chicago office of Morgan and Monroe. Ten years later, the Black woman was a member of the firm's executive committee. Katelyn had met her briefly on several occasions.

"Should I come back later? I have some work I need to finish."

"No, Suzanne told me to keep your appointment on her calendar."

While she waited, Katelyn fidgeted. She'd returned from the courthouse to an unexpected project that had to be completed before the end of the day. Combined with putting in an appearance at the victory celebration and meeting Robbie for dinner, her schedule was going to be tight.

Finally, Lisa picked up her phone and turned to Katelyn. "Go in. They'll see you now."

"Both of them?" Katelyn asked in surprise.

"Yes."

Katelyn entered the gleaming office decorated with modern art. The two lawyers were seated at a small, round table across the room from Suzanne's desk. Valerie Pinson was several years older than Suzanne and much more conservative in her wardrobe. She was wearing a dark blue skirt and a white blouse. Her dark hair was sprinkled with gray. She extended her hand to Katelyn.

"Good afternoon," Valerie said in a voice that reflected her Dallas roots. "Congratulations on the part you played in the verdict this morning."

"It was a great win for the firm," Katelyn replied.

"I've been keeping Valerie up-to-date on all your work," Suzanne said. "She's here for a couple of days, and when the jury returned a verdict this morning, we decided to hold a meeting with you today rather than tomorrow."

The fact that the encounter with the two powerful women was prearranged sent Katelyn's mind spinning.

"Yes," Valerie said, picking up the conversation. "The executive committee met a few weeks ago, and one item on the agenda was your future with the firm. You're on a strong partnership track, and we want to best prepare you for what's ahead."

"Which should be good for both you and the firm," Suzanne added. "There's nothing I enjoy more than mentoring a young woman like you and helping her succeed, but it also means I can't hold on too tight. When Valerie contacted me, I was both happy and sad. But mostly proud."

Katelyn wasn't used to this kind of unqualified praise from Suzanne, who held everyone around her to such a high level of perfection that most cracked under the pressure.

"We want to offer you a position at the Chicago office," Valerie said. "You'll be part of my group. The litigation emphasis would be different than here because you would oversee the matters assigned to you. The cases wouldn't be large at first, but it would give you the opportunity to hone your management skills. Everyone on the team would report to you."

Katelyn was stunned. This was one of her goals. But she'd thought its realization was at least two or three years in the future. Driving the car, even if it had a small engine, would be a huge paradigm shift.

"Wow," she managed, then quickly realized how unprofessional it sounded. "I mean, I appreciate the opportunity."

Valerie handed her an envelope. "Inside are details of the changes in compensation associated with the move. I think you'll find the increase significant. All moving expenses will be covered, along with a three-month stipend for temporary housing until you find a permanent place to live. If you find someplace to live quickly, the stipend will convert to bonus salary."

"I told Valerie about Robbie's interest in working with youth,"

Suzanne said. "There should be no shortage of jobs for someone with his interests and skills in Chicago."

As she listened, Katelyn looked at Suzanne and realized how much she appreciated and respected the senior partner.

"Suzanne, you've been more than I ever could have hoped for as a mentor. I don't know how to—"

"No," Suzanne said and held up her hand. "You can save that speech. Also, I don't want to get emotional."

"And I won't attempt to fill Suzanne's shoes," Valerie said. "A few years from now the three of us can get together and celebrate what's taken place today. We'd like to have you up and running in the Chicago office within sixty days."

"You'll love it there," Suzanne added. "I spent four of my favorite years with the firm in Chicago."

"Thank you," Katelyn managed. "To both of you."

"See you later for cocktails," Valerie said.

Returning to her office, Katelyn opened the envelope. The increase in salary broke the glass ceiling in associate attorney's pay. Firms like Morgan and Monroe lured top students with generous first-year salaries, but pay raises thereafter were meager for five or six years. Everyone knew that was how the system worked. Suzanne had funneled above-average bonuses to Katelyn, but the move to Chicago would increase Katelyn's base pay by thirty percent, a clear sign that a partnership offer was in her future. She immediately thought about calling Robbie but decided against it. News this big had to be shared in person. They would be able to get totally out of debt and buy a place of their own. There was only one nagging uncertainty in the back of her mind.

Later, at the victory celebration, Valerie caught Katelyn's eye and raised her glass in her direction. Valerie and Suzanne were in the center of a huddle of lawyers who wanted to be close to power-ful people and crowded around them. Katelyn didn't try to force her way closer. When she encountered Mr. Bancroft at the hors d'oeuvres table, he completely ignored her. As soon as she could, Katelyn slipped away to call Robbie and left a voice mail.

Crossing the Potomac into Arlington, she beat Robbie home. Charlie, their three-year-old whippet, greeted her at the door of the town house. Built like a miniature greyhound, the dog with light brown and white coloring instantly bonded with Robbie and always tried to keep him in sight. His relationship with Katelyn was more casual, which suited her fine. She patted him lightly on the head, and he returned to one of his favorite spots where he could watch squirrels hop from trees to the ground in the commons area of the complex.

Walking through the townhome, she felt nostalgic. They'd had a lot of fun decorating the forty-year-old residence to their taste and making it uniquely their own. The good news was they were near the end of their lease. The timing for a move couldn't be better.

After changing clothes, Katelyn called the restaurant for a res-ervation and plopped down on the blue-and-white sofa. Charlie jumped up beside her.

Robbie called. "Where are you?"

"Sitting on the couch with Charlie."

"I was held up in a meeting about a kid who may be placed next week but still thought I'd beat you home. How was traffic?"

"Not bad, but you know it's getting worse by the minute. Do you want to meet at the restaurant?"

"Sounds great."

Katelyn took the memo about the job offer with her and read it several times while waiting for Robbie.

When he arrived, he gave her a quick kiss on the lips. "How was the celebration?"

"I couldn't wait to leave so I could be with you."

The hostess led them to a table directly overlooking the Potomac. Robbie was wearing jeans, a short-sleeved blue shirt, and fancy cowboy boots. Noticeably in shape, with curly brown hair, a well-trimmed beard, and blue eyes, he was the kind of man capable of making other women jealous. But it wasn't primarily his good looks, love of the outdoors, and kid-like exuberance that drew Katelyn to him. Like her, he'd experienced more than his fair share of pain and disappointment, some of it due to his own bad choices. But Robbie had come out of his tunnel with an emotional sensitivity that allowed Katelyn to open up and relate to him in a way she'd never been able to do with another man. Because of that, his degree from a community college and lack of a high-paying job hadn't disqualified him as a spouse.

"Want to go all-sushi?" Robbie asked. "That's what this place is known for."

"No," Katelyn replied slowly. "I'm going with the regular menu."

"Why?" Robbie asked in surprise.

"That's what I want to do."

Robbie liked heat, even when the food was cold. Katelyn had never seen him intimidated by a hot pepper or hot sauce. It was a trait he shared with his father. Robbie ordered a spicy shrimp roll and a spider roll. Katelyn selected a salad with a combination of seafood as the protein.

"What more can you tell me about the verdict?" he asked after the waitress left with their order.

Katelyn gave him a condensed version of the events in the courtroom.

"Oh, do you remember Phoebe Jacobs, one of the lawyers for the other side?" she asked. "I had lunch with her a few weeks ago. She left the courtroom before the verdict. Later, her paralegal told me that Phoebe was in labor and on her way to the hospital. In some ways, that's bigger news than a jury verdict."

"Yeah, I would say that's true in the universal scheme of things," Robbie replied with a slightly puzzled expression on his face. "I heard some dramatic news today too. David called while I was on my way here."

"Is everything okay with your dad?" Katelyn asked quickly.

"Yeah, his last checkup with the cardiologist was good. It has to do with Camp Seacrest. The director was fired for misappropriation of funds."

Katelyn's eyes widened. She and Robbie made modest but regular contributions to the nonprofit organization.

"How much?" she asked.

"Over $95,000."

"How is that possible? Don't they audit the accounts?"

"Yes, which is how they caught Chris. He didn't steal a lot at once. He did it in increments of a few thousand at a time, mostly charged to accounts for repairs that were never done or supplies that were never purchased."

Katelyn's legal mind shifted gears. "Is your father still on the board of directors?"

"No, he rotated off eighteen months ago. And David turned them down when they asked him a few months ago to sign up for another term."

"I'm glad neither one of them can be criticized for lack of oversight."

Robbie took a bite of spicy shrimp roll.

"That's terrible," Katelyn continued. "And even worse when it involves a nonprofit."

"Yeah, I really love the camp and want the best for the kids."

Katelyn reached for her purse.

"I have more news," she said. "And it might mean we can do more for the camp than we have so far."

David, Nanette, and their two children lived in a two-story brick house tucked away at the end of a quiet street about fifteen minutes from the law office. Mature live oaks lined the streets of the neighborhood. David pulled into the driveway and stopped the car. Blocking the way was his eight-year-old daughter. Courtney was decorating the concrete with sidewalk chalk. With blond hair and hazel eyes, the slender girl looked like her mother's side of the family. David got out and inspected her artwork—four huge daisy-like flowers with multicolored petals of red, blue, orange, purple, and yellow.

"Those are beautiful," he said.

"And I've named them Rebekah, Emmaline, Lillian, and Natalie because they're my best friends."

"Where's your flower?" David asked. "I think you should have one."

"Oh, these are to give away," Courtney replied. "Maybe if I show 'em to Mommy, she'll let me invite them over to play tomorrow. Will you ask her for me?"

David smelled a parent trap. "Have you already asked her? Did she say no?"

"But you haven't asked her," Courtney replied with emphasis. "She always says yes to you."

"Really?" David laughed. "I'll remind her about that."

The house was surrounded by mature bushes. There was a large, fenced-in backyard. David passed through the kitchen and den into a small downstairs study that Nan used as a home office and personal retreat. Slender like her daughter, Nan had blond hair that reached past her shoulders. Her blue eyes were complemented by high, patrician cheekbones. Her family roots in the area went back over two hundred years. Longtime residents of Wilmington were familiar with the name Wakefield. She and David met when they were in high school, dated for a while, broke up, and reconnected when they both went to Wake Forest. Nan's degree was in psychology, and she served as David's favorite sounding board. Being around lawyers wasn't new for her. One of her grandfathers was an attorney and judge in New Bern. As David entered the room, he found her sitting in a comfortable chair reading a book.

"Looks like you've had an easy day," David said.

Nan smiled and stretched. "I was just about to grab a box of bonbons but didn't want to spoil my appetite for supper."

"If you have any bonbons in the house, you need to hide them from me. Have you seen Courtney's artwork on the driveway? It's an appeal for friends to come over tomorrow after school."

"And I told her maybe next week."

"She claims if I ask, you'll agree to anything."

"Then ask for next Wednesday."

"Done. Where's Andy?"

"On his tablet in his room. He saved his screen time for late in the afternoon and earned an extra hour by working in the backyard."

Andy, a sturdy eleven-year-old with sandy-brown hair, was a clone of David and Carter. When they posed for family pictures, it was clearly three generations in the frame.

"What did he do?"

"Dug up the stumps of the two trees you cut down six months ago. I took a video. He was slinging the mattock like a steam shovel."

The saplings were about six inches across. David was going to let them rot in the ground for a year before taking out the stumps. Nan handed him her phone. Wearing a pair of David's old work gloves that were too big for him, Andy used both the digging and the cutting features of the mattock.

"My dad would enjoy that video," he said, returning the phone.

"I'll send it to him. Tell me about your day."

"I did some stump-digging too. Only the stumps needed to be pulled out of people's hearts. The clients gave me permission to share with you."

Nan loved the story about the Jordan family.

"The part about their mother is beautiful. Maybe I should try that the next time Andy and Courtney get in a fuss. I'll march them into the kitchen and see how long it takes for them to make things right."

"I'd like a video of that."

"But I'm not clear exactly how you got them talking about their personal relationships when they scheduled an appointment to discuss the business."

"Your prayers."

Nan smiled. "Okay. I'm just praying for what's obvious. You have a knack for listening and giving good advice."

"I left out one of the most important parts. One of the scriptures I read this morning was Proverbs 22:6, about training up a child. That was the trigger."

"That gives me goose bumps," Nan said as she rubbed her arms. "It's like the Lord sent an angel who whispered what to say in your ear, then walked over to the sister and reminded her what their mother used to do."

Nan was quicker to talk about divine supernatural intervention than David.

"Maybe. There's one other piece of not-so-good news. It has to do with Camp Seacrest."

"Tell me while you throw together our salad. I promised the kids a homemade pizza."

FOUR

WHEN KATELYN DROPPED THE NEWS OF THE JOB
opportunity and move to Chicago, Robbie laid his chopsticks on
the table and stopped eating. She took the memo from her purse
and handed it to him. His eyes widened when he saw the new salary.

"That's a lot of money," he said. "Will you have to work more
hours? If so, I don't see how that's possible."

"The hours won't change, but this is a huge leap forward in my
career. I'll finally be in charge of something. Suzanne and Valerie
have pegged me as one of the women they're grooming to be part of
the next generation of leaders at the law firm."

"Chicago," Robbie said. "I've never been there. I guess we need
to fly up and check it out as soon as possible. We could add the
moving stipend to what we've saved and make a down payment on
a place of our own. That's been our next step."

"Right, but I haven't accepted the offer. And there's more to our
plan than just buying a place to live." Katelyn paused. "If I accept
the job and we move to Chicago, it will be at least two or three years
before I'll be in a position to take time off to have a baby."

"Are you sure about that? I didn't read anything about restrict-
ing propagation in the memo."

"It's implied."

"You should ask Suzanne if that's the case."

"Not possible."

"Off the record."

Katelyn was silent for a moment. "No, I can't do that. Breaking into top management like Valerie isn't my goal, but I'd like to make partner. Once that happens, I'll have the ability to shift into practice areas more friendly to having a family. Becky Algren hired a nanny and leaves the office at a reasonable time during the week." Katelyn took a deep breath before adding, "And I'd want to cut back on my hours. I rarely see Becky at the office on Saturday and Sunday."

"I like the sound of that. How about stress? The stress you deal with now is crazy. Would it increase in the new position?"

"Yes, but working for Suzanne has prepared me for that. Valerie Pinson seems more low-key; however, I would have the responsibility of running my own little group. If we don't perform well, I'll get blamed."

Robbie leaned back in his chair. "I'm not worried about your performance. There's not much to discuss. Let's do it. I'll start looking for places where I can land. I'm sure there's no shortage of opportunities to work with disadvantaged kids. And I've already promised to modify my work schedule if we decide to have a baby and one of us needs to be at home more."

"I want to take time to think this through. You know I hate making spur-of-the-moment decisions."

"Since you're cooking one pizza, do you think you could make two?" David asked as he sliced a tomato for the salad.

"What do you want on your pizza?"

"It could be our pizza."

"I can feel your hunger from across the room. Did you skip lunch today?"

"No, Dad and I went to Lupie's."

Nan nodded. "Wednesday is chicken casserole day. You guys are so predictable."

"Is that bad?"

"I assume you also want pepperoni, mushrooms, black olives, and then to douse it with red pepper flakes," Nan said as she opened the refrigerator door.

"All of the above."

David prepared the second pizza.

"What's going on at Camp Seacrest?" Nan asked when she'd closed the oven door and set the timer. "You have eleven minutes."

David broke the news of the embezzlement.

"Has Chris been arrested?" Nan asked.

"No. And the board may try to avoid that because of the negative publicity."

"What did your father say about it?"

"He was upset. He regrets not agreeing to serve another term on the board, but I told him it's better that he's not close to the problem." David paused. "And the way he talked at lunch made me realize he's starting to think more about retiring."

The timer sounded for the pizza.

"Call Courtney," Nan said. "Make sure she washes her hands."

David went into the little girl's bedroom. Courtney had graduated from the unicorn phase to self-expression in her own artwork. Multiple crayon and colored-pencil drawings decorated the walls. They went into the bathroom she shared with her brother.

"Did you talk to Mommy?" the little girl asked as she lathered her hands and arms with soap that immediately took on the color of the chalk.

"Yes, and I have good news. She's going to let you invite your friends over next Wednesday."

"That's what she already told me. What if it rains between now and then? My flowers will wash away, and they won't get to see them!"

David didn't know the weather forecast, but like most places along the coast, Wilmington often experienced an afternoon shower. It would take only a few drops for the chalk flowers to wilt.

"I'll take a picture of the flowers on my phone and print it at the office. That way, you can give the girls a copy."

Courtney didn't reply. She finished rinsing her hands and turned off the water. David handed her a towel.

"Okay," she said as she dried off. "But I want a picture for each girl that just has her name on it."

"Great idea. I'll do it right after supper while it's still light outside."

"And I want to be in the picture too."

"That will make it even better."

Robbie's quick willingness to support the move to Chicago wasn't surprising. To him, any opportunity for change and adventure was a green light. And Katelyn knew she'd earned the promotion the right way. She'd avoided backstabbing law firm politics and let her work stand on its own merit.

When they arrived home, Robbie took Charlie out for a walk.

After they returned, Charlie continued to follow Robbie through the house as if connected by a leash.

"How was the walk?" Katelyn asked.

"Okay, until we encountered Kevin."

Kevin was a massive black-and-white Great Dane.

"You've always said Kevin was friendly."

"He is, but he saw a squirrel and let out a woof that made Charlie want to crawl up my leg. It took a minute to restore calm." Robbie leaned over and scratched the dog's head behind his ears. "I asked Charlie what he thought about moving to Chicago."

"What did he say?"

"That he's going to need a new winter vest and earmuffs. He's heard that the wind coming off the lake can be brutal."

They spent the next couple of hours conducting virtual tours of the real estate options in Chicago. Homes within a reasonable distance of the law firm's office were expensive. But so was the cost of housing in DC.

"Something will turn up," Robbie said, leaning back against the sofa. "Although when I was camping out of the back of my truck, I never thought I'd be thinking about spending this much for a place to live."

"It would have been cozy, but I'm glad we didn't have to start our marriage living in your truck."

"One thing you should do is ask for time off between moves so we can enjoy a decent vacation."

"Agreed. I already thought about that."

In the middle of the night, Katelyn woke up. It was 4:00 a.m., and Robbie wasn't in bed. The light was on in the living room, and Katelyn found him sitting on the couch with his feet propped up on the coffee table. In his lap was the homemade leather-bound journal he used to record ideas and information for fishing and hunting trips. On occasion, he still offered guide services to longtime clients. When Katelyn appeared, he closed the journal. She joined him on the couch.

"Are you okay?" she asked.

"Yeah. I was having trouble sleeping."

"Why?"

"Thinking about the move to Chicago."

"Are there good places to hunt and fish?"

"Oh yeah. Lake Michigan is a different environment than anyplace else I've been before. There will be a learning curve, just like Alaska. And some of the largest white-tailed deer in the country are in Upper Michigan and Minnesota. Real trophy animals."

Robbie yawned. Katelyn patted him on the leg.

"Come to bed so you can dream about deer with massive antlers."

———

Most mornings, David dropped the kids off at school. Courtney held David's phone in her hand as she studied the photos taken of the chalk flowers.

"I'm not smiling in the one for Emmaline," she said from the rear seat. "Can you take another one after school?"

"If it doesn't rain, but I think they're all good. Just in case, I'll make color copies for you today."

Andy, who was riding in the front seat, rubbed his arms.

"My arms are hurting," he said. "I should have asked Mom for some medicine. Is it okay if I go see the nurse at school?"

"There's nothing wrong with your arms," David replied. "Your muscles are sore from all the work you did yesterday digging up the stumps. They'll be fine tomorrow, and you'll be a little bit stronger."

David told them a story about how their grandfather strengthened David's muscles by having him saw lumber by hand for a storage shed.

"Is that where he keeps his riding lawn mower?" Andy asked.

"Yes. I was about twelve when we built it. I couldn't figure out why he told me to go back and forth between sawing with my right arm and my left arm. That way, both arms got a workout."

"I think you're strong," Courtney said. "You have big muscles."

"Thanks, but I'm coasting at this point."

"What does that mean?" Courtney asked.

"It's like when you go down a hill on your bike and don't have to pedal," Andy said.

The children attended a new elementary school that didn't exist when David and Robbie were growing up. Andy got out of the car. Courtney leaned forward and hugged David's neck.

"I love you, Daddy," she said.

"I love you, sweetie."

Reaching the office, David greeted Meredith, the law firm office manager. Meredith was answering the phones because Candy had the day off. A plump, dark-haired woman in her late forties, Meredith had worked for Carter since she graduated from high school. During that time, she'd performed every job except the practice of law. And sometimes, she overstepped the line and offered advice to clients when the lawyers weren't available. David's father hadn't yet arrived.

"I set up an appointment this morning for you and Carter to meet with Zeke Caldwell," the assistant said. "I suggested he send you an email providing background about what's going on, but he wanted to talk to you instead. I'm sending Candy first thing to the storage facility to pull his file."

"I thought Candy had the day off."

"Change of plans. Her explanation included way too many details for me."

"That's fine. And we'll give Zeke as much time as he needs. He and my father go way back."

David fixed a cup of coffee in the former kitchen they used as a break room. Thirty minutes later, Candy came into his office with a harried expression on her face. She plopped a folder on his desk and brushed her sandy hair out of her eyes. Carter had hired the twenty-two-year-old eighteen months earlier after their longtime receptionist moved to Florida with her husband. Candy had the outgoing personality suited to the greeter position but hadn't increased her skills.

"It's hot in that storage unit," Candy said. "I had to move a bunch of boxes to get to the right cabinet."

"Thanks. I'll try to get over there and straighten it out."

"Or you could hire my little brother. I'll supervise him."

David smiled wryly. He knew he'd walked into a setup. But he didn't mind paying Candy's brother to perform manual labor.

"I'll approve five hours at twelve dollars an hour."

"Thanks," Candy replied. "That should take care of it. My daddy has hand trucks."

David placed Zeke's file on his credenza. Thirty minutes before the appointment, he finished reviewing it. Candy buzzed him.

"Mr. Caldwell is here," she said.

"Is my father available?"

"No, he just got on the phone with Mr. Swanson."

Ethan Swanson was one of the firm's biggest clients. He owned three businesses and a lot of rental property. Any call with him could be lengthy.

"I'll get started with Zeke in the conference room. Send in my father when he finishes with Mr. Swanson."

Two years younger than Carter Cobb, Zeke and Carter played together on the offensive line when they were on the high school football team. Zeke was shorter than Carter with broad shoulders, an ample stomach, and a strong handshake. His hair was sprinkled with gray, and he wore glasses. Today, he was wearing dark pants and a knit shirt with the name of the pharmacy embroidered on it. He had a magazine in his hand.

"Let's meet in the conference room," David said. "My dad is on the phone and will join us shortly."

The conference room was a former bedroom and contained an antique dining table surrounded by six chairs. On the walls were original oil paintings of famous Wilmington sites by a local artist.

"Thanks for agreeing to meet with me on short notice," Zeke said. "I know you're busy."

Zeke spoke with an accent influenced by the unique dialect developed by African Americans who'd lived for many generations on the Carolina coast. They sat on opposite sides of the table. David opened the file.

"I understand there's an issue with the drug patent my father helped you get a few years ago," he said.

"It's for one of my remedies I developed while investigating the medicinal qualities of mangrove bark. When I combined it with some other things, I came up with a formula that can be used to treat severe nausea without any negative side effects. I paid $5,000 in inheritance money to a lab in California that figured out what was in it. Carter helped me fill out the government paperwork."

Some of Zeke's products were based on recipes passed down from prior generations. But he'd also refined formulas and come up with new ones of his own. Carter had used what Zeke called "Heart Boost" drops after his heart attack and perked up faster than his cardiologist predicted.

"The examiner at the patent office turned us down at first, but we kept plugging away until it went through. After that, I contacted a bunch of drug companies to try to sell it, but no one was interested. That was a couple of years ago. Finally, I gave up."

Zeke slid the magazine across the table. "Recently, I was looking through a trade publication that comes to the pharmacy and read about a new medication named Relacan that's used to treat severe nausea. According to the technical data, it contains the same ingredients as my drug."

David skimmed the information in the magazine that included diagrams of the chemical chains for Relacan. He stopped when he saw the name of the company releasing the new drug.

"Brigham-Neal," he said. "That's one of the biggest pharmaceutical manufacturers in the country."

"They were one of the first companies I contacted when I tried to sell it."

David placed the patent data in the file beside the magazine. Even without technical training, he could see the similarity.

"Zeke, this could be huge."

"I know."

"But you're going to need a lawyer who specializes in drug patent litigation. That's an area that requires a level of expertise we don't have. Let's see what my father thinks would be the next step—"

At that moment, the door flew open and Candy rushed in.

"Come quick! It's Mr. Cobb! He's collapsed in his office. An ambulance is on the way!"

———

Katelyn usually didn't need an alarm to wake her up, but after her interrupted night's sleep, her phone beeped several times before she realized what was going on. She fumbled and dropped it to the floor before leaning over and grabbing it. She pressed the button to silence the alarm and fell back into bed.

"Are you okay?" Robbie asked.

"Yeah, I was sound asleep. How are you?"

"Fine. I'll take my shower first so you can rest a bit more."

"Okay."

Uncharacteristically, Katelyn dozed off. When she woke up the second time, Robbie had dressed and taken Charlie out for a morning walk. She lay in bed until she heard him return and then stumbled into the kitchen. Robbie handed her a cup of coffee with cream.

"I don't know what's wrong with me," she said.

"A lot of emotion yesterday emptied your tank. The trial, the job offer, finally eating at a new restaurant."

"Maybe."

Robbie kissed her. "I'm off."

Katelyn took her coffee into the living room and sat on the sofa. Charlie curled up on the floor at her feet. Noticing Robbie's journal on the coffee table, Katelyn casually picked it up and flipped it open. Her husband's use of technical hunting and fishing terms and personal shorthand made much of it indecipherable. But he also included an occasional black ink sketch of a camping spot, a person he knew, or a fishing fly he might tie later. Katelyn considered Robbie an artist. He scoffed and referred to himself as a doodler. She reached some entries made a couple of months earlier. One caught her eye, and she stopped. It was a prayer.

God, it's me. I remember camping on the marsh when David and I were kids. We would cook hot dogs and have a contest to see who could eat the most. Then Dad would suddenly start singing and scare us half to death. After that, he would pray and talk to you like you were right there with us. I tried not to laugh or think he was crazy. But I believed he was weird. Was he weird or was he right? I'd really like to know.

Beneath the prayer was a sketch of two boys and a man sitting around a campfire with hot dogs on sticks. Katelyn recognized Robbie because his hair was curly. David's hair was straight. Floating above Carter Cobb's head were musical notes that mingled with a few scattered stars. Katelyn closed the journal. This was personal. Robbie had never asked her not to read his journal. But he'd never invited her to do so either.

As she got ready for work, the words and sketch stayed with her. Faith had never been a significant part of Katelyn's life. She and Robbie loved the outdoors. The open sky was their "church."

After arriving at the office, she watered the small plant that sat on the corner of her desk and settled into her routine. Grinding out long hours with intense concentration was one of Katelyn's strengths. She was a marathoner, not a sprinter, which was the kind of work rhythm a big law firm preferred. Unlike other associates, she had no trouble reaching her annual time and billing quotas.

Late morning there was a knock on her doorframe. It was Franklin Deming.

"I received a memo that I'm supposed to coordinate with you on the McMillon matter."

"I've not gotten to it," Katelyn replied. "And probably won't until late this afternoon. Is there a deadline?"

"It's not a rush job, but I wanted to get as much guidance from you as I could before you leave."

Katelyn tilted her head to the side.

Franklin lowered his voice. "You know how hard it is to keep personnel matters quiet around here," he continued.

Katelyn motioned for the paralegal to come in and close the door. Even though everyone was trained to maintain strict client confidentiality, that didn't apply to law firm gossip.

"What did you hear?" she asked.

"That Valerie Pinson was in town to offer you a position at the Chicago office."

"That's pretty accurate," Katelyn said with a nod. "Except I suspect she and Suzanne discussed other matters too."

"Yeah, and it wasn't good news for Rebecca Algren."

"What's going on with Becky?"

"She's on her way out."

"But she made partner two years ago!"

Franklin shrugged. "That's what I heard. And it came from someone close to the source. But I'm not here about Becky. I want to put in a personal request."

"What is it?"

"I'd like to transfer to Chicago and be assigned to your group. I know you're going to run a litigation team, and I'd like to be closer to the action. After working here for five years, I know the only way

I can break out of document review is if a lawyer brings me along and assigns other responsibilities. You're the best person I've worked with, and I hope you've been pleased with my work product."

"Absolutely."

Katelyn had heard a handful of derogatory comments over the years about Franklin's background. Snooty superiority infuriated her, and she always defended him, pointing out his talent for his job.

"And you're willing to relocate to Chicago?" she asked.

"Yes, my fiancée is all for it. Jasmine wants a change when we get married, partly to create space between us and her relatives, who are always in our business."

Katelyn started to say that she hadn't decided whether to accept the firm's offer to relocate. But if Franklin talked to her, he'd talk to others.

"Okay," she said. "I'll keep your request in mind."

"And confidential."

Katelyn agreed but resisted the urge to point out the double standard related to confidentiality. After Franklin left, she spent a few moments wondering how wide the ripples of her decision might go. Working through lunch, she ate at her desk. Shortly before five o'clock, her cell phone vibrated. It was Robbie. After leaving work early the previous day, she was going to work into the evening.

"Are you home yet?" she asked.

"Yes, and I need to talk to you."

"I won't be leaving the office for another couple of hours."

"It's my dad. He's in an ambulance on the way to the hospital."

FIVE

DAVID SAT IN A CHAIR IN THE ICU WAITING AREA. IT
had been two hours since Candy burst into the conference room.
Zeke and David found Carter lying on his back, his eyes closed, his
breathing shallow. It looked like he'd tried to get up from his chair
and collapsed.

"Help, Lord Jesus!" Zeke called out.

David knelt and placed his hand on his father's chest and prayed
softly. Zeke paced back and forth, praying in a loud voice. The sound
of a siren in the distance came closer. Moments later, two EMTs
rushed into the office. David answered their rapid-fire questions as
best he could, confirming that his father took high blood pressure
medication and had suffered a heart attack five years earlier.

"We're taking him to NHRMC," a member of the team replied.

The New Hanover Regional Medical Center was the facility
where Carter had received care following his heart attack. The
EMTs put the large man on a stretcher and rolled him out of the
office. David and Zeke followed.

"Is there anything I can do?" Zeke asked.

"You're doing it," David answered.

"I'll send the word out through the prayer chain at my church."

David turned to Candy, who was clutching tissues in her right hand. Tears were streaming down her cheeks. Meredith was also crying.

"I don't know how long he'd been lying there on the floor," Candy sniffled. "I thought he was on a phone call with Mr. Swanson, but he called back and said they'd been disconnected. I figured Mr. Cobb must have gotten distracted by something. He didn't answer his phone when I buzzed him, and that's when I went in and—"

She stopped as more tears flowed.

"You didn't know," David said.

On the way to the hospital, he called Nan.

"I'm so sorry," she said. "Do you want me to get someone to pick up the kids so I can be with you?"

"No, and please don't mention anything to them until I know more what to say and how to explain it."

"Andy is going to be devastated."

"Let's hope for good news from the doctor."

David then called Robbie.

"If I can't get a flight, I'll drive down as soon as possible. Katelyn may not be able to leave immediately."

"You can stay with us."

"Thanks, but if it's okay, I'd rather go to Dad's place."

"Sure. I'll call you from the hospital as soon as I know anything else."

Dr. Spies, a local neurosurgeon who wasn't much older than David, entered the ICU waiting area.

"Mr. Cobb?" he asked.

David stood, and the doctor shook his hand.

"The records indicate you have a health-care power of attorney from your father," Dr. Spies said.

"That's right."

David followed the physician into a small, plainly furnished room with a table and four chairs.

"I've reviewed the CT scan of your father's brain. He had a hemorrhage, not a stroke. That means the damage is from a brain bleed, not a blocked artery. The hemorrhage is in a spot where surgery may help, but I can't put the odds at greater than fifty-fifty."

"Fifty-fifty for survival or improvement?"

"Improvement, although there's always the chance that someone in his condition won't survive surgery."

David thought for a moment. "If he was your father, what would you do?"

"Operate," the doctor replied. "He has the preexisting heart condition and hypertension, but I'd like to give him the chance for more years with a decent quality of life. We'd do a standard decompression procedure via craniotomy to relieve pressure on the brain, remove pooled blood, and try to repair the damaged blood vessels. The ability of the body to adapt to damage in the area of the brain where this occurred can be surprising."

This was a more optimistic prognosis than David expected.

"Let's do the surgery," he said.

Dr. Spies stood. "I'll start prepping, and one of the nurses will bring out the consent forms for you to sign. After surgery he'll return to the ICU."

"May I see him now?"

"Yes, but just for a few minutes."

When David entered the room, his father was lying peacefully in bed. Carter Cobb had always been a sound sleeper, and once unconscious it took a major disruption to wake him. It was a trait David and Robbie relied upon when they were sneaking into the house as teenagers after staying out too late. David pulled a chair close to his father's bed and bowed his head.

"Lord, I pray that my father will not leave this life one millisecond before the end of the exact time you've ordained for him to be on earth. Watch over him now and assign angels to accompany him into the operating room, and be with Dr. Spies and those performing the surgery."

David was still praying when the door opened and a nurse in scrubs entered.

"Mr. Cobb?" she asked.

"Yes."

"Here are the consent forms for the surgery."

David didn't bother to read the forms. This wasn't the time to negotiate the particulars of the hospital's informed consent policy. He knew the document included language intended to absolve the doctor and hospital from liability to the fullest extent possible. David quickly initialed and signed.

"Return to the waiting area," the nurse said. "Dr. Spies will come out as soon as we're finished."

David phoned Robbie. "Where are you?" he asked his younger brother.

"On my way and making good time. How's he doing?"

David relayed the discussion with Dr. Spies and the decision to proceed with surgery.

"I totally agree," Robbie replied. "Let's give him a chance to recover and improve. Dad's tough."

"Is Katelyn with you?"

"No, she couldn't get away from the office, but she's going to catch a flight tomorrow evening. Should I come straight to the hospital?"

"Yes, the surgery is going to take two and a half to three hours. Maybe you can make it in time to meet with the neurosurgeon."

———

Katelyn sent Suzanne an email letting her know about Robbie's father, then spent the next hour prioritizing what she needed to take care of before leaving. She received a follow-up email from Suzanne asking how long she thought she'd be gone. Katelyn had no idea. A funeral would involve a few days out of town, but Katelyn quickly shook her head to dispel the possibility of imminent death. She was fond of her father-in-law. Carter Cobb always greeted her enthusiastically and treated her kindly. Once he learned she liked fresh strawberries, he made sure to have some on hand when she visited. And in conversations around the dinner table, he went out of his way to ask her questions. It was clear he cared about other people. She received a text from Robbie informing her that Carter was undergoing surgery for a brain hemorrhage. Katelyn's eyes watered. She made a quick decision.

> I'll be in Wilmington at least through the weekend. By then, we should know my father-in-law's status.

Katelyn thought about adding more possibilities, but this wasn't a memo unpacking every contingency that might arise in a big lawsuit. She sent the brief response. Moments later, Suzanne answered.

Would you like to discuss the job offer before you leave? It would
be nice to communicate with Valerie sooner rather than later.

Katelyn felt her stomach tighten. She lightly touched the keys
of her keyboard without pressing any of them. She couldn't stall for
long. Suzanne expected a response.

I'll get back to you the first of the week. Thanks for your patience.

Katelyn stared with dissatisfaction at the words on the screen.
If she added that she and Robbie were blown away by the opportunity and the offer, it would be interpreted as tacit acceptance. She
decided to modify the last sentence:

And thanks for all you've done to make this happen.

She wasn't sure this was much better, but she pressed the send
button anyway.

A minute passed without a reply from Suzanne. That minute
turned into ten and then thirty. As she tried to work, she kept checking the bottom right corner of her computer screen for a notice that
she'd received an email from Suzanne. Katelyn's anxiety spun her
higher and higher. She considered barging into Suzanne's office
to make sure her email hadn't irritated the senior partner. Finally,
Katelyn clapped her hands together and stood from her chair.

"Stop it!" she said out loud.

Taking a few deep breaths, she ordered her emotions to obey
her brain. Her email didn't require a response from the senior partner. Silence was good. Driving home, she called Robbie to check
on him.

"I'm about an hour out from Wilmington," he replied. "I'm going directly to the hospital."

Katelyn heard Charlie's sharp bark. "What's Charlie doing?"

"Making sure no big trucks run over us. I don't need a rearview mirror. He lets me know when one gets close. How was the rest of your day?"

"I tried to stay busy."

"Did Suzanne ask you for an answer to the job offer?"

"Yes, in an email, but I asked her to give me a few days."

"I've been thinking a lot about it during the drive."

"Any second thoughts?"

"Maybe. I remember how much my life changed because I took the ski instructor job at the resort in Vermont. I had two other opportunities, one in Colorado and another in Northern California, both for more money. But if I hadn't gone to Vermont, I wouldn't have met you."

"I'm glad you went to Vermont."

"Me too."

"Call me as soon as you know anything about your dad."

———

David ate a turkey sandwich from a vending machine. Taking a drink of water from a bottle, he glanced up as the door to the ICU waiting room opened and Robbie entered. Always muscular, Robbie looked a little bit leaner than the last time David had seen him over the Christmas holidays.

"You look trim," David said, standing up to give his brother a hug. "I'm the one who should drop ten pounds."

Robbie held on to him a bit longer than expected. David gave him another pat on the back.

"Any word yet?" Robbie asked when they separated.

"No, the surgery is taking longer than expected, which I hope is a good sign."

The two men sat beside each other. David offered the water bottle to Robbie, who took a swig and returned it. The brothers had passed countless germs back and forth growing up.

"Tell me more about what happened," Robbie said.

David provided additional details.

"Do the kids know?" Robbie asked when David finished.

"No, I don't want to say anything until we know more."

"That makes sense."

The door opened and Dr. Spies, a surgical mask hanging around his neck, came into the waiting room. David introduced him to Robbie. The doctor's face didn't reveal anything.

"Your father is in recovery. Let's go to the consultation room."

Once they were seated, Dr. Spies placed both his hands on the table.

"He made it through surgery. But not without difficulty. Partway through, his heart rate became irregular. If we'd not already opened the skull, I would have called off the procedure, but I continued on. I was able to locate the primary site of hemorrhage, extract blood, and stabilize the vessels to reduce the chance of reoccurrence. We called Dr. Beaumont, his cardiologist, and she's checking the arrhythmia that's persisted post-op."

"What about brain damage due to the hemorrhage?" David asked.

"I remain guardedly optimistic, but we won't know for some

time. The swelling has to diminish first, and he needs to recover from surgery."

"What part of the brain was affected?" Robbie asked.

"The right, which controls the left side of the body along with having a big role in attention, memory, and reasoning."

"When will we be able to see him?" David asked.

"In an hour, but it will be a day or so before he's conscious. Even then, don't expect communication to be anywhere close to normal."

"Thanks for what you're doing," Robbie said.

The doctor left. The brothers stayed in the consultation room. They sat in silence for a few moments.

"I need to call Nan," David said.

"You stay here. I'll go into the hallway and phone Katelyn."

Nan answered on the first ring. "That sounds better than I feared," she said when he gave her a report. "It's been tough trying to act normal around the kids, especially when Andy brought up doing something on Saturday with Pops. They'd talked about taking the skiff out in the marsh to see if the redfish are running."

David had been emotionally stable the entire day—until that moment. Tears suddenly welled up in his eyes. He coughed and cleared his throat. His father's future relationship with Andy, if any, would be drastically different.

"Maybe Robbie and I can take him for a few hours. You have to time it right with the tide—" David stopped.

"How have you been holding up?" Nan asked.

David took a moment to compose himself. "Okay until you mentioned Andy."

"And Robbie?"

"Same as me, I guess. We haven't had time to talk much. Katelyn is flying down tomorrow evening. I invited them to stay with us, but Robbie brought the dog and wants to stay at Dad's place."

"Courtney would love having Charlie here."

"I know, but I'm not going to push it."

When David returned to the ICU waiting room, Robbie wasn't there.

Katelyn threw together a salad for supper, then logged on to the law firm server so she could work into the night. Without Robbie at home, she'd be able to grind out a few more billable hours and minimize the backlog that would be waiting upon her return from Wilmington. Three hours later, she stood and stretched her legs by taking a quick walk through the townhome. When she returned to her laptop, she'd received an email from Suzanne. It wasn't unusual for the senior partner to send a communication at any point of the day or night. The subject matter was listed as *KMC Follow-up*. Seeing her initials grabbed Katelyn's attention.

Members,

I strongly disagree with the decision by the executive committee to place Katelyn Martin-Cobb on a senior associate career track. Neither Valerie nor I communicated to KMC that the move to Chicago was a precursor to equity partner status, but that would be the only reasonable assumption Katelyn would draw. We need more female partners, not fewer. Making her coleader of the new Chicago group with Bryan McFarland will send the wrong message to both of them.

I wouldn't have been willing to lose Katelyn from my team for anything less than her upward mobility. I demand the opportunity to be heard on this matter prior to meeting with Katelyn, who is out of town for a few days due to a family emergency.

Suzanne Nixon

Katelyn was shocked, not only by what she read but by the fact that Suzanne sent her a copy of the email. Bryan McFarland, a Yale law graduate, was a few years older than Katelyn. More appellate lawyer than trial attorney, Bryan was an excellent writer who'd labored long and hard in the DC office. He and Katelyn rarely crossed paths, but he'd always been cordial to her.

She quickly scanned the list of recipients for the email. It included over twenty names, including the top attorneys in the firm. But one prominent name was missing: Kane Vanlandingham. The managing partner of the DC office hadn't received a copy. She checked again. Kane's name was absent. Katelyn sucked in a breath of air. That meant Suzanne mistakenly sent Katelyn the email because her name popped up as soon as the senior partner typed "Ka." Suzanne didn't catch the mistake. Her boss was clearly upset, which could lead to a careless error.

The email was a double blow—no partnership, no opportunity to be in charge. While Katelyn was trying to absorb the news, another email with the same subject line appeared. It was a Reply All from Dwight Kennedy, the chairman of the executive committee of Morgan and Monroe. Mr. Kennedy was in his mid-seventies and one of the most powerful partners in the firm. Katelyn knew him only from his photo on the website for the New York office.

Suzanne,

Lynwood and I are in agreement. The decision is final. No further discussion.

Dwight

So Lynwood Bancroft wasn't indifferent to her. He was an enemy. Reflexively, Katelyn sent the emails to the small printer she and Robbie kept at the townhome. Someone would likely notice the mistake and scrub the email from the computer server. The law firm hierarchy would be particularly concerned about Suzanne's statement regarding the need for more female partners. That could open the door to a discrimination claim. Thinking about that made Katelyn furious. She'd worked hard to be promoted on merit, not to scramble up through a back door, even if justified under the law. She walked over to the printer, picked up the emails, and read them again. She couldn't decide whether to cry or wad up the sheets of paper and hurl them across the room.

Katelyn doubted that the debate over her future had much to do with money. The most telling sentence from Suzanne's email was the reference to female partners. As much as corporate and legal America talked about the removal of glass ceilings for women, the reality was that limits still existed. Permanent associate status was better than termination, which at Morgan and Monroe was the fate of over fifty percent of the lawyers hired out of law school. Five or six years and out the door. As a permanent associate, Katelyn was looking at a good base salary, long hours, and the nagging question of why she didn't measure up. And she would always be, as she'd mentioned to Franklin, a worker bee.

Turning off her laptop, she went outside for a walk. She was sitting on a bench overlooking a pond at the edge of their development when her phone vibrated. It was Robbie.

"How's your dad?" she asked.

The seriousness of Carter Cobb's health crisis put her own situation in a different perspective.

"I'm glad you were able to get there in time to meet with the doctor."

"Yes. And I feel a bit of hope. I'm not ready to let him go."

"Of course not."

"How was your day?" Robbie asked.

"Long. I just finished working and went out for a walk. I'm sitting on a bench at the pond."

Katelyn paused. She didn't want to add an extra burden to Robbie's thoughts while he was at the hospital waiting to see his father.

"I may go to bed early tonight. I'm beat," she said.

"Okay, I'll be waiting for you at the airport."

The ache of separation from Robbie, even though brief, suddenly hit Katelyn. He'd always been a rock of emotional stability for her when, on rare occasions, she needed one. Tonight was one of those times.

"Love you," she managed.

"I love you too."

The call ended. Katelyn leaned back and closed her eyes for a few moments to clear her mind. One issue that she'd pushed to the sideline during the final few days of the trial was unwilling to retreat. Instead of returning to the townhome, she walked around the corner to a nearby twenty-four-hour pharmacy.

SIX

"DO YOU WANT TO SEE DAD BY YOURSELF?" DAVID asked.

"Not if they'll let us go together," Robbie responded.

A nurse was speaking to the members of another family. As soon as she finished, David asked about visitor protocol.

"Let me check. It depends on the patient's status."

David and Robbie sat beside each other and waited.

"You asked about Nan and the kids," David said. "What about you and Katelyn? Anything new in your world?"

"Looks like we're going to move to Chicago."

David and Katelyn had both graduated from law school and passed the bar exam, but their law practices were as different as paper plates and fine china. Robbie told him about the offer.

"Congrats to Katelyn," David said approvingly. "The door she's squeezing through is as narrow as it gets in the legal world."

"Yeah, she's a rock star."

"What are you going to do in Chicago?"

"When salary isn't crucial, it's easy to find a place to land. I really like working with kids."

"Hey, I believe the Lord will direct your steps."

Robbie turned his head sideways. "That's what I prayed last night."

"You prayed?"

"Yeah, over the past few months I've been doing that a lot more."

"Dad mentioned that at lunch yesterday but didn't add any details."

"We were going to talk later," Robbie said. "And then this happened."

A nurse opened the door to the ICU and motioned them forward. "You may both see your father now."

The nurse stopped in front of a room with "Carter Cobb—Dr. Spies" written on a whiteboard on the wall.

"You can stay for around fifteen minutes," she said.

David was shocked by the sight of his father hooked up to machines and monitors. Carter's head was wrapped in bandages. His mouth gaped open. For a split second David doubted the wisdom and mercy of opting for surgery to keep him alive.

"I guess it's good that he's breathing on his own," Robbie said. "I thought he might be on a ventilator."

"Yeah," David managed.

Robbie approached the bed. David held back. The younger son leaned over and kissed their father on the cheek.

"Hey, Dad," Robbie said. "During the trip down from DC, I listened to a podcast. It was an interview with a doctor who claims that even when people are unconscious, they retain the capacity to receive verbal information and store it away. I thought I'd try out his theory on you."

Robbie continued a one-sided conversation and talked to their father about things he knew would interest him. That included the fly-fishing lures he'd tied, Charlie's latest antics, and a guided fishing trip he'd led for smallmouth bass on the Upper Potomac. He ended up telling his father how much he looked forward to eating the smoked turkey Carter cooked every Thanksgiving.

"I always tell folks your secret is the two sticks of butter you melt and inject into the bird before putting it on the smoker. When that butter starts sizzling, it bastes the turkey from the inside. Genius idea."

"Will you change the subject," David cut in. "All I've eaten today is a turkey sandwich from a vending machine. The turkey meat in my sandwich was from a different species of bird than you're talking about. Listening to you talk about Dad's smoked turkey is making my stomach start basting itself."

"Toughen up," Robbie replied. "I want to give Dad a goal. Something to look forward to deep in his subconscious."

"Go ahead."

Robbie picked up their father's hand and held it in his. "Dad, I feel a need to repeat everything I said about the smoked turkey. But I'll move on to the last time you smoked a pork shoulder and brined it overnight in apple juice, brown sugar, salt, and some herbs. David ate so much that he had to lie down on the den couch for over an hour before he could eat dessert."

"I think it was two hours."

"Did you hear that, Dad? It was two hours. Anyway, I want us to do more things together as soon as you're able." Robbie paused. "Also, I'm going to be praying for you. I mean it. You've got to get better so we can finish the conversation we started the other day. God is really working in my life. So much of what you used to tell me is starting to make sense."

Chills ran down David's arms.

Robbie turned to him. "Okay. Your turn. Pray."

"Why me?"

"Because you have way more experience."

David bowed his head. He waited until he settled into a place where he could talk to God with confidence. Knowing that Robbie wasn't hostile or indifferent made it much easier to express what was on his heart. He prayed for their father until no more words formed in his spirit to be released through his lips.

"Amen," he said.

"And all God's people said amen," Robbie added in a quieter version of their father's usual prayer ending. "That was a solid B-plus prayer."

David chuckled. They quietly left the room.

As they were entering the elevator to return to the main level, David spoke. "The toughest thing I have to do is tell the kids about their Pops. Maybe you and I can take Andy fishing on the flats for redfish while you're here. That was one of the things he'd been looking forward to doing with Dad."

"Absolutely."

———

David sat on the edge of Andy's bed. At first, all Andy wanted to know was whether his Pops was going to live. He didn't cry; he wanted information. He peppered David with questions best answered by Dr. Spies. David attempted to communicate the truth in an optimistic way.

"Max Harrison's grandfather died a couple of months ago," Andy said. "He had a heart attack. That's what I've been worried about for Pops. Whenever he gets hot and sweaty, I ask if he needs to stop and drink some water."

"That's good."

"When will I get to see him?"

David didn't want Andy to see his grandfather in the ICU.

"After he gets out of the hospital," he answered. "Hopefully by then he'll be able to understand us and talk. The doctor told us not to be discouraged if it's a slow process. But I think Pops will enjoy hearing your voice even if he can't carry on a conversation. Uncle Robbie was telling me at the hospital that scientists believe people who are unconscious can still understand what's going on."

"Really?"

"Yeah. And Robbie and I may take you fishing for redfish while he's in town. We can use the skiff."

Andy sighed. "Pops has been tying extra crab and shrimp patterns. He was going to let me use one of his fly rods instead of my spinning tackle. I've been practicing in his backyard."

"I've never caught a redfish on a fly line."

"That's what Pops said. We were going to surprise you."

"Time to go to sleep," he said.

David and Nan had prayed individually and together with both children since birth. Often it was a simple prayer or blessing. Tonight, something more was in order.

"Mom already prayed with me before you got home," Andy said.

"Then I'll be quick."

"May I go first?"

Andy's request wasn't common.

"Yes."

Andy prayed a brief but heartfelt prayer for his Pops to get better and not be in pain. David didn't have much to add.

"Tell me again," Andy said. "Will the side of Pops's brain that's bleeding make it hard for him to cast with his right arm?"

"No, his left side will probably be worse."

Andy amended his prayer: "Lord, I ask that both Pops's arms will work just fine. Amen."

David tucked the sheet under Andy's chin and left for Courtney's room. Even though younger than Andy, Courtney was more of a night owl. When he told her about Pops, her hazel eyes immediately filled with tears.

"I want Mommy," she said.

David called downstairs, and Nan joined them. She held Courtney in her arms while David talked to her between the little girl's sniffles.

"I want to see him," she said. "And I'll draw a picture."

"Go ahead and get started on the picture, but a visit will have to wait until Pops feels better. Uncle Robbie is here, and he brought Charlie. He and Aunt Kate are going to be staying at Pops's house."

The children started calling Katelyn "Aunt Kate" at Courtney's suggestion based on a character in one of the little girl's favorite picture books. Katelyn quickly gave her consent.

"Can Charlie come over?"

"I'm sure he can."

"Okay," Courtney sighed. "I hate it when anyone gets sick. It stinks."

"We do too," David replied.

"Mommy, will you pray?"

Nan stroked Courtney's head while she prayed. They tucked her in and went downstairs.

"How is Andy?" Nan asked.

"A son we can be proud of."

David told her about Andy's questions and his prayer.

"And Andy's not the only person in the Cobb family besides us committed to praying for Dad," David said.

"Who else?"

"Robbie."

———

Relieved that Robbie's father had come through surgery, Katelyn still had a restless night inhabited by troubled dreams. Every time she woke up, she checked her in-box to see if anyone had discovered Suzanne's email error. Nothing appeared.

After taking a shower, she opened the pregnancy test she'd purchased the previous evening at the pharmacy. She was sure the results would be negative, but she'd bought the test to make sure. She placed the digital stick on the bathroom counter while she blew her hair dry. Glancing down after three minutes, she almost dropped the dryer. In the results window appeared a single word: *Pregnant.* Katelyn quickly checked whether the test had functioned properly. There was a single horizontal line in one window and a plus sign in the other. It was a valid test. Turning off the hair dryer, Katelyn stared at her reflection in the mirror.

Throwing on exercise clothes, she returned to the twenty-four-hour pharmacy and bought two more tests made by different companies. Rushing home, she repeated the tests. Both were positive. Katelyn was pregnant. She called Robbie, but it went to voice mail. She texted, asking him to call as soon as possible. No response. Robbie was notorious for unplugging.

Katelyn's mind was a swirl of thoughts and emotions while she got ready for work. Being pregnant changed everything. But she was going to have to figure out exactly how. She checked the airline to see if she could skip going to the office and catch an earlier flight to Wilmington. Nothing was available. Just as she was about to walk out the door of the townhome, her phone vibrated. She almost dropped it as she retrieved it from her purse.

"Where have you been?" she demanded. "I've been trying to reach you."

"Uh, I went out for a long run and left my phone at Dad's house. Are you okay?"

"I'm pregnant! I took a test this morning. Actually, three tests!"

Robbie didn't say anything.

"Well?" Katelyn asked.

"Are you sure?"

"Yes!"

"Uh, congratulations to us," Robbie managed. "How? Why?"

"You know the answer to both those questions. It must have happened when I worked late those nights preparing for the trial and didn't take my pills on time."

"Wow," Robbie said. "How do you feel?"

"Weird."

"What kind of weird?"

"I don't know how to explain it."

"Wow," Robbie repeated. "This is a shock. I'm not sure what to say. Are you excited?"

"Yes, yes. Of course. How about you?"

"One hundred percent. I wish we were together right now."

"Me too. I can't wait to see you. I tried to get an earlier flight but couldn't book a seat. Don't tell anyone yet. It's so early."

"Okay."

"See you soon."

———

David arrived at the hospital after leaving the house the next morning. There was no change in his father's condition. Carter looked the same as the night before. Eyes closed. Nonresponsive.

Continuing on to the office, David wanted to get a head start on figuring out what to do about his father's caseload. He particularly wanted to make sure there weren't any time deadlines lurking in the shadows. Most legal malpractice claims were linked to calendar mishaps. Given the stress of the day before, he had told Meredith and Candy not to worry about coming in until the afternoon. Midmorning, David heard the chime for the front door. Going into the reception area, he saw Zeke Caldwell standing on the front porch. David unlocked the door and let him in.

Zeke was wearing overalls and brown boots. "I was driving by and saw your car parked out front. How's Carter?"

"He had a brain hemorrhage. A neurosurgeon operated on him last night to stop the bleeding and relieve the pressure. Prognosis is guarded, but he survived the surgery."

David told him what they'd learned from Dr. Spies.

Zeke shifted his weight on his feet. "I was praying for Carter last night, and I believe I have a remedy that might help him, especially with memory issues. I've even seen improvement with people who have Alzheimer's."

"I don't know," David said and shook his head. "I remember your drops helping with the heart attack recovery, but this is way worse."

"There's a woman on the east side of town named Franny Lyman. Her family called me because she was getting more and more feeble and crazy-minded. Since using my drops, she's back to doing crossword puzzles. Do you know Oscar Lurwig, who worked for the power company?"

"Yes."

"He's another one. Oscar had a stroke and after using the drops for a month, he's driving to the store on his own. His physician is Dr. Mark Sparrow and can vouch for my remedies. I'll swing by the first part of next week and drop off a bottle."

"I know Dr. Sparrow. He's my father's family physician."

David didn't want to commit to anything he didn't intend to do. He walked Zeke to the door and onto the porch.

"Oh, how is your son doing?" Zeke asked. "I know he and Carter are really close."

"Andy seems to be coping fine. Robbie and I may take him fishing tomorrow to keep his mind off his grandfather's situation."

"What kind of fishing?"

"Redfish, if they're running on the flats. My dad's old skiff only draws a few inches of water."

"The reds are coming on the incoming tide near Reynold's Grocery," Zeke replied. "There's a spot where you can put in your boat about a quarter mile down a dirt road that starts behind the store."

"Off Highway 14?"

"Yep, that's it."

They reached the sidewalk. Zeke shook David's hand. "As soon as I get home, I'm going to prepare some drops for Carter. You can trust them. They're all natural, just like everything else I make."

Buying a hot tea at the snack bar on the main floor of the building so she could avoid the law firm break room, Katelyn went directly to her office. She tried to work, but it was impossible to concentrate and focus. Over and over, she found herself staring off into space. The shock of finding out she was pregnant, coupled with the dramatic shift in her possible future at the law firm, had shaken her world to the core. There wasn't a legal grid for analysis of this type of situation. She repeatedly stared at the photo on her phone of the positive pregnancy test. Her initial excitement was struggling in the face of her other circumstances. It was hard to know what to think and feel.

Before noon, she left for lunch. Sitting by herself at a table, she picked absentmindedly at her salad. Then a woman who reminded Katelyn of her mother entered the restaurant. It was a combination of the woman's face and hair and the way she moved. Not being able to share the news of becoming a mother with the woman who'd given her life caused sudden tears to sting Katelyn's eyes. It took a couple of minutes in the restroom doing repairs before she could return to the office.

Katelyn took a detour to lengthen the walk back to the building. Still unable to accomplish anything productive, she decided to leave early for the airport. As she was getting ready, her phone buzzed.

"Oh, you're still here," Suzanne said when Katelyn answered. "You were listed as out of the office this afternoon on my staff schedule."

Hearing herself described as "staff" emphasized to Katelyn the previous night's email.

"I'm about to leave for the airport," she said.

"What time is your flight?"

Katelyn told her.

"Great, you have time to swing by my office. See you in a minute."

Trapped, Katelyn stopped by the restroom to make sure she was presentable. She practiced the expression she wanted on her face when she met with Suzanne. A smile looked forced; seriousness came across as sullen. Katelyn settled on a pragmatic look based on the fact that countless lawyers would be thrilled to receive a job offer like the one she had on the table.

Suzanne was sitting behind her desk with two large stacks of papers in front of her.

"Sit down," the senior partner said. "How's your father-in-law?"

Katelyn gave a quick summary of what she'd learned.

"That's hopeful," Suzanne replied. "He's a lawyer, isn't he?"

"Yes. He has a practice in Wilmington with Robbie's older brother."

"There are good lawyers in small firms."

"I think they have a good reputation."

Suzanne paused, took a deep breath, and exhaled. The simple act told Katelyn everything she needed to know. Her heart started pounding.

"Right before I buzzed you, I was meeting with Kane and realized you were mistakenly copied on my email last night about your employment status and the offer in Chicago. I assume you read it."

"I did."

"And you know my opinion, and the response from Dwight Kennedy."

"Yes."

Suzanne looked directly at her. "Despite what he said, Dwight's statement isn't the last word on the issue. He'll eventually retire, and when that happens, things could change."

"What about Mr. Bancroft?"

"Yes, that hurt," Suzanne said. "But I can work with Lynwood. I've turned him in a different direction before."

"Wasn't the decision made by a majority of the executive committee?"

"Yes, but the committee is like a jury. There are leaders and fillers. And according to Valerie, some of those who went along with Dwight would have easily changed their minds if he hadn't been so adamant. He's the key."

A "filler" was a juror who would line up behind a dominant personality and follow along.

"Why would Mr. Kennedy and especially Mr. Bancroft be so against me?"

"To be blunt, I think Lynwood is jealous of your loyalty to me. As for Dwight, I'm not going to speculate."

"But you know."

"I trust you, but I can't go there. I'm already telling you too much and could get my wrist slapped for what I wrote in the email."

"I'm not interested in suing the firm."

"And I know that because I know you. Anyway, don't give up. Move to Chicago and keep doing the kind of work you're capable of. Things will come right eventually."

"Thanks again for being such a strong advocate for me."

"You're welcome. You earned it. It wasn't a gift. Now go be with your husband and his family."

Katelyn wasn't sure if she should be encouraged or not. Suzanne's personal commitment to her cause was inspiring, but the monolithic structure of the huge law firm still blocked her way.

———

When the plane landed in Wilmington, Robbie was waiting for her in the baggage claim area. He held a large bouquet of flowers in his right hand. A card on the flowers read "Congratulations." She hugged him tightly before planting a firm kiss on his lips.

"Yes, congratulations," she said. "To us."

"All three of us," Robbie replied.

Katelyn pulled back slightly. "Unless it's twins."

SEVEN

EMERSON SAT AT A SMALL TABLE IN THE KITCHEN OF
the two-bedroom apartment he'd rented on the outskirts of Raleigh.
The house he'd owned with his wife sold for less than he'd hoped.
After paying his divorce lawyer, Emerson's share of the equity in the
home went to satisfy his portion of the joint debts incurred during
the marriage. His wife received a third of his retirement account,
but he dodged the bullet of an ongoing alimony obligation. He was
free and broke.

Fortunately, neither his ex-wife nor her lawyer discovered the
existence of First Flight Research and Development, the company
that held the patent for the antinausea medication. Emerson lost the
$49,000 he'd received upon signing the agreement with Brigham-
Neal betting on who would be the Player of the Season in the
English Premier League. Abandoning his preference for long shots,
he placed his money on the favorite, an established soccer star. The
striker injured his foot, missed the last five matches of the season,
and fell to second in the voting.

In Emerson's hand was an envelope from Brigham-Neal. Fearing
it was bad news, he tore off the end of the envelope, blew into the
opening, and extracted what was inside. His mouth dropped open.

The envelope contained his portion of the initial payment from the pharmaceutical company. He read the numbers on the check three times in disbelief and then called Lance.

"Did you get your payment from Brigham-Neal?" Emerson asked.

"Yeah, it's a decent start."

Emerson had received $317,680.72.

"Decent? Your check should be for around $335,000."

"Yes, $339,647.28 to be exact."

Hearing the number, Emerson felt a deep pain shoot through his gut. All of that should have been his money.

"You should be happy," he managed.

"Based on how long I've waited, we're not level, but I agreed to the deal, and I'm a man of my word."

Emerson grunted.

"I also got a phone call from my lawyer," Lance continued.

After obtaining a majority interest in Emerson's company, Lance had insisted that his attorney be designated as the legal contact for the pharmaceutical manufacturer. All significant communication went through him.

"He says the company received a complaint that you infringed on someone else's patent," Lance continued.

"That happens all the time with new drugs," Emerson replied. "It's a common shakedown, but Brigham-Neal knows how to take care of spurious claims."

"My attorney says if the drug manufacturer has to pay damages on an infringement claim, they can charge it back to us."

"That's standard language, but it only applies if someone proves we did something wrong."

"If *you* did something wrong," Lance corrected him.

"That's what I meant. Didn't your lawyer tell you the indemnity provision was in the paperwork when he reviewed the contract?"

"If there's a problem, it's not my lawyer's fault. I'm holding you personally responsible if there's a charge-back."

"Do whatever you want," Emerson said in exasperation, then immediately regretted his words and tone of voice.

"I will," Lance answered coldly. "You can count on it."

"Did you call the hospital?" Katelyn asked when she went into the kitchen where Robbie was brewing coffee for himself, along with some hot tea for the mom-to-be.

"As soon as I woke up. The nurse says my dad is stable but no other changes."

"Stable is good."

"Yes, I was thinking about him in the night and believe he's going to pull through."

Katelyn had seen Robbie's journal on the nightstand but hadn't taken another peek.

They ate a light breakfast in the sunroom. Katelyn placed her flowers in a vase that she positioned in the middle of a glass-topped table. There were still a few exotic plants in the sunroom, but not nearly as many as when Robbie's mother was alive and filled it with orchids. The room provided a panoramic view of the backyard that was lush with green grass and flowering bushes. Sitting in a wicker chair with a thick cushion, Katelyn nibbled on a muffin from a local bakery. The automatic sprinkler system sprayed mist that created a jungle feel.

"This is nice," she said.

"And in the sunroom, you and the baby are protected from the mosquitoes and Burmese pythons."

"Have pythons made it this far north from the Everglades?" Katelyn asked in surprise.

"Not yet."

"I don't like snakes."

Charlie ran across the yard and began sniffing around the base of a bush.

"Charlie would chase off any snakes," Robbie said.

"Not if they were bigger than earthworms."

Katelyn took a sip of tea. She didn't want to spoil the morning mood, but she had to talk to Robbie.

"I need to tell you more about the job in Chicago."

Robbie glanced sideways at her. "Are we finished discussing snakes?"

"Not totally," she answered.

Katelyn left to retrieve the emails from Suzanne and Dwight Kennedy. She handed the copies to Robbie and watched his eyes as he read them.

"Did they catch the mistake in sending this to you?"

"Suzanne did."

Katelyn told him about her conversation with the senior partner. Robbie finished eating his muffin while she spoke.

"What are your thoughts about the Chicago job this morning?" he asked.

Katelyn sighed. "I don't want to think about it. Suzanne may be right about a future change in opinion on the executive committee; she may be wrong. It's so peaceful here. I just want to sit here and do nothing all day."

"You're working," Robbie answered. "Just on something new. I think I see the beginning of a baby bump."

Katelyn touched her flat abdomen. "Any bump is from that muffin. And I don't want my thoughts to be dominated by the law firm. I'd rather focus on your father getting well."

They sat in silence. Katelyn drank the last drop of tea. A ceiling fan stirred the air that brushed across her cheeks. She closed her eyes and let the tension flow out of her body. She didn't bother to see how much time passed. Robbie spoke.

"Stay here all day if you like," he said. "But I'm heading over to the hospital. I'd like to be with Dad in case he wakes up. I'd like the first face he sees to be a member of the family."

"I'll come with you."

"That's not necessary. Half an hour ago, you wanted to spend all morning in the sunroom."

"I'm pregnant, which gives me the right to change my mind on a whim."

"That's not the Katelyn Martin-Cobb I know, who tracks her outfits on a spreadsheet."

———

They pulled into the hospital parking lot. Katelyn usually tried to avoid hospitals. She grabbed Robbie's hand as they walked through the entrance and took the elevator to the ICU ward. On her wrist was the fancy watch that Robbie had bought her the previous Christmas. Carter had chipped in to help purchase the gift.

Katelyn had not seen Carter Cobb for several months. Following his heart attack, her father-in-law quickly bounced back and had been working a normal schedule for a couple of years. Katelyn braced herself for the shock of seeing the man Robbie had described over the phone. The nurse released the electric lock to open the door for the ICU.

Still as a corpse, Carter was lying on the bed. Katelyn involuntarily shivered. Robbie stepped directly up to his father.

"Good morning, Dad. I brought Katelyn to see you. She flew in yesterday, and we're staying at your house. I hope that's okay. We really enjoyed spending time in the sunroom this morning. Everything is going fine." Robbie glanced at Katelyn and whispered, "Should I tell him?"

Katelyn shook her head. "No, I want it to be confirmed."

"Except Charlie had an accident in the kitchen. He doesn't have the strongest stomach, and the change in location triggered something. I cleaned it up and sprayed air freshener."

"I didn't know about that," Katelyn said.

"It was before you finished your shower this morning."

"Maybe we should make him stay outside more."

Robbie redirected his attention to the unconscious man in the bed. "I spotted a couple of things that need to be fixed. The toilet in the guest bath needs a new flapper, and the flashing on the north side of the garage has some rot. I'll buy a new flapper, but I think we should ask a carpenter to look at the flashing. There might be some wood rot hiding behind the boards. I know Benjie Guion used to help you out with bigger repair projects, but I think he's retired. Let me know if you want me to ask David for a recommendation."

Robbie stopped and looked over his shoulder at Katelyn.

"I don't know how you can do this," she said in a low voice. "It seems weird to me."

"Do you want to try it?" he asked.

"No."

"It doesn't have to be a big speech. Just let him hear the sound of your voice."

Katelyn hesitated for a few seconds, then stepped forward to the side of the bed. Her father-in-law's chest rose and fell in a regular rhythm. His skin color was pale and pasty beneath the gray stubble on his face. Robbie had moved to the foot of the bed. With permission, Katelyn had adopted the same name for her father-in-law that Andy and Courtney used.

"Hey, Pops. Good morning."

"Morning," a weak voice said.

Katelyn jumped. She glanced over her shoulder at Robbie, who was clearly as surprised as she was.

"Say something else to him," Robbie urged her. "He responded to your voice, not mine."

Katelyn cleared her throat and leaned over slightly.

"It's Katelyn. Can you hear me?"

She watched his lips, but they remained motionless.

"I flew in from DC to see you."

"Hi, darling," Carter mumbled.

"That's what he called my mom," Robbie said. "He must think you're her. He's been close to death and maybe saw her."

Carter began to mumble unintelligibly. It went on for several seconds before he stopped. Robbie motioned for Katelyn to respond.

"Please say that again," she said. "I couldn't understand you."

One of the nurses came into the room.

"My father just said a few words when my wife spoke to him," Robbie said excitedly.

"Yes, he's waking up, although we've not heard him say anything we could make out. How clearly did he speak?"

Robbie told her.

The nurse nodded. "That's common. A patient will be in the past before returning to the present, coherent one minute and incoherent the next. Don't let that discourage you."

The nurse injected medicine into the IV port running into Carter's arm and then left the room.

"Try again," Robbie said to Katelyn.

"What should I say?"

"Tell him you love him."

"I do love him, but I've never said it to him in person," Katelyn protested.

"Maybe it's time."

Katelyn looked at Carter, whose eyes were now slightly open. He blinked as if trying to bring her into focus. Katelyn thought about an evening when the family went out to dinner as a group. During the meal, Carter leaned over and said to her in a soft voice, "I'm glad you married Robbie." It was the moment she first felt part of the greater Cobb family.

"I love you."

"I want to go home," he said.

"Not until the doctor says it's okay," she responded awkwardly.

Robbie rewarded her with a thumbs-up. They stayed for another fifteen minutes. Katelyn tried to coax more responses, but Carter didn't stir again.

"You brought him up into consciousness," Robbie said as they left the ICU area. "There was something about your voice. Maybe it's because you speak clearly and not with a North Carolina drawl like the rest of us."

"I'm sure that's it. But it really was sweet that he thought I was your mom. Is that why you wanted me to say that I loved him?"

"Yeah, it just popped into my head."

They reached the car.

"Ready to go home?" Robbie asked.

"You mean to your father's house?"

"Yes."

David and his family were surrounded after church by well-wishers asking about his father and promising to pray for him.

"When do we get to see Pops?" Courtney asked when they were in the family minivan. "All those people talking about him made me miss him."

"Not until he's in a regular hospital room or goes to a rehab center," David replied. "They don't allow children to enter the intensive care unit."

"Why not?" Courtney protested. "I know not to touch stuff."

"Most kids aren't as smart and well behaved as you are," Nan answered.

David glanced in the rearview mirror at Andy, who was staring out the side window.

"Andy, would you like to go fishing tomorrow morning with Uncle Robbie and me? I talked to a man who told me where the redfish may be coming onto the marsh flats to feed on the incoming tide."

"What about school?" Nan asked.

"Every boy needs to play hooky to go fishing at least once in his life," David replied nonchalantly. "We'll make it educational and talk about wildlife on the marsh. How about it?"

"Maybe," Andy mumbled.

David glanced at Nan, who shrugged.

"We'd need to get up early," David continued.

"I want to go," Courtney piped up. "And I'm not learning any-thing at school. I already know everything we study."

"No," Nan said before David could answer.

"I guess so," Andy said, turning away from the window. "Would I be able to fly-fish?"

"Yeah. Robbie's an expert."

Andy spoke slowly. "I really want to go with Pops, but I guess I can practice with you and Uncle Robbie."

———

David and Nan were finishing lunch when Robbie called to tell what had happened at the hospital the day before while he and Katelyn visited. David placed the phone on speaker so Nan could listen. The kids were outside playing.

"Along with the few clear words, there was a lot of nonsense," Robbie said. "One of the nurses said that was typical. If you want to take Nan to see him, Katelyn and I can come over and watch the kids."

David looked at Nan, who nodded.

"That would be great," he said. "I sat with Dad for a while early in the morning yesterday, but I didn't get any response from him."

"And I can bring over one of Dad's fly rods and let Andy prac-tice casting out back."

"Good, because we're on to go fishing tomorrow. I found out where the redfish are coming up on the flats."

"But it's Monday."

"Nan and I agreed to let Andy skip school for a day."

Nan punched David lightly in the arm and shook her head. David grinned.

"Awesome," Robbie replied. "I think that will be great for him."

Two hours later, David watched as Robbie and Andy headed to the backyard. Courtney curled up in Katelyn's lap with a stack of books to read together, and there was a promise of an ice pop.

"Robbie and Katelyn don't have a problem interacting with the kids," Nan said as they backed out of the driveway. "They'll be great parents."

"Who knows when that will happen? Katelyn's been offered a big promotion with the law firm. They'll have to relocate to Chicago, but it looks like the final step before partnership for her."

David and Nan's visit with his father was much less dramatic than what Robbie described earlier that day. Carter tried to speak, but it was nonsensical. When he briefly opened his eyes, he didn't recognize either of them, and seemed frustrated and upset. Both David and Nan tried to comfort him with soothing words.

Nan sighed. "I guess he's still fighting his way through the fog of the hemorrhage and surgery."

Seeing his father so unsettled was worse than David imagined. He desperately missed Carter's booming enthusiasm. His father mumbled, moved his head, and moaned.

David silently wondered if the home remedy Zeke had told him about could help him.

When they arrived home, Robbie and Andy were playing a video game in the den. Courtney was outside in an oversized portable plastic pool. Katelyn had positioned a small slide so the little girl could plunge headfirst into the chilly water. It was a warm afternoon, but there wasn't enough sun to warm up the water.

"Aunt Kate said it was okay so long as we fill it all the way to the top with water," Courtney said, jumping up and down as she wiped drops from her eyes.

"She told me it was allowed," Katelyn added with a quick glance at her niece.

"The pool, yes," David replied. "Not the slide. But it looks like you've set it up so that it's safe."

"I just said pool," Courtney interjected.

"Discussing rules with Courtney is like appearing in front of a judge who wants to dissect every phrase of a statute," David said. "Detailed clarification is part of the process."

"Got it," Katelyn said.

"The pool at the country club will open at the beginning of May," David said to Courtney. "If you prove to me that you can swim across the pool twice, I think you're ready to jump off the bigger diving board."

"Aunt Kate said she would teach me to dive."

"With permission from your parents," Katelyn added.

After wrapping Courtney in a towel, they went inside the house. Robbie and Andy were finishing their game. Robbie handed the controller to his nephew.

"Uncle Robbie is good," Andy said to David. "Even though he's never played the game, he almost beat me."

"And Andy made progress with his casting. I think we should take spinning tackle for backup, but he can give the fly rod a try."

The boy returned his attention to the game and set it for solo play.

"How was Dad?" Robbie asked.

"Incoherent and agitated."

"What does that mean?" Andy asked, hitting the pause button.

"He's confused, and his words don't make sense."

The adults moved away from the den and sat around a small table in the kitchen nook.

"If it's okay, I'd like to tag along on the fishing trip," Katelyn said. "I've never seen the marsh at dawn, and I enjoyed watching you teach Andy. I'm curious to see how he does."

David watched the surprise flash across his brother's face.

"Are you sure?" Robbie asked. "I thought you might have to work."

"I texted Suzanne and told her that I was unavailable until Wednesday."

"I'd love to have you join us," Robbie said.

"Me too," David added.

Katelyn glanced at Robbie. "There's been a bit of an upheaval at the law firm," she said. "Is it okay if I tell them about it?"

"Uh, sure."

Katelyn spoke calmly, but David could imagine the emotions and pressure his sister-in-law must be experiencing.

"I'm sorry," Nan said when Katelyn finished. "You've worked so hard. But it sounds like the executive committee might change their decision down the road."

David cleared his throat. "Maybe the Lord has something better for you," he said.

"Do you know something we don't?" Robbie asked.

"What do you mean?" Katelyn added with a puzzled look on her face.

"Nothing. But someone as talented as you are should have a chance to shine."

"Thanks," Katelyn said with a smile. "That means a lot."

A few minutes later, Robbie and Katelyn left. David and Nan went into the kitchen to clean up. David began loading the dishwasher while Nan wiped the counters with a damp rag.

"What were you thinking when you told Katelyn that God might have something better for her than transferring to Chicago?" Nan asked. "I can tell when those wheels of yours are turning."

"I wondered if she might be interested in coming to work at Cobb and Cobb. What would you think about that?"

Nan dropped the rag on the counter and faced him. "I'm not sure. Tell me more."

David took a deep breath. "Who knows when or if Dad will be able to practice law again? We have plenty of work. Nothing fancy. But solid, loyal clients who mostly pay their bills. It wouldn't be anything like Morgan and Monroe. I mean, Katelyn is like a Thoroughbred racehorse, and I'm more of a—"

"David, you're an excellent lawyer," Nan cut in. "And you have insight into people and situations that you can't learn in law school."

"I appreciate your confidence," he replied. "But not everyone appreciates me as much as you do. Salary would also be a big hurdle. I couldn't offer Katelyn half of what she's probably making in DC and wouldn't want to offend her. But as she talked, my heart went out to her because of what just happened, and I also thought about the need we have here."

"My heart went out to her too. What they did to her at the law firm made me mad. Maybe we should pray and think about it. We have a good relationship with Robbie and Katelyn now, but we don't see them except at holidays. This would throw us totally into each other's lives. It would be a huge change."

"There would be challenges."

"Yes."

"But you'd not oppose the idea?"

"Not if we're in agreement." Nan tossed the wet rag into the sink. "What would Robbie do if they moved to Wilmington? He'd love the fishing and hunting, but he'd need a job."

"Oh, that's easy. He'd be the new director at Camp Seacrest."

EIGHT

KATELYN SAT IN THE SUNROOM AS EVENING DESCENDED.
Robbie was playing hide-and-seek with Charlie in the backyard.
Each time, the agile animal quickly found the hidden dog toy. Robbie
came into the sunroom and took a long drink of water from a plastic
bottle.

"I didn't realize Charlie had a grandfather who was a blood-
hound," he said. "He's having a lot of fun. How about you?"

"Oh yeah. Dad used to play hide-and-seek with his Jack Russell
terrier. That's what gave me the idea."

Robbie took another drink of water. "Are you serious about joining the fishing trip in the morning? You'll see the marsh at dawn,
but whether Andy catches any fish is up in the air. Redfish can be
hard to hook, especially using a fly rod."

"Is that going to frustrate Andy?" Katelyn asked.

"I hope not."

"I want to go. See you in your element."

"Okay, I think you'll like it. Spending time on the marsh has
always been popular with David, my dad, and me."

Charlie appeared at the door of the sunroom with a miniature rubber Doberman in his mouth. Robbie threw it toward the rear of the yard. Charlie took off after it.

"I saw the drawing in your journal about eating hot dogs by the campfire with your dad and David. Was it okay that I looked?"

Robbie sat down close to her. "Yeah, there aren't any dark secrets in there. Most of those happened before we met."

"Not all of them?"

"All the really bad ones."

"And I read your prayer about wanting to know if God is real."

Robbie raised his eyebrows. "Did you stop there?"

"Yes."

"God answered my prayer."

Even though the ceiling fan was slowly turning overhead, the atmosphere in the sunroom became very still.

Robbie continued. "He said yes. Not out loud, but in here." He touched his heart. "And I've felt different ever since. I told my dad about it."

"What's different?"

Robbie paused. "More alive, if that makes sense. More aware of myself and other people. More at peace. A better person."

"If this makes you happy, I'm all for it," she said cautiously, wondering if this was simply a phase he was going through.

———

Katelyn slipped out of bed before the alarm went off and brewed some tea along with a pot of coffee. Robbie appeared in the kitchen with his unruly hair pointed in multiple directions. He ran his fingers over the top of his head without visible impact. Katelyn pointed out the futility of his action.

"I'll cover it with a cap," he replied.

"Do I need to worry about bugs while we're on the boat?" Katelyn asked.

"There's repellent in my dad's tackle box if we need it."

Twenty minutes later, they left with the skiff on a trailer behind Robbie's truck. He had no problem backing down the curvy driveway with the trailer attached to the rear.

"They don't teach that in law school," Katelyn observed as he smoothly navigated a bend with pine trees on both sides of the drive.

"David and I used to have contests. We'd set up obstacles and see who could do it the fastest. Dad made us take the boat off first."

"Who won?"

"Usually, I did. Otherwise, I wouldn't have brought it up."

David and Andy were waiting for them in front of the house.

"I brought a bunch of snacks," Andy said when he got in the rear seat of the truck. "Aunt Kate, do you like cashew nuts?"

"Yes."

"That's one of Pops's favorite foods."

"I've brought everything else," Robbie said. "I know how to take care of my important clients."

The interior of the truck was mostly quiet during the forty-five-minute drive to the country store Zeke mentioned. The nearby boat ramp was little more than an open space in the dirt. There wasn't a breeze, and at low tide the marsh grass stood upright at attention. Exposed mudflats defined the narrow canals of water that snaked through the grass and out of sight. Katelyn stood beside Andy while Robbie and David put the boat in the water.

"Are you excited?" she asked.

"Yeah. And a little nervous. I don't want to mess up in front of you and Uncle Robbie."

Katelyn put her arm around Andy and gave him a hug. "You're already a much better fisherman than I am. And Uncle Robbie likes teaching people how to do things. He's not going to criticize you."

"That's the way Pops is too."

Robbie jumped into the truck and pulled the empty trailer into a sandy clearing.

"All aboard!" David called out.

Katelyn had to take three steps in the squishy black mud to reach the boat. Her sandals sank down. David held out his hand and helped her into the boat. She glanced down at her feet.

"The mud is a natural barrier to insects," he said.

"Maybe I should roll in it," she answered.

Andy, who was standing beside her, laughed. Proud she could make an eleven-year-old laugh, Katelyn watched as he and Robbie jumped into the skiff, a classic shallow draft vessel with dark-colored wooden seats that shone from years of polishing. Robbie pulled the rope handle on the small motor, which coughed a few times and then died.

"It fired up last night at the house when I checked it, but you never know with an engine this old," he said.

After multiple attempts the motor stayed alive, and the boat moved slowly down the channel. Katelyn sat in the bow and savored each breath of the salt air. Looking down, she saw a cast of tiny crabs fleeing into their holes as the boat passed. White egrets stood motionless in the water, waiting for breakfast to come to them. One jabbed its bill into the water and came up with a tiny fish that it swallowed in one gulp. Clusters of oysters were exposed on the mud in the low tide.

"Based on what Zeke told me, there's a good place to begin a couple of hundred yards to the southeast," David said. "He claims the fish funnel through there, feed, then spread out as the water rises."

Robbie steered the skiff by moving the engine from side to side. Andy sat with his feet over the edge of the boat. A few minutes later they turned into a deeper channel. The number of egrets increased.

"This is it!" David said, pointing. "The baitfish are already pushing in."

"I'm going to anchor over there so we can finish setting up the gear," Robbie said.

Robbie turned off the motor. Only the faint sound of some seagulls disturbed the silence. With Andy watching, Robbie selected a fly and tied it onto the line at the end of a rod.

"I'm using twenty-pound fluorocarbon for this crab fly," he said. "A fish is more likely to cut the line on an oyster than break it by pulling too hard. Here, show your aunt Kate what a crab fly pattern looks like."

Andy held out the fly in his open palm. "You can touch it," he said. "Pops made it."

"Where's the hook?" Katelyn asked cautiously.

"That's what we want the redfish to wonder about too," Robbie answered. "It's barbless so it won't tear up the fish's mouth."

"Which makes it harder to land a fish," David added.

Katelyn picked up the fake crab by a tiny claw.

"I put some of Pops's flies without hooks on our Christmas tree," Andy said.

"Nan says they make perfect decorations," David added.

"I bet they do," Katelyn said.

While they were talking, she could tell the level of the water was rising slightly.

"There's one!" Robbie called out.

Katelyn looked into the opaque water but saw nothing.

"Another one!" Robbie pointed. "You can see its tail."

This time Katelyn followed the end of her husband's finger toward where the grass met the water. Sure enough, she could see a broad fish tail a few inches out of the water.

"It looks like it's standing on its head," she said.

"That's because it is," Robbie answered. "Andy, tell her why."

"The redfish is eating crabs and other stuff that live on the bottom. Pops says the fish will slam its nose into the mud to grab and swallow them."

Robbie handed a rod to Andy. "Do you think you can reach the edge of the grass from here?"

"I don't know," the boy answered doubtfully.

"Try."

Katelyn watched as Andy pulled line from the reel by hand. She'd fished for trout several times using a fly rod in the cooler water of streams and rivers north of Washington. With her husband as teacher, Katelyn had quickly progressed from a novice angler whose line ended up in a bird's-nest tangle to one who could usually place a fly where she wanted it to land. The order and symmetry of the back-and-forward motion was beautiful.

Andy was standing in the stern. He began to move the rod back and forth. Katelyn glanced at David, who seemed to be holding his breath. With a final forward thrust of the rod, Andy let the line go. The fly landed about twenty feet from the edge of the boat. Far from the grass.

"You pushed it too hard at the end," Robbie said gently. "Let the rod do the work. It's the same as in the backyard when you were trying to hit the plastic bucket."

Six or seven casts followed. None of them came within ten feet of the target area. Katelyn could tell Andy was getting frustrated. David remained silent and let Robbie do the coaching.

"I should just use my spinning rod." Andy turned and tried to hand the fly rod to Robbie.

"Maybe later," Robbie answered. "I'm going to move the boat closer."

Once the tide started flowing, it was surprising how quickly the water level rose. Robbie started the motor and drifted slowly down the channel about a hundred feet and then killed the engine. He pointed. "I saw one tailing over there."

Andy moved to the bow of the boat. Katelyn eased out of his way. This time they were closer to the grass. Andy resumed the rhythmic back-and-forth motion and released the fly. It floated over the water and came to rest at the edge of the grass.

"Let it sink," Robbie said. "Your fly is about three feet away from where I saw the fish tailing."

Katelyn stared intently at the spot where the fly landed. Suddenly, the water boiled for a couple of seconds and the line went tight.

"Got him!" David shouted.

"Hold up the rod tip!" Robbie yelled.

Andy took a few steps back toward the center of the boat. The slender rod was bent almost double.

"Now to the side!" Robbie said. "Strip line to set the hook."

Andy pulled the line back sharply a few inches with his free hand.

"He's strong!" the boy said.

"So are you," Robbie replied. "Don't try to muscle him in; just let the rod and the drag on your reel do its work."

The fight with the fish was like a conductor directing a symphony. In a calm voice Robbie gave Andy a mixture of soft instructions coupled with encouragement. Once, Andy tried to give Robbie the rod, but he refused.

"This is your fish," he said.

Several times, the fish came close enough to the boat that Robbie grabbed a long-handled net. But as if sensing the end was near, the fish would take off again. Finally, the fish swam past the bow of the boat and Robbie scooped it up.

"That's huge!" Katelyn exclaimed.

"Let's measure him," Robbie said.

Katelyn glanced at Andy, whose eyes were wide open in awe. Robbie held up the fish by the lower jaw while David checked the length.

"Twenty-seven inches," he said.

"It's a female," Robbie added. "They get bigger than the males."

The fish had a very large head and a thick upper body that swooped down to a much narrower section and a broad tail. Katelyn could tell Robbie was having trouble holding it.

"What does it weigh, Uncle Robbie?" Andy asked.

"I'd guess seven pounds. Come closer."

With Robbie's assistance, Andy held the fish. David took a succession of quick photos with his phone.

"Do you want to keep it?" Robbie asked Andy. "It's a legal size to keep in North Carolina."

"No." Andy shook his head. "Pops and I want the fish to be even bigger when we catch them again."

Robbie knelt and carefully lowered the fish into the water. It didn't dart away. Robbie held it for a few seconds until it slowly swam off.

"Why did it swim so slowly?" Katelyn asked.

"If Andy hooked you that long, you'd be winded too," he replied.

Over the next three hours, Andy caught a much smaller fish and lost a large one that broke the line. Robbie and David caught one each. As the sun rose, the bugs woke up, and they all applied repellent.

"Your turn," Andy said to Katelyn when they moved to a new spot and saw a fish tailing.

"No, I'm a spectator today. Maybe next time."

"Are you sure?" Robbie asked. "We're having a good day."

"I'm enjoying watching you."

Shortly after high tide, the water grew still, and Katelyn suddenly realized she could see to the bottom.

"It's so clear now," she said.

"Yeah, it can be murky one minute and clear the next when it's between tides."

Katelyn was quiet during the drive home. Andy's excitement continued. He wanted to relive the entire morning by asking his father and uncle questions. Robbie seemed to have all the answers.

"Dad, when will I be able to show Pops the pictures of my fish?" he asked.

"As soon as he's fully awake and can appreciate them."

Andy was silent for a few moments. "I'm going to pray that's soon."

The day had been an unqualified success, something Andy would remember the rest of his life. Throughout the morning, David debated whether to ask Katelyn if she was interested in coming to work in Wilmington. Bringing up the subject while on a skiff fishing would be a different way to do so, but it never seemed like the right time.

"Katelyn and I would like to take you out to dinner later this week," Robbie said when they neared David's house.

"Can I come?" Andy jumped in. "I don't want a babysitter to watch me."

"When I said you, I meant all of you," Robbie answered. "Including Courtney."

"It will be a celebration of your fishing success," Katelyn added.

"Sounds good," David said. "I'll tell Nan."

David and Andy unbuckled and prepared to get out.

"Thanks, Uncle Robbie," Andy said. "That was awesome."

"You're welcome, but you were awesome. I bet you dream about that first fish you landed."

"I hope so."

Inside the house, David listened to Andy tell his version of the day to his mother. Nan was impressed when she saw the photos of Andy's largest fish.

"You caught that all by yourself?"

"Yep. I held the rod while Uncle Robbie adjusted the drag on the reel."

"It was an epic battle," David said as he scrolled through more pictures, including the fish he and Robbie caught.

"Did Aunt Kate fish?" Nan asked when a photo with Katelyn appeared.

"Not this time. But she liked looking at the marsh and watching me."

When Andy left to take a shower, David lingered in the den.

"Did you talk to Katelyn about coming to work at the law firm?" Nan asked.

"What makes you think I'd do that?"

"There are different kinds of fishing."

"I wasn't sure that kind of fish was biting."

At the office later that afternoon, David faced a mountain of phone calls and emails. His natural work rhythm was deliberate, but, when necessary, he could engage a faster gear. He delegated calls inquiring about his father's health to Meredith while he focused on legal matters. It was 5:40 p.m. when he responded to the final email. He texted Nan to tell her not to hold supper for him.

Arriving at the hospital, he ran into Dr. Spies in the hallway outside his father's room. The surgeon was making his evening rounds.

"How's my father doing?" David asked.

"Satisfactory. We did a postsurgery MRI, and the swelling in his brain is reduced. He's beginning to regain consciousness."

"What about cognitive functioning? On Sunday, all he did with my wife and me was mutter incoherently."

"Too soon to know."

David found his father resting peacefully, his breathing normal. Pulling a chair close to the bed, he decided to try the same approach to communication as Robbie. In a normal tone of voice, he told his father about the fishing trip. It was awkward at first, but as he relived the morning, he became more animated. Pulling out his phone, he held it in front of his father's face.

"Here's Andy's fish. His first redfish caught on a crab fly pattern that you tied. It was a beauty, twenty-seven inches and seven pounds."

His father's eyelids fluttered for a second, then opened. David held the phone closer.

"Uh," his father said, blinking. "Nice fish."

David's mouth fell open. "Dad, can you understand me?"

"Water," he replied in a croaky voice.

David grabbed a plastic cup, filled it with water, and placed the straw against his father's lower lip. He took a tiny sip, then a longer one that made him choke. David quickly removed the straw. His father settled down and his breathing became regular. He was asleep. David lowered his head and rested it on the bed in thanksgiving.

That evening as he was spending time with Andy, he told him what had happened at the hospital. Andy's eyes widened.

"I haven't prayed yet," Andy responded. "I thought we'd do it now."

"What you said today in the truck was a prayer, and God answered it."

Andy closed his eyes and spoke words of thanksgiving. All David did was add an "Amen."

David told Nan about their son's prayer upon hearing the news about his Pops.

"He's grown up a lot in the last couple of days," she said. "As a fisherman and as a child of God."

"Yeah, it was a big day. Much more important than sitting in a school classroom."

"Don't push it too far. From what I've heard, you and Robbie played hooky any chance you got."

"Those stories have been exaggerated. But being with Andy and Robbie brought back a lot of memories."

Nan started to move away, then stopped. "Oh, Katelyn called. She and Robbie want to take the whole family out to dinner tomorrow night."

"Robbie mentioned that earlier."

"Katelyn is flying back to DC on Wednesday."

David was silent for a moment. "Maybe I should have mentioned the possibility of her working at Cobb and Cobb while we were fishing."

Robbie put away the boat, and Katelyn took a shower. She was fixing a salad in the kitchen when Robbie came in and announced he was taking Charlie for a walk.

"I made an entry in my journal about our trip, if you want to look at it," he said.

"Thanks. Any artwork?"

"No, didn't have time for that," Robbie said, then added, "and you can browse some of the other pages if you want to while you eat."

After Robbie left, Katelyn found the journal open on the nightstand and brought it into the kitchen to look at while she ate. The entry included the specifics about Andy's fish: the time of day, tide conditions, fly used, type of fishing line, and length and weight of the fish. He also listed who'd been on the boat and had underlined her name and put two exclamation points after it. Katelyn chuckled.

After eating a few bites of food, she tentatively flipped back a page and saw an entry about Carter's brain hemorrhage, followed by a prayer:

God, please touch my dad and restore his health so he can be a grandfather to our child. Amen.

Katelyn read the prayer several times. The words perfectly mirrored the desire of her own heart. She closed her eyes. Not to pray, but to imagine a healthy Carter, a huge grin on his face, proudly holding a baby in his arms. That was a hope she would love to see become reality. She started to close the journal but turned back one more page. At the bottom of the sheet, Robbie had written three words: "Director—Camp Seacrest." Nothing else.

As soon as Robbie and Charlie returned from their walk,

Katelyn called him into the kitchen where the journal was still open on the table.

"We need to talk," she said.

"Am I in trouble?"

She placed her hand on the leather-bound book. "No, but I read your journal. It started me thinking."

"Let me grab a water."

Robbie joined her at the table. Katelyn opened to the prayer for Carter, read it, and told him what she hoped for.

"I want this so much," she said. "It would be terribly sad if our child doesn't get to know Pops the way Andy and Courtney have."

"I agree."

"But that's not all."

Katelyn turned back a page and slid the book across the table. "What's this about Camp Seacrest?"

"Wasn't the water on the marsh beautiful this morning?" Robbie responded. "I'm so glad you got to see it at high tide. It's the same with the marsh near Camp Seacrest. That's where I first saw the water suddenly become clear as an aquarium."

"That's a nonanswer. Why did you write down 'Director' and 'Camp Seacrest' in your journal?"

"I forgot I'd done that when I told you to take a look."

"Can you clear that up for me? There's no drawing or words after it."

"You know what's going on with the director embezzling money. I care about the camp and its future."

"And? I know there's more."

Robbie sighed. "To be director at the camp would be my dream job."

Katelyn leaned forward. "That's what I thought," she said with satisfaction. "I watched you interact with Andy on the boat. You were amazing. And I'm not talking about the technical part of fishing. You were patient, challenging, and encouraging. I believe you'd be the same with any ten- to fourteen-year-old boy willing to let you into his life. When were you going to talk to me about it?"

"I was going to mention it as a wild idea at the seafood restaurant, but when you pulled out the Chicago offer from the law firm, I was glad I'd kept my mouth shut. Your career has always been way more important than mine. Applying to be director at Camp Seacrest makes no sense for more reasons than we can list."

"For money, yes. But what about influence on people? What I saw today on the boat could be duplicated over and over and over, not just by you but by counselors trained to be like you. The possible impact on hundreds of young boys would be huge."

"That's nice, but—"

Katelyn held up her hand. "I have the floor."

"Sorry, go ahead."

"You've supported me one hundred percent from the day I received the job offer at Morgan and Monroe. Maybe it's time for you to pursue your passion. You do good work now, but I can see how this might be perfect for you. It would at least be worth finding out if it's a possibility. If they're interested in hiring you, we can think about other options for me."

"What kind of options?"

Katelyn smiled. "Do you really believe it would be hard for me to land a job at a law firm? There are firms all over the country that would let me work remotely. If I did that, where we live would be irrelevant. And with what's happened at Morgan and Monroe, I'm willing to consider a different path."

Robbie was silent for a few moments. "I guess it won't hurt to find out the status of the search for a new director. I'd need to call

Frank Gates, the chairman of the board. He owns a local heating and air-conditioning company. I don't know him very well, but David does. The board may already have someone in mind. I suspect they'll want to act quickly to move on from the bad publicity caused by Chris Brammer's departure." Robbie paused. "But what about you and Chicago?"

"I'm not going to make a decision about the law firm until we see what happens here. I've loved being in Wilmington and staying at your dad's house. It's like the stress and pressure didn't make it off the airplane."

"I like that."

"Should you ask David to help set up an interview?"

Robbie picked up his phone. "No, I'm past the point of needing my big brother to open a door for me."

He found the number, placed the call, and set the phone on the table between them.

"Gates Heating and Air," a woman answered in a crisp voice.

"This is Robbie Cobb. I'd like to speak to Mr. Gates, please."

"If this is about a problem with your HVAC system, one of our technicians would be glad to talk to you."

"It has to do with Camp Seacrest."

"Just a minute."

Katelyn looked at Robbie. "Are you nervous?"

Robbie pointed to his chest. "Thump, thump, thump."

"Robbie," said a gravelly male voice. "How in the world are you?"

"Fine, fine, thanks for taking my call."

"Of course. The last time I talked to your father, you were living in the Washington, DC, area."

"Still am, but I'm in Wilmington right now. My father had a brain hemorrhage last week."

Katelyn listened as Robbie told Mr. Gates about Carter's health crisis.

"I hate that," Gates said. "As soon as he's able to have visitors, let me know."

"I will, but I'm also calling about Camp Seacrest. David told me what happened with Chris Brammer."

"It's bad," Mr. Gates replied. "Worse than David knows. We appreciate the support you and your family have given over the years."

"That's not changing." Robbie cleared his throat. "Has the board started the process of finding a new director?"

"Yes. We got the jump on that before the news came out about Chris's misconduct. We interviewed several candidates and settled on a man in his early fifties with a lot of camp experience and a good track record as a fund-raiser. I can't reveal his name, but he was in charge of a similar camp out west for the past fifteen years. We offered him the job last week, and he accepted. It will all be public in a few days. Of course, I want you and David to meet him. We'll schedule a dinner to formally announce the decision and introduce the new man to our key supporters."

As Katelyn watched Robbie's face, she was glad they weren't sitting in the same room as the chairman of the camp board. Robbie's disappointment was painfully clear.

"I may be back in Washington, but I'm sure David will attend. I'm glad you found someone who will do a good job."

"It was a huge relief. And don't forget to keep me updated about your father."

"Will do."

The call ended.

"That was a punch to the gut," Robbie said. "But after listening to Frank, it makes sense for the board to hire someone with that kind of experience."

Katelyn reached out and touched Robbie's arm. "I still believe everything I said about you."

NINE

"UNCLE ROBBIE AND AUNT KATE ARE GOING TO BE here in a few minutes!" David called upstairs to the children.

David loosened his tie. He'd worked later than usual, left the office, and made it home just before Robbie and Katelyn were scheduled to arrive. They were going to ride together in the minivan to dinner. Nan, dressed casually, came out of their bedroom.

"Are you going to wear a tie to Jordan's Restaurant?" she asked.

"I wasn't going to take the time to change, but I guess I am now. I don't want people to think you're my college-aged daughter."

Nan kissed him on the cheek. "In that case, keep the tie."

The doorbell chimed. David could hear the sound of the children as they bounded down the stairs to greet Robbie and Katelyn. He changed shirts and put on a pair of navy pants. When he came out, Robbie and Andy were watching a fishing video, and Courtney was showing Katelyn a picture she'd drawn for her aunt. Nan wasn't in sight.

"That's you," Courtney said, pointing to a figure with short dark hair.

"I knew it immediately," Katelyn replied. "And that's Charlie."

David came close enough to see more clearly. The crayon drawing of the woman and dog was well done.

"How did you learn to do that?" he asked her.

"Mom showed me a trick," Courtney answered. "You start with little circles in pencil."

"And there's artistic talent in your genes," Katelyn said. "Robbie can sketch anything."

"Not true," Robbie replied from the sofa.

"Daddy, I want a dog like Charlie," Courtney said. "I promise to take care of him. I'll give him food and water and play with him. Emmaline has a new puppy. Can she bring him over when my friends come over? It will be good practice for me."

David wasn't sure Nan would want to supervise the girls and a puppy.

"Not until the puppy is housebroken," he replied.

Nan came in from the garage. "What puppy?" she asked.

Courtney repeated her plea for a dog to her mother.

Andy heard the second version. "If we get a dog, Courtney will lose interest in it, and I'll have to take care of it," he said.

David looked at Robbie. "See how tough it is being the older sibling? You have to step in when the younger one drops the ball."

"I fed your turtle fresh fruit flies that I caught myself," Robbie responded.

"Let's go," Nan said. "No more talk about fruit flies before dinner."

Robbie and Katelyn interacted with the kids during the ten-minute drive to the restaurant. Andy and Robbie talked fishing. Courtney answered Katelyn's questions about friends.

Fran Jordan was the hostess for the evening at the restaurant. Her eyes lit up when she saw David.

"Now I'm glad I decided to work the supper shift," she said as she greeted them.

They sat at a round table for six. David didn't bother to look at the menu. For him, it was a choice between fried chicken with white gravy, lasagna, or local fried flounder. Nan was reading the menu.

"Are you going soul food, Italian, or seafood?" she asked David.

"After our trip yesterday, I'm leaning seafood."

"Do they have redfish?" Katelyn asked.

"Redfish on a restaurant menu is usually raised on a fish farm," Robbie answered. "I wouldn't want to eat it."

"How did you learn so much about fish?" Courtney asked.

"Your uncle Robbie has a very high fish IQ," David quickly replied.

Robbie kicked David under the table.

"All right, boys," Nan cut in. "If you can't behave, we're going to have to leave right now."

"You started it," Robbie retorted to David.

"I don't want to leave," Courtney objected. "We just got here and haven't eaten."

"Your mother is teasing," David answered. "Your uncle Robbie and I will behave."

When the food arrived, Andy spoke. "Dad, may I pray?"

"Absolutely," David replied.

Andy bowed his head and squeezed his eyes shut. "God, thank you for answering my prayer for Pops and for this food. Amen."

Robbie opened his eyes and faced David. "What's he talking about?"

"During my visit with Dad yesterday, I showed him the photo of Andy's fish and he said, 'Nice fish.'"

Robbie nodded. "If anything can coax Dad back to consciousness, it's a great fish."

During the meal, Courtney talked about the reasons she liked each one of her friends.

"With her insights, she may end up being a professional coun-selor," Nan said.

"Or lawyer," Katelyn said.

Courtney was carefully coating the end of a french fry in ketchup. "Aunt Kate, please move here," she said. "That way you can come over to see me anytime you want."

Katelyn glanced over at Robbie. "We agreed to tell them," she said.

"Are you sure?"

"Yes."

Robbie put his hands together in front of him. "With Katelyn's support, I decided to apply for the director job at Camp Seacrest. I called Frank Gates as the first step."

David's heart skipped a beat.

"This is confidential, but it will be out in the open soon," Robbie continued. "They've already offered the job to someone who's accepted. They started the search before Chris's problems leaked out. The new director has experience running a boys' camp and is a good fund-raiser, which is a huge part of the job. It was a smart move by the board of directors to have a smooth transition in place."

Robbie spoke in a matter-of-fact tone of voice, but David sensed his brother's disappointment.

"I think it would be awesome if you were the head of the camp," Andy said. "All of my friends would like it too."

"Thanks." Robbie smiled at his nephew. "But it's not up to me."

"That was a bold step on your part," Nan said to Katelyn.

"Yes, and I appreciated it a lot," Robbie said.

"Part of what influenced me was seeing Robbie interact with Andy the other day on the fishing trip," Katelyn said. "I imagined how wonderful it would be if that was repeated in the lives of other boys. Everything we do shouldn't be dependent on my career."

"But the conversation with Frank Gates shut the door," Robbie said.

"What are you talking about?" Courtney asked. "I don't understand."

"Uncle Robbie and Aunt Kate wouldn't consider moving to Wilmington unless Uncle Robbie could get a good job," Nan answered.

Courtney was silent for a moment. "That's easy," she responded perkily. "He could work with Daddy and Pops. They have an empty room with a big desk and chair in it. That's where I play on my tablet when I go there, but I wouldn't mind Uncle Robbie using it too."

"That's sweet, Courtney," Robbie said. "But Katelyn is the lawyer in our family, not me."

Mulling over Robbie's news, David ate a bite of flounder as the dinner conversation flowed in another direction.

Later that night, David was in Andy's room for their evening time together.

"I'm glad you prayed before the meal tonight," he said.

"I was thinking about it when everyone was ordering their food. I was a little bit nervous."

"We couldn't tell."

Andy was silent for a moment. "Would it be okay if we prayed that Uncle Robbie would get the job at camp? I had a good time at camp last year, but it would be way better if he was there. Mr. Brammer smiled all the time, but I didn't like him that much. He was kind of fake."

David didn't respond.

"What did he do wrong?" Andy persisted.

"It had to do with money."

"Did he steal?"

"Yes, but I believe he's going to pay it back."

Andy closed his eyes. "God, I ask you to let Uncle Robbie get to be the director of Camp Seacrest." He paused. "And help Mr. Brammer stop being fake. Amen."

The young man opened his eyes and looked up at David. "You can pray too."

Unlike his son, David didn't see things so simply. There was the career of the new director with experience who'd already accepted the job. What would happen to him? And to rescind an offer and bring in someone like Robbie who'd never led a camp or raised money might appear as nepotism because of the Cobb family's longtime involvement. David lifted up a generic prayer that "God's will be done."

"Thanks," Andy said.

David pulled up the sheet and kissed Andy on the forehead. "You're the best," he said to his son.

Downstairs, David told Nan about his time with Andy and their prayers for Camp Seacrest.

"What went through your mind at the dinner table when Robbie brought it up?" she asked. "I know you like the idea."

"Mixed. Robbie would be great with parts of the director job, but I have doubts about his ability to handle the finances. Not that he would be dishonest, of course. But would he be competent to oversee the books? The only business Robbie ran failed miserably, and the last thing the camp needs is back-to-back financial disasters."

"Are you glad now that you never mentioned a job to Katelyn?"

"Yeah, sometimes I confuse my imagination with God's will."

"Imagination can be sanctified," Nan said with a smile. "If your heart is in the right place."

David was silent for a moment. "Do you ever think about the $40,000 we lost investing in Robbie's boat business?"

"Not really. It stung at the time, but I knew why you and your father wanted to do it. You were trying to pull Robbie out of the ditch. That's why I went along."

"Thanks again for not giving me a hard time about it."

"That took a while, if I recall."

"At lunch the day before his brain hemorrhage, Dad told me he lost $80,000. I'm not sure it was all boat-related."

Nan's eyebrows rose. "I wonder if Katelyn knows about it," she said. "That all happened at least a couple of years before they met."

———

Katelyn and Robbie spent the morning in the sunroom before she left for the airport. She'd slept later than normal, and Robbie took Charlie out for a long walk before she was out of bed.

"Are you going to change diapers during the night?" she asked as she sipped a cup of tea.

"Yes, but don't expect me to nurse him. Will you go to the office this afternoon?"

"Do you think I should?"

"Your choice."

"And every choice has consequences that flow from it," Katelyn replied.

"You're making my head spin."

"Good," Katelyn teased. "No woman should be overly predictable. It's in our secret job description."

Robbie looked directly at her. "Are you thinking about turning down the job offer?"

"If I did, what would you say?"

"Great."

"And if I accept it?"

"Chicago, here we come. I'm along for the ride, wherever it takes us. You've known all along that adventure is in my job description. There's no secret about that."

———

Once on the ground in Washington, Katelyn drove directly to the office. She spent a few hours trying unsuccessfully to engage with work. Her phone buzzed. It was Lisa.

"Suzanne wants to see you. She's on a conference call but wanted to make sure you didn't leave."

"I'm not leaving," Katelyn said, then realized the statement had multiple meanings.

"Hold on. She's off now."

It was over a minute before the assistant came back on the line. While Katelyn waited, she started feeling nervous.

"Suzanne will see you now."

Walking down the hallway, Katelyn thought about her bold statement to Robbie that women are designed to be unpredictable. It might be true for some aspects of life now that she was pregnant, but it didn't necessarily transfer to the law firm. When she entered Suzanne's office, the senior partner rose from her chair to greet her.

But something was different. To Katelyn's surprise, the sense of authority and power that Suzanne wore like an invisible cloak was gone. She looked like an ordinary woman in her mid-fifties. Katelyn shook her head as if to clear the fog over her brain, but the change was undeniable. Instead of anxiety, she felt a strange peace.

"How's your father-in-law doing?"

Katelyn told her while internally trying to process why she felt different in Suzanne's presence and what it meant.

"I hope he improves," Suzanne said. "If you need to take more time off to be with your family, let me know. It won't be a problem."

"Thank you," Katelyn replied.

"Are you ready to move forward with the promotion and relocation to Chicago?"

From the tone of Suzanne's voice, Katelyn knew further delay wasn't an option. She took a deep breath.

"Suzanne, I respect and appreciate you enormously. You've been both my mentor in the practice of law and my advocate at the firm. I couldn't begin to list all the ways you've helped me, and I can't thank you enough for how you stood up for me in the email to the executive committee."

Katelyn stopped. Even she was surprised by the sentence on the tip of her tongue.

"But it's clear that my time at Morgan and Monroe has come to an end."

A flash of emotion crossed Suzanne's face. Katelyn wasn't sure if it was shock, anger, disappointment, or a combination of all three.

"Is your decision final?" Suzanne asked tersely.

"Yes."

"Do you have plans to join another firm?"

"No, not at this time. I've not sent out my résumé or made any inquiries. I've been loyal to you."

Suzanne shook her head. "I was going to tell you that Valerie and I had come up with a plan to rally support for you on the executive committee. But we don't want to expend capital on a lost cause."

Normally, Suzanne's words would have caused Katelyn to panic.

"That's one more example of how supportive you've been to me," Katelyn said.

She stopped. Suzanne didn't speak. This, too, would typically make Katelyn nervous. Today, she simply waited.

"All right," Suzanne said. "Type a letter of resignation effective immediately and give it to Kane, along with your building access card. You know the drill. Gather your personal belongings, and we'll lock you out of the system. There's no need for anyone to personally supervise your departure."

They stood. Katelyn didn't know whether to shake hands or give Suzanne a hug. Neither happened. Walking down the hallway, she encountered Franklin Deming.

"Katelyn, I need to talk to you," Franklin said. "Is it okay if I stop by later?"

"Make it soon," Katelyn replied and kept walking.

Alone in her small space, she closed the door and took a deep breath. She'd quit her job. The calm she'd felt in Suzanne's office faded, and accusing voices stepped forward, demanding to be heard. She hurriedly typed a brief resignation letter, printed it, and signed it. At that moment, the thought shot through her head that she'd made a terrible mistake, one she would regret for the rest of her life. Her suggestion to Robbie that she could work remotely as a cog in another law firm machine and be satisfied doing so seemed totally foolish.

The mental assault intensified as she retrieved some empty boxes from the copy room and began to pack her personal belongings. All her hard work. Countless hours of intense research and preparation. The pressure of multimillion-dollar responsibility. Every fiber of her being dedicated to achieving success. Financial security. Prestige and esteem. Tossed away in a moment like a sandwich wrapper from a fast-food restaurant. She saw herself running down the hall to Suzanne's office to apologize and ask for a chance to continue with the firm in any role available.

But Katelyn couldn't change her mind. Maybe it had to do with being pregnant and her desire to devote herself to a child she'd not yet met. Perhaps it was something else. But in the actual moment of decision, she'd felt no other path lay open but to leave. Right or wrong, that was what she had to do. The link between her and Suzanne was severed. Figuring out exactly why that happened would have to wait for another day.

Once the boxes were full, Katelyn went through the drawers one more time to make sure nothing was being left behind. Her cell phone vibrated. It was the number for Cobb and Cobb. She assumed it was David. She'd intended to call Robbie to break the news as soon as she was in her car. Her brother-in-law wasn't the first person on her need-to-know list. Reluctantly, she accepted the call.

TEN

"ZEKE CALDWELL CALLED TWICE," MEREDITH SAID when David returned from lunch.

"Did you talk to him?"

"Yes, he has a special potion that he believes will help Carter and wants to bring it by as soon as possible. He left a voice-mail message."

"Yeah, he mentioned that the other day."

David went into his office and listened to the recording.

"Hope your daddy is doing better," Zeke said in his unmistakable voice. "And I've come up with something different, not just the Alzheimer's drops I told you about the other day. One thing that happens when a person gets very sick is the chemicals in the body get out of balance. I have mixed together a remedy that takes care of that along with confusion of the mind. Three drops under the tongue, twice a day, should fix him right up. And don't try to pay me. This one is on me."

David buzzed Meredith and asked her to come in and listen to the message.

"That's what he mentioned on the phone," she confirmed.

"My dad's blood work isn't right, and he's definitely confused, but it's hard to imagine his neurosurgeon adding a home remedy to the medication list. I'll have to figure out a way to tell Zeke thanks but no thanks without hurting his feelings."

"Good luck," Meredith said. "Candy texted me. She's coming home early from vacation and will work the rest of the week."

"She doesn't have to do that."

"Let her," Meredith answered. "I need the help."

"Okay."

A chime signaled the opening of the front door. Meredith quickly left the room and returned less than thirty seconds later.

"It's Zeke," she said. "Looks like you're going to have to tell him in person."

Zeke was wearing his pharmacy uniform and an Atlanta Braves cap. In his right hand was a small, brown paper sack.

"I didn't know you were an Atlanta Braves fan," David said.

Zeke touched the cap. "I'm not. I have so many hats that I just grab one before I head out the door. Did you get the message I left you?"

"Yes."

"I have the special remedy for Carter. Like I said on the phone, there's no charge. I mixed in ingredients that will help his thinking and also regulate his blood chemistry. They work hand in hand. I want to see him up and about as soon as possible." Zeke took a thick envelope from his back pocket. "Do you have time to talk for a few minutes?"

David led Zeke into his office and offered him a seat. Zeke handed the envelope to David.

"A month ago, I sent a certified letter to Brigham-Neal about my patent and included a vial of my stuff. When I didn't hear back, I thought they threw it away. But after we talked the other day, I received this from a lawyer who works for them."

David opened the envelope. The letter was two pages long with multiple attachments. Emblazoned across the top was "Brigham-Neal Pharmaceuticals." It began with an acknowledgment of the communication received from Zeke. The lawyer, a man named Russell Detar, then analyzed Zeke's patent and listed five reasons why Relacan was materially different. The lawyer's arguments seemed persuasive, and David was impressed that the company's in-house counsel treated the inquiry from Zeke with respect, not disdain.

"What do you think?" Zeke asked.

"It's a lot more technical than I suspected, and they took the time to explain why they don't believe their formula infringes your patent."

"Both drugs are designed to treat the same condition," Zeke replied. "It says so right there at the beginning. And did you see how closely related the chemical compounds are to one another? It's even more clear than from the information in the magazine I showed you the other day."

"I've forgotten what I learned in high school chemistry," David said. "But if there's even a little difference, I suspect that would be important. May I make a copy of this letter to show any lawyer I talk to about helping you?"

"That's why I brought it. I thought it would help you."

While David stood over the copy machine, he asked the Lord how to best help Zeke. When he returned to the office, an amber vial was on his desk.

"That's the remedy for Carter," Zeke said. "Don't worry about what else he's taking. The body knows what to do. The blood sends it straight to the part that needs it. People sneak my stuff into the hospital all the time. All it takes is a few seconds to put three or four drops under his tongue, then watch the results."

"I'm not sure," David said doubtfully.

"I know what Carter would do. He was glad to get what I mixed up for him when he had his heart attack a few years ago. Did he ever tell you about it?"

"He believed it helped."

"That's right." Zeke rose to his feet. "I have another delivery to make before I head to the house. You know Mrs. Dorothy Canterbury, don't you?"

"Yes. The last time I saw her, she was in a wheelchair."

"She has crippling arthritis, but she's up walking around."

"Good for her."

David escorted Zeke to the reception area.

"Don't be afraid of what the Lord provides in his creation," Zeke said.

"I hear you," David replied.

"And keep me posted about Carter. I expect quick improvement."

After Zeke left, Meredith looked up at David. "Looks like you couldn't figure out a way to tell him thanks but no thanks," she said.

"It's hard to say no to someone who really wants to help."

"I don't think there's any harm in giving it a try. There's a woman I know who swears by Zeke's stuff."

David reread the letter from the in-house lawyer at Brigham-Neal. Picking up his cell phone, he scrolled through his list of contacts. No attorneys he knew seemed to be a reasonable referral source. Going through a second time, he saw the name "Katelyn Martin-Cobb." He'd never heard his sister-in-law mention any involvement in a drug patent case. Morgan and Monroe represented big companies with deep pockets, not individuals. But she might have a recommendation for a reputable plaintiff's firm.

———

Katelyn accepted the call from Cobb and Cobb.

"Is Carter worse?" she asked.

"No, and I'm sorry if seeing my name caused worry," David replied. "I know you're always busy, but do you have a few minutes to talk?"

"A few."

"I'll try to be quick."

Katelyn listened as David told her about a local herbalist named Zeke Caldwell who'd patented a home remedy and now believed a pharmaceutical company had infringed his patent. While he talked, she placed the phone on speaker and continued to pack up her office.

"What's the name of the company?" she asked.

"Brigham-Neal. They're based in Hartford, Connecticut." David paused. "Has Morgan and Monroe ever represented them? I should have mentioned that at the outset."

"It doesn't matter," Katelyn answered as she placed a picture of her and Robbie in a box.

"Why not?"

"I've resigned. But I don't want to say anything else about it until I talk to Robbie."

"You quit your job?"

"Yeah."

David was silent for a moment. "I wanted your advice about finding a lawyer for Zeke Caldwell in his drug patent infringement claim, but that can wait."

———

Katelyn estimated it would take three trips to carry the boxes to her car. After the first load, she noticed curious eyes following her when she passed by her coworkers. Carrying the second box, she debated whether there was anyone she wanted to say good-bye to now, or if she should put off any conversations until she'd had time to organize an explanation. Returning to her office, she found Franklin waiting for her. The earnest young man had a serious expression on his face.

"Were you going to tell me?" he asked.

"I was going to talk to you later."

"Did you get an offer from another firm?"

"No."

"Was there a problem with the job in Chicago? I need to know in case they offer it to someone else and I try to make the move too."

"There was a problem, but I'm not going to give you the details. You obviously have sources of information close to the top. But as far as I know, there's nothing about the position that would be a negative factor for you. I've been thinking about the direction of my life and what's most important. My job is huge, but it's not everything."

"So it's true that you resigned?"

"Yes."

"Stunning." Franklin shook his head. "You're leaving on your own terms. No severance. Nothing. That took guts."

"Only enough guts to say the words and then not try to pull them back," Katelyn replied. "I do have one favor to ask."

"What is it?"

"Tell anyone who asks about my leaving that I think Suzanne Nixon is a great attorney, wonderful mentor, and outstanding person. Will you do that?"

"Yes. And what else? That's not going to satisfy most folks."

Katelyn thought for a moment. "That for the first time in my life, I'm truly open to the next step. Up until now, I've had a plan for my life and executed it flawlessly. That journey ended a few minutes ago."

Once she was in the car, Katelyn put both hands on the steering wheel, rested her head on her arms, and took a few deep breaths. Leaving the parking lot, she drove a couple of blocks to a small park and pulled into a space alongside the curb so she could call Robbie. He seemed out of breath when he answered the phone.

"What are you doing?" she asked.

"Cooling down after a run along the river. It may be flat, but the humidity is high today, and that sapped my energy. How are things at the office?"

"Changed. I talked to Suzanne."

"And?"

"I resigned. It's like my connection with her was broken. That sounds weird, but it's the best I can come up with."

Robbie listened as she told him about her conversation with the senior partner.

"How do you feel?" he asked.

"It's been a rough sixty minutes, but I'm okay. How about you? This morning you said you were up for the adventure, but now it's real."

"I would have been surprised if you'd done anything else. The job in Chicago paid more money but didn't check your other boxes. And starting a family means beginning a new chapter for both of us. Six months from now, I may have a problem remembering the name of the firm."

Katelyn smiled. So long as she and Robbie were united, they could navigate any transition.

"We have no income except your salary."

"Who knows? I might quit too."

"No, you can't!"

"I'm kidding. I'm proud of you. And I'm really looking forward to spending more time with you."

Katelyn felt a wave of emotion surge up from within. "Thanks," she managed.

"Is there any reason for you to stay in DC?"

"No, I'll pack up my car and drive to Wilmington this evening. Let me know if there's anything you want me to bring. Oh, and David knows I quit. He called me right after it happened, and I told him."

"Why did he call?"

"Looking for a referral in a case. We'll talk about it later."

———

Still processing Katelyn's news, David drove to the hospital. Before going inside, he took the amber vial from the front pocket of his shirt, unscrewed the top, sniffed the contents, and caught a faint odor of peppermint. As the entrance doors to the hospital slid open, he saw two security guards standing nearby and wondered what answer he would give if they suddenly decided to search him and demanded to know the nature of the strange contraband he was transporting into a medical facility.

He waited ten minutes before being allowed in to see his father. Carter was asleep with his eyes closed and his mouth partly open. A young woman who was part of the janitorial staff was cleaning the bathroom.

"You must be Mr. Cobb's son," she said. "I can see the family resemblance. Your father represented my mother years ago when she had a problem with her landlord. He got everything worked out and only charged her $100. I still remember how much she appreciated his help."

It was the kind of story David had heard many times before. He looked at the unconscious man in the bed.

"Has he said anything to you?" David asked.

"Just nonsense. It seems like he wants to talk but can't put his words together. A few minutes ago, he looked at me and started jabbering like he wanted to say something important but then went back to sleep."

The young woman left. David slipped the vial from his pocket, shook it, and unscrewed the dropper. He glanced over his shoulder. Squeezing the top of the dropper, he positioned it just inside his father's open lips and deposited three drops beside his tongue. A fourth drop slipped out.

"Good afternoon!" a man's voice boomed behind him.

It was Dr. Spies. David closed one hand around the vial and clasped the dropper in the other. He stepped away from the bed with both fists clenched.

"Hello," he replied, hoping the doctor wouldn't try to shake his hand.

The neurosurgeon was holding a tablet. "Glad I caught you," the doctor said.

"Uh, me too," David managed.

"The surgery site is healing nicely, but your father's blood pressure is elevated and his blood work isn't where we want it to be. I consulted with his cardiologist, and we've ordered some changes in his medications. Has he been awake during any of your visits?"

"A little bit."

"We'll hope for more. I'm going to transfer him to a regular room in the morning with the goal of placing him in a rehab facility pretty soon."

David was startled by the change of pace. "Where would you recommend for rehab?"

"River Oaks would be my first choice. A social worker can help you with the placement."

Dr. Spies left. While the neurosurgeon was in the room, Carter had closed his mouth. He remained asleep. David spent fifteen uneventful minutes before leaving.

On his way home, his phone vibrated. It was Nan.

"Where are you?" she asked.

"Five minutes from the house."

"Good. Robbie is joining us for supper. He said Katelyn is on her way back from DC but won't be here until late tonight. It's odd that she would fly up there this morning and immediately turn around and drive back."

"She quit her job."

"What!" Nan exclaimed.

"I don't know any details, but I called to ask for help in finding a lawyer for Zeke Caldwell, and she told me."

"Did you say anything about—"

"No."

"Can you pick up a bag of lettuce mix for a salad? The kids want spaghetti, so it wasn't hard to add more meat to the pan and noodles to the pot. A side salad for the adults would be nice."

When David arrived home, Andy, Courtney, and Robbie were playing with Charlie in the backyard. David leaned on the fence to watch. Robbie threw a rubber chew toy in his direction, and David caught it.

"That toy belongs to Charlie," Robbie said. "Don't put it in your mouth no matter how much you want to."

David threw the toy so Charlie could chase it. "Is it true that a dog's mouth is cleaner than a human's mouth?" he asked.

"No, they have tons of bacteria. That's why a dog bite can so easily become infected."

David glanced past Robbie and saw Charlie licking Courtney's face. Even if she knew about dog germs, Courtney wouldn't let that deter her. Robbie came over and stood beside David.

"That was a strong move by Katelyn," David said. "I told Nan about it."

"Yeah. I'm glad. I would have supported the move to Chicago if that's what she wanted, but things at the firm were moving sideways rather than forward."

Before David could ask another question, Nan called from the rear deck: "Supper's ready!"

"I hope you're in the mood for spaghetti," Nan said to Robbie when they entered the kitchen.

"Always."

Andy and Courtney made sure each of them sat on one side of Robbie at the round table. Nan placed the salad in the middle of the table. David asked the blessing. He included a prayer for a safe trip for Katelyn.

"Aunt Kate is coming back?" Courtney asked. "I didn't know she left."

"It was a quick trip," Robbie said.

They passed around the spaghetti.

"Did you stop by to see Dad this afternoon?" Robbie asked.

"Yes, but he was asleep."

"I went earlier," Robbie said. "He was awake, but his speech was slurred and didn't make sense."

"Does that mean Pops is getting worse?" Andy asked with a concerned look on his face.

"Not necessarily," David quickly replied. "It's going to take time to see how much he recovers. The fact that he recognized the photo of your fish was amazing."

Andy grew quiet. By the time they finished the meal, there wasn't a noodle left in the bowl. While the kids cleared the table, Nan went into the kitchen and returned with slices of coconut cream pie on plates. After dessert, the children went upstairs to take showers.

"What do you think Katelyn is going to do?" Nan asked.

"I'm not sure. She'll have options, but I don't want her to settle for just anything. I'd rather wait for the right opportunity."

David looked at Nan, who shook her head.

Robbie took a drink of water. "Why did you say you called Katelyn again?" he asked.

"I had a legal question about Zeke Caldwell."

"I've always liked Zeke. He was one of my favorite speakers at camp when we were kids. Is he still cooking up his home remedies?"

"Yeah," David answered. "A few years ago, Dad helped Zeke patent a formula designed to help relieve severe nausea. It even works for people taking chemotherapy. Now a big drug company may have infringed the patent by manufacturing a similar product. Zeke was at the office to talk about it when Dad had the hemorrhage."

"What were you going to ask Katelyn?"

"For a referral to a law firm that might be able to help Zeke. It's a very specialized area of the law."

"That makes sense," Robbie said.

David cleared his throat. "When he found out about Dad's brain bleed, Zeke brought by a vial containing a mixture that is supposed to help with memory loss and restore the body's correct chemical balance. He suggested we add it to the medicines Dad is getting from his doctors."

"Did you give it to him?" Robbie asked.

"Just a few drops under his tongue," David said, speaking rapidly.

"What?" Robbie blurted out.

"Did you check with Dr. Spies?" Nan asked. "There could be a danger of an adverse reaction with the prescribed drugs he's taking."

"Zeke told me not to be afraid of anything the Lord provides in his creation."

Nan and Robbie exchanged a look.

"I didn't think it could cause any harm," David continued defensively. "Zeke reminded me that Dad used a home remedy after the heart attack. Remember how amazed we were at how quickly his energy came back? Maybe it was because of what Zeke gave him."

"He bounced back great," Nan replied. "But I didn't know he took a home remedy. Zeke's poison ivy cream stinks like sour milk when you squeeze it out of the tube."

"But it works," David said. "And penicillin originally came from a natural source. There's an organic base to more drugs than people realize."

"Are you going to keep giving it to him?" Robbie asked.

"Only with your permission."

David told them about his close call with Dr. Spies.

Robbie chuckled. "You never could keep anything secret from Dad and Mom," he said. "I was the one who stepped out of line and didn't get caught."

"What about the drops?" David asked.

Robbie paused for a moment. "I want to do everything we can to help Dad recover. If something Zeke cooked up has been beneficial in the past, I'm in favor of using it now. But I think you should tell Dr. Spies, just to make sure it's safe."

"I agree with Robbie," Nan said. "Zeke researches what he creates and should be able to provide a list of ingredients."

Katelyn pulled into the driveway at Carter's house. She was physically exhausted and emotionally drained. All she wanted was a long hug from Robbie, followed by a quick shower and a good night's sleep. She received her hug as soon as she entered.

"I really needed that," she said when they parted.

"I'm available twenty-four-seven."

Instead of going straight to bed, Katelyn wrapped herself in a robe and joined Robbie in the darkened sunroom.

"Tell me again that you believe I did the right thing," she said.

"You did the right thing," he replied.

"Not good enough."

"I'm proud of your courage and believe you made the correct decision to leave the law firm. You squeezed every drop of training and experience you could from Morgan and Monroe, and I'm looking forward to the direction your career will take in the future. I'm especially excited about spending more time together. How's that?"

Katelyn smiled into the darkness. "Better. Tell me about your day."

"Not much to tell. I messed around here. You should see Courtney playing with Charlie. He likes her so much that I struggled with jealousy."

"That's the kind of jealousy I can handle," she said.

Robbie told her about Zeke Caldwell's home remedy and the reason David had called her.

"No law firms come to mind," Katelyn said with a yawn. "All my expertise is with industrial patents. Pharmaceutical patents are a completely different world and a specific subspecialty of the law. It sounds like something David should stay away from."

"That's what he said too."

They listened to the night noises until the crickets went to sleep.

ELEVEN

THE FOLLOWING MORNING, ROBBIE'S TRUCK WAS IN the hospital parking lot when David pulled in beside it. As they walked into the hospital, Robbie showed him a text message on his phone.

"I just received this from Frank Gates."

> If you're still in town, I'd like to meet with you and David about the future of Camp Seacrest.

"He didn't text me," David replied.

"I guess he knows which of us is the more important supporter of the camp."

David checked the office calendar on his phone. "I can squeeze in thirty to forty-five minutes later this morning."

Robbie replied to Frank and suggested a time.

"Do you have Zeke's medicine?" he asked.

David patted the front pocket of his pants. "And I'm going to let you give it to him so that both of us are culpable."

"Don't use those fancy legal words on me. I thought we agreed you were going to talk to Dr. Spies."

"I didn't agree when you were at the house, but Nan made me sign an agreement after you left. I'll ask Zeke for a list of ingredients."

They reached the room. Carter, his eyes shut, was sitting up straighter in bed. One of the RNs was working with him.

"We were able to feed him a few bites of soft food this morning," she said.

"He likes scrambled eggs," David said.

"And we gave him oatmeal too."

"That would be a first. Did he say anything?"

"No. He's still sleeping a lot, which is to be expected."

"How about his blood work?"

"It's looking better."

They waited as the nurse finished her tasks. When she left, Robbie touched their father on the arm.

"Good morning, Dad!" he announced in a loud voice.

"There's nothing wrong with his hearing," David said.

"This is my turn to communicate with my father, and I'm going to do it my way," Robbie replied. "How were the scrambled eggs you ate for breakfast?"

Carter Cobb's eyes fluttered open. He made a soft grunting sound.

"Good or bad?" Robbie asked.

"Bad," Carter answered and closed his eyes.

Robbie cast a triumphant glance at David.

"What about the oatmeal?" David asked.

Carter partially stuck his tongue out of his mouth and gave them an expression that made both brothers chuckle.

"I bet the eggs needed hot sauce," Robbie said. "I've been staying at your house for a few days. Did you know that you have five bottles of the same brand of hot sauce in the pantry? Are you preparing for a hurricane?"

Carter opened his eyes and cut them toward Robbie. "Take one."

"I will," Robbie replied. "How are you feeling?"

"I woke up with a terrible headache."

It was Carter's most complete and complex communication since he'd suffered the brain hemorrhage. David wanted to shout.

"That's great," he said. "I mean, not that you had a headache, but that you know what's going on. Do you want something for pain?"

"No. What happened to me?"

David glanced at Robbie.

"You had a brain hemorrhage," Robbie said. "They performed surgery last week, and you've pretty much been out of it since then."

Their father let out a long sigh.

"You've been through a lot," David said.

"When you're up to it, Dr. Spies, the neurosurgeon, can explain it in more detail," Robbie added.

"The office," Carter said softly in a muffled voice.

"I'm taking care of everything," David reassured him. "I'm on top of all the deadlines."

"Good," Carter said, then seemed to relax. In a few moments he was asleep.

"That was awesome," David said to Robbie.

"It's all about using the right tone of voice to stimulate him."

David punched his brother in the arm. "I can't wait to tell Andy," he said. "He wants an update every night before he goes to sleep. It's been tough telling him there's nothing new."

Robbie stared down at their father. "Do you think Zeke's drops helped?" he asked.

"After one dose? I doubt it, but at least they didn't seem to hurt."

Carter's lips were closed, his breathing regular.

"Give me the vial," Robbie said.

David handed it to him. Robbie unscrewed the top.

"Four drops, right?" he asked.

"Three or four. Are you going to give him a dose?"

Robbie took out the dropper. His hand seemed to be heading toward Carter's nose.

"Don't put them in his nose!" David said.

"I'm not, although that would probably work."

Robbie stopped and returned the dropper to the bottle.

"I don't want you to get in trouble with Nan," he said.

They stood side by side for a moment.

"We don't have to get Dr. Spies's permission to pray," David said.

Robbie stared down at Carter. "God, we thank you for the work you're doing in restoring our father to health," he said. "Please continue to touch and heal him. Amen."

David glanced at his brother and said, "Amen."

Fifteen minutes later they left the room. Robbie checked his phone.

"Frank says to come over anytime this morning."

"Let's go now. Follow me. Frank moved his business to a bigger facility a year or so ago."

Gates Heating and Air occupied half a block at the edge of an industrial area of the city. Five shiny white vans with the name of the company emblazoned on them were in front of the office area. David and Robbie parked in spots reserved for visitors.

"Business must be good," David said as they walked toward the front door. "I see Frank's vans and trucks all over town."

The reception area was small and spartan. A young woman behind a desk greeted them.

"I'll let Mr. Gates know you're here," she said.

"No need, Veronica," the business owner said in his booming

voice from the entrance to a hallway. "I saw them pull in. Good morning, gentlemen. Follow me."

Frank Gates was a short, stocky man in his early sixties. His father had started the business with one van and a helper, but it didn't start growing until his son came on board. Frank was a natural salesman. He took them into a conference room with a large whiteboard on one wall. The board was covered with diagrams.

"We had a training session early this morning," Frank said, motioning to the board. "The equipment we install is so high-tech that we use computers to diagnose the problems. They simply plug the equipment into a tablet. My dad could tell what was wrong with an AC compressor by listening to it."

David and Robbie sat beside each other, with Frank across the table.

"Thanks for coming by on such short notice. How's your father doing?"

"We just came from the hospital," David replied. "He's showing signs of improvement."

"Great." Frank placed his hands on the table. "I'll get straight to the point. The situation with the camp has been keeping me up at night and waking me up in the morning. I had no idea when I agreed to be on the board that it would turn out like this."

"I'm sorry it's been stressful," David said.

Frank shrugged. "It is what it is. Anyway, I was thinking this morning about your family and how much you've given of your time and resources over the years. Carter has been there time and again when we had special needs. The latest twist hit us late yesterday afternoon. The man who accepted the director job sent me an email asking for more money. I forwarded it to the other members of the board, and we're meeting tonight to discuss his demand."

"Did he give a reason?" Robbie asked.

"Yes. He has a son who's going to be a freshman in college this fall, and because the family is moving to North Carolina, the boy won't be eligible for in-state tuition. The new director is asking us to cover the additional cost. The son is going to stay in Colorado, establish his own residency, and will qualify for reduced tuition as a sophomore."

As Mr. Gates talked, David knew the chairman of the board was going to ask for a contribution. With Katelyn quitting her job and the loss of his father's revenue at Cobb and Cobb, a significant gift might not be a possibility for either one of them.

"I sympathize with his situation, but it hit me the wrong way," Frank continued. "We'd already agreed on the terms of his hiring."

"How much were you going to pay him in the original agreement?" Robbie asked.

Frank told them. "And the extra amount is over $30,000. What if he stays a year and leaves? The board will look irresponsible, or worse."

Even though he knew the answer, David asked, "What do you want from us?"

"I'd like to be able to tell the board what you think. I don't want to treat the issue like I would if it happened at my business. In that case, I'd send the guy on his way. I'm setting up phone calls and meetings later today with a few other folks who have been longtime supporters to ask them the same thing."

David glanced at Robbie but couldn't tell what his brother was thinking. David's heart began to beat a bit faster.

"Are you considering another candidate?" David asked.

"The current search was a big effort. We vetted twenty candidates and flew in five finalists for in-person interviews. Our number two choice has already accepted another job. Number three decided to stay where he is. The thought of having to repeat the process is the biggest motivator to paying the extra cash so we can move on from Chris."

"Maybe the next director of the camp is sitting at this table," David said.

"David!" Robbie said sharply. "That's not why Frank asked us to come."

"Would you be interested in the job?" Frank asked Robbie in surprise.

Robbie was silent for a moment.

"Tell him," David prodded.

"All right," Robbie admitted. "That's the reason I called you the other day. But I wouldn't want my interest to be a distraction to the board or keep it from hiring the right person. I love the camp and have plenty of experience working with kids, including those from less-than-ideal homes, but I've never had to run a program or raise funds, which I know are big parts of the job."

"That's true," Frank replied thoughtfully. "But if the program offered to the boys isn't first-rate, nothing else matters. Isn't your wife an attorney with a big firm in Washington?"

"Until yesterday," Robbie said. "She resigned."

"What?" Frank replied in surprise. "Did you quit your job too?"

"No, but it's not a reason to stay in DC. It would be easy for my boss to transition my caseload to other folks who work at the agency."

Frank was silent for a moment. "I bet at least half the members of the board know you, and everyone is aware that the Cobb family are big supporters of the camp."

"This has to be on my merit as a candidate and nothing else," Robbie said.

"Of course, but with your existing connections in the community, you'd have a head start as a fund-raiser and in restoring trust. The more I think about this, the more I like it. Can you put together a résumé and send it to me so I can bring it up to the board?"

"You'll have one in your in-box by early this afternoon," Robbie said.

"And would you be available to meet with the board tonight if they want to do so?"

"Yes," Robbie said.

"Great. I'll set it up."

Frank clapped his hands together and stood. "I like this idea a lot more than the other reason I wanted to meet with you."

"What was that reason?" David asked.

"Oh, I was going to hit you up for money to help cover the additional $30,000, if that's the way the board wanted to go. I was willing to put in $5,000 to avoid the headache of starting over."

"If I'm hired, my first act will be to come by and pick up that $5,000 check," Robbie replied. "There are plenty of other places where that money can be spent to improve the camp facilities or programs."

Frank laughed. "You're not going to have any trouble raising money."

When David was alone in his car, he immediately placed a call to Robbie. He didn't want to offend his brother but had to bring up an issue they'd not discussed with Frank.

"Hey, I didn't want to mention it just now, but should you ask Frank to delegate some of the day-to-day financial responsibilities of the job to someone else? That sort of thing can be a real drag."

Robbie replied, "I will, but not just for that reason. There needs to be a division of responsibilities to avoid what happened with Chris. And I think the director should have to get secondary approval for any checks over a certain amount."

David was impressed. "Good thinking."

Katelyn spent the morning doing something she'd not done for years—reading a book for pleasure. Robbie returned in time to take her to lunch.

"I know you're unemployed, so I'm buying," he said.

It was a sunny day with small clouds pinned against a brilliant blue sky. Katelyn took a deep breath. They were too far from the ocean for a hint of salt to be in the air, but the sea breezes made the inland air naturally fresh. Robbie drove in the direction of the river.

"This place is new but has good reviews," he said as he pulled into the parking lot of a sandwich and salad shop.

They were a couple of blocks from the river, so there weren't any scenic views, but the restaurant was bright and clean. Robbie ordered a salad with seafood, and Katelyn selected a sandwich. They waited at the counter and took their meals to a booth. When they were seated, Robbie told her about the visit with his father at the hospital.

"That's positive," Katelyn said. "But it didn't take up the whole morning. What else did you do?"

"David and I went to see Frank Gates. They've hit a speed bump in the hiring process for the new director at Camp Seacrest." Robbie took a breath before continuing, "And during the conversation I brought up the real reason I called him the other night."

Katelyn lowered her sandwich to her plate. "What did he say?"

"That he wants a copy of my résumé to show the board at an emergency meeting tonight."

"Robbie!" Katelyn exclaimed so loudly that the people sitting at an adjacent table turned and stared at them for a second.

"And I want to ask you the same question you had for me last night. Did I do the right thing?"

"Yes," Katelyn answered. "Absolutely, you did the right thing."

"If the initial reaction is positive, I'll head over to Frank's office this evening to meet with the board in person."

"What was the problem with the other candidate?"

Robbie told her. "I reassured Frank that our son was several years away from college."

"No, you didn't."

"And he has to go to camp first."

Katelyn hadn't touched her food.

"You need to eat so he'll get stronger," Robbie said.

"I'm too excited. If I hadn't quit my job, would you have brought this up at the meeting?"

"Who knows? But it was a lot easier this way. And don't assume they're going to offer me the position."

"Of course they're going to offer you the job," Katelyn said dismissively. "You're perfect."

Robbie took out his phone. "Could you repeat that last bit so I can record it and play it when needed later?"

During supper, David told Nan and the kids about the meeting with Frank Gates.

"After Robbie sent the résumé, Frank called and told him to be on standby for an interview with the board this evening."

"That's fast," Nan said.

"Frank won't let them procrastinate. It's not his style."

"I hope he gets to be the director of the camp," Andy said. "What would I call him? Uncle Robbie or Mr. Cobb?"

"Camp Director Mr. Cobb, sir," David replied.

"Is that supposed to be funny?" Andy asked. "I'm not laughing, and neither is Mom."

After supper David and Nan played a fast-paced board game with the kids. Toward the end of the game, he received a text from Robbie.

On my way to meet with the board.

David showed the message to Nan and Andy.

"Can I stay up to find out what happens?" Andy asked.

"No, it could be late tonight," David said. "We'll let you know in the morning."

On the other hand, David knew it was futile to try to sleep before he heard from Robbie. Nan stayed up with him. They were reading in bed when Robbie finally called around 10:30 p.m.

"How did it go?" David asked.

"They left me waiting an hour. You could feel the tension when I entered the room, and Frank looked upset. He's probably used to getting his way instantly when there's a meeting at his business."

"His name is on all the trucks and vans."

"Right. Anyway, Frank introduced me to the members of the board who didn't already know me. They all had copies of my résumé, which Katelyn helped me put together after lunch."

"I hope it didn't have your picture on it," David said.

"Quiet, and let him talk," Nan said.

"Frank gave a very nice little speech about who I am and how much our family has meant to the camp. Based on what he said, it was clear the board hadn't made a final decision whether to move on from the man who'd accepted the job and wanted more money. After that, he threw it open for questions. The new folks focused on my lack of administrative and fund-raising experience. One guy said this wasn't an entry-level job and recommended I apply for an assistant position someplace else."

David bristled. "Who said that?"

"I'm keeping that confidential."

"Right. Go ahead."

"When the questions slowed, Frank asked me to tell the board about Levon Norwood."

Levon was a young boy in foster care who came to the camp when he was twelve years old. Robbie was his counselor for three summers and maintained contact with him over the following decade. When Levon graduated from college at East Carolina University, he asked Robbie to sit in the parent section during the ceremony.

"After I finished talking, two of the women on the board were wiping their eyes with tissues. There were only a couple more questions. The final one had to do with my lack of bookkeeping or accounting experience. Before I could answer, Frank said if the board hired me, he was willing to donate five hours a week from his accounting department to help with the books. He made the point that having increased outside oversight made sense after what happened with Chris and would lessen the administrative burden on me. Then they sent me out of the room so the jury could deliberate."

"What was the verdict?" David asked.

"Thirty minutes later they brought me in and offered me the job. I accepted."

"Congratulations!" David pumped his fist. "How does it feel?"

"Like a big responsibility."

"It is," Nan said. "But you're up for it. What did Katelyn say when you told her?"

"She cried too. She's been so unselfish about this. Even though she didn't say it, I think she believes all that's happened to us is going to work out for our good."

"We believe that too," Nan said.

The call ended, and they turned out the lights. David still couldn't go to sleep.

"Are you awake?"

"Yes," Nan answered.

"There's one other situation I'd like your opinion about."

———

As the grandfather clock in the foyer sounded 11:30 p.m., Katelyn and Robbie sat in the dark in the sunroom and listened to the night noises. Charlie was curled up on the floor at Robbie's feet. Robbie was overflowing with ideas about what to do at the camp and wasn't ready to go to bed. Katelyn listened, amazed at her husband's energy. Finally, he grew quiet.

"Is that an owl?" Katelyn asked.

"Yes. There must be a pair. I've been listening to them talk back and forth for several days."

"What are they saying?"

Katelyn could faintly see Robbie's silhouette.

"Mostly it's the female giving the male orders about proper construction of their nest. He replied that she needed to stop hooting about it because he'd been spending most of his time hunting mice, chipmunks, baby rabbits, and squirrels to feed their chicks."

Katelyn laughed. "How much of that is true?"

"Some of it. Listening to them, I believe it's a pair of great horned owls. They visit the coast to breed but don't build nests and often use abandoned osprey nests. I've tried to spot them during the day. By this point in the year their chicks are fledged, and the family will leave soon before it gets too hot."

"Living in Wilmington, I won't have the option to fly someplace cooler."

"We'll crank up the air-conditioning."

They sat in silence for a few moments. The owls called back and forth again.

"And you don't have a nest in Wilmington," Robbie said. "Our money will go a lot further here in Wilmington than in DC or Chicago."

"And I'm not in a rush to leave this house, especially if it becomes necessary to set things up for your father to live here."

"You're not going to be his caregiver. We'll need outside help for that."

"I know, but I could keep watch until we know he's being well taken care of." Katelyn went on, "I've thought some more about what I might like to do. What do you think about me looking for work with a local law firm?"

Robbie was silent for a beat before asking, "With David?"

Even though she couldn't see him, Katelyn heard the skepticism in Robbie's voice.

"Possibly," she said.

Robbie chuckled. "You would raise the IQ in the place considerably the moment you walked through the door. What would make you consider it?"

"A chance to see how things are done differently in a small firm. It could help me decide on the direction I want to go."

"I don't know specifics, but I suspect David and my father run their office more like an old-fashioned general store than a twenty-first-century law firm."

"You think it's a bad idea?"

"No, but it would be important to manage expectations on the front end. For everyone."

"True."

"Just a word of caution from a guy who usually jumps off the cliff and then starts looking for the ground."

Katelyn laughed. "Okay. There's no need to decide anything about that tonight. We've made enough decisions for one day."

The owls continued to call back and forth.

"The owls agree," Robbie said.

———————

In the morning, Robbie left early for a breakfast meeting with Frank Gates. Katelyn stayed in bed. For years, even when they were on vacation, a portion of her mind was always devoted to what was going on at the law firm. But no longer. She decided that this was what retirement must feel like. When she got up, she sat in the kitchen and ate a cup of yogurt, one tiny spoonful at a time. Her phone vibrated. It was Nan.

"Good morning. I hope this isn't too early to call."

"No, Robbie left for a meeting with Frank Gates about the new job."

"Would you like to come over for a second cup of coffee or tea?"

"It will be my first. Give me a few minutes."

"Take your time. It looks like rain, so park in David's spot in the garage."

The early morning sky was overcast with dark clouds. A few drops of rain fell on the windshield during the short drive to David and Nan's house. The garage door was open. As soon as she turned off the engine, the sky opened and a deluge of large raindrops descended. Nan opened the house door and pointed at the water already flowing down the driveway.

"That's one reason David and I moved from the house on Henderson Street," Nan said. "I didn't like getting soaked when I carried in groceries."

"That's something I'll remember when Robbie and I go house-hunting."

They went into the kitchen. David and Nan had an espresso machine.

"I'm having a caramel latte. Would you like one?" Nan asked.

"You know, this seems like a good morning for hot tea."

"On second thought, that sounds good to me too."

While Nan brewed the tea, Katelyn sat at a table placed next to a large window whose panes were streaked with water.

"Is this what it's like being a stay-at-home mom?" she asked when Nan placed the cup in front of her.

"Pretty much." Nan smiled. "Deciding between a pumpkin spice or vanilla cream is the toughest decision of the day."

"I know that's not so."

"Full disclosure . . . The first year with Andy was very stressful. Especially when he had colic and I didn't sleep more than two hours at a stretch for three months. And then from the time Courtney was two until she turned four, it would take an hour and a half to get her to settle down in her bed. She wasn't being bad, just restless. Her mind kept churning even after her little body was ready to shut down. I guess every stage of life has its challenges."

Nan joined her at the table.

"They're great kids," Katelyn said.

"Yes, and they love having you and Robbie around."

Nan took a sip of tea. "How are you feeling this morning?"

"Better than I expected. Maybe it's relief that the decision is made. Or it could be I'm pretending to be on vacation. Sooner or later, reality will hit."

Katelyn told Nan what she'd mentioned to Franklin Deming about starting a new journey without a plan in place.

"I like that," Nan replied.

"And while I wait on the next step, I told Robbie I could help if Carter is released home from the hospital. With assistance, of course."

"Yeah, it's better when the whole family works together. David and I would want to do our part."

Katelyn told Nan how much she'd enjoyed sitting in the sunroom at Carter's house and described the back and forth calls between the owls the previous evening.

"We hear owls too," Nan said. "But David and I don't know much about them. That sort of information just flows out of Robbie."

"I guess David is going to be extra busy with Carter out of commission," Katelyn ventured.

"Yes, he's already putting in a lot of hours trying to figure out the status of cases. Carter kept a lot of things stored in his head."

Katelyn lowered her cup to the table. "What would you think about me working at Cobb and Cobb? Maybe on a temporary basis."

Nan smiled. "David asked me the same question before we went to sleep last night."

"He did?" Katelyn's eyes widened. "What did he say about it?"

"That he'd like to discuss it with you. He knows it would be vastly different from the law firm in Washington."

"If it was the same, we wouldn't be having this conversation."

"What does Robbie think?" Nan asked.

"It's hard for brothers to be objective about each other. Robbie reacted as if it would be him, not me."

"They would spend more time teasing each other and acting like teenagers than working," Nan said.

"Exactly. So what's your opinion?" Katelyn asked again.

Nan looked directly into Katelyn's eyes. "If the two of you want to give it a try, I totally support you."

TWELVE

EMERSON CHAPPELLE SAT IN A COFFEE SHOP NEAR the river in Wilmington. He was feeling great. Three days before, he'd won a big bet and doubled the payment he'd received from the pharmaceutical company. In his mind, he viewed his gambling winnings as payback for the percentage he'd been coerced into handing over to Lance.

Rather than placing another big bet, he'd paid cash for a brand-new BMW and driven to the coast to scout out options for a beach house. Gambling income wasn't reported to the IRS, which meant the money went further. Emerson wasn't going to splurge on a beachfront property and told the agent he wanted a third- or fourth-row house. He didn't mind a short walk to the beach and valued the extra protection from flooding and storm surges.

He left the shop for a stroll along the riverfront. Tents for a local craft fair were set up in a vacant lot. A piece of iron sculpture in the form of a brown pelican caught his eye, and he stepped in for a closer look to see if it would fit the decor of his beach house. Upon closer inspection, he noted that the welds for the bird's wings were a bit sloppy. Two stalls deeper into the fair he saw a row of small amber bottles placed on a plain wooden table. A simple sign for the booth announced "Zeke's All-Natural Remedies." The size and color of the bottles on display were identical to the one a friend had given him three years before.

The friend, a history professor at Duke, had a chronic problem with severe nausea. Doctors could never find a physical explanation for his condition and concluded it was a by-product of stress. Psychotropic medications didn't help. Then someone gave him a home remedy. He took it and within a few days improved. The history professor wasn't the type of man who would exaggerate. When he mentioned his results to Emerson, the chemist thought about the problems his mother experienced during her cancer treatment and asked the professor for a sample.

Emerson took the bottle to the lab and began the process of identifying the contents. Working sporadically, he created with a synthetic version after several months. He then asked the professor to give it a try. It, too, worked, and Emerson began the patent application process that led to the development and sale of Relacan.

A large woman was standing in front of the booth. Emerson inched closer as she posed a question to an older Black man who was sitting in a cane chair beneath a white canopy.

"And you say this will make me lose weight?"

"It burns fat cells like bacon grease poured into a campfire," the man replied. "But you have to cooperate by cutting fatty foods from your diet so it can go after the ones you already have."

The woman scrunched up her face and read the label. "Does it keep you from getting hungry?"

"No, it works with your own metabolism to go after fat," the man said. "It regulates the chemical makeup of the body to the way it's supposed to be. Three drops under the tongue thirty minutes before meals and no late-night snacks."

"Do you offer a money-back guarantee?"

"No. But you can buy two bottles for $29.00. One is $19.00."

"Sounds like a diet to me," the woman sniffed, returning the bottle to the table. "And I don't do diets."

She moved on. Emerson stepped closer. There were small, handwritten labels taped to the table identifying the purpose of each bottle. Multiple bottles were clustered behind each label.

"Are you Zeke?" he asked.

"All my life."

"What's your last name?"

"Caldwell."

"Are you from Wilmington?"

"Yeah, my kinfolk have been living around here for over two hundred and fifty years."

There was a group of bottles behind a label that read "Sour Stomach." Emerson picked one up.

"Is this one for nausea?"

Zeke leaned forward in his chair. "There are two different ones. That one takes care of acid in the stomach. The one on the end is for throwing up."

"Really?" Emerson picked up a different-shaped bottle. "And this is for headaches?"

"Yes, it's brand-new."

"Would it work for migraine headaches?"

"Yes." Zeke nodded. "It also contains the ingredients I use to relieve an upset stomach, because some people have nausea with their headaches. It costs $24.99 for one bottle and $39.99 for two."

"Why is the shape of the bottle different?"

"Oh, that's nothing. I ordered the empties from a different company, and that's what they sent me."

Emerson was silent for a moment. "What did you include to treat the pain from a headache?"

"That's confidential."

"I understand," Emerson said. "If I buy four bottles, will you tell me? I like to know what's in something before I put it in my body."

The older man eyed Emerson, who felt himself beginning to sweat. It was folly to come up to Zeke's booth.

"I can tell you it's a form of seaweed, but not the exact one," Zeke said after a moment passed. "You likely wouldn't know it anyway. It only sprouts in marshy water."

Emerson suspected he was referring to Salicornia, locally known as pickle grass. Various forms of the plant were used in home remedies in Asia and other parts of the world. It was a halophyte, which meant it could tolerate being submerged in salt water for a period of time.

"I'll take six bottles," he said.

A large smile creased Zeke's face. "I'll bag that right up for you."

"Do you take cash?" Emerson asked, reaching for his wallet.

"I prefer it." Zeke pointed to a scuffed-up tablet. "That thing is temperamental with debit cards. Half the time it rejects them."

———

First thing that morning, David printed out the list of ingredients in Zeke's remedy and slipped it into his pocket. Hoping to see Dr. Spies, he drove directly to the hospital. The neurosurgeon was standing at the nurses' station when David entered the ICU area.

"How's my father?" David asked.

"Improving," the doctor replied. "We had a decent conversation about what he's been through. You can go on in to see him."

David cleared his throat. "I have a question. My father has a friend who makes home remedies. Would it be okay to include one of those in what he's receiving? I have the list of ingredients."

As he asked the question, David's voice got softer and softer until it trailed off. He handed the sheet of paper to the doctor, who quickly read it.

"Oh, I know Zeke Caldwell," Dr. Spies replied. "He's a true herbalist who stays away from stimulants, alcohol, and sugars. I've been by his booth at local craft fairs."

David relaxed. "Mark Sparrow is my father's family doctor," he said. "I know he allows some of his patients to take Zeke's remedies."

"It's fine with me." Dr. Spies handed the sheet back to David. "You can give this in moderation if your father wants to take it. I don't discount the impact this sort of treatment can have, whether due to what's actually in it or the confidence patients have in the treatment."

"Three or four drops a day?"

"Yes."

Carter was sitting up in bed while a nurse's aide held a cup with a straw to his lips.

"That's great, Mr. Cobb," the young woman said. "One more swallow. I promise I'll bring cranberry juice, not apple juice, the next time."

Carter saw David and managed a crooked smile. It was one of the most beautiful sights of David's life. The aide wiped the corner of Carter's mouth with a paper napkin.

"Are you ready for your visitor?" she asked.

"Yes, thanks for your help," Carter answered in a voice that more closely resembled his normal tone than anything David had heard since the ambulance came to the office.

The aide left. David pulled a chair close to the edge of the bed. "How are you feeling?"

Carter raised his right hand and shakily touched his nose. He tried to lift his left hand but only made it a foot off the bed.

"This arm isn't working very well," he said.

"Do you know what you've been through?" David asked.

"I met the surgeon this morning. What's his name?"

"Dr. Spies."

"He told me about the brain bleed and the operation. What do you know?"

David took his time to explain everything that had taken place. Partway through, his father shook his head and closed his eyes.

"Dad?" David asked.

"I'm here," Carter replied. "It's a lot to take in."

"Do you want me to stop?"

"Yeah. I know I've got to take it a day at a time. How are Nan and the kids?"

David showed him the photo of Andy's fish. His father didn't remember seeing it before.

"Did you know that Robbie and Katelyn are in town? They're staying at your house."

"Okay, so that wasn't a dream," Carter replied. "I thought they came, but my mind has gone some crazy places."

"One other thing," David said. "Zeke Caldwell knows you're here and cooked up one of his home remedies that's supposed to help restore your mental capacity and balance your blood chemistry. I checked with Dr. Spies, and he said it was okay to give it to you if you want to take it."

"That's nice of Zeke. You asked the doctor?"

"Yes. He's heard of Zeke and is familiar with what he does."

Carter managed another weak smile. "Sure, Zeke is famous."

"I'll tell him you said that."

David took the vial from his pocket and unscrewed the top. "Open up."

Carter parted his lips, and David deposited the drops beneath his father's tongue.

"Hold it there for a few seconds," he said.

Carter closed his eyes. Moments later, he swallowed and opened his eyes.

"Your turn," he said to David.

"Me?"

"Don't you want to be smarter and have good blood?"

David laughed. The return of his father's wit was another wonderful sign.

"Oh, and bring me some photos to put in this room," Carter continued. "Some from the house—and print out the one of Andy and his fish. That will cheer me up."

Katelyn left Nan's house and decided to drive toward the coast. The beachfront communities near Wilmington were strung together like white, sandy beads. At the southern end of Kure Beach were the ruins of Fort Fisher, a Confederate fortification known as the "Southern Gibraltar." The fort protected the entrance to the Cape Fear River and the port of Wilmington. The first attempt by the Union Army to capture the fort in December 1864 failed, and it wasn't until January of 1865 that it was captured by Union forces. One of those Union soldiers was Katelyn's direct ancestor, a twenty-one-year-old lieutenant in a

Vermont regiment. After the war, he returned to New England and lived to be ninety years old.

It had been several years since Robbie and Katelyn visited the remains of the fort, which was now little more than large mounds of sandy earth. Katelyn walked along a path and up to one of the overlook platforms. It was a beautiful, calm day, completely unlike what it must have been for her ancestor when he faced the massive earthen walls and the muskets of those who defended it. Billowing smoke and the smell of gunpowder would have filled the air.

Katelyn laid her hand on her abdomen. A tiny person directly descended from the nineteenth-century soldier lived within her. When thinking about children in the past, she'd never had a preference for a boy or a girl. But today, the scales tipped slightly in one direction. Her forebear's name on her mother's side of the family was Jedidiah Spencer Overstreet.

"Jedidiah Cobb," she said softly, then chuckled. That name on a lunchbox would create a heavy load for a little boy to carry to kindergarten.

"Spencer Cobb," she said. That sounded more manageable. Maybe Spence for short with Robert as the middle name. That would make Robbie happy.

Katelyn stayed on the platform for several more minutes and daydreamed about little boys.

Robbie was standing in the kitchen when she returned to the house for lunch. "I just left the hospital, and my dad is better," he said.

Katelyn listened as Robbie described the visit with his father.

"Not that he was normal," Robbie said. "His memory short-circuits if you ask him about what he said a few minutes earlier, but he can carry on a conversation that makes you forget for a moment what he's been through. We talked about Camp Seacrest. He was glad I applied and got the job. Then I told him you'd resigned from the law firm."

"Was he surprised that we're moving to Wilmington?"

Robbie leaned against the counter. "He was so happy that he cried."

"Aww," Katelyn said.

"I became emotional too," Robbie added. "He wanted to talk more about it but was so tired that I left so he could rest."

"Did you tell him again that we're staying at his house?"

"Yes. He also asked how you're doing."

"What did you tell him?"

"The truth."

"What part of the truth?"

"Not that you're pregnant. But I said a couple of nice things that popped into my head in the moment. Maybe we can visit him tomorrow. I'll be curious what he remembers from the conversation today."

Robbie opened the refrigerator door, took out some cold cuts, and started making a sandwich. "I'm starving. Did you eat lunch?"

"No, my stomach is feeling odd."

Robbie stopped.

"No, no." Katelyn held up her hand. "Morning sickness usually doesn't happen this early in a pregnancy."

"Did you eat breakfast?"

"A yogurt followed by tea with Nan."

While Robbie fixed a sandwich, Katelyn told him about the time spent with her sister-in-law.

"I mentioned working at Cobb and Cobb, and she told me David wanted to talk to me about it. She thinks it's a good idea."

"Hmm," Robbie replied.

"Temporarily, to see if it's a good fit," Katelyn continued.

"I'm not sure. But it's your call." Robbie took a bite of his sandwich. "If you do it, I'd be glad to discuss the terms of employment with David."

"How much negotiating did you do with the board of directors?"

"None. I desperately wanted the job."

"I can handle my own negotiations."

Katelyn took a bottle of water from the fridge. "After I left Nan's house, I drove to Kure Beach and went to Fort Fisher."

"Why?"

"I didn't really know. But standing on an overlook, I thought about my ancestor who fought there and our baby."

"What was his name? Jeremiah?"

"Jedidiah. If we have a son, what do you think about calling him—"

"No." Robbie shook his head.

"Jedidiah's middle name was Spencer. I like the idea of a heritage name."

"Maybe."

―――――

David read a text from Nan about Katelyn's interest in working at Cobb and Cobb and immediately called home.

"She brought it up, and I told her you had the same thought," Nan said.

"I could use her now," David replied. "Things are already starting to back up. Is Robbie on board with it?"

"I'm not sure. She said he treated it like a joke."

"Typical. I'll text and ask him."

"Why not a phone call? This is an important decision for the whole family."

"Because I haven't thought through the details yet."

After the call with Nan ended, David took out a legal pad and started making a list of points to discuss with Robbie and Katelyn. One page became two pages. He was halfway through a third page of questions when he stopped, reviewed what he'd written, and realized it sounded more like dealing with a stranger than a family member. Ripping the sheets from the pad, he tossed them in the trash and sent a text to Robbie.

What do you think about Katelyn working at the law office?
No long-term commitment on either side. If it doesn't work
out, no hard feelings.

In return, he received a simple thumbs-up emoji. David called Katelyn.

"Sounds like we both had the same idea," he said.

"Yes."

"Would you like to come by the office Monday morning to discuss?"

"Sure, and I turned down Robbie's offer to represent me in the negotiations and wanted to let you know."

Katelyn's lighthearted comment helped David relax.

"I'll be on my own too. How about ten o'clock?"

"See you then."

The next morning, Katelyn was feeling better, and Robbie wanted to show her his new workplace. She was agreeable to going for a ride on what had turned into a beautiful day. A large sign on the highway announced "Camp Seacrest for Boys—Founded 1948." They turned down the unpaved sandy road that wound its way for over a mile past large live oaks draped with Spanish moss.

"How much land does the camp own?" Katelyn asked.

"Over a thousand acres. When the men who founded the camp bought the property, it was scrubland unsuitable for successful farming. They paid between $25 and $30 per acre."

"What about the beachfront area?"

"Even less. People thought only a fool would live on the beach and risk the full brunt of a hurricane."

Katelyn smiled. "Things change."

"Yes, selling part of the beach property has been a topic of debate for years. There's a gap where Nichols Creek creates a natural separation from the main beach used by the camp. We always called the smaller area South Beach. There's no direct road access to it, but developers would jump at the chance to buy the land and build one."

"What do you think about the idea?"

Robbie turned into the parking area for the main building, a long, low wooden structure whose planks had turned gray from weather and sun. It was known as the "Big House."

"A week ago, I would have opposed it," Robbie said. "Now that I'm tasked with raising money, I think it's worth considering as long as we would retain access to half the Nichols Creek watershed, and the development would need to be limited to single-family homes. No condos or high-rises."

To the left of the Big House were five cabins used by the younger boys, and on the right were five cabins occupied by the older campers. The counselors stayed in the cabins with their individual groups. There were two bedrooms in the Big House, including one reserved for the camp director. Robbie took a large ring of keys from his pocket.

"Do you want to see our summer quarters?" he asked.

"Do I have to stay here during camp season?" Katelyn asked.

"Why would you want to miss all the fun when boys sneak out after curfew and we chase them through the woods with flashlights?"

"I think that's my answer."

A long porch stretched the length of the Big House. During the summer, it was lined on weekends with cane-backed rocking chairs. Robbie tried multiple keys before he finally found the right one.

"My first job is to label the keys," he muttered.

A large open room served as the dining hall. Wooden tables and benches were pushed against the far wall. The floor was made from wide pine planks that glistened with long-dried resin.

"These floors are spectacular," Katelyn said.

"Yeah, everyone says that. All the lumber for the buildings was milled on the property."

To the right was the kitchen. Everything looked clean and tidy.

"In spite of his problems, it looks like Chris kept things neat," Robbie said.

Katelyn didn't try to count the number of massive pots and kettles. There were two four-burner gas cooktops and a walk-in cooler. Robbie picked up a pot that was on the stovetop and placed it in a sink.

"Seeing the kitchen makes me hungry for grits with bits of sausage sprinkled on top," he said. "And biscuits with bacon jam."

Grits and Katelyn had never become friends. "How much weight are you going to gain over the summer?" she asked.

"We'll have to see about that."

Two bedrooms occupied the corner of the building not dedicated to the kitchen. The camp director's quarters consisted of a bed constructed with thick posters cut from the same pine as the floors. A chest of drawers rested against one wall. There was a bathroom with a tub-and-shower combination. Katelyn touched the bedspread decorated with coastal images.

"This looks handmade," she said.

"It probably is. Creating handmade quilts won't be part of your job description either."

There were three screened windows. Robbie looked outside and patted the screens.

"See, the mosquitoes can't sneak in to feast on you," he said.

"Until I go outside."

"Or you develop herd immunity."

Katelyn had never heard about herd immunity from mosquitoes until she met Robbie. He claimed that by the end of the summer, he and David would have been bitten so many times that new bites had little effect on them.

"I don't want to test your theory."

Robbie lay down on the bed. "At least check this out."

Katelyn joined him. The mattress was nicely firm. "Okay, I could sleep on this maybe once a week."

"On the weekend. That's when the director's wife is on duty."

Katelyn hadn't seriously considered her role. She turned onto her side so that she faced Robbie. "Please don't expect me to jump in and prepare food for a hundred and fifty campers when one of the regular cooks calls in sick."

Robbie stroked her hair. "No worries. No expectations. I'm just excited about being here. You can do as little or as much as you like."

They continued their tour of the sleeping cabins, which were little more than large, open rooms filled with bunks, a single lavatory, two toilets, and two shower stalls.

"I'm relieved," Robbie said when they finished a quick inspection. "Except for some problems in cabins four and seven, everything looks to be in good shape. With Chris siphoning off money, I was worried things might have deteriorated."

"Do you have counselors lined up?"

"According to Frank Gates, almost all the slots are filled. I'll be going over the list and setting up precamp training. Even with the negative news about Chris Brammer leaving, registrations are strong for campers, and there is always a last-minute flurry."

They walked back to Robbie's truck.

"Do you want to go down to the beach?" he asked. "Frank says they've constructed a new ropes course and zip line."

"Sure."

It was about two hundred yards to the beach. When the camp was built, the directors placed the Big House on the highest point in the area. It was only seven feet above sea level, but that seven feet and two hundred yards distance from the water meant the buildings had never been seriously damaged in a hurricane. They parked beside a long shed where the kayaks and other watercraft were stored. There was a nice breeze blowing off the ocean. Standing at the edge of the sand, the view was as unspoiled as when the first settlers arrived from England.

Robbie pointed to the right. "You can't see Nichols Creek, but it's around the bend. The property we might sell is beyond that."

"I'd vote against it," Katelyn said. "People would trespass, and you'd have to run them off."

"Remind me not to nominate you to join the board."

"Are you serious about wanting to sell land to a developer?"

Robbie squinted as he looked out over the water. "Nope. I'd rather have a donut sale as a fund-raiser."

David, Nan, Robbie, and Katelyn were spending time with the kids in the backyard after supper on Sunday evening. Robbie was coaching Andy, who was casting with a fly rod and trying to get the end of the line to land in a plastic clothes basket. David was throwing a Frisbee with Courtney, who'd not yet mastered the art of making a flat disk fly straight. Katelyn and Nan were watching from the back deck.

"Don't hook your sister!" Nan yelled when Courtney chased an errant throw and ran in front of her brother as he released the line.

"Robbie hooked a girlfriend once," David said to Katelyn.

"Is that true?" Katelyn called out to her husband.

"What?" Robbie replied.

"That you put a fishhook in a girlfriend."

Robbie came over to them. "No, that's impossible," he replied. "I never had a girlfriend before I met you."

Katelyn rolled her eyes.

Robbie continued, "But there was a girl I barely knew who went fishing with me one time. I landed a hook in her jaw on a backcast."

"Did you get it out?" Katelyn asked.

"Yeah, but it took a while." Robbie shrugged. "It was in pretty deep."

"Bonnie Simpson," David said. "She eventually married a plastic surgeon who fixed her up. You can't even see the scar."

"I'm not believing any of this," Nan said.

"You could ask Bonnie," David said. "But it would be cruel to bring up such a painful memory."

Later over supper, Robbie gave a summary of the condition of the camp. "I need to find a good contractor who can come in and do the repairs," he said.

"Call Rodney Hornbuckle," David suggested. "He'd be good for a job like that. I'll text you his contact info."

"Any new ideas for the camp program?" Nan asked.

"They used to keep a small herd of goats. David, you remember, don't you?"

"Getting to ride in one of the goat carts was a huge reward. And the goat cart races on Saturday afternoon were a highlight of the week."

"I'm thinking about bringing back the goats. If I do, we'll end up with nanny goats that need to be milked, which would be another great activity for the boys."

"Robbie was a natural at milking the goats," David said. "He could squeeze out a pint faster than most people could drink one."

"Way faster than I would want to drink it." Nan smiled.

"And we'd make goat's milk ice cream. It was always fun watching the reaction of the parents when they realized what was being served on their peach cobbler," Robbie remembered.

"Seriously, you'll need the right health permit to bring in the animals," David advised.

"Katelyn can take care of that as part of her duties at the law firm," Robbie said.

"Yeah," she replied. "I'd love to develop a niche practice in goat law."

After saying good night to Courtney and Andy before the kids headed up to bed, David and Katelyn exchanged confirmations about her arriving at the firm at ten o'clock the next morning.

During the drive home, Katelyn yawned. "I'm tired even though I didn't do anything."

"You're working twenty-four-seven," Robbie said. "When can we tell them our biggest news?"

"After my appointment with the doctor."

In the morning, the queasiness she'd felt a couple of days earlier returned, only stronger. It wasn't enough to make her nauseous, but it was a step closer. Feeling thankful that she wasn't due to meet David until ten o'clock, she mentioned how she felt to Robbie, who was trying to adjust Carter's archaic coffeemaker.

"You've not thrown up once during our entire marriage," Robbie said.

Katelyn held her hand in front of her mouth. "Past history isn't having much influence on how I feel right now."

"Does anything sound good for breakfast?" he asked as the coffee began to drip into the pot.

"This morning, I'd like hot English tea with honey and lemon."

"Are you serious?"

"It doesn't have to be English tea."

Robbie opened the pantry door. "I'm not sure Dad has honey and lemon in the house, especially lemon. Check the fridge for lemon juice in one of those little bottles."

"No, I want fresh-squeezed lemon juice."

"Should I go to the store?"

"No, that's not necessary."

Robbie shut the pantry door and poured coffee into a travel mug. "Back in ten minutes," he said. "I won't be able to focus if I know you're longing for hot tea with honey and fresh-squeezed lemon juice."

Katelyn wanted to tell him not to go, but she really did crave the drink.

"I'll take Charlie into the backyard," she said.

Barefoot in the grass, Katelyn watched Charlie run excitedly in a series of smaller and smaller circles until he ended up panting at her feet.

"I don't want to run in circles," she told the dog. "I want to move forward in a straight line."

Robbie called to her from the house. "Your butler has returned with English tea, fresh lemons, and locally sourced honey!" he said.

"Being pregnant has its advantages." Katelyn smiled when she saw the items on the kitchen counter. "But I'm worried you're going to spoil me."

"Me too," Robbie replied with an expression of mock concern on his face. "Let's make sure that doesn't happen."

When she felt well enough to get dressed, Katelyn wasn't sure what to wear for the meeting with David.

"Should I dress as if I were interviewing for a job in New York?" she asked Robbie.

"This is Wilmington, not New York, and you're meeting with your brother-in-law, not a stranger who doesn't know anything except your academic and professional credentials. Go business casual."

"That's easy for a man in khakis. It's tougher for a woman."

"Do you want me to go through the outfits you brought from the townhome?"

"No! I'll find something."

She settled on a yellow top and a skirt with a subdued pattern.

"You look fantastic," Robbie said when she came into the kitchen.

"Any last words of advice?"

"Don't accept his first offer. Double it and then accept half the difference."

"I'm not going to force anything today. This is the first step of the dance."

"David's a terrible dancer. All the rhythm and coordination in the family landed on me."

Katelyn chuckled. "You're a better dancer than I am."

"And you're a smarter lawyer than David. But seriously, in thinking more about it, this is about helping him out until you decide what you want to do professionally. Like you said yesterday, look at it as temporary."

"A temp job."

"And while you're impressing David, I'm going to call the agency in DC and let them know I won't be coming back."

"How do you feel about it?"

"A little sad, but I believe I'm doing the right thing. Fortunately, the two new guys they hired last year have the capacity to absorb my caseload. The hard part for me is thinking about the boys I've been helping. I won't get a chance to see them complete the program."

Katelyn left the house. It was a pleasant morning with a clear sky. Much of the ten-minute drive to the law office was through tree-lined residential streets. No traffic snarls. No honking drivers. Getting to work wouldn't be a source of stress. Close to the office, Katelyn slowed down as the building came into view. It was nicely landscaped across the front and still retained the welcoming look of a residence, which made sense for the type of clientele Cobb and

Cobb wanted to attract. There were two reserved parking spaces in front for the lawyers with small signs identifying them. Both spaces were empty. Katelyn didn't park in Carter's spot.

Candy greeted her in a thick Southern drawl. They'd met previously during one of Katelyn's visits.

"David isn't back from an early meeting with a client," the receptionist said.

"I'm early. How are things going here with Carter in the hospital?" she asked.

"Hectic. But we're doing our best to keep up."

Katelyn could see the computer monitor on Candy's desk. "What are you working on?"

"Trying to help Meredith with the finances, but I'm more lost than found."

"What software do you use?"

Candy mentioned something unfamiliar to Katelyn.

"We've had it a long time," Candy added. "Oh, and David said for you to wait in the vacant office if you'd like."

Katelyn went into the former bedroom that was twice as large as her office at Morgan and Monroe. She sat behind the desk and looked out the windows at the trees. It wasn't like the sunroom at her father-in-law's house, but it was a peaceful place. There was a desktop computer and monitor that looked dated. She took out her tablet and continued reading the book she'd started earlier that morning. Fifteen minutes later, she heard David's voice in the hallway.

"What do you think?" he asked when he reached the doorway.

"It's a good place to read a book."

"And as a place to work?"

"More than adequate if I have the tools I need."

David sat across from her and pointed at the computer. "That needs to be replaced, but we can get to that in a few minutes. What's the most important thing we need to discuss? I want to start there."

"How can I best help you? What cases require immediate attention?"

"Not with the salary?" David asked in surprise.

"That's important, but I believe you'll be fair."

In an apologetic tone of voice, David mentioned a figure within the range Katelyn had anticipated. Together with the pay raise Robbie would receive in his new job, they would be able to pay their bills, her student debt, and continue saving toward the purchase of a home. That goal might be closer in Wilmington.

"I'll discuss it with Robbie, but that sounds reasonable until we see what value I bring to the firm," Katelyn replied. "How many hours a week?"

"Full-time, if you're willing to do so. Forty hours. Bill whatever is warranted during that time period. We've never had a quota."

Katelyn smiled. "Do you know how many weeks I've only worked forty hours in the past five years?"

"Not many?"

Katelyn shaped her index finger and thumb to form a zero. "And billable hour quotas were a part of life."

"That no longer applies. Dad never tried to make me do anything that he didn't want to do himself. Anything else?"

"I checked on reciprocity for my Virginia, New York, and DC law licenses. I've met the experience requirement, so all I have to do is pay a fee to be admitted to the North Carolina bar. In the meantime, it shouldn't be a problem letting me work on cases as long as you sign everything too."

"Sure, and the firm will pay your admission fee."

"And I'll want to be admitted to practice in the federal courts."

"I'm admitted to the Eastern District, but I've never filed a case there. Most of our litigation is in state court. Let's check out the other open litigation files."

THIRTEEN

KATELYN FOLLOWED DAVID INTO THE LARGE OFFICE
formerly occupied by Carter Cobb. Like many lawyers who'd practiced more than thirty-five years, Carter hadn't fully transitioned
into the electronic age. There was a lot of clutter. Katelyn quickly
counted six large stacks of paper files in different parts of the room.
David pointed to one of the piles.

"Those are the most pressing litigation matters," he said. "I went
through them the other day and dictated memos that Meredith is
typing up. That should help you get up to speed on what needs to
be done. Most of them are different types of business disputes. No
current personal injury claims."

"Anything on an upcoming trial calendar?"

"Thankfully, no. But there are depositions that need to be
scheduled and discovery answered."

"Any concerns about time deadlines?"

"Yeah," David answered as he leaned over and pulled one file from
the stack. "The statute of repose is going to run out on this construction
claim in six weeks, and we obviously need to file suit even though the
opinion from our expert is shaky. There are another half dozen cases in
my office that I've not reviewed. Should I just turn those over to you?"

"Yes. They'll go to the top of my list."

David gave her a wry look. "I'm a little embarrassed about how disorganized we are compared to what you're used to. Our systems work, but maybe not at the highest efficiency."

"I get that. I'll go through them in here if that's okay."

"Great."

Katelyn paused. "And how much autonomy will I have in overseeing the cases in litigation?"

"Total, at least until my dad can offer an opinion from his hospital bed. Even then, you're a much more experienced litigator. He's still something of a generalist and will take in business that I'd turn away or refer to someone else."

"Are you still focusing on representing small businesses?"

"They're not all small," David replied. "I mean, none are Fortune 500 companies, but they're significant for Wilmington. I represent a couple of shipping companies that own several massive container transports and—"

"Sorry," Katelyn cut in. "I didn't mean it that way."

"And I've been building my estate planning practice," David finished.

"I wouldn't be much help in the estate area, but if I can assist with the business matters, I'd be glad to try."

After David left, Katelyn sat in Carter's oversized leather chair. She unsuccessfully tried to adjust the height so that her feet could touch the floor. She phoned Robbie and told him what David had offered to pay her and her anticipated schedule.

"Only if he says, 'Yes, ma'am,' and 'No, ma'am,' when he talks to you," Robbie replied. "Are you okay with the money? It's a big cut, but we knew that would be the case."

"I'm fine with it, and David needs help that I can provide, especially with the litigation files."

"And I love the work schedule."

"That will be a change I enjoy immediately."

Ending the call, Katelyn faced Carter's computer. Her father-in-law had written his password on a small note and attached it to the side of the monitor. Katelyn smiled and entered the collection of initials from his two grandchildren and their dates of birth. She checked out the research service utilized by the firm. David returned with more paper files in his arms and set them on the floor beside the others.

"You logged on?" he asked.

Katelyn pointed to the yellow note. "I saw this."

"Yeah." David acknowledged the note and cringed slightly. "I told him not to do that, but our IT guy made us change the passwords a few weeks ago, and Dad didn't want to forget it."

"How often do you change them?"

"Uh, it's been a while. Maybe every two or three years."

At Morgan and Monroe, the in-house IT department changed the complex access codes for each attorney every ninety days.

"I know," David said before Katelyn could reply. "That's terrible."

"The threats are greater with a big firm," she said.

"You're here forty-five minutes, and I'm already realizing how much better we could be doing things."

"I'm not trying to make you uncomfortable—"

"No, this is good."

"Would it be okay if we purchased an inexpensive litigation software suite? And add some parts to the research suite? I'll only include something that will earn its value."

"Go ahead. Meredith has the law firm credit card."

Katelyn quickly prepared a simple employment agreement and emailed it to David. A few minutes later he brought it into the office, already signed and dated.

"Looks good," he said. "Have you done this before?"

"Yes. I've consulted for other law firms. Morgan and Monroe would farm out services for specific functions based on our expertise."

The phone on the desk buzzed.

"Please answer it," David said. "Candy knows I'm in here."

Katelyn swiveled the chair toward a beige phone that looked as old as she was.

"Yes?" she said, pressing the speakerphone button.

"Zeke Caldwell is here to see David."

"Ask him to have a seat in the lobby," David replied.

David turned to Katelyn. "I'm not sure why he's here today, but he recently received a letter from an in-house lawyer at Brigham-Neal refuting a claim of patent infringement. That's why I called you the other day. But if you don't have a recommendation for a law firm to represent him, I'll talk to him myself."

"I'd like to see the letter and sit in on the meeting."

"I'll take him into the conference room. You can join us there after you read the letter."

————

"How's your father?" Zeke asked when David appeared in the lobby.

"Better."

"Did you give him the drops?"

"For the past few days."

"They work fast, don't they?"

"Yes."

Zeke nodded with satisfaction. "That was a good batch. I took some myself just to check it out, and I've had all kinds of energy."

"I'm not going to argue with success."

"I didn't have an appointment and stopped by because I had a delivery in the area. I mostly wanted to check on Carter but also wondered if you've made any progress in finding a lawyer for me."

"Not yet. But my sister-in-law is looking over the letter you received and is willing to meet with you. She's a lawyer who's handled complicated litigation."

"Robbie's wife?"

"Yes, her name is Katelyn Martin-Cobb. She went to law school at Cornell and worked for a big law firm in Washington, DC. She and Robbie are moving to Wilmington because he's accepted a job as the new director for Camp Seacrest."

"That's awesome news," Zeke said with a smile. "He could be a bit ornery back in the day. Now he'll be the one to enforce the rules."

"Exactly."

David led the way to the conference room.

"Did you go fishing the other day with Robbie and your son?" Zeke asked. "Were the redfish coming up on the flats?"

"Yes and yes," David replied. "Let me show you a picture of the fish Andy caught on a fly rod using one of my dad's crab patterns."

David scrolled through the photographs on his phone.

"Here it is." David handed the phone to Zeke.

"That's a nice one. And he caught it on a fly rod?"

Katelyn entered the room. David introduced her to Zeke.

"I tagged along on the trip," she said. "The marsh is beautiful early in the morning, and it was fun watching Andy."

"Did you get eaten up by bugs when the sun came out?" Zeke asked.

"Not too bad. We had strong insect repellent."

"DEET isn't good for you," Zeke said with a frown. "I make a cream that stays on the skin like one of those metal coats of armor they used to wear. That's why I call it Bug Shield. David, have you tried it?"

"No."

"It's pretty new," Zeke said. "I had to study the bugs we have in this area and see what they didn't like. Then I had to figure out how to put it in a bottle. Did you know there are animals the mosquitoes won't bite? It has a lot to do with odors, not that bugs have a highly developed sense of smell, but . . ."

David let Zeke ramble on. Not all the herbalist's remedies were effective. One of David's friends had tried Zeke's cure for baldness. It proved as ineffective as a sandcastle trying to stem the incoming tide. And if the insect repellent smelled as foul as the poison ivy cream, David couldn't see Nan using it on herself or the kids. Finally, he stepped in.

"Zeke, let's get to business," he said. "Katelyn, what did you think about the letter from the drug company's lawyer?"

Katelyn placed the letter and attachments on the table. "I would have expected a single paragraph," she said. "They are taking this matter seriously."

"That was my impression," Zeke said with a nod.

"A lot of the letter is boilerplate and not really relevant to the claim," Katelyn continued. "How well do you understand the chemical formulas in the patents?"

"I'm not a trained chemist, but I have a lot of lay knowledge. I've worked for years as an assistant at a local pharmacy. When I was working with Carter on the patent application, I hired a lab in California to put together the technical data. The guy I worked with told me the tricky part is figuring out what's an active ingredient and what's filler."

"The drug company did that," Katelyn said. "And even though

there are obvious similarities between the patent applications, that's an area of difference. I could see that pretty quickly."

Zeke's face fell. "Does that mean I can't complain about them stealing from me?" he asked.

"Not necessarily," Katelyn answered. "But I believe you're going to have to take your chemical analysis to a more sophisticated level to rebut their arguments."

"What will that look like, and how much would that cost? I don't have a lot of money."

"I'm not sure, but in my opinion it's a prerequisite to taking the first step in arguing that patent infringement occurred. That's probably what the chemist in California was telling you. And no competent lawyer would file a complaint without knowing there's a provable similarity in the active chemical compounds and how they counteract nausea."

Zeke was quiet for a few seconds as he processed Katelyn's explanation. "I think I follow you. Should I contact the lab in California?"

"That would be a good place to start."

"And what should I ask them to do?"

"Show them what you've received from Brigham-Neal and find out if they can prepare a response."

Zeke sighed. "I was hoping the letter from their lawyer was an invitation to try and settle our claim in return for a license fee. I read that's what usually happens in these cases."

"After they've been litigated for months or years," Katelyn responded. "Big companies can't develop a reputation for rolling over and paying money every time someone comes to them with his hand out."

"One of my friends suggested that would be my next step," Zeke answered. "You know, send them a demand letter."

"How much would you ask them to pay?" Katelyn asked.

"I'm not sure. But I'd put a high price on it. It's easier to go down than up."

"What's a high price? And how would you justify it?"

"I really don't know," Zeke said. "And hearing what you say makes me realize that might not be a good idea."

"At this point there's no way to calculate damages. Any claim has to be based on facts that can be supported by evidence. The drug company must believe a party is serious and willing to go all the way through a trial. There's nothing in the letter indicating an interest in paying you so that you'll go away, which gets back to the cost of this type of litigation. And I'm not talking about attorney fees. I've been involved in patent litigation related to manufacturing processes, but not drug cases. Either way, it's a very expensive type of lawsuit."

"How expensive?" David asked.

"The last patent infringement case I worked on, our client spent around $3 million on scientific reports, economic analysis, and expert witnesses. It was an industrial patent, not a pharmaceutical patent, but the protocol is similar."

David knew he registered as much shock as he saw on Zeke's face.

"Wow," Zeke managed. "Where does that leave me?"

"Exactly where you were when you came through the door this morning," David said. "Looking for a lawyer who will not only represent you for a percentage of any recovery but also finance the case."

"And the attorney fee will be at least forty percent," Katelyn said. "With no recovery for you until all expenses are paid."

This was a lot for Zeke to consider. David felt sorry for his father's friend.

"What would you charge?" he asked Katelyn. "I'd be glad for you to make money so long as I do too."

"You need a contingency lawyer who's set up to handle this spe-cific type of case. That way, they won't have to reinvent the wheel but can plug the claim into their system and try to put the squeeze on the drug company."

"Which brings us back to our conversation the other day about identifying a lawyer to represent you," David said. "Katelyn and I will do some research and let you know what we find out."

"Okay," Zeke said with a nod of his head to Katelyn. "Thanks for meeting with me. I can tell how smart you are, and I wish you'd think it over."

"Give us a week," David said. "Do I have permission to share the letter with any lawyers I contact?"

"Sure," Zeke answered.

"And could I mention the claim to Nan? She'll pray for us."

"Absolutely," Zeke replied.

Katelyn spoke. "Before you go, I'd like to prepare a document for you to sign authorizing David and me to speak to other lawyers on your behalf."

"That's a great idea," David said.

Katelyn left the conference room.

"I bet she's hard to beat at Scrabble," Zeke said.

"Yeah." David chuckled. "There's a lot of horsepower under her hood."

Zeke leaned back in his chair.

"What's the plan for Carter's long-term care?" he asked. "Even with the drops, it will take a while for him to bounce back."

"Most likely a rehab facility for a while, then he'll return home with assistance based on his status."

For the next few minutes, they discussed the pros and cons of various facilities in the greater Wilmington area. With his large family, Zeke knew them all. Katelyn returned and placed a copy of a two-page document on the table in front of Zeke and David.

"Do I need to read this, or can I just sign it?" Zeke asked. "I trust David one hundred percent."

"Take your time to read it," Katelyn said.

David picked up the authorization. It contained fewer uses of "wherefore" and "hereinafter" than he would have suspected and covered issues he wouldn't have thought to include.

"Where did you find this?" he asked as he reached the top of the second page.

"I had to craft it myself. That's why it took me longer than I'd hoped."

David was even more impressed.

"Looks fine to me," Zeke said as he signed the authorization.

"This meeting is worth at least a couple of tubes of Bug Shield," Zeke said when they finished. "One for each of you. I always like to barter when I can."

———

After the meeting with Zeke, Katelyn returned to her father-in-law's office and began going through the litigation files. The folders were thin, and organization of the intake information and documents was nonexistent. It looked like Carter simply threw anything related to the cases into a folder and returned it to a filing cabinet. That might be okay at the early stages of a simple lawsuit, but it would quickly snowball into a significant time thief if information wasn't organized and had to be located each time a file was reviewed.

Katelyn began with the construction claim facing a deadline, scanned the documents into an electronic folder, and created an index. It wasn't something David had asked her to do, but her standards for excellence were ingrained. She was in the middle of inputting data from a third file when there was a knock on the office door.

"Come in!" she called out.

Robbie entered. "You're not my father," he said.

Katelyn leaned back, then had to grab the arms of the chair to steady herself as her feet left the floor. "And I'm not certified to operate this chair," she said.

"That's obvious. How's it going?"

"Fine. I'm organizing litigation files. And we met with Zeke Caldwell. He's an interesting man."

"That's an understatement. Does he have a case?"

"Too soon to know. Our assignment is to locate an attorney to represent him."

"Are you available for lunch?"

"Yes."

"Have a good time!" Candy called out cheerily as they passed her desk and left through the front door.

"None of the receptionists at Morgan and Monroe ever said that to me," Katelyn noted. "They were required to write down when everyone left and what time they returned."

They got into Robbie's truck.

"Anything to add about your morning?" he asked.

"Being busy kept me from dwelling on what's going on today in DC. I'm sure my departure from the law firm is at the top of the gossip chain, and they're busy reassigning my cases. It's odd to think that I won't have any input into issues I considered extremely important a matter of days ago."

They stopped at a small place that featured salads. Katelyn had eaten there before and liked it.

"I didn't think the practice of law could be so different from one firm to another," she said after the waitress left with their order. "Not that the way your brother and father run their office is wrong, but there are so many ways to improve their organization and processes. You were right. It was like stepping into a time machine and going back thirty or forty years."

Robbie chuckled. "I'm sure what they do reflects their personalities. My dad is all about getting to know people, and I've heard him say that David is more counselor than lawyer."

Katelyn ate a piece of grilled chicken before continuing the conversation. "If we're able to find a lawyer for Zeke, maybe I should shadow the case to make sure they're treating him fairly. And see how a plaintiff's lawyer operates from the inside."

"That makes sense. Did you suggest that to David?"

"No." Katelyn hesitated. "I don't want to come on too strong with a lot of new ideas."

"The stronger the better."

Later that evening Katelyn tried to read in bed, but her eyes wanted to close. Robbie was writing in his journal on a small table in the corner of their bedroom.

"I'm going to sleep," she said, putting down her book.

"What time did David tell you to be at the office?"

"He suggested nine, but I'll come up with a schedule and probably go in earlier, since that's my most productive time of the day."

"Do you want me to go out to the den so I don't keep you awake?"

"No, you can stay here. It won't bother me."

In the early morning hours, Katelyn woke up. Robbie was sound asleep beside her. Slipping out of bed, she went into the kitchen to get a drink of water. Retrieving her laptop from the den, she logged on and read an article about the development of her unborn child. Both she and Robbie had downloaded apps that gave them a day-by-day progress report. Katelyn also did some follow-up research about ob-gyn doctors in the Wilmington area, including the group Nan recommended.

While her search screen was open, Katelyn thought about Zeke and entered a query about plaintiff lawyers in patent infringement claims against pharmaceutical companies. Some were clearly unsuitable because the lawyers had either poor credentials or an absence of proven success. She then searched federal court records for cases in which the lawyers from the better firms appeared as counsel. A legitimate group would have a judicial track record. It took an hour and a half to refine the process to a level that yielded valid results.

Six law firms made the cut: two in California, one in Florida, one in New York, one in Virginia, and one in Georgia. The Virginia and Georgia firms were geographically the closest, but the firm of Craft and Bosworth in Miami seemed the best fit. They had represented clients in multiple reported cases, including one in the Eastern District of North Carolina that ended up before the Fourth Circuit Court of Appeals in Richmond. The firm ultimately lost the case, but that didn't discourage Katelyn. Any lawyer who regularly goes to court is going to lose sometimes. It was clear that the firm knew what it was doing. They hired chemical and medical experts, economists, and consultants. The academic backgrounds for the two named partners in the six-person firm were stellar, and the four associates seemed highly qualified. Reading about the lawyers awakened a twinge of curiosity in Katelyn. If she'd not gone to a huge, multistate practice like Morgan and Monroe, she might have enjoyed the more freewheeling style of a high-end, sophisticated plaintiff's practice. One associate particularly intrigued her, and Katelyn sent her an email laying out the gist of Zeke's claim. Yawning, Katelyn turned off her computer and returned to bed.

FOURTEEN

AFTER DROPPING THE KIDS OFF AT SCHOOL, DAVID stopped by the hospital to see his father. Carter was sitting up in bed as a nurse's aide fed him breakfast. The regular room was lighter and cheerier than the one in the ICU.

"I don't have much breakfast to share," Carter said to David. "And neither one of my arms is cooperating enough so that I can feed myself."

"You're doing great, Mr. Cobb," the aide said. "And this is much better than a feeding tube."

"How close was he to getting a feeding tube?" David asked.

"I can't say for sure, but it's not uncommon with patients who have suffered a similar stroke or hemorrhage."

"It would be hard to fit bacon-wrapped jalapeños into a feeding tube," Carter said.

It was the second attempt at humor David had observed from his father since the brain hemorrhage. He chuckled.

"You really are getting better," he said.

Carter accepted a forkful of scrambled eggs, then coughed as he choked.

"Sorry, that bite was too big," the aide said as she held a cup with a straw up to his lips.

Carter took a small sip, coughed again, then managed a larger swallow of water. "That's okay," he said, clearing his throat. "It's a reminder that I'm alive."

David watched as his father eventually ate everything on the plate. The woman brushed Carter's teeth. The gentle, deliberate way she did so made David appreciate the people who served at the hospital.

"That feels way better," Carter said after he spit into a small trough. "Now I don't have to worry about chasing my son from the room with my breath."

The aide left, and David scooted a chair closer to the bed. "Ready for some of Zeke's miracle drops?"

"What?"

"You don't remember? I've given them to you before."

"No, I don't even remember you coming to see me. My short-term memory must be shot."

"Don't give up. I think you're improving every day."

David explained again the purpose of the remedy and gave it to his father.

"We also need to talk about where you're going when you're discharged from the hospital," David said.

"That's easy. Home."

"Or a professional rehab facility. That's what Dr. Spies mentioned."

Carter's face saddened. "No, David. Even if it's supposed to be temporary, I don't want to do that."

"I understand. But if you come home, we'll need to find someone to help. Maybe a couple of people."

"The woman who was in here only works part-time at the hospital," Carter said. "Maybe she'd be willing to come on her days off."

"Are you sure she's part-time?"

Carter hesitated. "No. I may be thinking of someone else."

"Speaking of help, what would you think if I told you I offered Katelyn a job at the law firm?"

"Katelyn?"

David realized his father might have forgotten about Robbie going to work at Camp Seacrest, Katelyn resigning from Morgan and Monroe, and their move to Wilmington. He started to explain.

"No, I remember that," Carter said, cutting him off midsentence. "But is Katelyn interested in working at a firm like ours?"

"She started yesterday."

"Why didn't you ask my opinion about it?"

David froze. He didn't know what to say.

"We're equal partners," Carter continued. "I haven't forgotten that, even if you have."

David cleared his throat. "Uh, I assumed you might not be able to return and someone would need to handle your business."

Carter closed his eyes. David pressed his lips together tightly for a moment.

"Dad, I'm sorry. I should have come to you first. There was so much momentum in the way it came up that I went with it. Both Katelyn and I had the same idea. She needed a place to land and has the litigation experience to make sure your clients' interests are protected. She isn't interested in a general practice, but I can already see how she will be a huge asset across every aspect of the firm."

Carter's eyes remained closed.

"Did you hear me?" David asked.

There was no immediate response. A few moments later, Carter opened his eyes.

"Yes," the older man sighed. "But I'm not ready to quit. I want to hang in there for several more years."

"What should I do about Katelyn?"

Carter was silent for a moment. "Nothing for now."

On the way to the office, David called Nan and told her about his father's reaction to Katelyn joining the firm.

"He's right," David said. "I should have talked to him instead of acting like he's no longer here. I apologized but still felt bad."

"Don't be too hard on yourself. And don't say anything to Katelyn."

———

Katelyn didn't wake up until the sun peeked around the edges of the plantation blinds on the windows. Instead of hopping out of bed, though, she moaned. She tried lying on her back, but that made things worse. There was a volcano in her stomach. Stumbling out of bed and into the bathroom, she threw up. When she emerged after splashing water on her face, Robbie was looking at her with his eyes wide.

"Did you just—" he started.

Katelyn extended her right arm, palm out. "If you say it, I'll do it again."

Robbie's mouth snapped shut. Katelyn crawled back into bed and pulled the sheet up to her chin.

"Is there anything I can do to help?" Robbie asked.

"Don't make the bed move. Not one millimeter."

Katelyn closed her eyes, but that didn't help. Her best position was lying on her side. Several minutes passed.

"Can I get out of bed?" Robbie asked. "I need to go to the bathroom."

"Go," Katelyn muttered.

Miserable, she tried to lie as still as possible. She peeked open her eyes when Robbie, walking softly, returned to the room. He had a small plate in one hand and a cup in the other.

"I read up on morning sickness. Scientists believe it may be caused by an increase in a hormone called HCG."

"That sounds like an acronym for 'here comes the gagging' to me."

"Doctors recommend eating and drinking something so your stomach isn't empty. I brought you a piece of dry toast and a cup of the hot tea you craved yesterday."

Robbie placed the plate and cup on the nightstand.

"I can guarantee you my stomach is empty," Katelyn said as she managed to sit up.

Neither the tea nor the toast looked appetizing, but she forced herself to eat a bite of toast and take a sip of tea. She braced for a violent rejection. It didn't come. While Robbie watched, she ate and drank some more. Her stomach started to calm down.

"Thanks," she said. "This helps."

"I also read that morning sickness isn't limited to mornings. Women can become nauseous at any time of the day."

"I knew that," Katelyn answered. "But thanks for reminding me."

"Sorry."

"No, you're being sweet."

Katelyn glanced at the clock on the dresser across the room. It was later than she thought. Even though she didn't feel well, she must have dozed off.

"I'd better get going if I want to make it to the office on time. It would be awkward to be late or call in sick on the second day."

"Not if it's true. And David Cobb isn't Suzanne Nixon."

"But I'm still me."

"Only different because you're pregnant."

Katelyn ate the last bite of bread. "Did you make two pieces of toast?"

"Yeah, but I ate one myself. Do you want another one?"

Katelyn thought for a moment. "No, but I'd really like a cinnamon raisin bagel with cream cheese."

Robbie laughed. "I'll be back in ten minutes."

Katelyn emerged from the bedroom after her shower. Robbie was in the kitchen. He'd cut open her bagel and evenly spread each half with cream cheese.

Katelyn sat at the table and ate a bite of bagel. She closed her eyes. "This is the best bagel I've ever eaten," she said.

Robbie gave her a puzzled look.

"I'm serious," Katelyn continued. "How many did you buy?"

"Uh, one. It came from the in-store bakery."

"Try it," Katelyn coaxed as she pushed the plate toward him. "Half is enough for me."

"Not if you're loving it so much."

"I want to share."

Robbie took a bite.

"Well?" Katelyn asked. "How is it?"

"Fantastic."

Katelyn laughed. A streak of sunlight raced across the kitchen floor. She ate every bite of her bagel.

"I'm ready for the day!" she announced. "What are you doing?"

"Spending the morning with the bookkeeper at Frank Gates's office. I need a working knowledge of the camp finances even if I'm not hands-on with all the day-to-day details. And I've set up three meetings this afternoon with people who have given money in the past. I want to reassure them that the camp is going to go forward with integrity as we serve the boys."

"Are you going to stop by and see your dad?"

"I'd like to."

"Let's go together."

David arrived early at the office. Meredith was answering the phone until Candy came in.

"I visited Carter yesterday," the office manager said brightly. "He was doing much better than I thought. He asked how my aunt Sally is doing. She had kidney surgery six months ago, and I'd only mentioned it once. Do you think he'll be able to come back to work?"

"I'm not sure. It's way too soon to know."

Meredith's face fell. "I'm going to hold on to hope. This place won't be the same without him."

"That's true. I miss him too. Did he mention Katelyn?"

Meredith averted her eyes for a moment. As a key employee, the office manager's support was important.

"Yes, and he asked me what I thought about her joining the firm."

"What did you say?"

"Oh, something like, 'It's too soon to know.'"

"Did you spend any time with her yesterday?"

"Not really," Meredith replied with a slight edge to her voice. "Except when she went over her list of demands."

"I approved her requests. And whatever she needs to order to get set up in the vacant office is fine with me. Based on our conversation yesterday, she should be in around nine o'clock."

In his office, David said a quick prayer for the relationship between Katelyn and Meredith. An hour later, Meredith buzzed him.

"Didn't you say that Katelyn was coming in at nine?" she asked.

"Yes."

"She's not here yet."

"I'm sure she's on her way."

At ten, David was about to send Katelyn a text when she appeared in his doorway.

"Sorry I'm late," she said. "I was unexpectedly delayed this morning."

David didn't ask the reason. "First order of business is for you to set up your office the way you want," he said.

"I have my laptop and cell phone, and I know the password for your research service. That's enough for now. I spent some time last night trying to locate a lawyer for Zeke Caldwell and identified some options. Do you want me to prepare a memo for you or communicate directly with him?"

"Let's both talk to him."

"Okay, set it up, and I'll be there. In the meantime, I'll continue working on the litigation files."

David called Zeke and arranged a meeting in the afternoon. Checking his calendar, David had a lunch date scheduled with a local CPA. He buzzed Katelyn to ask if she'd like to join them.

"He's a good referral source with a lot of connections," David said. "As soon as he finds out you're here, he'll talk about it in his network."

"Okay."

Shortly before noon, the CPA called to cancel. David went across the hall to Katelyn's office. She was staring intently at the computer. He knocked on the doorframe.

"Do we need to leave?" she asked, looking up.

"My lunch appointment fell through."

Katelyn leaned back in her chair. "Let's go anyway. I need to eat; plus, I have a few things to go over with you."

They went to a restaurant in an upscale shopping area not far from the office. It was crowded. After ordering their food, David looked for an empty table. A man in a booth toward the rear of the restaurant raised his hand and waved them over. David pointed him out to Katelyn.

"He's a client named Tyler Crandall. The CPA we were supposed to meet with referred him to me a few years ago."

They approached the table where Tyler was sitting alone with a half-eaten salad in front of him.

"Would you like to join me?" he asked.

David and Katelyn sat across from the middle-aged man with short dark hair and a bushy black mustache. David introduced Katelyn simply as a lawyer and his sister-in-law who had recently joined the firm. If they'd been meeting with the CPA, he would have gone into much more detail about her qualifications and experience.

"Her husband, Robbie Cobb, recently accepted the job as director for Camp Seacrest."

"I heard about their problems," Tyler said. "I'm glad someone good is taking over. Both of my sons are signed up to attend the camp this summer. The older boy went last year and loved it."

A server brought their food to the table. David said a quick blessing over the meal.

"My wife would love it if I could pop out a prayer like that, but it's not in my wheelhouse," Tyler said.

"It's not hard," David replied. "My eleven-year-old son volunteered to say the prayer the other night at Jordan's Restaurant."

"Yeah, but kids aren't self-conscious or worried about being hypocrites."

"You don't have to be perfect to avoid being a hypocrite. Just in process."

"I hope it can be that way for me someday, but I'm not there now."

"You could be. It's like taking a long walk with someone who wants to guide you in the best way to go. Similar to what you do with people's money. It all begins with the first step, which is Jesus calling you to follow him on the journey. You answer with a yes."

Tyler turned toward Katelyn. "Tell me more about you," he said.

Tyler was in the financial planning business. He'd started out on his own and now had three other people working for him. David had prepared the employment agreements for his staff to sign. He was a persistent salesman.

"I'd love the chance to sit down with you and your husband to see ways that I might be able to help you," he said. "I've tried to get David's and Carter's business, but someone roped them in before I came along."

David wasn't sure if he should step in to rescue Katelyn or not.

"I've been working with a financial adviser who administered the profit-sharing plan at my previous firm," Katelyn said. "Over the past five years our rate of return has averaged eighteen percent per year."

"That's good," Tyler said, raising his eyebrows. "I'd be interested in knowing their portfolio mix."

David tried not to chuckle. Tyler's phone, which was on the table, vibrated. He picked it up.

"Hey, I've got to go. I'm meeting with a woman who may come to work with me. If I offer her a job, I'll need another employment agreement."

"Just let me know."

"Nice to meet you," he said to Katelyn.

Tyler left and David switched to the other side of the table. Katelyn ate a bite of salad.

"Eighteen percent?" David asked her. "That got Tyler's attention. Most financial guys like him are proud if they can beat an index fund."

"We had some unusual products that were proprietary. I'm not going to share our information with him."

"I understand." David took a drink of tea. "What did you want to talk about?"

"Before we get to that, what else would you have said to Tyler about hearing from God if he hadn't changed the subject?"

"Most people don't hear a voice that comes out of nowhere." David touched his chest. "You hear the call in here. That's when the journey begins."

Remembering what she'd read in Robbie's journal about her father-in-law talking to God around the campfire, Katelyn thought for a moment. Robbie's prayer wasn't much different from what his brother had just suggested to Tyler.

"I hope that didn't make you feel uncomfortable," David continued.

"No, I think Tyler was the one who was uncomfortable."

"Possibly. As far as I know, he's a good dad to his boys and a decent guy. This was a chance for me to see if he's interested in God's call on his life."

"I've never heard anyone do that before."

"Sometimes people are interested, sometimes not."

Katelyn took her phone from her purse. "We talked about office procedures in general terms yesterday, but I made a few more detailed notes to discuss with you."

"I'm listening."

Katelyn outlined for David how she'd like to systemize the office and provided a cost-benefit analysis. He didn't interrupt with questions and waited until she finished.

"What's the most pressing need?" he asked. "Is that the litigation suite?"

"No, I believe it's a client and case organization system because it cuts across the entire practice."

"Okay. If you can get Meredith and Candy on board, let's do it."

"You want me to talk to them?"

"Yes, because you'll be the in-house support person, not me."

After returning from lunch, Katelyn asked the two women to come into her office and told them what she had in mind. It was fun to have a blank canvas to paint on, and Katelyn realized that she enjoyed administrative creativity as well as legal analysis.

"I love it! I love it!" Candy responded. "I want to learn how to do more stuff. I get bored when the phones aren't ringing and there's nobody to talk to in the waiting area."

"You'll need to make sure your computer screen isn't visible to clients or visitors, and close it if you leave the room while you're accessing personal data," Katelyn said.

"And no more solitaire," Meredith added.

"Carter told me it was okay if I didn't have anything to do."

"That won't be the case from now on," Meredith said.

"And this software is going to help you as well," Katelyn said to Meredith.

"How?"

"All the time you spend searching for conflicts of interest and multiple entries for receipt and payment of funds will be drastically cut because the data will populate the entire system."

"I don't know how to do that."

"I'm going to teach you and walk you through it until you do. Based on your years of experience, you'll eventually get to the place where you can bill some of your time to clients for paralegal-type work."

Meredith's eyes widened. "Paralegal? I thought you had to be certified to do that."

"No, it can be based on experience."

Katelyn explained some of the functions that could be billed.

Meredith nodded. "I've always assumed that stuff was clerical."

Katelyn suddenly felt queasy. She put her hand to her mouth. "I need something to settle my stomach."

"We have medicine in the break room," Meredith said.

"No, maybe a snack."

"I have crackers in my desk," Meredith offered.

"Could I have a few?"

Meredith returned with the saltines, then left. Katelyn closed her eyes and leaned back in her chair. There was a knock on her door.

"Come in," she said.

"How did it go?" David asked.

"So far, so good. Meredith is halfway on board. She's the one I'm going to have to convince."

"Let me know if I need to reinforce the need to cooperate."

"Are you sure you don't want to be part of the training?"

"Positive." David smiled.

"When is Zeke coming in?"

"Later this afternoon. Are you ready for the meeting?"

Katelyn turned toward her computer. "I will be."

Preparing a memo was like riding a bike for Katelyn. The process was second nature. Zeke was smart, but she was careful to cut out any legalese. Two hours had flown by when Candy buzzed her.

"Mr. Caldwell is here."

Katelyn made some final changes before printing out copies for everyone. David and Zeke were waiting for her. Zeke was wearing khakis and a shirt with the pharmacy logo embroidered on it. His face lit up with a smile when he saw her. When the lawyers at Morgan and Monroe filed into a boardroom for a meeting with a client, they were rarely greeted with huge smiles.

"Good to see you," Zeke said.

"And you," she replied. "I've been working on finding a lawyer for you."

Katelyn explained her process. "Instead of sending an email through the firm website, I contacted one of the associate lawyers directly. She hasn't replied yet, but I thought we could call while you're here."

"Sounds good," Zeke said.

Katelyn placed her cell phone in the middle of the table, pressed the speaker button, and entered the direct number for the lawyer at Craft and Bosworth.

"Hello, this is Regina Abernathy," a woman said.

Katelyn identified herself and the reason for the call.

"I received your email and passed it on to one of the paralegals who screens our cases," Regina replied. "They should respond within thirty to forty-five days."

Katelyn knew this was a reasonable amount of time. "Thanks, but I'm with the client right now and have a few basic questions. If your firm is interested, what would be the terms of representation for fees and costs?"

"We have a forty percent contingency contract if the case is resolved prior to trial and fifty percent if a jury is selected. There is a $10,000 nonrefundable deposit for costs. The law firm advances the rest of the litigation expenses subject to reimbursement from settlement proceeds or verdict. Expenses can run into six figures for these cases."

While Regina talked, Katelyn watched Zeke. His face didn't reveal his thoughts.

"I saw on the website that your firm has handled quite a few drug patent infringement cases."

"Yes. And based on your email, I believe Mr. Caldwell's claim is worth a preliminary look. I personally settled a case against Brigham-Neal last year for over $2 million. If we agree to take the case and want to file it in North Carolina, would you be available to serve as local counsel?"

Katelyn looked at David, who didn't respond.

"I'm licensed in New York, Virginia, and DC and in the process of admission in North Carolina via experience and reciprocity," Katelyn said. "I can appear pro hac vice if you file in federal court. David Cobb, the principal of the firm, is admitted in the Eastern District of North Carolina. It would be up to him if he wanted to serve as local counsel."

"If none of that works, I'm sure we can find local counsel. That's never a problem for us. Any other questions?"

David and Zeke shook their heads.

"Not at this time," Katelyn said. "I appreciate you taking my call and look forward to hearing from you."

"Absolutely."

The call ended.

"What do you think?" Katelyn asked Zeke.

"What was that Latin stuff about?"

"Basically, a way for either David or me to be involved as your local attorney even though we wouldn't be the ones doing the major work."

"I like that idea. Is the amount the lawyer would charge fair? I thought it would be a third."

"That's in car wreck claims," David said.

"He's right," Katelyn said. "This type of case carries a lot more risk for the attorney. And the $10,000 deposit for costs and expenses sounds reasonable too."

"That's a lot of bottles of remedies," Zeke said ruefully, shaking his head. "I don't have that much in my bank account."

"Is there a family member who might be willing to help?" David asked. "What about your nephew Amos?"

"He doesn't earn that much as a teacher, but he's real savvy with his money and has saved enough to buy a couple of rental houses. I could ask him. He believes in what I do."

"I want to talk something over with Katelyn," David said. "Excuse us while we go into my office for a minute."

David held the door open for Katelyn as she entered.

"Are you thinking about advancing the $10,000?" Katelyn asked before David said anything.

"No, what made you think that?"

"I don't know. It was a guess."

"It's about the lawyer you called. Something about the way she talked made me feel uneasy."

"Uneasy? What do you mean?"

"I'm not sure they will really do what they promise."

"First, they haven't accepted the case, so we don't know what they'll think or promise or do."

"It doesn't feel right." David shook his head.

"Do you mean intuition?"

"Maybe," David said and then paused. "Let's put out a fleece. It's a biblical term for determining what to do."

"I know what it means. But I'm not sure how it applies here."

David took a deep breath before he spoke. "My concern is the Miami firm will take the $10,000 and never do anything. You heard what the lawyer said. It's nonrefundable. That's a red flag to me. The fleece would be that if she comes back within the next couple of days and says they fast-tracked the evaluation of the claim and are ready to come on board as soon as they receive the cost deposit, we shouldn't recommend them to Zeke because they're more interested in the advance money than vetting the merits of the case."

"That's the craziest way to make a decision I've ever heard."

"Could you maybe substitute the word 'unorthodox'? The idea popped into my head when we were in the conference room, and I couldn't shake it. I've learned not to ignore that inner prompting."

Katelyn threw her hands up in the air. "I told Regina Abernathy you were in charge of this firm, so it's your call. Are you going to tell Zeke what you're thinking?"

"Yes. I believe he'll understand."

They returned to the conference room, and David explained his suggestion.

"That makes sense to me," Zeke said. "The part about plopping down $10,000 without knowing where it's going rubbed me the wrong way too."

"It would be spent on investigating the claim," Katelyn said. "Hiring an expert, conducting a chemical analysis of your remedy and the drug issued by the pharmaceutical company. Things like that have to be done in a case like this. And when the deposit is gone, the law firm would pick up the tab for everything else. This could be your only opportunity. I bet the Miami firm turns down way more cases than they accept."

"I hear you, but I've always trusted Carter and David when it comes to legal matters," Zeke replied.

Katelyn opened her mouth again to speak but remained silent. David escorted Zeke to the reception area.

"I appreciate you being cautious," Zeke said. "But I'll talk to Amos about loaning me the money if I need it for that firm or someone else."

Apprehensive, David went to Katelyn's office. His sister-in-law was putting her laptop computer in a leather case. David suddenly wondered if she was quitting.

Katelyn looked up. "This has been an interesting day," she said.

"Will you be back tomorrow?"

Katelyn gave him a wry smile. "It depends on what happens when I put out a fleece."

FIFTEEN

KATELYN MET ROBBIE IN THE HOSPITAL PARKING lot. He got out of his truck and stretched. She joined him.

"I'm tired," he said. "Looking at numbers all day wears me out like nothing else does. How are you feeling?"

Katelyn told him about her short bout with nausea. "But I ate some crackers, and it went away right before David and I met with Zeke Caldwell."

"You should have asked Zeke if he has a potion that cures morning sickness."

"That might have been too big a clue for David that I'm pregnant."

"Yeah, even he would pick up on that."

They started walking across the parking lot.

"I need to talk to you before we see your father," Katelyn said. "Let's stop in the lobby."

"Okay," Robbie agreed.

Once they were seated, Katelyn looked Robbie directly in the eye. "Your brother is crazy," she said.

"That's old news."

"I'm serious. A question came up about how to best help Zeke

Caldwell, and David wants us to make our recommendation by putting out a fleece."

Katelyn explained what happened.

"That's David," Robbie said, nodding. "He's always marched to the beat of a drum no one else hears. That makes him different, but not crazy."

"Maybe that wasn't the right word. He preferred 'unorthodox,' but I felt uneasy. It's a different kind of control. Not the heavy-handed kind that was standard procedure at Morgan and Monroe. This was slippery and impossible to interact with." Katelyn stopped and shook her head. "Now I'm sounding like David. Basing events at the office on my feelings."

"Just go with the flow. He's in charge, and any mistakes land on his desk."

"I hate blame-shifting."

Robbie stared at her for a moment. "When was the last time I told you how much I respect you?"

"Okay, okay. Thank you."

"Ready to see my father?"

"Yes. But I sure would like to hear what David says to Nan about the meeting with Zeke."

"It will be good. She's a positive, stabilizing influence. Just like you with me."

Katelyn laughed. They walked over to the elevators.

"Should we have brought a plant or flowers?"

"No." Robbie reached into his pocket and pulled out some small red candies wrapped in cellophane. "This is what he's craving. They're a mixture of cinnamon and tamarind and hot as firecrackers."

"Could he choke on one of those?"

"Maybe I should cut one into little pieces. The only problem is

I didn't bring gloves. If one of the candies touches your skin, it can cause third-degree burns."

Katelyn gave Robbie a wry smile. "Then how can you put one in your mouth?"

Carter was propped up in bed watching TV when they entered his room. He looked a lot better than the previous time Katelyn visited. He turned off the TV with the remote and greeted them.

"I've had several visitors today."

"Who stopped by?" Robbie asked.

Carter stared blankly at him. "If you hadn't asked, I would have been able to tell you." He thought a moment. "Alex Maxwell was one of them."

"I doubt that," Robbie said slowly. "He's been dead for years. Was it his brother Joe? They look alike."

"That's it." Carter nodded. "We talked about Alex. That's why he's on my mind."

Robbie looked over his shoulder at the door, then took the candy from his pocket and placed it on the tray table.

"I brought these. Do you want one?"

"Yes," Carter answered. "Unwrap it for me. My fingers won't cooperate enough with my brain to do that."

Robbie removed the cellophane. Carter was able to pick up the candy with his right hand and navigate the route to his mouth.

"That will tell my brain to wake up," he said after several seconds passed. "But it doesn't seem as hot as normal. I know you don't want one. What about you, Clara?"

"Dad, this is Katelyn," Robbie said softly.

Carter gave them a pained look. "I know. Why did I say that? I apologize."

"It's okay," Katelyn said. "You made the same mistake the other day. It was very sweet and showed how much you still love her."

"Would you bring the photo of us at Ocean Isle Beach that's in the den?" Carter asked. "I'd like to have it in my room."

"Sure," Robbie said with a glance at Katelyn. "And we have some good news to share. Katelyn is pregnant. We've not said anything to David and Nan, so keep it a secret for now. It's still early."

Carter looked at Katelyn. She could see her father-in-law's eyes begin to water. He sniffled. Seeing his reaction removed any reservations Katelyn had about sharing the news with him.

"This candy is making me cry," he said.

Robbie chuckled. Katelyn reached over and squeezed Carter's hand.

"I hope those are happy tears," she said.

"They are," Carter replied with a crooked smile. "I just hope I'm around to watch the baby grow up."

They stood in silence for a few moments. The door opened, and an orderly entered with supper.

"Mr. Cobb, I've brought your rib eye cooked medium-rare," he said.

Robbie quickly scooped up the candies from the tray.

"Are those what I think they are?" the young man asked.

"They have a kick," Carter said. "Would you like one?"

"No, but my great-aunt loves them."

Robbie handed the young man three pieces. The orderly lifted the dome off the plate. It contained pot roast, runny mashed potatoes, and green peas of a hue Katelyn had never seen.

"Hope you enjoy," the young man said and left.

"Will you pray a blessing?" Carter asked Katelyn. "I love hearing a woman's voice talking to the Lord."

"I'll do it," Robbie jumped in. "Even though my voice is an octave too low."

Carter closed his eyes, and Robbie prayed. Katelyn watched and listened. Robbie didn't just thank God for the hospital food; he also thanked God for his father. It was a touching tribute. He ended with the familiar closing.

"And all God's people said, 'Amen!'"

"Amen!" Carter added enthusiastically.

Katelyn tagged on a much more sedate "Amen."

They stayed until Carter ate all that he wanted.

"Are you still taking the drops Zeke cooked up for you?" Robbie asked.

Carter concentrated for a moment. "Yeah, but I don't know where they are."

Robbie found them in the drawer and gave his father a dose.

"Keep taking these, and you'll be solving brainteasers in no time."

After supper, David and Andy worked on a science project. Andy had wanted to do something connected to predicting the weather, and they came up with a protocol that involved Andy taking his own barometric, temperature, rainfall, and other readings and checking satellite images. He recorded the data and made his own forecast. Then he compared his predictions to what actually happened. This had been going on for six weeks, and tonight he was pulling together all the information and calculating his accuracy. David gave guidance, not answers.

"You know what I'd like to do next?" Andy asked when they finished. "I want to figure out the best weather for catching redfish."

"You'd have to do a lot of fishing to get enough data."

"Yeah." Andy smiled. "I already thought about that."

At that moment, Nan stuck her head into the doorway of Andy's room. "I thought you were working on a science project. I walked past the door and heard someone mention fishing."

"That's next year's project," David replied. "There's nothing wrong with planning ahead."

Downstairs with Nan, David sat in a recliner and propped up his feet. Nan placed her book on a side table next to her chair.

"How did things go with Katelyn at the office?"

"Pretty good. She's going to update our office technology and work with Meredith and Candy to learn the new systems. It needs to be done and will be a big help. We went to lunch together at the new salad place on the east side, and she explained what she thinks we should do for the upgrade. Later, we met with Zeke Caldwell about trying to help him find a lawyer for the patent case I told you about. Katelyn contacted a firm in Miami that might be able to help, but I wasn't sure about them. I suggested we put out a fleece to determine if they're the right ones to help."

"How did that go over?" Nan asked, her eyes wide.

"She was skeptical. I don't think they did that at Morgan and Monroe. But she made a joke about it before she left work."

"What was the joke?"

"She said she was going to put out a fleece before deciding whether to come back to work tomorrow."

"Was she smiling when she said it?"

David thought for a moment. "Actually, I think she was."

The following morning David and the kids were finishing breakfast when Nan came into the kitchen dressed to go out.

"What do you have this morning?" David asked.

"I'd like to stop by the hospital to see your dad. Can you meet me there after you drop off the kids?"

"Yes."

"When do I get to see Pops?" Courtney asked.

"Saturday," David replied.

"Why not today? It's okay if I'm late to school. Emmaline is late all the time and doesn't get in trouble."

"Emmaline's mother is always late too," Nan answered, then turned to David. "I'll run by the drugstore and meet you in the lobby."

Nan left.

"How is Pops doing?" Andy asked. "Will he recognize me when we visit him?"

"Oh yeah, and he'll talk to you. But a few minutes later he might not remember what he said." An idea popped into David's mind. "Do you still have the lure you used to catch your biggest redfish?"

"Yes, but it's missing two legs. I think the second fish I caught ripped them off."

"He'll still enjoy seeing it. That's the sort of thing that may help bring his memory back."

Andy brightened up. "Okay."

"What should I take Pops?" Courtney asked.

"Draw him a picture."

"I could draw a picture of Andy fishing."

"It won't be right," Andy said. "You weren't there."

"That's a great idea," David said to her.

Nan was waiting for David in the hospital lobby.

"What made you think about visiting my dad this morning?" he asked.

"I was praying for him this morning and felt a nudge. You've been obeying your divine hunches recently, and I thought I'd join in."

Carter's breakfast tray was gone, and he was lying flat on the bed with his eyes closed.

"I don't want to wake him," David said softly.

His father's eyes opened. He blinked sleepily a couple of times and then yawned.

"Sorry, I didn't cover my mouth," he said to Nan. "I can raise my hand but not very fast."

"That's okay," she replied.

Carter demonstrated his ability to move his right hand.

"That's great," David said. "Are you able to feed yourself?"

"I did this morning," Carter said as he pressed the button to elevate his upper body to a more upright position. "I can't cut meat yet, but the occupational therapist is pleased with my progress."

There was a plastic fork on the tray table. Carter picked it up and brought it to his mouth. At the last second, he missed his mouth and poked his cheek.

"That's what I get for bragging and trying to show off," he said.

"Not bad," Nan said. "And the kids really want to see you. We thought we might bring them to visit in a few days."

"I'd love that. I'm getting bored in here."

While David watched, his father picked up a cup and positioned the straw so he could take a drink.

"What do Andy and Courtney think about having a little cousin?" Carter asked after he returned the cup to the tray.

"A cousin?" David asked. "Neither one of Nan's sisters is pregnant."

"Katelyn's baby."

Nan gave David a startled look. He stepped closer to the bed.

"Are you sure about that?" David asked gently. "Your short-term memory has been off quite a bit."

"It will be easy enough to find out if Katelyn is having a baby," Carter replied gruffly. "Give her a call."

"Okay, calm down," David said.

"And Robbie is going to be the new director at Camp Seacrest," his father continued. "They're moving to Wilmington and staying at my house for the time being. They found my stash of hot sauce in a kitchen cabinet. And I'm okay with you hiring Katelyn to work at Cobb and Cobb so long as we deduct her salary from your draw. I'll draft the agreement as soon as I get back to the office."

Nan was standing at the foot of the bed. "That was an impressive speech," she said.

"Except for the part about me paying Katelyn's salary," David said.

"I remembered you telling me about that and being upset." Carter smiled crookedly. "But I don't know if I talked to Katelyn about it or not. Anyway, I could get used to the idea, especially if she brings the new grandchild to the office to see me."

Katelyn finished her first training session with Meredith. Although initially less enthusiastic than Candy, the longtime assistant was slowly warming up to the changes at the office.

"Let's focus on the client information component," Katelyn said. "Having everything in a central location where you and Candy can access it and avoid retyping the same data over and over will be a big help."

"Unless it takes me as long to find the data as it does to type it," Meredith replied.

"That will change as you become familiar with how to navigate the program. We'll start on files that begin with A through C and move them over to the numerical system."

"Okay," Meredith sighed. "I know you're right. What we've been using at the firm is as outdated as the Dewey decimal system in a library."

Once she was alone in her office, Katelyn ate a third pack of crackers. She'd awakened at dawn, nauseous and tired. Over Robbie's objection that she should stay home and rest, she'd insisted on coming into work.

So far, she believed she'd made the right decision. David hadn't appeared, which gave her uninterrupted time to work with Candy and Meredith. Katelyn checked her email in-box. There was a huge difference from the volume she'd received every day at Morgan and Monroe. She'd received three emails the previous day, two from the NC State Bar about her admission application and another from one of the firm's clients who, on David's recommendation, wanted to consult with her about filing a lawsuit. As she faced her monitor, a new email popped up. It was from Regina Abernathy, Esq., in Miami.

Hi Katelyn,

It was great to connect with you yesterday about the drug patent infringement claim. I checked out your bio and saw that you worked at Morgan and Monroe in DC. I interviewed with their New York office for a summer clerkship when I was in law school but went with another firm. Small world! Anyway, I expedited review of your client's claim and got the okay to proceed. Attached is the contract we'd ask the client to sign. It includes wiring instructions for the $10,000 cost deposit, or he can send a cashier's check. Once the contract and deposit are received, we'll get started. Given your background, you would be perfect local counsel.

I look forward to working together!

Regina

As she reread the email, conflicting emotions swirled through Katelyn's mind. She opened the contract. It was a garden-variety contingency agreement. The initial payment was nonrefundable, but the firm assumed responsibility for all other expenses of litigation subject to reimbursement from any recovery. The attorney fee percentages were clearly set out in all capital letters. She debated whether to immediately forward it to David but decided not to.

Thirty minutes later, she heard David's voice in the hallway outside her door. Her brother-in-law stuck his head through the opening.

"Good morning," he said. "Just wanted to let you know Nan and I had a good visit with my dad, then I stopped in to see a client."

Katelyn braced herself to mention the email from Attorney Abernathy.

"One odd glitch with his short-term memory," David continued. "He's convinced you're pregnant. Maybe one of the hospital staff is pregnant, and he managed to confuse her with you."

Katelyn felt the blood rush out of her face. When she didn't respond, she saw the expression on David's face change.

"Are you pregnant?" he asked.

"Yes, maybe five or six weeks," Katelyn answered. "We weren't going to mention it to anyone until after my first ultrasound, but Robbie told your father on the spur of the moment. Carter was so happy that I was glad we did. Robbie reassured me that he wouldn't remember the news."

"Congratulations!" David said with a smile. "I can't wait to see Robbie as a father."

David turned to leave.

"There's one other thing," Katelyn said. "I heard this morning from Regina Abernathy in Miami. They've agreed to accept the Caldwell case."

David faced her. "Did she still insist on the nonrefundable deposit?"

"Yes, but you need to read the email," Katelyn added quickly. "There's nothing about it that gives off a bad vibe. Regina even interviewed with Morgan and Monroe for a summer job in the New York office. I think we'll be able to work together. I know what you said yesterday, and Zeke agreed with you about the fleece idea, but I believe we should let him make his decision in light of this new information."

Having run out of arguments, Katelyn waited for David to reply.

"Are you surprised?" he asked.

"Yeah. I was shocked."

"Send me the email, and I'll discuss it with Zeke."

After reading Regina Abernathy's email, David understood why Katelyn wanted to recommend that Zeke hire the Miami law firm. Where else would he find legal representation for such a sophisticated type of claim? He forwarded the message to Zeke with the request for a follow-up phone call.

Midmorning, Candy buzzed his office. Tyler Crandall was on the phone.

"Do you remember our conversation yesterday at the restaurant?" the financial planner asked in a hurried voice.

"Which part?"

"About God. I went over what you said with Lori last night, and she started crying."

David tensed. He didn't want to get blamed for upsetting Tyler's wife.

"And then I started crying too," Tyler continued. "We weren't heading for divorce, but I apologized for stuff I knew was wrong in our relationship and hadn't considered a big deal. It's a good thing the boys were in bed, because by the time we finished, both of us were a mess. When I walked out of the house this morning, it seemed like the sun was shining brighter."

"That's great."

"I'm super busy at work but had to give you a call. I'll be in touch soon about the new hire I mentioned."

"Maybe Nan, Lori, you, and I could get together soon."

"Yeah, we'd like that. Gotta go for now."

After the call ended, David paused to pray briefly for Tyler and Lori. Nothing he'd said during lunch related to marital problems, but apparently that didn't limit what God could do with the conversation. Buoyed by Tyler's call, he worked steadily all morning. He had a new client interview about estate planning scheduled for 12:30 p.m. Candy buzzed him.

"Dr. and Mrs. Brighton are here," she said.

Sitting in the reception area was a young couple. The slender-built man was wearing glasses and had dark hair bound in a ponytail. The woman had striking blond hair and was pregnant. David escorted them to his office.

"Here's the information form you emailed us," the woman said as she handed the pages to him.

Ray and Annalisa Brighton had two children ages four and two.

"You're a professor at UNC Wilmington?" David asked as he read the form. "What's your area of instruction?"

"General and upper-level biology with an emphasis on natural sciences."

"Do you work outside the home?" David asked Annalisa.

"Not now. Ray and I met when we were graduate students at NC State, but I've been at home for the past three years. I tried to go back to lab work after our son was born but stopped when I became pregnant with our daughter. Now we're waiting for girl number two."

"Every so often you take on a contract job," her husband said.

"Yeah, I have a master's degree in chemistry but never applied to a doctoral program. My consulting work is usually very routine. Crunching data. Nothing interesting. But it gives me a chance to use a bit of what I studied so hard to learn."

The couple had a last will and testament written before the children were born. The biggest question now was who would take care of the kids in case both parents were killed in a common disaster. The form listed Annalisa's parents.

"My folks live in Florida and are more suited to caring for children than Ray's parents, who like to travel all the time," Annalisa said.

"Do you know if they might end up caring for any other grandchildren?" David asked.

"We should ask about that," Ray said as he looked at his wife. "Do you think your sister and her husband included them in their wills?"

"Let me check." Annalisa took out her phone.

"How many children does your sister have?" David asked.

"Six, including a set of twins who are a year old," Annalisa said, her focus still on her phone.

"We're not in a birthing competition with them," Ray said wryly. "They have the trophy."

They sat in silence while Annalisa continued to text with her sister.

"Delana and Jeff designated someone in their church," she said, looking up. "We can put down my parents."

"If circumstances change in the future, it's easy to modify the will through something called a codicil," David said. "That way you don't have to rewrite the entire document."

An estate plan for a young couple without a lot of money wasn't complicated.

"I should have a draft for you to review next week. Would you like to set a return appointment?"

"We should avoid next week because Annalisa has a consulting project," Ray said. "I'm watching the kids two days in a row."

"May I ask what kind of project?" David said.

"I have a niche in the analysis of polymers, alloys, coatings, and composites used in industrial settings that's led to a few opportunities, mostly double-checking someone else's work."

"Have you ever done any pharmaceutical analysis?" David asked, sitting up straighter in his chair.

"No."

"Would you be able to?"

"Maybe, if I had access to the right kind of equipment." Annalisa turned to her husband. "Do they have a GC-MS or infrared spectroscopy machine in the lab at the university?"

"I have no idea," Ray answered.

"What's a GC-MS machine?" David asked.

"Gas chromatograph–mass spectrometry device. It can identify what's in a substance."

"I don't know anything about chemical protocols," David said. "But I have a client who may have a patent infringement claim. We need to compare what he developed with a drug manufactured by a big pharmaceutical company. The patent applications are similar."

"I could take a look at the data," Annalisa said. "But it would take HTCS, or high-throughput chemical screening, to identify how the chemical compounds interact with things like proteins. That is way beyond my expertise."

"Everything you just said is beyond my expertise," David replied. "Are you saying that HTCS analysis would determine active compounds that affect the body?"

"That would be the goal."

"How much would it cost to do what you can do?"

"It depends on the fee to access a lab."

"Would it be a lot of trouble to find out about the availability of the equipment and cost of running the tests?" he asked.

"You could contact Dr. Jackson at Duke," Ray said to his wife. "He'd be glad to point you in the right direction."

"I don't know," Annalisa said as she shook her head. "He's all about academic research. He'd have to jump through a bunch of bureaucratic hoops to allow me into a lab for something that has commercial implications. And you'll still need someone who could perform HTCS analysis."

"What's the guy's name in Raleigh who was interested in developing new medicines?" Ray asked. "You had a seminar class with him."

"Emerson Chappelle," Annalisa replied. "He'd certainly be one to ask about HTCS analysis and might be able to do it himself. He was an adjunct professor. Many of them work in the private sector or for the government and teach on the side."

"Would you be willing to look into it?" David asked.

"A phone call is easy," Annalisa replied. "But like I said, I've never done anything like that. I'm a technician."

"I think you should do it," Ray said. "I always tell people you're way smarter than I am."

"I have a few brain cells left that I've not donated to my children," Annalisa replied with a small smile. "It would be interesting to see what I can do, as long as expectations are low. I have a due date in the delivery room that takes priority over everything else."

"Thanks," David said. "And keep up with your time. I'm not asking you to do this pro bono."

SIXTEEN

KATELYN LEFT THE OFFICE EARLY TO TAKE AN AFTER-
noon nap on the sofa in the den with Charlie curled up at her feet.
The sound of her cell phone vibrating on the wooden top of the coffee
table jarred her awake. She grabbed her phone, almost dropping it
onto the floor. It was David.

"I know you're at home, but are you available for a conference
call with Zeke Caldwell?" he asked. "He's on hold. His nephew has
agreed to help finance the litigation."

Katelyn rubbed her eyes and sat up straighter. "Does he know
about the email from Regina Abernathy?"

"No, I wanted to give you the opportunity to tell him."

"I have a printed copy of the email in the kitchen. Give me a
second to get it."

Katelyn retrieved the email and sat at the kitchen table. Her
heart started beating faster.

"Got it."

There was a brief pause before David spoke again. "Zeke, you're
connected with me and Katelyn. She received an email this morning from Regina Abernathy, the attorney in Miami. I'll let her go
over it."

Trying to avoid any inflection in her voice that advocated for Regina's proposal, Katelyn read it.

"That answers that," Zeke said as soon as she finished. "We're not going with that law firm."

"Are you sure?" Katelyn asked. "If I turn her down, that will close the door for the future, and we don't have any other options on the table."

"I don't feel right sending that outfit in Florida $10,000 without any guarantee of results."

"No attorney can guarantee anything in a case like this," Katelyn said.

"Please tell Ms. Abernathy we're going to pass on her offer to represent me," Zeke said.

David was silent.

"Okay, I'll do that," Katelyn replied reluctantly.

"We may have another option, at least regarding the preliminary aspects to the claim," David said. "I had an interesting conversation earlier this afternoon with a professor from the university and his wife who's a chemist."

Katelyn sat at the kitchen table and listened as David told about his meeting with the Brightons. She rested her head in her right hand as he talked. She knew where this was heading.

"I don't know what Annalisa will charge to do the research," he said. "But at least we'll have an idea about the underlying facts of the case so we can better evaluate your chances in a lawsuit."

"Does that mean you're going to represent me?" Zeke asked in an excited voice.

"Nothing has changed about our lack of experience in this type of case," David replied. "We'd just be managing the initial research. Katelyn, what do you think?"

"If Ms. Brighton can give an opinion that supports potential infringement of the patent, that would be a huge step. If not, you'd know that as well. David, did she say what it would cost to do what you discussed with her?"

"No, but she's going to make some phone calls and get back to me."

Katelyn rolled her eyes. David's recommendation was based on the flimsy threads of a slightly damp fleece and a vague offer of help from a non-PhD chemist with no expertise in pharmaceutical research.

"Let's do it," Zeke said. "Amos and I agreed that we shouldn't let this go without a fight."

"I'll send the patent documents to Annalisa," David said.

The call ended. Katelyn was thirsty and poured a drink of purified water from a jug in the refrigerator. Her phone vibrated again. It was David.

"Thanks for going along with my idea," he said.

Katelyn took a sip of water. "In the end, the client is the boss, and Zeke clearly wants to give this a try. I've seen worse decisions made by big corporations when the monetary stakes were a lot higher."

An awkward silence followed. She heard David clear his throat.

"I wanted to invite you and Robbie over for supper so you can share your news with Nan."

Katelyn felt out of sorts, due to either the pregnancy, the situation with David and Zeke, the massive changes in every area of her life, or a combination of the three. She wanted to say no, but Robbie would be bursting to share their news once he found out his brother already knew.

"Except for the meal at Jordan's Restaurant, we've been coming to your house all the time," she said. "I don't want to wear Nan out."

"It's not a problem. I'll buy steaks and cook them on the grill. How about fillets medium-rare and topped with sautéed mushrooms? That's what I fixed when you visited last fall."

David was an excellent grill master.

"Okay. Do you want Robbie and me to bring something?"

"Anything that goes with steak."

Remaining in the kitchen, Katelyn turned on her laptop and composed a short email to Regina Abernathy telling her the client was not ready to sign a contract at this time. She couldn't resist adding a sentence about keeping the door open for future communication. She sighed as she pressed the send button and returned to the couch. That's where Robbie found her an hour later.

"David sent me a text that we're eating steaks at their house tonight," he said when he entered the room. "Do you feel up to it?"

"Red meat sounds good to Charlie and me," she said, nudging the dog with her toe.

Normally, Charlie would have jumped down immediately to greet Robbie, who leaned over and scratched the dog's head.

"Has there been a shift in your loyalty?" Robbie asked his pet.

"Not when he has an accident in the house that needs to be cleaned up. Then he's totally yours."

Katelyn sat up so Robbie could join her on the couch. When he did, Charlie jumped into Robbie's lap.

"That's more like it," Robbie said. "Tell me about your day."

"I'd rather hear about yours."

Courtney let out a squeal when Katelyn announced at the end of the meal that she was going to have a baby.

"Is it a boy or a girl?" she asked excitedly.

"The baby is about the size of a pea," Katelyn answered. "We won't know if it's a boy or a girl for a while."

"I hope it's a girl," Courtney replied. "That way the girls will outnumber the boys."

The kids left the table with David and Robbie, who'd promised to play a game with them. Nan gave Katelyn a hug.

"You should have seen David trying to convince his dad that he was wrong about your pregnancy," Nan said. "Even with Carter lying in a bed in the hospital, they were like bulls butting heads."

"It was sweet when he heard the news."

"Loads of changes for you and Robbie."

"Yes, in every area."

"How are things at the office?"

Katelyn shrugged. "I'm adjusting."

There was a loud uproar from the den.

"Robbie, I can't believe you did that to me!" David exclaimed. "That is so crooked!"

"Sounds like the two younger bulls are butting heads," Nan said. "Let's either watch and be entertained or intervene for the sake of family peace."

After Robbie and Katelyn left and the kids were in bed, David and Nan relaxed in her study.

"That was a fun evening," David said.

"Do you say that because you won more games than Robbie and forced him to admit that he cheated?"

"He did cheat!"

"Only because he didn't know the rules, which was because you put them in your back pocket."

"In case I needed to refer to them at a crucial juncture."

"You guys are hopeless."

David propped his feet up. "The meal was great," he said. "I even liked the asparagus dish that Katelyn brought. I've never eaten two servings of asparagus in my life."

"You like garlic, not asparagus. And I can smell your breath across the room."

David left to brush his teeth. He returned and leaned over to kiss Nan.

"How's that?" he asked.

"Not very romantic, but most of the odor is gone."

David resumed his seat in his recliner.

"Katelyn seemed subdued when I asked her about the office," Nan said.

David told her about the turn of events in Zeke's case.

"It's understandable that my methodology is confusing to her. I mean, it can be confusing to me. But the timing of the meeting with the professor and his wife had God's fingerprints all over it. The Lord brought her along at the perfect time."

"Did you say that to Katelyn?"

"No. I don't want her to think I have a 'god complex' and believe I'm always right."

Nan chuckled.

"I don't act that way around here," David protested.

"I'm not criticizing you," Nan replied. "I'm glad you recognize what could be a problem. Maybe let Katelyn know that."

"Could I hire you to do it for me?"

———————

David found Candy with her eyes glued to her computer monitor the next morning. She didn't glance in his direction as he approached. Expecting to see a solitaire game on the screen, he greeted her.

"Good morning," he said.

"Good morning," she replied, leaning back in her chair. "I did it."

"Won your game?"

"No, sir," she replied curtly. "I correctly merged the data from over three hundred real estate files so that when you request a title search, we can provide background information to the examiner and pay for only an update, not a full search. Of course, there are more than a thousand files still to go."

Years before, Carter had handled a lot of residential and commercial real estate closings. It happened less frequently now because David didn't like to do them. He didn't quell Candy's enthusiasm by pointing out that the work might not be needed because his father wouldn't be coming back.

"Katelyn says it's an area where a practice like ours can generate steady income if it's systematized," Candy continued. "She wanted me to prepare a list of real estate agents who might be referral sources."

"Who's going to do the legal work?"

Candy gave him a puzzled look. "Usually, lawyers do legal work," she said.

David continued toward his office.

"Will you look over the Realtor list and get back to me?" Candy called after him.

David didn't reply. He waved in greeting at Meredith but didn't stop at her desk. The first item on his to-do list was to forward the competing patent applications and approvals issued by the US Patent and Trademark Office to Annalisa Brighton along with the letter from the attorney for Brigham-Neal. There was a knock on his door. Katelyn entered.

"What would you think about me reviving your father's real

estate practice?" she asked. "It could be a steady sideline that would supplement revenue from litigation."

"If you want to give it a go, I'd support you one hundred percent. I'll look over the Realtor list that Candy put together. Also, a few calls to bank officers we know at the local lenders and credit unions would restart the flow of business. Would you prefer to focus more on residential or commercial business?"

"Commercial. That would tie in with what you're doing."

"Okay. I'd prefer to keep that business in-house instead of referring it out."

———————

Emerson narrowed his search for beach houses in the Wilmington area. His focus on buying a vacation property partially filled the vacuum normally occupied by another high-stakes wager. But not totally. He'd spent the past thirty minutes trying to decide whether to bet $50,000 on a trifecta ticket for an upcoming horse race at Santa Anita in California or wager the same amount with Lance for three off-market prizefights in Trinidad and Tobago. The racing bet required him to pick the top three finishers and would pay out at 55–1. The fight offered even higher odds if he selected three underdogs and they all won. Emerson was about to pull the trigger on the Santa Anita wager when his phone vibrated and a Wilmington number appeared on the screen. Suspecting it had to do with one of the houses he'd looked at, he answered.

"Dr. Chappelle?"

"Who's calling?"

"You probably don't remember me, but this is Annalisa Brighton. My last name used to be Mauldin. I was in a master's-level seminar class you taught several years ago at NC State. Dr. Larry Jackson was my adviser in the chemistry department."

Emerson knew Larry Jackson, a lab rat and one of the most boring people on the planet.

"Sorry, but I can't place you," he answered.

"I'm married and living in Wilmington where my husband is a biology professor at the local UNC campus. We're raising a family, and I occasionally do side work, mostly fact-checking data and formulas related to industrial alloys. A different opportunity came up that has to do with analysis of a possible pharmaceutical product, and I remembered that you had expertise in that area."

"That's true, but I normally only work on my own projects."

"I understand, but I wondered if you could recommend where I might be able to gain access to a GC-MS or infrared spectroscopy machine."

Emerson used the equipment at either Duke or Chapel Hill but often buried his private projects in the middle of research sanctioned by the university as part of his teaching duties. As he listened to Annalisa talk, the sound of her voice jogged his memory.

"Are you a tall blond from someplace in Virginia?" he asked.

"Yes, Richmond."

Emerson remembered taking the class outside for some of their sessions during a spring semester. He cleared his throat.

"Do you want to associate me on the project?" he asked.

"If you're interested. After the initial testing it would be necessary to conduct—"

"HTCS protocol," Emerson cut in.

"Yes, and that's outside my sphere."

"What's your budget?"

"That's what I'm trying to determine to advise the client."

"Would you be able to come to Raleigh?"

"Yes."

Emerson quoted a fee less than half of what he might normally charge for a consultation.

"That's very reasonable," Annalisa responded. "I'm up against a deadline. What's your availability?"

"I have a class that ends in a few weeks, so it would be best to work it in while that's going on, and I'll be in the lab anyway."

"Great. I really appreciate you doing this."

"No problem. Send some dates and times for us to get together. I look forward to seeing you."

The call ended. Instead of returning to his debate over the best wager to place, Emerson went onto social media to locate a recent photo of Annalisa Mauldin Brighton.

Katelyn and Robbie liked the young doctor at the ob-gyn clinic. Confirmation of the pregnancy by a medical professional made everything seem official. They stopped by the pharmacy to pick up prenatal vitamins, then Robbie drove Katelyn to the law firm.

"Now that the pregnancy is doctor-certified, I guess I'll need to drive you to work every day," Robbie said.

"Yes, the suspension in your truck will be especially nice the further along I get."

"I'll start carrying a pillow."

"See you at five o'clock," Katelyn said as she opened the door to get out.

"Deal. And what do you think we should have for supper?"

"I'll see how I feel when you pick me up, okay?"

An hour later, she was working on one of Carter's litigation files when her cell phone vibrated. It was Franklin Deming from Morgan and Monroe. Katelyn hesitated before answering the call.

"Hey, Franklin," she said. "How's it going?"

"You know what happens in this office when someone leaves," the paralegal responded. "I've done all I can to protect your reputation, but some of the rumors have been crazy. The worst is that—"

"Spare me the drama," Katelyn said before he could continue. "But I have big news that's true. I'm pregnant."

"Congratulations."

"And Robbie has accepted a job in Wilmington where he grew up. We're ending the lease prior to renewal on our townhome in Arlington. It's all worked out for the best."

She left out the news about starting work at Cobb and Cobb. That information in the wrong hands would create its own negative spin cycle.

"Huge changes," Franklin said. "I wanted to let you know that Bryan McFarland is going to be manager of the new litigation group in Chicago. I've not worked with him at all. Do you think I should jump on his train or not?"

"They're putting Bryan solely in charge?" Katelyn asked in shock.

"Yeah, that's the word. From what I've been able to find out, he's a decent guy."

"He's primarily an appellate lawyer, not a litigator."

"Which in my mind means he'll need people with litigation experience like me. Do you know why Suzanne didn't ever ask him to work with her?"

"I have no idea. But Lynwood brought him into some projects. Maybe that's why he's getting an opportunity in the Chicago office."

"That's what I've heard, but I wanted your nonbiased thoughts."

"Have you talked to him?"

"That's my next step, though I don't want to burn through my capital lobbying for a position I'll regret taking later."

Law firm politics could give Machiavelli a headache. Katelyn thought for a moment.

"Don't tell anybody about your interest in moving to Chicago, and see if Bryan or Kane Vanlandingham mentions a position to you. For that to happen, the people in charge would have already decided to offer it to you. Sitting tight, you won't risk rejection, which can be a negative for future opportunities."

"That's brilliant," Franklin said. "And takes the pressure off me to try to make it happen."

"Talk it over with your fiancée to make sure she agrees."

"Okay." Franklin paused. "Hey, I miss you. You were intense, but only because you wanted to be the best and expected everyone you worked with to be the same way. Most people like that are jerks."

"Thanks. And you were always up to the challenge."

Still processing the news from Morgan and Monroe, Katelyn had trouble concentrating. Setting aside the litigation file, she turned on her laptop and began the process of setting up the vacating of their townhome in Arlington. She and Robbie had decided not to attempt a do-it-yourself move. That route might be okay for newlyweds moving from college dorms into a first apartment, but at this point they didn't want to do anything except move their clothes and a few personal items like Robbie's fishing rods. Everything else would be boxed and labeled by a moving company.

Katelyn was surprised at the number of companies offering full-service moving options. She selected one that described itself as a "concierge relocation company" and made arrangements for a representative to enter the townhome and give an estimate.

Checking her email account at Cobb and Cobb, she found a new communication from Regina Abernathy.

Hi Katelyn,

I checked with my managing partner and received approval to accept a $7,500 deposit for your case, but only if confirmed and paid this week.

Let's make great things happen!

Regina

The tone of the message struck Katelyn as odd, more like something a used-car salesman would say than a lawyer in a successful law firm. She retraced the steps of her initial research and confirmed the Miami firm's involvement in federal litigation in pharmaceutical cases. Regina wasn't listed as counsel on any of the lawsuits. This wasn't surprising because multiple lawyers might work on a claim, but only the senior partners or chief associates would be identified by the court. And settlements would be confidential. Katelyn continued digging and identified several lawyers who'd formerly worked for Craft and Bosworth. She decided to call one who now worked for a small firm in Houston. A receptionist transferred the call.

"Chris Brunswick," he said.

Katelyn identified herself. "I told the receptionist I was looking for a reference about associating Craft and Bosworth in a drug patent case," she said.

"Did they request a nonrefundable deposit?" he asked.

Katelyn was surprised by the first question. "Yes."

"That means the likelihood they'll actively pursue the case is very small. When I was there, the firm only asked for up-front money in dubious claims. There will be an impressive legal analysis explaining why they're not going to file suit, but it's mostly boiler-plate. They won't deliver anything substantive."

Katelyn was shocked. "That's fraudulent."

"Your words, not mine. But it was enough to make me uncomfortable and explains why I took your call. When Craft and Bosworth commits to a case, they do a good job, and Jeff Bosworth is a great trial lawyer. Otherwise, most people should avoid them. Hope this helps."

"Yes, thanks."

The call ended, and Katelyn shut down her laptop. Sometimes, it's not bad to be wrong.

When David returned from lunch, he had a voice mail from Annalisa Brighton indicating she had an update for him about his request for her help.

"You already talked to your former professor?" he asked when she told him what she'd done.

"Just a preliminary conversation, but he's willing to provide a consultation if I meet him in Raleigh. I also reviewed the patent applications and the approvals issued by the government. I can see why your client thinks there might have been infringement. There is a lot of similarity in the chemical structures, and the differences may not be important. That's what we need to determine."

"How much time have you spent so far?" David asked.

"Don't worry about it. I've only put in a few hours when the kids were down for naps, and it was more enjoyable than sneaking in a TV show or playing a game on my phone. I'm a chemistry nerd who loves anything that has to do with different permutations of carbon atoms."

The more he talked with Annalisa, the more comfortable David felt about having asked her for help. "Did you set a date and time to get together with your professor?"

"He asked for options within the next week or so. That's good for me. Once he and I talk, I'll have a better idea what he's going to charge. He quoted a lower rate than I expected for the initial consultation, but sometimes that can be a smoke screen because the expert inflates the hours to meet a targeted financial goal."

"I guess lawyers aren't the only ones accused of doing that."

"I've seen what my previous clients paid other people and can spot it. One other thing. I talked this over with Ray, and there may be a place for him as a biologist since your client claims he developed his drug from natural sources."

"Good idea."

The call ended. David sent Zeke a text message letting him know they needed to talk as soon as possible. He then went into Katelyn's office and told her about the conversation with Annalisa Brighton.

"Would you be willing to draft the contract with the Brightons to cover their services?"

"Sure. What about the professor in Raleigh? What's his name?"

David checked his notes. "Dr. Chappelle. I didn't write down a first name. But nothing is going to happen until Annalisa meets with him in the next week or so."

"How much information is she going to give him? If they talk, there should be a confidentiality agreement and sufficient consideration paid that it prevents him from using anything she tells him for personal benefit or on behalf of someone else."

"Isn't that being a bit paranoid?"

"Call it what you like, but these cases boil down to a battle of experts, and we want to remove him from the game if the drug company ever contacts him for an opinion. A jury is often more open to a local expert than one flown in from out of town."

"Let's wait until after her initial meeting. I'll make sure Annalisa knows to be careful about what she shares with him. If we move to the next step, we'll pay him something because he'll actually be working."

"Sounds like I should also draft an agreement for Zeke to hire Cobb and Cobb to represent him."

"All we're going to do is get the claim ready for another lawyer to take the case."

Katelyn paused. "If we were fishing and Zeke's case was the fly, I'd say you already have the hook in your mouth."

SEVENTEEN

KATELYN HAD WITNESSED BATTLES OVER EXPERTS that were the key to success or failure. Properly dealing with expert witnesses wasn't a matter to leave to a handshake and verbal reassurance. Professional hacks and academic guns for hire were plentiful, but in sophisticated litigation, there was often only a handful of people whose expertise and credibility could carry the day and convince a jury.

It didn't take long to identify Dr. Chappelle as Emerson J. Chappelle, a PhD chemist who obtained his doctorate from the University of Florida. Chappelle stayed over ten years at his alma mater, then bounced around several schools, each stint being shorter than the last. Finally, he ended up as an adjunct professor who taught seminar classes at both North Carolina State and Duke. Recently divorced, he had no children, and his current residential address was in an apartment complex. He'd never published an article in a peer-reviewed journal or listed any experience testifying as an expert witness. Nothing about his academic or professional history made Katelyn think Dr. Chappelle should be seriously considered as a chemist to be paid for work on a case that would end up in federal court. She prepared a memo and sent it to David.

She then turned her attention to preparing a document for Ray and Annalisa Brighton to sign. Locating a form via the new research suite she'd asked David to authorize, she made a few modifications and forwarded it to David. Within less than a minute, he responded.

This is great!

Katelyn knocked on his office door.

"Come in!" he said.

David had papers spread all over his desk.

"Did you actually read the form I prepared for the Brightons to sign?" she asked.

"I glanced over it and assumed it was fine."

"Please have my back, and I'll do the same for you. It's not wise for either one of us to assume the other won't miss something important. Corrections and suggestions aren't the same as criticism."

"Okay," David replied with a chagrined look.

"More importantly, what about Dr. Emerson Chappelle? Judging from the minimal amount of information available, there's no way he qualifies as the kind of chemist worth hiring as an expert."

"But he's the contact Annalisa knows. At least it's a start, even if it's only a consultation."

"That may not lead anywhere. Zeke should know that."

"I'll make sure he does."

"Okay. I'll prepare a document for Dr. Chappelle to sign as well."

"And I promise to read it carefully."

Katelyn returned to her office and spent over an hour drafting the agreement for Dr. Chappelle to sign. Once he provided any type of consulting services, the chemist wouldn't be available to Brigham-Neal because of an explicit conflict of interest. Not that he was the type of expert to be feared. Cross-examining someone with his checkered professional background would be fun.

Robbie picked up Katelyn at five o'clock on the dot. She was too tired to even think about dinner plans, and as soon as they arrived home, she stretched out on the couch and fell asleep within minutes.

When Robbie heard her stir an hour later, he quietly entered the room. "Don't get up," he said to her. "I'm fixing supper."

"What do you have in mind?"

"There's a taco kit in the pantry, and we still have ground beef from the other night when you made your awesome homemade spaghetti with onions and fresh garlic. We know there's plenty of hot sauce on hand."

"Check the date on the taco kit."

A minute later Robbie returned with the box in his hand. "We have twenty-eight days," he said.

"That sounds great." Katelyn yawned. "Don't let me sleep too long though. I want to be able to fall asleep tonight."

Katelyn jerked awake when Robbie touched her toes. Her sudden movement caused Charlie, who'd assumed his customary place at her feet, to yelp.

"How long have I been unconscious?" Katelyn asked, stretching her arms.

"Forty-five minutes. I could hear you snoring while I fixed dinner."

"You're lying."

Katelyn shuffled into the kitchen. The table was set with china and the silverware owned by Robbie's mother. The flame of a single white candle in a silver base flickered in the dim light.

"This is a little bit fancy for tacos, isn't it?" she asked.

"It would be if we were having tacos."

Robbie pointed to a large pot of boiling water on the stovetop. "I decided I'd rather let a couple of lobsters go for a hot swim."

He opened the refrigerator and took out two large objects wrapped in white paper.

"Where did those come from?" Katelyn asked.

"Maine. I bought them yesterday at a fish market and hid them in the meat keeper. There's also corn on the cob that I'm grilling in the husks. I thought we might eat the lobsters tomorrow night, but this seemed right."

Katelyn hugged him and gave him a kiss. "You're right. As much as I love tacos from a box, this is better."

The lobster meat was firm, sweet, and glistened with melted butter. The corn was nicely charred and seasoned with spices. During the meal, Katelyn enjoyed listening to Robbie talk about his day. He was clearly getting his legs beneath him as the one in charge, a position he'd never held at any of his previous jobs.

"At first I thought I'd only enjoy the duties directly related to camp operations with the kids, but the enthusiasm carries over. One of the donors I met with today agreed to double his previous contribution, and another committed to a sizable amount each year for five years. I'm almost looking forward to the next board meeting."

"When is that?"

"Next month. Normally, they meet quarterly, but with the recent crisis, that changed."

Robbie took a final bite of lobster. Katelyn was lagging behind.

"Are you full?" he asked.

"I don't want to be, but I think my stomach is telling me not to load up on too much rich food."

She placed the rest of her lobster on Robbie's plate. "Yes," she said when he started to protest.

Robbie took a big bite and sighed. "Anything else happen today?" he asked.

"Franklin Deming called wanting advice about whether to try to request a transfer to Chicago. It looks like Bryan McFarland will be given primary authority over the new group there."

"I don't remember him."

"He played football at either Brown or Columbia and then went to law school at Yale. He's more of an appeals specialist than a trial lawyer."

"How did that make you feel?"

"Glad that I left. Anyway, I suggested to Franklin that he put out a fleece and see if the firm contacts him rather than actively seeking the transfer."

"Is that the way you described it to him?"

"No, but it was the same principle. He liked the idea." Katelyn paused. "It certainly worked for David in the Caldwell case. I uncovered some troubling information earlier today about the law firm in Miami that I wanted to associate. I'm glad they're not going to get involved."

Katelyn told him what she'd found out. Robbie wiped his mouth with a napkin.

"Did you tell David?"

"No."

"I understand," Robbie said. "I don't like to admit when he's right either."

The following morning, David arrived at the office early for a staff meeting with Katelyn, Meredith, and Candy. The first item on the agenda was the new office software.

"I doubted at first," Meredith said with a glance at Katelyn. "But after a couple of days and comparing notes with Candy, I can see how this is going to ramp up our efficiency for both financial matters and case management."

Candy's comments were more disorganized than Meredith's, but what she lacked in substance, she made up for with enthusiasm.

"Okay," David said and held up his hand. "I think that's enough for now. Katelyn, will you be able to help with some of the questions they have?"

"Yes. Meredith, I'll get with you around ten thirty; Candy, let's meet first thing this afternoon."

The two women left David and Katelyn alone.

"You were right," David said as soon as the door closed. "This is going to make a bigger difference than I would have thought."

"And you were right," Katelyn replied.

"What do you mean? It was your suggestion."

David listened as Katelyn told him what she'd discovered about Craft and Bosworth.

David nodded. "That's what my gut was telling me."

"My gut has been talking to me too," Katelyn said. "But it's mostly about morning sickness."

"I should have thought about that when I set up this meeting."

"I'm okay. Your brother fed me lobster last night. Apparently, that's what I need to eat on a regular basis, because I felt great this morning."

"Nan loves lobster," David said with a grin. "Once she finds out it's at the top of your preferred menu, it will give her an excuse to buy some and invite you over to share."

Katelyn smiled. "I won't turn down that invitation."

***

Early Monday morning, discussing the patent case was the first order of business. "Have you talked to Zeke Caldwell?" Katelyn asked.

"Late Friday afternoon. I explained the situation with Dr. Chappelle, and he still wants to go forward. I went over the agreement for Dr. Chappelle to sign and I have a few questions. I'll get it back to you today. Also, the Brightons are coming in to sign their wills tomorrow, and I'd like to have their agreement in final form by then."

The phone rang, and David picked it up.

"Dr. Scott Spies would like to speak to you."

"I'll take it."

"Do you want me to leave?" Katelyn asked.

"No, please stay."

David placed the phone in the cradle and pressed the speakerphone button.

"I just left your father," Dr. Spies said. "And I'm very pleased with his improvement. It looks like he'll be discharged by the weekend. Where are you in the process of finding a rehab center? The social worker said you'd not talked to her."

"I'm here with my sister-in-law now. She and my brother are temporarily living in my father's house. We'd like to bring my dad home and hire a caregiver, if that's okay."

"A few days ago, I would have told you that's not feasible, but your father is making remarkable progress," the doctor said. "Even his ambulation has improved dramatically. He still requires a walker, but he's much more stable. And the occupational therapist says he's doing well with his activities of daily living, even though the left hand remains mainly supportive only. I recommend he receive ongoing OT after discharge."

"We'll get right to work on locating a caregiver."

The call ended.

"Do you have anyone in mind?" Katelyn asked.

"No, but the need to find one just jumped to the top of my to-do list."

The next morning, Katelyn and Robbie ate breakfast in the sunroom. He finished his cup of coffee.

"I'll see you at two o'clock to interview caregivers for my dad," he said. "Are you sure we shouldn't do it at the house since this is where they'll be working?"

"David suggested we narrow the field and then do a second interview here for those who make the cut. That will give us two chances to check them out before introducing them to your dad."

"I'm interested in meeting the woman who helped take care of Lindsey Dempsey's father. That's a solid referral from a family we know well."

"And there's the former hospital orderly suggested by Dr. Spies."

"Either one of them would be fine. What else is on your calendar today?" Robbie asked.

"Continuing to organize your father's litigation files. And the local chemist who's offered to help with Zeke Caldwell's case is coming in with her husband to sign their wills. After that, we're going to talk about Zeke's claim."

When Katelyn returned to the office from a late lunch, Ray and Annalisa Brighton were meeting with David.

"Good," Candy said as soon as she saw Katelyn. "The Brightons came early. You can be one of the witnesses so I don't have to leave the phone unattended. I hate it when a call goes to voice mail. Everyone is in David's office."

"Should I just barge in?"

"Oh yeah. I do it all the time."

Katelyn knocked on the door and entered. David introduced her. Seeing Annalisa Brighton in her advanced stage of pregnancy previewed Katelyn's own status in seven and a half months. Witnessing the wills was an age-old function of the practice of law but something she'd never done before. As soon as they finished, Meredith left to make copies.

"Let's shift gears to Zeke Caldwell's case," David said. "Katelyn worked for a large law firm in Washington, DC, and she has expertise in patent infringement cases."

"But not for pharmaceuticals."

"My background is in industrial applications, so this is new to me too," Annalisa said. "But the more I've been digging into this particular situation, the more it appears to have merit."

"Katelyn prepared agreements for you and your husband to sign. Let us know if you have any questions."

David handed the paperwork across the desk to Katelyn, who gave it to the Brightons. No one spoke for several minutes.

"This looks fine to me," Ray said. "I don't have any questions. As a biologist, I'd like to meet Mr. Caldwell. I reviewed the patent and found it fascinating. His reliance on natural ingredients intrigued me."

"That can be arranged," David replied. "He loves to talk to people about his work."

"No questions from me about what you prepared," Annalisa said.

"I also prepared an agreement for Dr. Chappelle," Katelyn said. "Does he know you're meeting with him about a potential lawsuit? That wasn't clear to me."

"No, all I mentioned was that I wanted to obtain analysis of a medicinal product."

"Good," Katelyn responded. "His credentials aren't the best, and I'd rather be cautious in bringing him on board."

"His qualifications as a chemist are way better than mine."

"I understand, but we have to approach him as a potential expert witness. Legally, it can be a very nuanced situation because of the rules of discovery that apply down the road. I don't want to create evidence that is adverse to Mr. Caldwell's claim that has to be revealed to the drug company's lawyers. When Dr. Chappelle signs his agreement, we can eliminate that possibility."

Annalisa furrowed her brow. "I'm not sure I'm up to this. Would I need to explain the legal document you prepared to him? Also, should I give him a copy of the letter sent to Mr. Caldwell by Brigham-Neal's lawyer?"

"When is your meeting with him?" Katelyn asked.

"This Thursday, unless my daughter decides to come early."

Katelyn made a quick decision. "How do you think Dr. Chappelle would respond if I came with you?"

"I don't know, but I'd love it. That way I could focus on the science while you take care of the legal part. I'd want to make sure it was okay for you to be there beforehand. How would I bring it up?"

"Tell him that we hired you, and I asked to be present to answer any questions he may have. Oh, and don't send him a copy of the letter Mr. Caldwell received from Brigham-Neal. That might taint his opinion. We'll provide him with the two patent applications."

"What about a sample of Zeke's remedy?" David asked.

"Maybe," Katelyn replied.

"Hopefully, he'll be so interested that he can't wait to get to work on it," Annalisa added.

"Anything else?" David asked.

"I'll get in touch with him and let you know what he says about you being there when I meet with him," Annalisa said.

The Brightons left.

"I like her," Katelyn said to David.

"And I'm glad you brought up attending the meeting with Dr. Chappelle. I was thinking the same thing."

The door opened and Robbie entered. "Is this what a high-powered meeting at Cobb and Cobb looks like?" he asked.

"Pretty much," David answered, checking his watch. "Are there any candidates for the caregiver job in the reception area?"

"There's a guy who's at least six feet four inches tall and weighs around 275 pounds."

"That's the former orderly Dr. Spies mentioned," David said. "We'll start with him."

Two hours later, they'd finished the interviews. David, Robbie, and Katelyn were alone in the conference room.

"What do you think?" David asked. "I think at least three of them are well qualified, but because the person is going to share the house with you and Katelyn, your opinion is more important than mine."

"I really liked the woman who worked for the Dempsey family," Robbie said. "And it's hard not to consider the former orderly who has experience working with stroke and brain hemorrhage patients."

"Plus, he likes to fish," Katelyn added.

"Is that important?" David asked.

"No, but someone needed to say it. Both of you mentioned it several times when talking to him."

"I'd hire the orderly," David said. "But not because he likes to fish. He's strong enough to pick Dad up if he falls."

"True," Robbie said.

"Are we ready to make a recommendation to Dad and set up an interview?" David asked.

Katelyn and Robbie looked at each other. "No," they both said.

EIGHTEEN

KATELYN AND ANNALISA BRIGHTON MET AT THE LAW office on Thursday morning for the two-hour drive to Raleigh. To Katelyn's relief, Dr. Chappelle had quickly agreed for both women to be present. A manila folder contained the two patent applications and the agreement hiring Dr. Chappelle as a consultant. A bottle of Zeke's remedy was in her purse.

Annalisa shifted back and forth as she tried to settle into the passenger seat of Katelyn's car. She repositioned the seat belt across her swollen abdomen.

"Are you going to be okay?" Katelyn asked.

"As a relative term, the answer is yes. As an empirical fact, the answer is no."

Katelyn laughed and started the car's engine.

"The last thirty days of hauling a baby around inside your belly never seems to end," Annalisa said. "With the first one, I couldn't wait for her to be born and end the misery. Then, when she turned out to be very fussy, I wanted to tuck her back inside me so we could both get some rest."

"And this is number three?"

"Yes, which should tell you something about how amazing I

believe it is to be a mom. My oldest is now four and full of questions. My two-year-old son constantly makes me laugh and amazes me with the amount of food he can eat. Each stage is like starting a new chapter of a book."

"I'm about seven weeks pregnant," Katelyn confided.

"Congratulations!" Annalisa said.

"And a week and a half into morning sickness. Today wasn't that bad, but I may want to stop for a snack on the way to Raleigh."

"Take as many breaks as you like, for any or no reason."

Instead of two hours, the trip, with stops, took two hours and forty-five minutes. Katelyn had factored in extra time in case they ran into a traffic issue. None popped up. But the conversation made the time fly by. Katelyn hadn't anticipated how much she would appreciate the wealth of pregnancy-related information that poured effortlessly from Annalisa.

"There was a lawyer on the other side in a big case in DC who would have helped me if we'd not moved to Wilmington," Katelyn said. "But talking to you has been so much better."

"Glad to do it. Every pregnant woman needs a friend to go along with what she reads online that scares her to death. My sister filled the gap for me. She has six kids, including a set of one-year-old twins."

"What!" Katelyn exclaimed. "How does she survive?"

"You'd think she'd be super organized, but she's not. That's part of her secret. She doesn't get stressed out when things don't go according to plan. Her house is a mess. Not dirty, just piles of clean clothes and toys scattered all over the place. Once a week, she takes the children who aren't in school for a long ride in their van and out to lunch while a cleaning crew rolls in, picks up, and cleans. Within thirty minutes of her return the tide has brought back the chaos. That would drive me crazy, but she can handle it."

Katelyn tried to picture such a scenario but couldn't. The GPS signaled a final turn into the parking lot for a collection of small office buildings built to look like houses with a federal style of architecture.

"We barely talked about what we're going to say to Dr. Chappelle," Katelyn said.

"If he's still the same as before, he'll want to be in charge. You handle the law; I'll cover the science."

The chemist's office was on the second floor of the two-story building.

"No elevator," Annalisa said, looking around.

They trudged up the stairs and down a short hallway, stopping at a door with a name plate reading "Dr. Emerson Chappelle, FAACC."

"What does FAACC mean?" Katelyn asked. "I didn't see that when I researched him online."

"Fellow of the American Academy of Clinical Chemistry. It accepts chemists who work in research to improve patient health."

———

Emerson had taken extra care with his appearance. There had been plenty of times over the past few years that he'd not shaved for three or four days and worn the same shirt more times than he should have. Today wasn't one of those days. Wearing a collared shirt and neatly creased khakis, he'd straightened up the office he'd rented with a second, smaller royalty check from the pharmaceutical company. The business space gave him an excuse to leave the loneliness of his apartment and feel like he had purpose and direction. There were three chairs arranged close together. There was a knock on the door.

"Ms. Mauldin?" he asked when he faced the two women.

"Annalisa Brighton," the woman said, extending her hand. "And this is Katelyn Martin-Cobb, the attorney I mentioned whose client has an interest in this matter. Thanks so much for agreeing to meet with us."

Emerson turned to the attorney, an attractive young woman with short, dark hair. The lawyer's presence wasn't a problem. In his experience, most attorneys' knowledge of chemistry was as rudimentary as what could be learned from a mail-order kit used by a middle school student.

"You're not from the South, are you?" he asked Katelyn when they were seated.

"No, Vermont," she answered with a slight smile.

"Where did you go to school?"

"Tufts University undergrad and Cornell Law School."

"I have a friend and colleague who teaches chemistry at Cornell, but of course you wouldn't have taken any chemistry classes in law school."

Emerson turned to his former student and saw that her ankles were severely swollen.

"What can I do for you?" he asked briskly. "I don't want to take up too much of your time."

Annalisa handed him a manila folder. "Here are patent approvals for two drugs. The chemical formulas are strikingly similar, but as I explained to Ms. Martin-Cobb and her law partner, that doesn't necessarily mean they're the same substance when it comes to interaction with the human body. That's why I'd like to run GC-MS testing, followed by an HTCS protocol."

Emerson didn't open the folder. "It would take several weeks to set something up, and given your current situation, you might not be available."

"Correct," the former student replied. "But if possible, I'd like to assist, and I'm interested in learning what I can, but it would be great if you could provide a cost estimate whether I'm involved or not."

"Your fees would be paid by the law firm," the attorney added. "With a view toward retaining you as an expert witness should the claim proceed to litigation. Would you be open to that possibility?"

Testifying in a lawsuit could be lucrative.

"It depends on what my research shows."

"Of course. I wanted to make that possibility clear at the outset of our conversation. You would need to sign an agreement that's also included in the folder."

"Sure."

"The client isn't very sophisticated," the attorney continued. "He doesn't have any formal medical or chemical education. He sells his products at flea markets and craft fairs, mostly in the Wilmington area."

Fear suddenly shot through Emerson, making him feel sick to his stomach. "What's the purpose of the medicine?" he managed.

"Treatment of severe nausea with minimal side effects," Annalisa replied.

"That's needed," he answered. "But this type of testing and analysis isn't something I have the bandwidth to take on at this time."

He returned the unopened folder to Annalisa, who had a surprised expression on her face.

"But you mentioned on the phone—" she started.

"And I apologize that you wasted a trip."

"Is there someone else you could recommend?" the lawyer asked. "Perhaps your colleague at Cornell?"

"No, Dr. Spellman wouldn't be interested in something like this, and I'm not sure who would be."

Emerson stood.

"Are you sure that—" Annalisa began.

"Absolutely. Have a good day."

Emerson went to the door and held it open until they left. He then went to the window and watched the two women cross the parking lot and get into a small car. He began to pace back and forth across the room. Why did he panic? A former grad student with no PhD or expertise in the medical drug field wasn't a serious threat. And the attorney was clearly shopping for a hired gun.

He regretted how abruptly he'd terminated the meeting. He could have pretended to read the information in the folder, told the women why the herbalist didn't have a claim, and sent them on their way. Emerson slammed his fist against his desk as he passed by. He should have come up with a way to end any threat. But unlike with many high-risk bets he'd placed, he'd lost his nerve.

———

It was close to five o'clock. David had been out of the office all afternoon in a contentious meeting with a business client's board of directors. Unlike with the Jordan family, there'd not been a breakthrough in the fractured relationships, and round two was scheduled for the following week. David was curious to find out what Katelyn and Annalisa learned in Raleigh, but he'd promised Nan that he wouldn't stay late at the office. He sent a text message to Katelyn asking when she would return. She responded immediately.

Five minutes. Don't leave.

David swiveled in his chair and answered several emails. His door was open, and he heard the chime that sounded when someone entered the reception area. Katelyn and Annalisa Brighton were involved in an animated conversation.

"Conference room or your office?" Katelyn asked.

"Uh, my office," David answered.

Katelyn brushed past him.

"How are you feeling?" David asked Annalisa. "I know this has been a long day."

"Running on my last ounce of adrenaline. Ray may expect me to help with the kids this evening, but it's not happening."

Annalisa and Katelyn sat in chairs across from him. The two women exchanged a glance.

"You go first," Annalisa said to Katelyn.

Katelyn looked directly at David. "Dr. Emerson Chappelle is the chemist who filed the patent that infringed Zeke Caldwell's formula."

David sat upright in his chair. "He admitted that?"

"No. But while Annalisa was talking to him about helping us, I glanced over at a bookcase where there were a bunch of pill bottles lined up in a row. Toward the end of the line was one of the amber dropper bottles that Zeke uses for his remedies."

"Those can come from other places."

"Or from Zeke. When Annalisa gave him a folder that contained the competing patents and a consulting agreement, she told him a little bit about the origin of Zeke's patent, without mentioning his name. Chappelle didn't even bother to look at the information. He abruptly told us he couldn't help and escorted us out the door. We weren't in his office for more than a few minutes."

"You could see the color drain out of his face," Annalisa added. "I didn't know what was going on until Katelyn and I were out of the building. But it makes perfect sense. Why else would he be so cooperative on the phone, set up a quick meeting, and then back away in a split second?"

David was still absorbing the news. "Dr. Chappelle's name isn't on the patent," he said. "What's the name of the company?"

"First Flight Research and Development," Katelyn said. "Before leaving Raleigh, I checked the corporate filings with the Secretary of State's office, and the principal owners of the company are Emerson J. Chappelle and a man who lives in Texas named Lance Tompkins. I couldn't find out anything about Tompkins, but I assume he's an investor."

David shook his head. "All this would have come out eventually, but in a deposition, not sitting in the opposing party's office. I wish you could have inspected the bottle on the shelf."

"Even if he denies it, we know what happened," Katelyn said.

"Before he realized what was going on, Dr. Chappelle mentioned a chemist at Cornell in New York," Annalisa said. "His name is Dr. Spellman. I checked his background. He's worked for years in the medical field as a researcher."

"But if he has a close relationship with Chappelle, he probably isn't a good option," Katelyn added. "Who knows? He may have collaborated on this project."

David turned to Annalisa. "What can you do at this point? You still don't have access to the kind of equipment you need to do preliminary testing."

"Try to locate it and find out what it costs. What we did today was so much more exciting than conducting an experiment to determine if a metallurgical process will withstand temperatures below freezing without being compromised. It was like being on a TV show."

Annalisa checked her phone. "I've got to go," she said, getting up from the chair.

"Thanks so much," Katelyn said. "We'll be in touch."

David and Katelyn remained in his office.

"I wish we could be sure the bottle you saw in Chappelle's office was the same as the ones used by Zeke," David repeated.

"If there had been a way to get Dr. Chappelle out of the room for a minute, I could have gotten a closer look, but I'm almost positive. It wasn't like he had it locked up. It was sitting in plain view. Annalisa was right. He changed in a flash. And if that was a bottle of Zeke's remedy in Chappelle's office, it wasn't a smoking gun; it was a smoking cannon. Here's the bottom line: Anything Brigham-Neal throws at us down the road trying to deny there's been a theft of Zeke's patent is smoke, not substance. This is a legitimate case worth pursuing. We have a huge responsibility to Zeke."

David was silent for a moment before asking, "Do you think we should handle it ourselves?"

"With the right help." Katelyn pressed her hands together tightly for a moment. "I've had this in the back of my mind since the first time we met with Zeke but kept pushing it down. An opportunity like this doesn't come along very often and gets me more excited than Annalisa was about our little bit of detective work today. I've fought a lot of big battles in which I could see merit in the other side's position, even if I didn't agree with it. This is different. It's why I became a lawyer—to help a simple, honest person who's been seriously wronged. The thought of going to war for a just cause fires me up."

Listening to Katelyn was like standing in front of a gushing fire hydrant. She continued, "We'll have to come up with a plan to finance the litigation beyond the money Zeke and his relatives can provide. And whoever represents the drug company will have the same kind of resources as Morgan and Monroe. First step is to meet with Zeke and tell him what happened. Who knows, he may have met Dr. Chappelle without knowing who he is."

Katelyn was clearly ready to take charge of the case.

"Okay, I'll set up a meeting with Zeke."

———

Nan had her back to David when he entered the kitchen.

"Sorry I'm late," he said.

"And I know you have a legitimate excuse," she said. "But first, go upstairs and congratulate Courtney. Her teacher sent home a note that they're going to have a school art exhibition and several of Courtney's drawings were selected. Ms. Nevins also asked her to submit more drawings. It sounds like Courtney is going to be the star of the show."

"When's the exhibition?"

"In two weeks. It's on a Wednesday afternoon at four o'clock."

David took out his phone and entered the date on his calendar. Upstairs, the door to Courtney's room was open. She was sitting at her desk with colored pencils scattered around.

"What are you drawing?" he asked.

"A zoo," she replied. "And the animals are going to be in their natural habitat."

She was working on a female lion that was very well proportioned. David was impressed with both her artistic skill and her vocabulary.

"That's good," he said.

"Thanks," she said somewhat listlessly.

"What's wrong?"

"It's Myra. She's jealous and is talking about me behind my back to the other girls. She says I've been cheating and not really doing my drawings. And that's not all."

David sat on the edge of Courtney's bed. "What else?"

After listening without interrupting for several minutes, David wished that Nan was in the room. Boys might wrestle in the dirt to solve a conflict. Female relationships became more complex at a much earlier age.

"Let's talk to your mom about it after supper. She usually has great ideas."

"Okay."

After supper, David and Nan met with Courtney in Nan's little office. By the time they finished, David's respect for Nan's ability to help their precocious child navigate little-girl conflict rose to a new level. Equipped with a strategy that they used role-play to practice, with Nan pretending to be Myra, Courtney scampered upstairs to brush her teeth.

"You're amazing," David said to Nan when she left.

"I'm passionate about healthy relationships."

"I saw a bit of Katelyn's passion for the practice of law today," David said. He told her about Katelyn's trip to Raleigh with Annalisa Brighton and their meeting with Emerson Chappelle.

"What a crooked thing for him to do!" Nan replied indignantly.

"Yeah, and Katelyn was fired up and ready for us to take on Zeke's case. That's a huge swing from a few days ago when she wanted to refer the case to a law firm in Miami. Now she sees it as a fight for justice."

"I agree," Nan said. "A lot of Katelyn's sense of self-worth is tied to being a lawyer. That's not bad, but it's different from you."

"What's my self-worth tied to?"

Nan grinned. "Making me happy."

Katelyn was preparing supper. Usually, she cooked in the kitchen, but this evening she turned on Carter's gas grill so she could prepare salmon seasoned with salt, pepper, olive oil, minced dill, and lemon juice on cedar planks soaked in cider.

"I've been looking all over the house for you," Robbie said when he found her on the stone patio in the backyard. He leaned over to inspect the food on the grill.

"I'm hungry enough to eat the planks," he said.

"Help yourself. I soaked them for an hour in cider. And there's a sautéed vegetable mix in a pan on the stove."

"I know. The onions are just right."

They ate at a table in the corner of the sunroom. After supper, Robbie cleaned the dishes and took Charlie out for an evening walk.

"I'll be gone for a while," he said. "I need to stretch my legs after sitting all day at work. While I'm gone, there's an entry in my journal I marked that you might like to read."

"Are you sure?"

"Yes. It was from a few weeks ago. Before you first looked at it."

Katelyn propped her feet up in the sunroom to relax. The last rays of the sun reached across the grass. The owls began to talk to each other. After sitting for a few minutes, she went into the bedroom to retrieve Robbie's journal. He'd inserted a scrap of paper to mark the place he wanted her to read. It was a day or two after the campfire scene.

Lord, thank you for hearing and answering my prayer. What I've been feeling and experiencing is so real, I can't deny it. Even if I wanted to. Which I don't. Sitting on the park bench today during my lunch hour was amazing. And then during the drive home thinking about my love. Will you talk to her? Not sure that's how it works. Anyway, I place her in your hands. If you only answer one prayer, let this be the one. You love her even more than I do.

Beneath the words was a sketch of Robbie sitting on a park bench. He'd drawn it from the back. Several birds were perched on the bench and his shoulders. There was a lot of detail. Katelyn decided it was the most beautiful picture she'd ever seen, better than anything in an art gallery. She read the prayer again and checked the date of the entry. It was during the first weeks of the aircraft navigation trial. That was during cold weather in DC, but Robbie drew the picture as if it were spring. She carefully closed the journal and returned it to its place.

The sunlight faded, and she sat in the gathering darkness. The entry was so personal; the love Robbie had for her was undeniable. She wanted to respond. And she wanted it to be sincere. She thought for a few moments and decided simple was best.

"God, I'm listening."

It was the first prayer mixed with a tiny seed of faith that she'd uttered as an adult. The words hung in the air. She waited. No answer came. Thirty minutes later, Robbie returned. He turned on an overhead light before entering the sunroom.

"Why were you sitting in the dark?" he asked.

Katelyn blinked her eyes at the sudden brightness. "Just being quiet," she said. "I read your journal. I loved the sketch of you on the park bench. I'd like to get it framed so I can enjoy it every day."

Robbie leaned over and kissed her. "I'm so glad I'm married to you," he said.

"I believe you," Katelyn said. "And I told God that I'm ready to listen."

"Did anything happen?"

"No."

"It will."

The following afternoon, David and Katelyn met with Zeke to tell him about the meeting with Dr. Emerson Chappelle.

"This is better than what we were hoping for!" Zeke exclaimed.

"Not exactly," David replied. "Eventually, we would have known that Dr. Chappelle is the one who applied for the patent because he is one of the owners of the company that filed the request."

"But he had a bottle of the remedy in his office. That proves he copied my formula."

"Which we would have to prove when he denies it," Katelyn replied. "It's important for us to know that Chappelle stole the formula, but it's still going to come down to scientific evidence."

"What's next?" Zeke asked.

"Katelyn, you tell him," David said.

"Zeke, we'd like to represent you. I'd still like to find another firm that handles these cases on a regular basis to come alongside us, but I want to be involved to make sure you get justice."

Zeke's smile spoke more than words. "Hallelujah!" he said.

"I've never had that reaction from a client before," Katelyn replied. "I've prepared a contract for you to look over."

She slid the document across the table.

"This is the contract hiring Cobb and Cobb to represent you. David and I are charging a third of any recovery, not the higher amount that was in the proposed agreement from the law firm in Miami. If we determine that we don't have a case, any of the money remaining that you've paid toward expenses will be returned to you."

David had been hired hundreds and hundreds of times, but he couldn't remember a situation in which watching a client sign an agreement for legal services caused a lump in his throat. Zeke signed.

"I'll make a copy of the contract for you," Katelyn said, getting up to leave the room.

"This is very kind of you," Zeke said to David. "I know part of the reason you're willing to help is because of your dad and me. He's been a good friend for over forty-five years."

"That's true, but without Katelyn this wouldn't be possible. She was a top lawyer in a big firm in Washington, DC. I don't have the experience for this kind of high-dollar litigation. She came back from Raleigh fired up about your claim. Also, with your permission I'd like to keep Nan in the loop about the case. She'll pray."

"Absolutely," Zeke replied. "Could you get the police to search Dr. Chappelle's office?"

"No, it's not a criminal case. And never will be. At this point it's safe to assume that Dr. Chappelle knows or suspects we're representing you. If he went to the trouble to apply for the patent, he researched you as well."

Katelyn returned and pulled up a photo on the screen of her laptop and turned it so Zeke could see it. "This is Emerson Chappelle. Do you think you've ever met him?"

It was a head shot of the scientist from the Duke University website.

"A lot of folks stop by my booth," Zeke said doubtfully.

"The picture has to be several years old," Katelyn said. "He's lost more hair since the photo was taken."

"Maybe, but I can't be sure," Zeke said. "It's hard for me to remember a face unless I have a name to hook to it. He looks kind of familiar, but I have a bunch of customers, and they often buy for family and friends. My stuff gets around. I had a woman from Colorado stop by a few weeks ago. She'd been given a bottle of my headache remedy by a niece in Florida, who got it when she was here on vacation with her husband's family. The woman thanked me and bought every bottle I had with me."

"We still need to find someone to conduct the chemical analysis required to justify filing a lawsuit," David said. "Katelyn and Annalisa Brighton are going to work together locating someone."

"Annalisa is about to have a baby, which may slow us down, but she really wants to help," Katelyn added.

"I'll be glad to give her as much free stuff as she wants," Zeke said. "You too. And I'm going to look for another job to earn extra money. Ralph Hester told me this morning that he's going to cut back my hours. I'm already part-time, so I really need to find something else that won't interfere with making and selling my remedies."

"What kind of job would you like?" David asked as a simple solution occurred to him.

NINETEEN

THE NEXT DAY, KATELYN WAITED IN THE HALL OUT-
side Carter Cobb's room while Robbie helped his father get dressed
for his discharge from the hospital. David hadn't arrived yet.

"We're going to miss Mr. Cobb," said a gray-haired nurse with
an ID badge around her neck. "He's quite a storyteller."

Katelyn knew this side of her father-in-law but wasn't aware
how much the ability had returned.

"He never mentions any names, but I guessed who he was talking about in one of them that involved my aunt Susie," the woman
continued. "He didn't realize my connection to her when he was
talking about the lawsuit over a bunch of watermelons at the farmer's
market, but I picked right up on it. There were things I learned that
I didn't know."

"Did he represent your aunt?"

"Yeah."

"It would be better if she doesn't find out he said anything
about it."

"That's not a problem," the woman replied. "She's been dead for
ten years. It did my soul good to have a laugh with Mr. Cobb about it."

Katelyn glanced past the nurse and saw David approaching.

Fully dressed, Carter was sitting in one of the chairs near his bed. It had been several days since Katelyn had visited. He looked stronger and more alert.

"Good morning, Clara," Carter said when he saw her.

"I'm Katelyn," she said in a soft voice.

"I know," her father-in-law said with a smile. "Robbie told me how I got you mixed up with his mother a few times. I don't know how it sounded to you, but I'm sure I meant it as a compliment."

"That's the way I took it."

Carter yawned. "Who would have thought that putting on my clothes would wear me out?"

The nurse who'd talked to Katelyn returned. When Carter made the transfer from the regular chair to a wheelchair, both Robbie and David had to help him stand and then steady him. The simple process reinforced the need for an in-home caregiver. When Dr. Spies told the family that Carter required only practical assistance, not skilled nursing care, Zeke Caldwell's willingness to take the job made everyone happy, most of all Carter. Zeke had been granted a thirty-day leave of absence from his job at the pharmacy. Multiple people greeted Carter as the nurse wheeled him down the hallway.

"Dad, you either need to run for mayor or apply to be director of personnel at the hospital," David said as they waited for the elevator.

"Politics never tempted me," Carter replied. "And trying to run the law office was enough administrative responsibility."

"Katelyn's done a good job of taking over those duties," David said.

"Just trying to help things get better organized," she said.

The elevator doors opened, and they rode to the main level. At the exit, the nurse patted Carter on the cheek.

"If you ever get bored and need someone to talk to, call me," she said. "I put a card with my phone number on it in your bag of personal belongings."

Outside on the sidewalk, Carter looked up at the sky. The sun was climbing over the tops of the nearby trees. It was a pleasant morning on the coast.

"This is nice," he said. "You don't know how much you miss something until you lose the chance to enjoy it."

"Dad, do you think that nurse wants to date you?" Robbie asked. "I noticed that she wasn't wearing a wedding ring."

"Molly Bridges? No, she's just friendly. All her people are like that. I represented one of her aunts years ago. I can't remember her name, but she was the same way."

"Aunt Susie," Katelyn said.

Carter squinted and looked up at her. "I think that's right. How did you know?"

"It's hard to forget a good case about watermelons. Molly mentioned it to me when I was in the hall waiting for you to get dressed."

Carter smiled. "Yeah, after that was over, I didn't want to see another watermelon for a year. Oh, Robbie, I hope you've bought Katelyn some fresh strawberries."

"He's taking good care of me," Katelyn replied.

Robbie and David positioned their father in the minivan.

"We'll meet you at the house," Robbie said as he closed the passenger door.

Katelyn and Robbie walked across the parking lot to his truck.

"At this point, your dad's problems seem more physical than mental," Katelyn said.

"It looks that way this morning, but when David was here yesterday, Dad was very confused."

Zeke was waiting for them at Carter's house. As soon as they all pulled into the driveway, Zeke came outside with a walker. After seeing Carter's difficulty ambulating at the hospital, Katelyn doubted whether the walker would provide enough support. They'd purchased a wheelchair as well.

"I think we may need the wheelchair," she said.

"Let's try this first," Zeke replied.

Carter looked out the side door of the minivan at his former high school teammate. "Ezekiel!" Carter called out.

"Please, no," Zeke replied with a smile. "The only time I heard that name was when I was in trouble. Are you ready to give this walker a workout?"

Zeke set the walker in front of the car door. Positioning his hands under Carter's armpits, he maneuvered him with surprising ease. Carter grabbed the handles of the walker, and with Zeke standing behind him to provide extra support, he was able to shuffle his feet down the walkway to the house and inside.

"Impressive," Robbie said to David.

"I'm expecting you to do that for me when I'm old," David replied.

"No way." Robbie shook his head. "That will be Andy's job."

"Quit it," Katelyn said. "That's depressing."

Inside, they watched Zeke efficiently assist his old friend into bed.

"How did you learn to do that?" Robbie asked.

"Practice. I helped take care of two of my great-uncles. Both of them were at least as heavy as Carter."

"Thanks, Zeke," Carter said in a weak voice with a smile on his face as he rested his head on the pillow. Moments later, he was asleep.

Zeke positioned himself in a chair in the corner of the room. He reached into his pocket and took out an amber vial.

"I mixed this up to replace what you've been giving him," he said. "I'll start dosing him when he wakes up. I think it will speed up the healing."

———

At the office on Monday morning, David had several projects demanding his attention. Shortly before noon there was a knock on his door.

"May I interrupt?" Katelyn asked.

"Come in," David said, leaning back in his chair. "I'm finishing up the first draft of a commercial leasing agreement."

"I wanted to run something by you about the Caldwell case. What do you think about me contacting Suzanne Nixon to discuss the claim with her?"

"What would you ask her? Morgan and Monroe isn't a plaintiff's firm."

"Find out if she might be able to help us find a chemist. The firm has access to a database of top experts in virtually every field imaginable. She might be willing to point us in the right direction."

"Are you sure she'll take your call?"

"I hope so."

"Let me know how it goes."

"I will." Katelyn hesitated. "Would you pray for me about it?"

David didn't try to hide his surprise. It was one thing for Katelyn to observe him praying for others. Asking him to pray for her was on a completely different level.

"I'd be glad to," he said.

Thirty minutes later, David had a lightness in his step as he left the office for a lunch meeting. On his way to the restaurant, he received a call from the office. It was Candy.

"I'm sorry to bother you," the receptionist said in a soft voice. "But when I went to the kitchen a minute ago, I passed Katelyn's office, and it sounded like she was crying. The door was cracked open, and I heard her sniffling and catching her breath like she was really upset."

"Where is she now?"

"Still here."

David's heart sank. "I may know what it's about. She'll probably call Robbie to talk it over."

"Are she and Robbie having problems?"

"No, no. If she's still there when I return from lunch, I'll see if she wants to talk to me."

"I hate to see anyone upset."

David thought about the prayer he'd offered up for the call. He'd been optimistic and upbeat about how Suzanne Nixon would respond. Now he wondered if his prayer had been more about his own hope and desire than anything else. During the drive back to the office after lunch, he was apprehensive about facing Katelyn. Her car was gone.

"Where's Katelyn?" he asked Candy.

"Took off not long after I called you. I asked if she was going to lunch and returning. All she said was 'No.'"

———

When Katelyn entered the house, she heard Carter yelling from the bedroom. She rushed in to see what was wrong. Zeke was standing beside the bed with a Styrofoam cup in his hand.

"Carter, you had a bad dream," Zeke said in a soothing voice. "Take a sip of water."

Zeke turned toward Katelyn. "He's been asleep all morning but woke up agitated."

"Am I bleeding?" Carter said, lifting his right hand to his face.

"No, buddy," Zeke said.

"What's this on my head?"

"That's where you had surgery. It's still healing."

Carter took a drink of water. His breathing sounded choppy. He mumbled something unintelligible.

"You came home from the hospital just a couple of days ago," Zeke continued. "I'm helping take care of you for a while."

Carter turned toward Katelyn. "Where's Robbie? And David?" he asked frantically.

"Both of them are at work."

"Are they okay?"

"Yes."

Carter closed his eyes for a few moments. He reopened them and sighed. "That dream seemed so real."

"It wasn't," Zeke replied. "Are you hungry? I'd be glad to fix you something."

"Yeah. I'd like some scrambled eggs. With hot sauce."

"Sounds good to me too," Zeke said.

Katelyn wasn't sure whether to stay with Carter or go to the kitchen with Zeke.

"You stay here," Zeke said before she asked. "I know my way around his kitchen."

Katelyn pulled a small chair close to the bed. Her father-in-law was lying with his eyes closed. She hated that he'd been so upset. She could hear Zeke whistling in the kitchen. Carter opened his eyes.

"Zeke's a champion whistler," he said.

"He's a man of many talents," Katelyn replied with a smile.

By the time Zeke returned with the food on a tray, Carter seemed almost normal. Katelyn's phone vibrated. It was a text from Nan asking if they could bring the kids over to see their Pops late in the afternoon.

"Would you like to see Andy and Courtney in a few hours?" she asked.

"Yes," Carter immediately answered, then added, "unless you think seeing me like this will upset them."

"Let the young'uns come," Zeke said. "They love you just like you do them. There's no pretense with them."

Katelyn went into the kitchen and fixed a sandwich for herself. Later, when she looked in on Carter, she saw that Zeke had set up a checkerboard on the bed. Zeke made a move and helped Carter steady his hand to respond.

"This is going to be better than most of our games," Zeke said to Katelyn. "I may have a chance of at least getting to a stalemate."

"Not if you have to crown me one more time," Carter replied.

Katelyn spent the rest of the afternoon reading and relaxing. Before everyone arrived, Zeke helped Carter shower, shave, and get dressed. He looked close to normal. Zeke positioned him in a recliner in the den.

"I'm going to run on," Zeke said, patting Carter on the shoulder. "I'll see you tomorrow."

Katelyn walked with Zeke to the door. "Thanks," she said.

"It makes me feel good in here," Zeke said and placed his hand on his heart. "Jesus said he came to serve, not to be served. That's easy to obey when it's someone like Carter."

David rang the doorbell.

"Why don't we go right in?" Andy asked. "Pops never makes me ring the doorbell."

"Because Uncle Robbie and Aunt Kate are living here. We need to respect their privacy."

Robbie opened the door.

"Where's Pops?" Andy asked. "Is he in the bed?"

"No, he's waiting for you in the den," Robbie said.

David watched the kids' interaction with their grandfather. Both Andy and Courtney were tentative around him at first, but after Pops praised the artwork Courtney brought him and admired the photos of the redfish Andy caught, the children acted more naturally. David stayed quiet and avoided eye contact with Katelyn.

"Would anyone like coffee?" she asked.

"Not me," Carter replied.

"I want some, please," Nan said.

Nan joined Katelyn in the kitchen. David followed, leaving Robbie with Carter and the children.

"I didn't get to talk to you after lunch," David said to Katelyn, clearing his throat.

"Yes, I decided to leave and check on things here. Right when I walked through the door, Carter was coming out of a bad dream."

David and Nan listened to what had happened.

"Zeke handles him really well," Katelyn said. "I'm so glad we have help from someone who's known your father for so many years."

"Yes," Nan said.

"And after my phone call with Suzanne Nixon, I didn't feel like working."

David winced. "It was that bad?" he asked.

"Oh no," Katelyn replied. "It was incredibly positive."

"What?" David asked.

Katelyn turned to Nan. "David said a prayer before I made the call. I started out by asking Suzanne for advice in locating expert witnesses in the case we're handling for Zeke. She was very willing to help and promised to get back to me soon. But instead of ending the call, she kept talking and opened up in ways she's never done before. It was exactly one of the things David mentioned in his prayer. He asked God to open Suzanne's heart, which at the time made no sense but came back to me when she started talking."

"I don't remember saying that," David said.

"It's okay, honey," Nan said, patting him on the arm. "God's memory is better than yours."

"Suzanne comes across as one of the most self-confident people on earth," Katelyn said. "But she shared some of the struggles she's faced in her personal life. I knew she'd gone through two divorces but wasn't aware that she's estranged from her daughter. She mentioned some other situations that are so private I don't feel comfortable repeating them. That's when we both started crying."

"It's amazing how she opened up to you," Nan agreed. "She respects you."

"And I'm relieved," David said.

Later, lying in bed, David didn't fall asleep as quickly as he usually did. Instead, he followed up some of the events of the day with silent prayers, ending up with a request for blessing upon the three precious people sleeping in the house.

In the morning, David dropped the kids off at school. Pulling into the parking area for the office, he received a text from Katelyn.

Not feeling well. In later.

As soon as David entered the reception area, Candy asked him a question: "How's Katelyn?"

"Sick but great."

"What?"

"She has morning sickness and is going to stay home for a while. But the reason she was crying yesterday wasn't because something bad happened."

"So they were happy tears?" Candy asked.

David thought about the reason for Katelyn's emotions. "Not really."

"What other kinds are there?"

"The ones you cry when you share another person's pain or feel their hurt."

TWENTY

EMERSON CROSSED THE CAPE FEAR MEMORIAL
Bridge into Wilmington on the way to his new vacation home. After
meeting with Annalisa Brighton and the dark-haired lawyer, he'd
considered shutting down his promising work on the new headache
remedy developed by Zeke Caldwell. But knowing that his work
would be subject to future scrutiny gave him a new strategy. All he
needed to do was camouflage the substance he created. By boiling
Salicornia and skimming off the residue, he'd obtained a substance
that, when combined with the active ingredients in Relacan, created both an analgesic and an antinausea compound. But he'd not
deconstructed the Salicornia component via HTCS analysis into its
various compounds. When he did, he planned to include at least ten
inert compounds.

Regarding a potential lawsuit over the Relacan patent, Emerson
didn't doubt the power of Brigham-Neal to squash any claim. His
concern was with Lance, who'd called earlier in the week. When
Lance's name appeared on his phone, Emerson immediately took
the call. They'd received another six-figure license fee payment, and
he thought Lance was calling to celebrate.

"My lawyer tells me Brigham-Neal had to file a response to the people claiming you stole their patent," Lance said. "If that doesn't scare them away, he says a lawsuit is likely."

"I'm focused on the positive, like the money sent to us the other day," Emerson replied with a nervous laugh. "And Relacan works. It's gaining traction in the market. The only way forward is up, with higher profits for everyone."

"I've seen a lot of high rollers take a big tumble. I want to protect my investment. If this thing goes south, you're going to reimburse me every penny for any charge-backs in attorney fees."

"If there's a problem, I wouldn't have the funds—"

"I'm telling you what I expect you to do. I'll have my lawyer draw up the paperwork and send it to you."

When Lance used that tone of voice, Emerson knew he would eventually surrender. There was no use delaying the inevitable.

"Okay, but I don't think this is necessary," he said, trying to regain his composure.

"I'll be the judge of that. Also, Nick tells me you've been quiet on your account. You're not being unfaithful to us, are you?"

"No, I placed a few small bets in Vegas, but I bought a beach house, and I'm getting that set up."

"Where is it?"

"Kure Beach near Wilmington."

"What's the address?"

Emerson had placed ownership of the house in a new corporation to mask his ownership. He glumly repeated the address.

"Maybe I can visit you later this summer. I've never been to the North Carolina beaches."

"They're nothing spectacular."

Several days had passed without Emerson receiving anything from Lance's lawyer, and he began to hope nothing would come.

But then an email popped up with an indemnification agreement attached. It was more stringent than anything Emerson had ever signed for a bank loan. He'd signed it electronically and returned it.

Once over the bridge, Emerson didn't head directly to the beach. He followed the GPS directions to the law office of Cobb and Cobb. His heart beat a little faster as he approached the address. The sign in front of the building listed the names "Carter R. Cobb and David A. Cobb, Attorneys at Law," without mention of a female lawyer. Emerson drove down the street, turned around, and passed by again. When he did, a man in his thirties with light brown hair was leaving the building. Emerson instinctively sped up, which caused the man to glance in his direction. At the end of the street, Emerson stopped again and picked up his cell phone.

———

It took several extra crackers to calm Katelyn's stomach so that she could get out of bed, shower, and dress. After brewing a late-morning cup of tea, she checked on Carter. Her father-in-law was napping, and Zeke was sitting in a chair tapping on a tablet.

"What are you working on?" Katelyn asked.

"Another patent," Zeke replied. "Now that I've done one, I think the second one will be easier. I call my remedy 'Migraine Melody' because it sends a migraine headache packing and calms the stomach all at the same time."

"Did you get the lab in California to figure out what's in it?"

"No. But it has many of the same ingredients as my antinausea drops, plus something from the pickle grass plant that grows in the marsh. I did some research, and pickle grass has known medicinal qualities. It's used in Asia and other places but not in the way that

I'm using it. I plugged the chemicals I found online into my formula since I don't have to tell the exact amounts in the patent application."

"Zeke, I'm not sure that's going to work."

"I know." Zeke shrugged. "But I'm going to try. And once we collect money from that crooked chemist and Brigham-Neal, I'll go back and fill in the gaps."

"Don't spend any of that money yet."

"That's why I'm doing it this way."

When Katelyn arrived at the office, Candy greeted her.

"Feeling better?" the receptionist asked.

"So far, my morning sickness has stayed true to its name."

"I'm glad you're here. I had some questions about the new software that Meredith and I couldn't figure out."

Katelyn spent the next fifteen minutes helping Candy.

"You're getting close to the limit of what I can help you with," Katelyn said. "It's impressive how fast you've picked this up. I'll talk to David about locating someone who can provide professional IT advice."

David's door was closed, and Katelyn went into her office. She listened to a voice mail from Suzanne providing the names, credentials, and contact information for three experts who might be able to help with the Caldwell case. Her former boss was never one to procrastinate. Katelyn sent her a short email thanking her. There was also a voice mail from Annalisa Brighton. Katelyn called the chemist.

"Have you had any luck finding someone to run the tests?" Annalisa asked.

"I spoke with my former boss at the law firm I worked for in DC. She gave me a few names."

Katelyn rattled off the information for Annalisa.

"Never heard of them, but that speaks more about me than

them. Those are the kind of academic credentials you'd like to have for an expert in this field."

"I'll start working through the list in alphabetical order."

"I did some detective work on my own," Annalisa said, then paused. "I hope I didn't mess things up."

"What do you mean?"

"I called Dr. Spellman at Cornell."

Katelyn almost dropped the phone. "But he's friends with Emerson Chappelle!"

"I didn't mention Dr. Chappelle," Annalisa replied quickly. "I just told him who I was and what I was interested in doing. I also explained that I was looking for someone in our part of the country who might be able to help, and that we had a limited budget. Dr. Spellman was really nice."

"Did he have any suggestions?"

"The first name was Dr. Chappelle, and he offered to contact him for me."

"That figures."

"I thanked him and asked if he had another recommendation. He mentioned a professor in the chemistry department at North Carolina State and a medical researcher affiliated with Emory in Atlanta."

"Did you cross paths with the professor in Raleigh when you were in school at Duke?"

"No, but there are people I know who can tell me more about her. She received her doctorate in chemical biology from Cornell. That's how Dr. Spellman knows her. The medical researcher at Emory went to Yale and cowrote some papers with Dr. Spellman."

Katelyn paused for a moment. "Do you think Dr. Spellman will call Emerson Chappelle and tell him you contacted him?"

"Maybe. I started to ask him not to, but that would have sounded odd. Anyway, I acted on the spur of the moment when the kids were down for a nap. I panicked when he mentioned Dr. Chappelle's name. I should have talked it over with you before I did anything."

"Dr. Spellman is probably very busy. And even if he notifies Dr. Chappelle, it's not going to make a difference. Chappelle already knows we're coming after him."

"Ray told me not to worry about it. He says I have enough on my plate, but I've enjoyed trying to help you and doing something connected to my professional training."

"Do you want to contact the people Dr. Spellman recommended?" Katelyn asked.

"No, I think you should do it so I don't say something I shouldn't. But it might help if I send you an email outlining what I believe the person needs to do for us."

"That would be great. And if you're available, do you still want to be involved in the chemical analysis?"

"Yes, and I'll adjust my fee so Mr. Caldwell isn't paying two people for the same work."

Every time she interacted with Annalisa, Katelyn liked her more. "We'll figure out a way that's best for you and him."

"I'll work on the email as soon as I can grab a few free minutes."

"Okay."

———

David was on his way to lunch when his phone vibrated and flashed Unknown Caller. He usually ignored unknown calls, but there was a possibility it was a client who needed to reach him.

"This is David Cobb," he said.

"Mr. Cobb, this is Dr. Emerson Chappelle. Do you know who I am?"

"Yes," David replied as he swerved into a convenience store parking lot.

"I was trying to reach Katelyn Martin-Cobb, but the reception-ist at your office said she wasn't available and gave me your number. It's my understanding that you're the principal attorney at the firm."

"That's true. What can I do for you?" he asked, then shook his head in frustration at his choice of words. "What's the reason for your call?"

"Am I correct that your firm has been retained to handle a possible claim involving Relacan, a medication I developed and licensed for treatment of severe nausea?"

"Yes."

"And based on my conversation with Ms. Martin-Cobb and Ms. Annalisa Brighton, you're trying to determine if my patent infringed on a patent filed by your client."

"Yes."

"Are you recording this conversation?"

"No."

David felt like he was being cross-examined.

"I am," the chemist replied. "Do you have a problem with that?"

"No, but I'll start recording as well."

"Fine with me."

David pressed the record button on his cell phone.

"Who is your client?" Chappelle asked.

"Mr. Zeke Caldwell. Mr. Caldwell has developed plant- and animal-based home remedies for many years. He owns the patent in issue."

"Why do you believe my patent infringes the one filed by Mr. Caldwell?"

David hesitated. "We would need to discuss that in a different context."

"Because you don't know, correct?"

"Dr. Chappelle, I'm not going to debate the merits of the case with you in a phone call. If you have a lawyer, I should talk to your attorney."

"I don't have private counsel at this time. I'm speaking for myself."

"Why did you call?"

"We'll get into that another time, if I choose to do so. Until I have a lawyer, should I talk to you or Ms. Martin-Cobb?"

"Either one of us is fine."

The call abruptly ended. David stared out the windshield and tried to figure out what had just happened and why.

Meredith was answering the phones when David returned to the office. He mentioned the call to his cell phone from Dr. Emerson Chappelle.

"I've told Candy not to hand out your cell phone number like she does hers." Meredith shook her head. "I'll say something to her."

"No, I'm glad he called. Although I'm not sure why he did. Anyway, I saw Katelyn's car in the parking lot. Is she busy?"

Meredith glanced down at the switchboard phone. "She's been on the line the whole time I've been up here."

David tapped on the door to Katelyn's office and cracked it

open. She motioned for him to enter. She had someone on speaker while she typed notes on her computer.

"If that's what you recommend, I want to understand why so I can explain it to the client," she said.

A woman on the other end of the call used several acronyms that meant nothing to David except for GC-MS. The caller seemed to believe additional testing protocols were in order.

"I understand your recommendation to be three-tiered," Katelyn said. "You'd perform an initial analysis with multiple samples because you suspect there's a lack of uniformity in what our client produces. After the initial discovery phase of the lawsuit, a second round of tests would be necessary to evaluate the application submitted by the company that filed the patent, and then a final chemical analysis of the manufacturing process used by Brigham-Neal. Otherwise, there can be arguments raised about proper comparison at every relevant stage of development."

"Correct. If your client is cooking batches of this substance in a kitchen, not a controlled environment, the possibility of contamination and statistically significant variations is likely. It will be necessary to have enough data to argue that what he came up with falls within the range of efficacy for the therapeutic agent in the drug you contend infringes the patent."

Katelyn looked at David as she asked the next question. "What would be your budget to do what you're suggesting, not taking into consideration time spent preparing for and participating in a deposition or testimony at trial?"

"If we can work all the way through to a solid conclusion, $50,000 to $75,000. Washing out at phase one would be in the $25,000 range. A lot of the cost involves obtaining access to the equipment needed. I couldn't use the lab at the university."

"And your current availability?"

"Good for the next three months. Summer is my least busy time of the year."

"Anything else I should ask you?"

"No, I'll send you the paper I mentioned. It will help you understand my interest in natural compounds. It's technical, but your local expert can help interpret it for you."

"Thank you, Dr. Middlebury."

Katelyn turned to David after the call ended. "What did you think about Dr. Middlebury?" she asked.

"Who is she?"

"An NC State professor Annalisa suggested I call. Dr. Spellman, one of Dr. Chappelle's chemistry buddies, recommended Dr. Middlebury."

"Why would he do that?"

"I'll explain later."

"The professor is talking about a lot of money."

"Not if you'd listened in on my conversations with the other experts I've interviewed. I spoke with a couple recommended by Suzanne Nixon. Dropping her name along with Morgan and Monroe got me immediate access, but they each wanted a $50,000 retainer with no guarantee of anything other than an initial report. After that, the serious money kicks in."

"How serious?"

"They didn't commit up front, but both said several hundred thousand. We have to remember that in a typical case like this, the parties have so much money to spend that $50,000 here, $100,000 there doesn't cause any heartburn."

"I didn't eat anything spicy for lunch, but I'm feeling heartburn right now."

"And I want to focus on the merits of the claim, not get

sidetracked by what it will cost to get there. But this is part of the process. There's no getting around it."

"Better to do it now rather than later. What else?"

Katelyn motioned toward her computer. "I'm putting together a master plan for the litigation. There will be at least ten to twelve lay depositions, maybe more based on who we talk to at the drug company. As for experts, that could run into the same number when you include the chemists, biologists, and medical researchers who work for Brigham-Neal. Delegating different aspects of decision-making authority to multiple people is common. And in a lot of complex litigations, each side will have two tiers of experts, the ones they use to educate themselves about the case and don't have to be disclosed, and the ones they intend to present to the jury. With Dr. Middlebury, we'd get two for one."

David was silent.

"What are you thinking?" she asked.

"I'm still stuck on figuring out a way to finance the litigation."

"Let me finish putting together my overall plan. It's obvious, but part of that will be deciding how much Cobb and Cobb is willing to invest in the case. Then we'll see if there's a way to move forward in smaller increments."

"Okay."

David took out his cell phone. "You weren't the only person who had a significant phone call about Zeke's case today."

Katelyn listened to the portion of David's conversation with Emerson Chappelle that her brother-in-law had recorded.

"What do you make of this?" he asked.

"Play it again."

David did so.

"Chappelle tried to sound in control, but he's scared," Katelyn said. "He thought he could get away with stealing Zeke's remedy and never suspected Zeke had patented it too. Now he's stuck. There's no way he told the drug company he was copying what someone else developed. Even if he lies in his deposition, it's going to be a problem for him. There may be a provision in his license agreement with Brigham-Neal that authorizes them to charge him the costs of litigation caused by negligence or malfeasance on his part."

"I hadn't thought about that."

"Big companies like those kinds of clauses. Law firms love them because they guarantee future work."

"Chappelle is concerned about the costs of a lawsuit, just like us."

"Maybe. That can be tough to find out even after we file suit. It's not relevant to us, only between the licensee and the licensor of Relacan."

"He didn't threaten or bluster."

"That goes back to him being scared. He doesn't know what to do."

David was quiet for a moment. "I felt kind of sorry for him."

"No!" Katelyn shook her head emphatically. "There's no room for that sentiment. Think about what he did to Zeke."

After David left, Katelyn talked to the final expert recommended by Suzanne. The chemist, a man named Wallace Fletchall, had worked for twenty-five years with one of Brigham-Neal's major competitors. He brought up the names of two scientists who had been mentioned in the letter Zeke received from the drug company's in-house lawyer.

"Yes, they are cited in the letter," Katelyn said.

"They're the first and weakest line of defense. When you push deeper, you'll encounter the more sophisticated arguments," Fletchall advised. "It's all part of a litigation strategy developed over decades. And when Brigham-Neal is dealing with a layperson like your client, they will request and obtain multiple samples of his product and demonstrate why they're so different that it's impossible to properly protect via a patent. There will be variances between what's described in his patent and what he puts in his bottles."

"I heard that earlier today from another chemist."

"You'll hear it until you're sick of it."

Katelyn was silent for a moment before responding. "That will be the basis for a motion for summary judgment to get the case tossed out," she said.

"You're the lawyer, but that's right. No matter what you come up with, the challenge of making your client's substance perfectly match the patent application is going to stand in the way. These cases are determined on chemical minutiae."

"But if we can show the active ingredients are identical, that should give us a chance."

"Until the company explains how their manufacturing process creates a product that is purer, longer-lasting due to additives, more consistent in sustained delivery to the body. It's not just the active ingredients you have to worry about. It's everything."

While the chemist talked, Katelyn was living her future in depositions trying to combat arguments that would batter her like a hailstorm. But if she could survive the discovery phase, all the procedural hurdles, and get the case in front of a jury, anything could happen.

"You know more about how this really works than anyone else I've talked to," she said. "What would you charge to help us?"

"I wouldn't want to take your money. Even if your client is right, I'm not sure you're going to be able to connect the dots."

"Oh," Katelyn managed.

"But you may be able to run a big enough bluff to squeeze costs of litigation, which isn't a paltry sum. I've been in corporate meetings when that was the basis of conversation. Risk management is real. I don't want to offend you, but that's often influenced by who's on the other side. How many of these cases did you handle at Morgan and Monroe?"

"None. I was involved in a lot of multimillion-dollar cases that went to trial, but not in this area. I have no experience."

"Good luck. And I mean that sincerely."

After the call, Katelyn spent time making notes. The ebb and flow of litigation took a lot of internal fortitude. Many times, she'd faced moments when all seemed won or lost, only to have the scenario flipped. Rather than being discouraged, she used the conversation with Dr. Fletchall to steel her resolve. Better to know what lay ahead than to blunder into it blindly. By the time she finished her notes, she was thinking of ways to solve the problems. Totaling all the figures for the cost of the litigation, she drew a box around the final number: $250,000.

TWENTY-ONE

BEFORE THE END OF THE DAY, DAVID RECEIVED TWO
more calls from unknown numbers. Each time, he felt his heart beat
a little faster, thinking it might be Emerson Chappelle again. After
the second call, he put the chemist's name and number in his list
of contacts. He shared the same information with Katelyn so she
wouldn't be caught off guard if Chappelle called her.

David made sure he arrived home early from work. Supper of
baked chicken and rice was chaotic because Andy had to finish writing a paper so that he could go on a class field trip later in the week.
He'd put off the project until the last minute.

"I don't have time to eat," he said when he entered the kitchen.
"I have to work on my paper."

"Not negotiable," Nan replied.

"Is it not negotiable or nonnegotiable?" David asked.

Nan cut her eyes at him.

"Either way, sit down and eat," David said to Andy. "What's the
paper about?"

"Photosynthesis. I'm not interested in finding out how plants
change light and water into energy. I want to go on the field trip to the
marsh to see if I can spot any redfish tailing on the incoming tide."

"According to the memo from Mrs. Garrison, the trip is limited to the five students who write the best-researched and -written papers," Nan said. "If you want to go on the trip, you need to put in the effort."

"Everybody doesn't get a trophy?" David observed.

"They don't in Mrs. Garrison's class," Nan said. "And I'm not going to complain about it."

"They're using a boat that only holds a few people," Andy said. "Could I volunteer Uncle Robbie to take Pops's boat? That way more kids could come."

"Pops's boat isn't certified for school use," David said. "How much have you done for the paper?"

Andy glanced at his mother. "I've barely started the research."

Nan rolled her eyes. "This isn't going to be like it was when you were younger and I practically wrote your reports for you," she said to Andy.

"I write my own sentences without anyone's help," Courtney piped up. "And you can read my handwriting."

"I have to use five different sources and prove that I didn't copy the information," Andy said.

"Here's how to make your paper stand out," David said. "Use plants that grow in the local marsh. It will be good to know them so that if you notice a fish moving near a patch of smooth cordgrass or sea lavender, you'll know what you're seeing."

Andy's expression changed. "They talked about those plants at camp. I have some of the information up in my room."

"Which will give you a resource other than the internet," David said.

Andy finished eating and immediately returned to his room.

"You get the trophy," Nan said to David.

Courtney had saved time to play on her tablet, leaving David and Nan alone at the kitchen table.

"I have another plant question," David said. "Something related to plants at the office."

"Does it have to do with the case you're handling for Zeke?"

"Yes. How did you know?"

"I had a teacher like Mrs. Garrison."

David explained how and why the case was so different from anything else they'd ever handled at Cobb and Cobb. At one point, Nan started to interrupt.

"What were you going to say?" David asked.

"No, go ahead."

"Katelyn has taken ownership of the case, but I'm going to be involved to some degree," David explained. "Especially when it comes to financing the litigation. A case like this can involve a lot of experts, depositions, and—"

"How much?" Nan asked.

"Katelyn is working on an estimated budget, and we've told Zeke we will represent him. But I don't want to get sucked into a situation and not be able to get out of it." David paused. "Zeke's nephew loaned him $10,000 to help with costs, but it would easily take another $100,000, maybe more."

"And if you lose the case, all that money is gone," she said.

"Yes. Under our contract, it would fall on Zeke to pay us back, but everyone knows that wouldn't be possible. What are you thinking?"

"That if the case proceeds to the point where additional financing is needed, we should match whatever Katelyn and Robbie are willing to put in," Nan said.

David stopped. He'd not considered asking Katelyn to contribute.

"She's not a partner. I hired her as an employee."

"Treat her like a partner for this case."

"That means she would receive a percentage of any recovery, not just her salary."

"And share in the risk if the case is lost. Remember when you brought up the money we lost investing in Robbie's boat business?"

"Yes."

"In our hearts and minds we've forgiven that debt. But that doesn't mean we should assume all the risk, all the time, especially on something like this. Also, I think you should talk to your dad during a lucid moment and ask him what he thinks. He's still your law partner, and this will impact him."

"That makes sense."

Nan glanced around the kitchen and waved her hand at the cabinets. "I guess that means good-bye to our kitchen remodel. And the pool for the backyard. And the upgrades to the master bath."

"But if we're successful, we could do all that and more."

"I hope you're right. How do you think Katelyn will respond to your suggestions?"

"I'm not sure. For the time being, I'm not going to say anything to her about either the financing or the recovery share. The first step is to talk to my father. I don't want to repeat the mistake I made in failing to ask him about hiring Katelyn."

Nan was silent for a moment. "Do you believe taking on this case is something you're supposed to do?"

As soon as Nan asked the question, David knew the answer.

"Yes, it feels like that to me."

"I thought so. Don't pass off all the responsibility to Katelyn. I know she's very smart and has a lot of litigation experience, but with your father out of the office, you're in charge of the firm now.

Shouldn't you have the final say when it comes to settlement or resolution of the lawsuit?"

David hadn't anticipated putting that sort of restriction on Katelyn. "Yeah, she's used to working with partners who ultimately make decisions in cases."

"And that can be either not negotiable or nonnegotiable," Nan said. "It's up to you."

———

Zeke's case was also the main topic of conversation during Katelyn and Robbie's dinner.

"I'll do the vast majority of the work on the case while he covers the cost of litigation and the law firm overhead with his regular business," Katelyn said.

"And if you make a big fee, who gets it?"

"It goes into the law firm. David and your dad are the partners, so they would divide it however they handle that sort of thing."

Robbie ate a bite of lasagna. "How much is David going to have to put in to fund the case?"

"I didn't tell him yet, but I'm estimating around $250,000."

"He won't do that," Robbie replied immediately, then pointed toward the bedroom where Carter was taking a nap. "And neither will he, if he's able to offer an opinion."

"Then we need to tell Zeke we're not going to be able to represent him."

"Would that disappoint you?"

Katelyn had stopped eating to talk. "Yes. A lot. It would be a very challenging case, but I want to do it. I've reviewed the other litigation files in the office. There's work to be done, but nothing I'm excited about. Zeke's case is different. Maybe a once-in-a-career opportunity. And if I get a good result, it would be a huge step toward building my own reputation as a litigator, even if future cases aren't so big."

"Then I hope I'm wrong about David's willingness to gamble," Robbie said. "He took a big risk a few years before you and I met."

"What kind of risk?"

Robbie gave her an apologetic look. "I've never mentioned it to you because it was one of my lowest points and very embarrassing. David and my father invested in a boatbuilding business I started. I was going to do most of the work, but once I had the money, I hired too many people, spent some of the money partying, and over-estimated potential sales. It crashed in a little over a year. They lost everything."

Katelyn was shocked. "How much?"

"I don't even know. That whole time is a blur. At least $60,000. Dad kept me out of the gutter several other times. They've never bugged me about it, and I've tried to put it out of my mind, which is wrong."

"Yes, it is," Katelyn said, speaking rapidly. "We should pay it back. We have almost $30,000 in savings toward a down payment on a house, and I could cash in my profit-sharing account from the law firm. There would be a penalty for early withdrawal—"

"Slow down. Let me talk to David about it. Maybe he and Dad have discussed it."

Robbie had stopped eating with half the food remaining on his plate.

"Are you finished with supper?" Katelyn asked.

"Yeah, I lost my appetite. Let's check on Dad."

Carter was awake when Robbie and Katelyn entered the bedroom. He was propped up in bed watching TV.

"Are you hungry?" Robbie asked. "Katelyn fixed lasagna."

"That came from the freezer section of the grocery store, and I heated it in the oven," she said.

"I'll eat a few bites, but I'm mostly starved for conversation," Carter replied.

"Would you like to sit in the sunroom?" Katelyn asked. "It's pleasant this time of the evening."

"Yes."

Carter pulled his walker close to the bed. Standing up unassisted, he began moving across the floor toward the door.

"And I'd love a cup of coffee," he added.

"It has to be decaf," Katelyn replied. "That's on the sheet Dr. Spies sent home from the hospital."

"That's okay. I'll pretend it's real."

"Still drink it black?" Robbie asked.

"Yes. And put it in one of those cups that won't spill. I don't want to make a mess."

When Katelyn brought the lasagna out to the sunroom, Carter was sitting on a short couch. Robbie moved a chair so that he and Katelyn were facing him. Carter ate a bite of lasagna.

"This is good," he said after chewing a few times. "I've always thought the lasagna from the store was fine. Robbie, tell me about your day."

Robbie talked while his father listened and made appropriate comments. It was almost like times they'd spent together in the sunroom in the past. Carter was able to take several sips of coffee without a problem.

"I'm glad you've taken the job at the camp," Carter commented. "It makes me proud."

"I'm proud too," Katelyn said. "And I'm glad Robbie is excited about it."

Robbie cleared his throat. "Dad, do you remember the money you and David loaned me to start the boat business?"

Carter was looking down at the plate. He stopped and raised his head. "Yes, and I've forgiven that debt."

"I don't want you to do that," Robbie replied.

"It's not what you want; it's what I want," Carter answered. "You and Katelyn have moved here and are starting a family. It's the time for me to help you, not hold you back."

"You've always been willing to help me."

"Except for Alaska."

"Yeah, that's right. Your memory is better than mine on that. I would have wasted any help you gave me back then. I'm sorry I got upset with you when you turned me down."

"That's forgiven too. And there's no price that can be set on seeing the positive changes in your life over the past few months. I'm glad to be alive, but I could have died happy because of what God is doing in your life."

When Carter talked about faith, it had a different impact on Katelyn than listening to David over lunch. Carter yawned.

"Thanks, Pops," she said.

"Ask him about Zeke's case," Robbie said.

"Not if he's tired—"

"Don't talk about me as if I'm invisible," Carter said. "They did that at the hospital, and it irritated me. I remember Zeke calling about a problem with the patent I helped him get for one of his remedies."

"He's not mentioned it since he's been here?" Katelyn asked.

"Not that I can remember. If he did, it slipped my mind."

Katelyn gave a summary. Carter seemed to follow, except he had trouble keeping track of the people he didn't already know.

"Which expert is that?" he asked when she mentioned Dr. Middlebury.

"That's not important. The question is whether Cobb and Cobb should fully commit to the case and how to fund it if we do. One of Zeke's relatives put in $10,000, but it will cost a lot more than that."

"What does David say?"

"He wants to help Zeke. Both of us do. But we haven't figured out how to get over this hurdle. He's thinking about it."

"Zeke and I have been friends for decades, and I really appreciate him taking care of me. But you won't be doing him any favors if you start representing him but can't see it through."

"David and I talked about starting small."

Carter was silent for a moment. "I'd be fine with that if you and David decide it's what you think best. Keep me updated."

"Absolutely."

"If David wanted to fund the lawsuit beyond what Zeke put in, would that be okay with you?" Robbie asked. "I assume that decision would affect your revenue for the year from the law firm."

Carter tilted his head and looked at Robbie. "Are you my son who thought it was a waste of time to keep track of business expenses when he was a fishing and hunting guide?"

"Guilty as charged."

Carter yawned again. A few moments later, his head slumped toward his chest. Robbie lifted his father's legs and gently positioned him on the couch with a couple of cushions under his head. Carter began to snore.

"I'd recognize that sound anywhere," Katelyn said. "I never suspected a snore could be genetic."

"Our son will sound the same way," Robbie replied.

"Only cuter."

Robbie took a drink of water. "I felt a load lift off me when Dad told us not to worry about paying back the money he loaned me."

"All that past stuff needs to be sorted out with David too."

"When did you start representing David's interests?"

"Come on; be serious."

"Okay, but sometimes I slip back into that guy who didn't want to bother with anything that had to do with money."

"That won't work here. And Nan should be involved."

"Ouch," Robbie replied. "Her reaction to the boat business fiasco is something I've never wanted to know."

Katelyn and Robbie talked quietly for a few minutes. It was dusk and the crickets started to serenade them. Carter began to stir.

"The crickets must have woken me up," Carter said, rubbing his eyes. "Of course, that's not the first time I've dozed off on this couch."

Robbie helped his father sit up. "Ready to go back to bed?"

"Yeah. Were we talking about Zeke or did I dream it?"

"Yes, Katelyn told you about a case he's brought to the law firm. Someone stole the remedy for one of his formulas and sold it to a big drug company."

"Right, right. There's a streak of genius in Zeke. Did you know he won both the physics and the chemistry awards when we were in high school? I may have copied his paper in physics a time or two."

"Dad!"

"Don't worry. The statute of limitations has run out. They're not going to recall my high school diploma."

Katelyn said good night. Robbie helped Carter make his way to bed. Based on the evening's conversation, Katelyn wondered for the first time if her father-in-law's recovery might someday reach the point that he could return to work.

TWENTY-TWO

DAVID LISTENED AS KATELYN LAID OUT THE $250,000 cost estimate for the Caldwell case. He wasn't shocked by the amount. But that didn't keep the number from intimidating him.

"If we're going to do things in small increments, the first thing is to bring Dr. Middlebury on board and get a solid opinion from her," she said.

"No. First, I need to talk to my father."

"Sorry, I should have mentioned that. Robbie and I discussed it with him last night. I laid out the case, and he seemed to follow along pretty well."

"Does he think we should do it?"

"He's fine with taking initial steps and wants to be kept in the loop."

"And you're confident he understood?"

"In the moment, yes. But I think you should go over it with him too."

"Okay, I'll swing by to see him today."

Katelyn stood up to leave.

"There's one other thing," David said, clearing his throat. "I'd like final authority when it comes to decisions about the case."

Katelyn tilted her head to the side and gave him a puzzled look. "I assumed we'd discuss everything important."

"Yes, but I'm primarily responsible for everything that goes out of this office."

"That's true, but I'll be the one with my finger on the pulse of the case. Are you going to include Zeke in major decision making?"

"Of course, he's the client."

Katelyn sighed. "David, what are you trying to do? Where is this coming from?"

"I'm the partner in charge."

"That's fine, but I'm not promising to run in here every time I have to answer an interrogatory or decide how to cross-examine an expert witness on an issue that you've not researched."

"Let's just keep it to major decisions. That's what I mean."

"Why didn't you say so?"

"I'm just working through it myself."

Katelyn paused. "Anything else before I get to work?" she asked.

"No, that's it for now."

Katelyn left. David had ultimately agreed with Nan that he should have the final say in matters concerning the suit and settlement, but he knew he'd handled the situation poorly in informing his sister-in-law of that decision.

Before moving on to something else, he left the office and drove to his father's house. Carter and Zeke were playing checkers in the sunroom.

"Good morning," he said.

"It'll get a lot better when I get another king," Carter replied.

It was Zeke's move, and he jumped two of Carter's pieces, including one that was close to Zeke's side of the board.

"Ouch," Carter said.

"You told me to do my best," Zeke replied. "If you want me to let you win, just say the word."

"No, this is therapy," Carter answered.

"Dad, could I talk to you in private for a few minutes?" David asked.

"It's my break time," Zeke said, standing up. "I'm going to run to the store. Don't touch that board while I'm gone."

"When did you start taking a break?" Carter asked.

"Today."

Zeke left the room. David waited until he could hear the sound of the door to the outside of the house opening and shutting.

"Katelyn said she talked to you last night about Zeke's case," David said.

"Yeah," Carter replied. "But more importantly, Robbie brought up the money we loaned him for the failed boat business. It gave me a chance to forgive the debt. It had a real impact on Katelyn. You could see it on her face. She didn't know anything about it until recently."

"Really?"

"And I was able to tell Robbie how happy I am for what the Lord is doing in his life with Katelyn sitting there listening to me."

"That's wonderful," David said. "She didn't mention any of that to me when I saw her this morning."

"It's not her place to bring up the money debt. The four of you need to get together. That's what Robbie and Katelyn decided when they were talking and thought I was asleep."

"Nan and I are fine forgiving the debt. The issue is whether the firm should take on a much bigger burden in Zeke's patent infringement case."

Carter rubbed his hand across his face that was covered in gray stubble. "I need to get Zeke to shave me or find my old electric razor. My hand is too shaky to handle a blade."

"What about Zeke's case?"

"Oh, feeling my face distracted me. You need to go slow and manage Zeke's and Katelyn's expectations."

"Tell me what you mean."

"I think Zeke will be fine with whatever you recommend so long as you prepare him in advance. He trusts us. But Katelyn has the bit in her mouth and she's ready to go off to the races."

"Yes, and Nan suggested I treat her like a partner for this case. Should I ask Katelyn to contribute toward the costs in return for a percentage of the fee if we settle or win?"

Carter was silent for a moment. "That would be fine with me. But you need to stay involved and in charge. Don't just pass it off to her."

David chuckled and shook his head. "It sounds like you've been talking to Nan."

"I agree with Nan. Are we finished with our confidential conversation? If so, would you mind getting me some water? I'm using a cup that won't spill."

"Yes."

"Let Zeke know he can come back."

David went into the kitchen for the water and then sent Zeke a text. A few minutes later Zeke returned. He had a plastic bag in his hand and placed it in front of Carter.

"Here's a present."

Carter reached inside. It contained a bag of spicy-hot candies.

"Thanks, but I know what you're up to," he said. "You hope this will distract me, as if my dealing with a brain bleed wasn't enough of an edge for you."

Zeke opened the bag. He put a candy in his mouth and handed one to Carter.

"There, we're equal."

Carter sucked the candy for a few seconds. "This has more heat than the drops you're giving me."

"I could cook up something spicy using the hot peppers my niece grows," Zeke replied.

"I'll be your first customer," Carter said.

David patted his father on the shoulder.

"I think he's responded great to the remedy I prepared for him," Zeke said to David.

"They taste like peppermint mixed with garlic," Carter added.

"Which you like," David said. "Zeke, before you get back to your game, let me give you an update about your case."

David summarized what he knew about Dr. Middlebury.

"How much are we going to have to pay this expert to help us?" Zeke asked.

"Twenty-five thousand to start. But the law firm is going to help fund the litigation."

Zeke looked at Carter. "Are you good with this?"

"Yeah, it has to be done."

"But if we don't collect anything from Brigham-Neal, I'm going to owe you the money you spend. That's the way I read the contract I signed at your office."

"We understand the realities. That provision is mainly to make sure we're reimbursed from any settlement or verdict."

"But I'd feel terrible if you spent all that money and we lost."

"We're willing to take some risk," David said.

"Is there something else you could try?" Zeke persisted. "Do we have to spend all that money on an expert before filing suit?"

"It's not a legal requirement, but as a practical matter, it's the best way to go."

"I'm not sure about this," Zeke said slowly.

"Let him do it," Carter said. "That way we don't have to ask you to leave every time we want to talk about you behind your back."

"I'm not going to argue with both of you," Zeke said with a smile. "Two lawyers against me isn't a fair fight."

Robbie picked Katelyn up at the office to take her to lunch. When he asked her to join him, he didn't tell her where they were going, only that it would take a couple of hours.

"What do you have in mind?" Katelyn said when she slid into the truck's passenger seat. "Two hours sounds like an eight-course meal."

"A picnic," Robbie replied.

"I'm not dressed for a picnic."

"You are for a nice picnic."

Katelyn was wearing a gray skirt, a pale yellow blouse, and low heels. So far, only a few of her favorite outfits were uncomfortably snug. Robbie turned away from the center of town.

"How were things at the office this morning?" he asked.

"David and I talked about Zeke's case. At first, he came across like Lynwood Bancroft and wanted veto power over every decision, but then he became more reasonable. I think we have an understanding that major decisions will involve both of us along with Zeke as the client. I told him about our conversation with your dad. He left the office to meet with him, and I've not seen him since."

They picked up speed as the number of traffic lights decreased.

"Where are we going?" Katelyn asked.

"To Camp Seacrest."

"For a picnic?"

"Maybe alfresco dining is a more accurate description."

Katelyn laughed. "What are we going to eat?"

"That's a surprise."

It was a bright, sunny day. They drove across the flat landscape dotted with scrubby trees, bushes, and an occasional majestic live oak draped in Spanish moss. The Wilmington area was so different from anyplace else she'd ever lived.

"How would you feel about living this far out from town?" Robbie asked.

"We've passed a lot of trailers and run-down houses, but nothing that I'd like to consider buying or fixing up."

"It would involve buying a piece of land and building our own home."

"That sounds like a lot of work with a baby on the way."

"Just take a look."

Robbie slowed and turned off the highway onto a sandy road. "It's fifteen acres," he said. "A member of the board of directors owns it."

A quarter mile farther, Robbie turned onto an even narrower road that wound through a wooded area and ended at the top of a slight rise.

"This is the highest point," Robbie said. "Beyond that thicket it slopes down to the marsh. Do you want to get out and look around?"

"Not in these shoes."

Robbie reached behind the seat and pulled out a pair of Katelyn's sneakers. "I brought these for you."

"You've really planned this out."

Katelyn slipped on the shoes. It was quiet as they walked along a sandy path.

"Who made this trail?"

"Don't know. Maybe the people who've come here to hunt and fish over the years."

They rounded a group of low shrubs, and the marsh opened up before them. A slight breeze reached where they stood. Across the water, several large houses dotted the shore. From their location, the long docks for the houses looked as narrow as a strand of marsh grass.

"It's pretty, isn't it?" Robbie said. "What would you think about a sunroom with this as the view?"

"What's over there?" Katelyn pointed.

"East End Country Club. They pay big money for the view where we're standing."

Katelyn was silent for a moment. "This is a long way from town," she said.

"It took us twenty-seven minutes to get here. How long was your commute in DC?"

"Not a fair comparison. And this is so isolated."

"That part is true. It's another twenty minutes to camp."

"How far is it to the grocery store? And what about the schools?"

"We'll reach a commercial development with several stores in two miles when we're back on the highway. I have no idea about the schools."

"How much is the owner asking for the property?"

Robbie told her.

"That's all?" she asked in surprise.

"Yeah, and that's less than half the market value, which would make getting a construction loan much easier."

"Who would build our house?"

"You'll meet him at our picnic."

They lingered a few more minutes. Katelyn took in several deep breaths of salt-tinged air. She and her mother had lived in a rural area for several years. Their closest neighbors were a quarter mile away. Katelyn didn't mind isolation; she loved it. She just hadn't considered it for herself, Robbie, and their child.

"Will our baby get bitten by snakes in the spring and eaten alive by mosquitoes in the summer?" she asked.

"You like it, don't you?" Robbie replied.

"And how did you reach that conclusion?"

"Because we're still standing here and not walking toward the truck."

"It's not a definite no, but we should check out houses that are move-in ready."

"Absolutely."

They passed the retail shopping area. Everything was shiny and new.

"That's the East End Country Club effect," Robbie said. "The commercial development in this area is only going to get better and better."

Reaching Camp Seacrest, Katelyn saw several work trucks parked near the cabins. They went into the main building. People were moving around in the kitchen.

"What's going on?" she asked.

"The staff came in to prepare your picnic lunch. The woman married to the camp director is a VIP."

There were five workers, two men and three women, in the kitchen. Robbie introduced Katelyn to them. The manager was a woman who'd worked at the camp when Robbie and David were campers.

"They're doing a trial run of the food to serve when the parents drop off the kids for the first session in a few weeks," Robbie said. "Velma and her crew are cooking lunch for the workers, and I asked if we could join them."

"The picnic tables are set up outside," Velma said to Robbie.

Katelyn sat at one of the tables while Robbie talked to the construction crew. The wooden table was covered with a blue-and-white-checked tablecloth. Paper plates, plastic utensils, and napkins were at one end. Two men on the cooking crew started bringing out food on large platters and placing them in the center of the tables. They were having fried or baked fish, coleslaw, green beans, and yams. Several large circular pans of corn bread rested on hot pads. Tea was served in Mason jars. The construction workers waited for Katelyn, as the only woman guest, to go first. She sampled everything except the fried fish. Robbie sat beside her and introduced her to Rodney Hornbuckle, a short, stocky man in his late fifties with a light brown mustache. During lunch, the contractor took out his cell phone and showed her some of the houses he'd built in the Wilmington area.

"I took Rodney to the property yesterday," Robbie said as he ate a piece of lemon meringue pie. "He says there are several good building sites."

"You may want to hire an architect," the contractor said. "But I'd be willing to provide some rough drawings."

"Tell her what we discussed," Robbie said.

Katelyn was impressed with the concept the builder described. After the meal, they received a tour of the work being done on the cabins.

Back in the truck, Robbie spoke. "What did you think?"

"The baked fish was really good. I'm not a fan of yams, but the coleslaw was fresh."

"Spoken like a witness dodging a question. What did you think about Rodney building a house for us on the marsh?"

"I liked him, but I'm going to take the Fifth on the remainder of that question for now."

TWENTY-THREE

EMERSON REVIEWED THE ANALYSIS THAT ENABLED him to isolate the active components in Zeke Caldwell's antinausea remedy. When he'd first unraveled the herbalist's concoction, he'd experienced a rush as potent as scoring a win on a big bet. He was being more deliberate with the combined antinausea and headache remedy. He'd completed his HTCS analysis and had a similar eureka moment. He'd unlocked the secret of the remedy. But this time he didn't experience euphoria. He quickly moved on to identifying inert ingredients to add to his formula to make it appear different. His phone vibrated. It was Lance.

"What are you doing?" Lance asked.

"Working in the lab," Emerson replied in a tone of voice he hoped communicated extreme busyness.

"Coming up with any new ideas for medicines?"

"Not really."

"If you do, I'm in," Lance replied.

If Emerson obtained any other medical or drug licenses, he'd have to disguise his path even better than he did for his ex-wife and her lawyer.

"Often these licenses are a once-in-a-lifetime opportunity," he said.

"I've seen you put down a tiny bet with Nick when the odds were so extreme there was no way you were going to hit it."

Recently, Emerson had wagered $1,000 to avoid being harassed about his account. He lost, of course. Currently, he owed the bookie nothing.

"If I'd won, I would have banked half a million."

"In the future, be serious."

"Always," Emerson replied, trying to sound lighthearted.

"I just got off the phone with my lawyer. He's been talking to the general counsel's office for Brigham-Neal and knows a lot more about the bogus claim being made against our patent."

Emerson was relieved to hear the claim described as bogus.

"It's coming from a guy named Caldwell who lives on the Carolina coast and cooks up potions in his kitchen to sell out of the back of his pickup truck."

"That's sketchy," Emerson said.

"Yeah, but he's convinced a lawyer to help him. What are the chances that Caldwell lives near you? Do you know anything about him?"

"Of course not."

"Since he lives in your area, I'd like you to do some recon and find out more about him. You can combine it with a weekend at your new beach house."

"Why? There's nothing to it."

"Selling risk is my business," Lance responded. "But that doesn't mean I take any chances personally. I'd like to know more about Caldwell and why he thinks you've infringed on his patent."

Emerson tried to keep the panic from creeping into his voice. "What do you expect me to do?" he asked. "I can't knock on his door, introduce myself, and ask him why he hired a lawyer to send a threatening letter to Brigham-Neal."

"Pretend you're a private investigator. I'd like pictures of him, his house, his truck, where he goes, and what he does."

"I'm a chemist. If you want that sort of information, you should hire a private investigator."

"Why pay someone when I can use you for free? And it's not just the facts about this guy. My attorney recommends we obtain samples of the product he claims is the same as your medicine so it can be tested in a lab."

Emerson crept closer to a full-blown panic attack. "That's the drug company's job. They can demand a sample and develop the scientific data needed to disprove the infringement claim."

"Why get so upset and defensive?" Lance asked. "Don't you know the best defense is a good offense? I don't want this to go to the next level, especially if there's a chance the drug company will spend money that is going to come out of our pockets. Or your pocket."

Emerson took a deep breath. "It's just unnecessary. Like you said earlier, the claim is bogus. And I agreed to pay any charge-backs from the drug company for defending the patent."

"I'm sure you're good for the money, but who wants to go through the hassle? Listen, I don't have time to debate this with you. Do what I say and get back to me within the next week to ten days."

David was impressed with Andy's report about photosynthesis. The paper had turned into a project complete with diagrams and hand-drawn pictures of the different types of marsh grasses.

"The writing is very clear, and your illustrations are good too," David said.

"Courtney did those. Should I say that in the paper?"

"Insert a sentence at the end giving her credit."

Leaving Andy's room, David stopped by to see Courtney, who was stringing different-colored beads together to make a necklace.

"I saw the pictures you drew for Andy. They were really good."

"It was easy. Faces are the hard part."

"I'd like to see some of the other things you've been working on."

Courtney placed the necklace on the small table where she'd laid out all the pieces. "I'm making this necklace for Emmaline. She has a shirt with these same colors in it."

"Will your other friends be upset if you don't make something for them?"

"Rebekah might. I wouldn't give it to Emmaline in front of everybody."

"When you have a group of friends who are always around each other, it can be hard to keep everyone happy."

"Yeah. Do you remember the trouble I had with Myra?"

"Yes."

"I sat with her at snack time, but that made Brittany mad." Courtney pointed to another pile of beads. "Before that happened, I was thinking about making Brittany a bracelet. Now I'm not sure."

"Go ahead and do it. Show me more pictures that you've drawn."

The variety of work his daughter pulled from a large purple folder amazed David. There were a lot of nature scenes. She'd even drawn a picture of their house that was remarkably detailed. David held it up.

"Would you be willing to draw a picture of my office?" he asked.

"There's a lot of stuff in your office," Courtney said doubtfully.

"I mean the outside of the building."

"Maybe."

"If you do, I'd like to put the picture in a frame and hang it up where I work."

"You haven't seen it yet."

"I know it will be good."

Downstairs with Nan, David told her about his conversation with Courtney.

"Her ability has shot through the roof over the past couple of months," Nan said.

"Do you think she should have lessons?"

"Not yet," Nan replied with a smile. "She's in the third grade, and the teaching videos I find on the internet are enough for now. But I think we should let her experiment with different mediums. Buy her some good-quality watercolor paints, a nice set of colored pencils. Just so she can play around."

"Whatever you think."

"I like it when you say that."

"That's what I think Katelyn wanted to hear when we talked about the Caldwell case this morning."

David told her about the conversation.

"I thought if you had final authority over the case, it would cut down on arguments, not create them," Nan said.

"That may not be possible. But it's still the right thing to do. I went by the house to see my dad and Zeke. Dad agrees with you that I should give Katelyn a share of any recovery if she contributes to the costs, and that I should have ultimate say. Zeke is on board with whatever I recommend."

———

Shortly before dawn, David was reviewing verses that he'd memorized. He was about to close his Bible when he decided to check one more from the list on his phone. It was a familiar passage from the

Sermon on the Mount: "Settle matters quickly with your adversary who is taking you to court."

Chills ran down David's arms. Never had words risen from the pages of the Bible and become so practically relevant. He immediately knew what it meant and how it applied to Zeke Caldwell's case. His phone vibrated. It was a text from Katelyn.

> Can you come by the house for a meeting with Zeke? I've prepared a memo for him to review and would like to go over it together.

Attached to the text was a link to a document. The memo was a comprehensive and well-written plan of action for Zeke's case. It wasn't crafted like an argument in which an attorney was trying to achieve a particular result. All sides of an issue were explained. And when she gave her recommendations, she did so with multiple reasons. Thirty minutes earlier, David would have given Katelyn's advice his full approval. He pulled into the driveway, then entered the house. Zeke and Katelyn were sitting in the kitchen with cups of tea.

"Carter is taking a nap," Zeke said. "I got here early this morning."

"Which was a good thing because he'd been agitated and upset since four in the morning," Katelyn said. "Robbie sat with him while I tried to sleep."

"Why?"

"He woke up frustrated because he couldn't find the right words and his thoughts and sentences wouldn't come together. It was very different from a conversation Robbie and I had with him yesterday."

"He was good when I talked with him too."

"Robbie tried to reassure him that he's doing better, but he wasn't buying it."

"I arrived shortly after six and fixed breakfast," Zeke added. "The food seemed to help, and he nodded off."

"Do you think we should mention this to Dr. Spies?" David asked.

"It's up to you," Zeke replied. "I kind of expected Carter to have good days and bad days along with good nights and bad nights."

"Okay, let's see how he's doing when he wakes up."

On the table were copies of the memo Katelyn had prepared. She handed one to Zeke.

"This summarizes where we are with the investigation and what I believe we should do next. David, did you get a chance to look it over?"

"I did."

David watched Zeke's eyes as he read the memo.

"Whew!" Zeke said when he finished. "This case is like my remedies. I ask the Lord to show me what's hidden in a plant and how it can help cure people. Then I pray that sick folks will get well and no one will ever be hurt by anything I give them. Just like I told David and Carter, if you believe this is the way to go, I'm fine with it."

"I'm one hundred percent positive," Katelyn said. "We have to spend the money on a chemical analysis of your antinausea remedy to make sure we aren't kicked out of court."

"The summary judgment thing you mentioned in the memo," Zeke said. "Explain that a little bit more."

"Even though we believe Emerson Chappelle stole your formula, that's not enough to prove a case. We can't rely on him admitting what he did. People don't always tell the truth, even when they're under oath. We have to have independent proof to prevent the case from being thrown out by the judge without the chance to present evidence to a jury."

Zeke turned to David. "What do you think?"

David had been rehearsing what to say since he left his house. He cleared his throat. "Everything Katelyn put in the memo is accurate. And I'm like you. I pray about my law practice. This morning, I believe the Lord showed me our strategy moving forward. Do you remember what Jesus said in the Sermon on the Mount? 'Settle matters quickly with your adversary who is taking you to court.' Brigham-Neal and Emerson Chappelle aren't taking us to court. We're taking them to court. But when I read that verse, I realized we're supposed to settle quickly with them, not enter into prolonged litigation. That means we should resolve the case without spending tens of thousands of dollars."

As he talked, David saw the shock register on Katelyn's face.

"Do you mean send a letter to Brigham-Neal telling them we're really, really serious about the claim and they should therefore pay us a bunch of money?" she responded. "David, you know there's no point in trying to run a bluff on a case like this, and it's wrong to give Zeke the impression that it might work."

"No, I think we should file the complaint, then talk with Russell Detar, the drug company's in-house lawyer, and tell him we're willing to resolve the case prior to both sides spending a lot of money in litigation. I believe he'll agree to do so."

"Without any evidence backing you up?" Katelyn exploded.

"Other than what we have. Settle quickly. That's the key."

Katelyn opened her mouth but immediately shut it.

"I like David's idea," Zeke said. "I'm not looking to get rich, just something reasonable. Isn't there a minimum level of information that would allow us to do this?"

Katelyn shook her head. "I wouldn't be willing to put my name on the complaint if this is the way you choose to go. It's barely ethical. A lawyer isn't supposed to make an allegation in a lawsuit that has no basis in fact. Facts can be disputed, but they can't be made up. This could open us up to Rule 11 sanctions and assessed attorney fees for filing a frivolous claim."

"It's ethical because we know what Chappelle did," David said. "And I'm not worried about Rule 11."

"You should be," Katelyn shot back. "The lawyers who'll represent Brigham-Neal won't have any qualms about going after Cobb and Cobb for their fees if you make allegations without any evidentiary support and the case gets thrown out by a judge who's irritated with you for clogging the docket."

"I'll keep to simple notice pleading," David replied. "Just a few paragraphs to get things started and avoid specifics that could create problems."

"And that's going to work?" Katelyn looked at him incredulously. "If this is about not spending the money to develop the case, just say so. Don't hide behind a Bible verse."

"Please don't get into an argument because of me," Zeke said.

"It's too late," Katelyn retorted.

"What if we file the lawsuit and only do the amount of investigation that my money will pay for?" Zeke said. "I'd be okay with that."

"When we agreed to take it slowly, that didn't mean do nothing," Katelyn said. "This approach won't get us ten yards from the starting line."

"I believe it will work," David replied.

Katelyn looked directly at her brother-in-law. "What if I talk to Robbie and see if we can contribute to the costs? That would spread the risk. Would that change your mind about developing the case?"

David shook his head. "No, but I'd still want your help. Would you at least be willing to draft the complaint to minimize the chances of our getting slapped with fees and sanctions by the judge?"

Katelyn didn't respond for several seconds. "I guess so, but I don't want to sign the pleadings or request permission to be listed as an attorney of record for the case."

"Understood," David said.

"I'm not sure I understand," Zeke added. "But I'll go along with whatever you decide."

Katelyn picked up her copy of the memo. "I'm not coming into the office. I'll work from here."

———

David sat at his desk but found it hard to concentrate. He believed he was doing the right thing but couldn't deny that it didn't make sense. The greater danger wasn't from a judge under Rule 11, but in disobeying the direction he'd received from the Lord. Never before had he felt so strongly the fear of God. Explaining that to Katelyn wasn't an option.

Toward the end of the day, he received an email from Katelyn with the subject line "Caldwell Complaint—First Draft." Attached was an impressive document. Even more so because he'd tied his sister-in-law's hands in terms of the allegations she could include. Relying solely on logic and the undisputed contents of the patent applications, she had laid out a commonsense series of paragraphs explaining why Emerson Chappelle's patent was a copycat of the earlier patent filed by Zeke. She included multiple allegations based upon "information and belief" that detailed what they hoped their expert witnesses would conclude without identifying the source of the opinions. It was a skillful way to present the case.

He started to send Katelyn a quick response complimenting her but decided against it. To do so would send a signal to her that he'd not reviewed the document carefully. Better to read it more thoroughly and come up with a suggestion or two. David went through the complaint word by word, line by line, and paragraph by paragraph. He considered several changes, but nothing he came up with was as good as what Katelyn had already done. He didn't want to offer an inferior suggestion. Stepping into the reception area, he was surprised to find Candy still at her desk a half hour after the time to go home.

"I stayed after clocking out to practice using the new accounting software," she said. "I'm going to surprise Meredith tomorrow by showing her what I've learned. Katelyn says we need a better system of safeguards for the regular and trust accounts. I'm going to help Meredith avoid mistakes and keep her from stealing."

"Meredith isn't stealing."

"I believe that she could siphon off small amounts from the regular account, and no one would notice for a long time. Isn't that what happened to the man who was fired as director for Camp Seacrest?"

"Yes."

"Of course, because the trust account contains client money, it has to balance to the penny," Candy continued. "If money is missing from the trust account, it could cause you to lose your law license."

"Every lawyer knows that. And don't tell Meredith you've learned these new skills because we're suspicious of her."

"I'd never do that, but don't you believe it's good for someone to double-check the financial records? There are examples in the tutorial of embezzlement I'd never considered. A law office has to have systems in place to operate professionally. We can't be sloppy."

"Right," David said.

"Let me show you."

While David watched, Candy went through three scenarios for theft. One of them was new to him too.

"It's all about redundancy," Candy said. "I can't wait to use that word in a sentence with my dad. It will really impress him."

"I'm sure it will. Now go home. And I hope you don't have nightmares about duplicate account payable entries for commonly purchased office supplies."

They walked out of the office together.

"And when you surprise Meredith tomorrow, be careful how you come across. Present it to her as a way you can help her out. That's why we decided to do this in the first place."

"Do you want to be there when we talk?"

Normally, David would have declined. Columns of numbers made his eyes glaze over. "Yes. Wait until I'm finished with my first appointment, around nine thirty. Like you said, I don't want us to be sloppy."

After Zeke left for the day, Katelyn went to the sunroom, propped up her feet, and let her mind go blank as she watched Charlie nose around in the bushes. Preparing the draft complaint in the Caldwell case had been both therapeutic and torturous. She relished the challenge of making the document strong and persuasive under difficult guidelines but was tormented by the reality that there was no real substantive evidence backing up her words. Even though she wasn't going to sign it, her commitment to professional excellence wouldn't allow her to throw together something that would satisfy David but fall below her own high standards. In the end, it was a relief that the unavoidable deficiencies in the pleadings would be tied to David's signature, not hers.

Katelyn checked on Carter. Her father-in-law was sitting in a recliner that had been moved from the den into the bedroom. Wearing khakis and a light blue knit shirt, he looked normal. The TV screen on the wall was tuned to a sports network that was broadcasting a fishing show. Carter pointed the controller at the screen and turned it off.

"You didn't have to do that," Katelyn said.

"I know what's going to happen," Carter replied. "The star of the show always catches a nice fish during the last ten minutes. The producers probably make it work that way when they edit the film footage."

"Sorry I've not checked in on you. I spent several hours working in the guest bedroom. How was your day?"

"Which part?"

"Any part."

Carter tapped his head at the place of his scar. "This is mostly working better, but there are times when I draw a complete blank on what word I want to use, and it takes a second or two for me to sort it out. When Robbie gets home, I need to apologize for giving him such a hard time last night."

"He understands."

"Yeah, but that's not like me."

"Overall, you're doing great."

Carter pointed up and then at the nightstand where Zeke had organized his medicines. "You can thank the Lord, and the drops Zeke gave me, for that. Most doctors wouldn't put much stock in Zeke's remedies, but I believe they've helped."

"That's certainly possible."

"What's going on with the case you and David are handling for him?"

Carter's question caused Katelyn's frustration to well up. She suppressed it before answering. "That's what I was working on this afternoon. I drafted the complaint."

"Already?"

"Yeah," Katelyn said and stopped, hoping her father-in-law wouldn't ask any follow-up questions.

Carter was silent for a moment. "What were we talking about?" he asked.

"The good and bad parts of your day," she replied in an attempt to redirect the conversation.

"Oh yeah. I had a hard time making my legs work. We had to cut my exercise session short. I want to increase my stamina every day. Zeke and I walked all the way down the driveway, but then I couldn't take another step. He had to roll me the rest of the way in the wheelchair. Yesterday, or maybe the day before, I made it the whole way using the walker."

"You'll get there."

Carter rubbed the side of his nose with his right hand. "You say you dictated the complaint in Zeke's case? May I read it?"

"It will put you to sleep."

"So does everything else I read. But I'd like to see what you put together. Will you file it in federal court?"

"Yes. The juries there are usually more sophisticated."

Katelyn didn't move from the chair.

"Are you going to get me a copy?" Carter repeated.

"Okay."

Katelyn left, returned with a copy, and placed it on the bed beside her father-in-law. He picked it up. "This has some weight to it."

"I wish it had more legal weight."

Carter put on his glasses and started reading. Katelyn returned to the sunroom. Fifteen minutes later, Carter called out, "Katelyn!"

Not knowing what to expect, she returned to the bedroom.

"I didn't fall asleep," Carter said. "Didn't even get drowsy. You're an excellent writer. It drew me in like a good story."

"That's what it is at this point—a story. We don't have any expert witnesses on board."

"But you're working on getting some. That's going to be the key to success."

Katelyn kept her answer short. "Yes."

Carter yawned. "Don't let me sleep too long after Robbie gets here," he said. "I want to apologize to him."

"No need to apologize," Robbie said from the doorway, where he'd been standing unnoticed. "I've kept you awake at night plenty of times."

Robbie came over and gave his father a kiss on the cheek.

"Don't forget about her," Carter said.

Robbie hugged and kissed Katelyn.

"Out then," Carter said, shooing them away.

"He's a different man than he was last night," Robbie said as they walked into the kitchen. "There was no reasoning with him then."

"I just had a decent conversation with him."

"What did you talk about?"

While they collaborated in preparing a salad garnished with leftover grilled salmon, Katelyn poured out what had happened with David and Zeke.

"David is wrong," Robbie replied with a shrug. "I'm not a lawyer, and even I can see that much. I thought he was beginning to listen to you. You've been much nicer to him than you should have been."

"You haven't heard his side of the conversation."

"I don't have to. And Zeke will go along with him because they've known each other for so many years."

"Yes, he trusts him."

"Would you let me talk to David?"

"Do you think that might make a difference?"

Robbie waited a few seconds before replying, "Not likely. But I might do it anyway."

TWENTY-FOUR

AFTER THE CHILDREN WERE IN BED, DAVID TOLD NAN about Zeke's case.

"Do whatever your heart tells you. And even though you don't mean to, try not to come across as superior or condescending."

"I was pretty confident during the meeting with Katelyn and Zeke this morning, but now the weight of responsibility has hit. If I'm wrong, this is going to be a disaster."

Nan leaned forward and kissed him on the cheek. "I'm with you."

David looked at her gratefully. "And that means the world to me."

———

The following morning David wrapped up the meeting with Meredith and Candy satisfied that no feathers were ruffled. In fact, Meredith had a positive reaction to Candy's increased involvement in the law firm's finances.

Katelyn hadn't arrived at the office, and David wondered if she would show up at all. Ten minutes later there was a knock on his door, and his sister-in-law entered. The expression on her face was all business.

"I didn't hear back from you about the draft complaint," she said.

"It was very good. I considered a few minor changes, but they would have only made it different, not better."

"Still going to file it?"

"Within the next couple of days."

Katelyn paused. David waited with a sense of foreboding.

"Your dad wanted to read it, so I gave him a copy."

"What did he say?"

"That getting the right expert witnesses was the key to success."

David swallowed. "I'm glad he recognized your good work when he saw it."

"Yes, it was a relief to see his mind sharp after the tough time he had in the middle of the night."

Katelyn left. David stared at his computer monitor for a few moments before returning to work. Half an hour later, he received a text from Robbie asking if he was available for lunch. David replied.

Today at noon at Jordan's Restaurant

Fran Jordan greeted David when he entered. "I know who you're meeting," she said with a smile. "I've been hearing good things about Robbie taking over as the director for Camp Seacrest."

"He's excited about the opportunity."

David followed Fran across the dining room to a table for two in the back corner. Robbie was already eating a piece of corn bread.

"Couldn't let this get cold," he said. "Dig in. It's still hot enough to melt butter on contact."

David applied a pat of butter that obediently disappeared into the yellow square.

"I never could find decent corn bread in the DC area," Robbie said. "You'd think it would be available since we were so close to Virginia, but most places turned out a product that could serve double duty as a doorstop. I even asked Katelyn to make some. Do you know what she said?"

"Do it yourself?"

"She did a bunch of research and cooked some muffins that weren't as tasty as this, but they were good enough to satisfy me. That's just one of the times I've learned never to underestimate her."

David took a breath before responding. "Is that a parable about Zeke Caldwell's case?"

"That's up to you."

"Look, I'm not underestimating her," David said. "And I know she's upset with me, but I believe this is the way to go."

"I'm not going to argue with you about legal strategy because it's not my area of expertise, and Katelyn wouldn't want me to. But when I don't pay attention to Katelyn, I usually regret it."

The waitress arrived and took their orders.

"I'm sure what you're saying about Katelyn is true. But I believe I have a word from the Lord on how to proceed."

David told him about the verse from Matthew.

"That may be true in some situations, but what if you're wrong about this one?"

"I can't let that control what I do."

Robbie leaned forward. "David, from what I've heard, this could be a multimillion-dollar case. If you mess it up, it's not going to be easy to put behind you. Take it from someone who's made more than his share of mistakes. And every time you see Zeke Caldwell, it will remind you of your failure."

"I know."

"Give yourself the space to change your mind. Will you do that?"

"I'll pray about it."

"And I'll consider that a no," Robbie said, shaking his head. "There's another situation I need to talk to you about."

David's thoughts immediately went to their father.

"Something about Dad?"

"No, Katelyn."

For the next fifteen minutes, David listened to the full story of Robbie's reconnection with the Lord. If he hadn't been so stressed about Zeke's case, David probably would have teared up.

"Ever since that first night with Dad in the hospital, I could sense something was going on with you, but nothing like this," he said. "What have you shared with Katelyn?"

"Some of it, but not a lot. There's a way to approach her about change. Or at least there was until the past few weeks when so much has happened so fast. My goal was to nudge her in the same direction. For me, what I've heard since I was a kid is coming alive. That's not in her background."

David had eaten less than half his food. Suddenly, he had no appetite.

"And you're upset because you think I'm driving her away from faith, not drawing her in," he said.

"Your actions don't make sense to me. How do you think they look to her?"

"That I'm irresponsible or crazy."

"And I don't blame her or see a way to fix the damage."

Robbie's words stung.

"What do you think I should do?"

"Go to Katelyn and tell her this is your decision. Don't attach God's name to it."

"But that's not true."

"Then figure out something that lessens the fallout. She's going to view this objectively based on results."

Deeply troubled, David left the restaurant not sure what he could or should do. On the way back to the office, he received a text from Nan.

I'm taking dinner to Carter, Robbie, and Katelyn tonight.

At a stoplight, David typed a reply.

Are we going to eat with them?

Of course.

Katelyn was in the kitchen when Robbie walked through the door a few minutes before David and his family were scheduled to arrive.

"You're late," she said.

"Sorry, but my last meeting ran over."

"I've used that line before."

At that moment, the side door burst open and Courtney dashed into the house with Andy close behind her.

"Quiet!" Andy said to Courtney. "Pops may be trying to sleep."

"How could I sleep when I'm so excited about seeing you?" Carter said.

Their grandfather was standing in the kitchen doorway. He came forward, pushing his walker in front of him. Courtney grabbed her grandfather's right arm and hugged it. When she released her grip, Carter raised his arm and moved it slowly back and forth.

"What does that look like?" he asked Andy.

"You're about to cast your fly line," the boy said with a big grin on his face. "Do you think you'll be able to go fishing again?"

"That's one of the main goals of my rehab."

David and Nan entered the house carrying dishes of food.

"Anything else?" Katelyn asked.

"Yes, there's one more dish in the back of the van," Nan said. "It's hot, so use the pot holders to carry it."

Katelyn went outside. The gate of the van was open. Beside a casserole dish on the floorboard was a folder. Sticking out of the folder was a piece of paper with Katelyn's name written in vivid purple pencil. She slipped the paper out of the folder. Courtney had drawn a remarkably accurate picture of Katelyn standing on the beach holding a baby in her arms. Katelyn's dark hair was blowing in the breeze. The baby was wrapped in a light blue blanket. Included in the picture was a small, white stuffed bunny with a pink ribbon and bow around its neck. Leaving the folder, Katelyn brought the dish inside the house, placed it in the middle of the kitchen table, and took off the lid. Inside was a squash casserole with melted cheese on top. Carter, who was standing nearby, leaned over to look.

"I love your squash casserole," he said to Nan. "It's my favorite dish you make."

They'd also brought a seafood pasta, Caesar salad, and steamed broccoli. Katelyn could see scallops, shrimp, and mussels in the pasta. They helped themselves to the food and took their plates into the dining room. When they were all seated, Carter spoke.

"I'd like to pray," he said.

The room instantly became quiet. Andy and Courtney stared wide-eyed at their grandfather.

Carter didn't offer a perfunctory blessing. He began by thanking God for preserving his life and asked for the restoration of his health. He then went around the table and mentioned each person by name. Carter offered up thanks for Robbie's new job and prayed that he would be the best director in the history of the camp, one with a deep and lifelong influence on the campers.

Katelyn was sitting next to Robbie. "And, Lord, thank you for Katelyn. May she know more than ever the love you have for her and the love Robbie and the rest of us have for her. I ask for your blessing on everything she puts her hand to here in Wilmington, and the new life she is bringing into this family."

The mention of love brought back the words from Robbie's journal and caused a shiver to run down Katelyn's back. Carter concluded by praying for Courtney and Andy, who were sitting beside their grandfather. Katelyn heard Nan sniffle at the words for her children.

"And all God's people said, 'Amen!'" Carter concluded.

"Amen!" echoed the other voices at the table, including Katelyn's.

"I hope the food didn't get cold while I rambled on and on," Carter said.

"Dad, that was like something out of the Bible," David said. "It reminded me of Jacob blessing his children before he died at the end of Genesis."

"If God answers my other prayers, it's not my time to go," Carter replied with a smile.

"And all God's people said, 'Amen!'" Robbie responded.

"Amen!" everyone replied, including Andy and Courtney in very loud voices.

"Where are the pictures that I drew for Pops and Aunt Kate?" Courtney asked excitedly. "Did I leave them at home?"

"No, they're in the van," Nan said, returning a tissue to the front pocket of her slacks. "We can look at them after supper."

"I want to get them now. Pops, you don't want to wait to see it, do you?"

"I'll get the folder," Katelyn volunteered. "I saw it when I brought in the casserole."

When Katelyn returned, Courtney took one of the pictures out of the folder with a flourish and gave it to her grandfather.

"I love it," he said. "It's so good I want to put it in a frame and hang it where I can look at it whenever I want."

"Pass it around the table," Robbie said.

"Only if you promise not to get any food on it," Carter said as he handed it to Robbie.

Katelyn looked over her husband's shoulder. Her niece had used colored pencils to draw a picture of Carter's house.

"You're an artist," Katelyn said.

"I had a photo of Pops's house to make sure I didn't forget something," Courtney replied. "And Mommy showed me a picture of a house by a real artist, and I copied it."

"It was an architectural rendering that I found online," Nan said, turning to Katelyn. "I believe it was a farmhouse in New England. Show Aunt Kate her picture."

Katelyn acted surprised, but she didn't have to pretend that she loved the beach scene. It wasn't like a photo; it created a mood. Robbie commented on the color of the blanket.

"Did your daddy suggest that you wrap the baby in a blue blanket because we're going to have a boy?"

"He told me to pray about it and see what God said to me. So I held up a blue pencil and a pink pencil, and the blue pencil felt right to me. But I put a pink ribbon on the bunny."

"Whether it's a boy or a girl, I'm going to hang this in the baby's room," Katelyn replied.

Carter was quiet during the rest of the meal. He ate squash and a few bites of pasta.

Katelyn leaned over to him. "How are you feeling?" she asked.

"Tired but happy," he said with a smile. "Very happy."

"Pops, I'm glad you're happy," Andy said. "That makes me happy too."

Carter reached over and gently placed his hand on his grandson's shoulder.

The following Monday morning, David asked Meredith to make sure the law firm PACER account with the local federal court was active so they could transfer the filing fee for the Caldwell case. The complaint would be filed electronically. The era of bringing in a legal document on red-lined, fourteen-inch paper to be stamped by the clerk of court was gone.

"You're good to go," the office manager replied a few minutes later. "When are you and Katelyn going to file the complaint?"

"Today, but Katelyn's name isn't going to be on the pleadings."

"Right." Meredith nodded. "She's not yet been admitted to the bar in North Carolina."

"That's not the reason. It's her preference. She's not comfortable proceeding without an expert witness or two in our back pocket."

David explained his strategy without mentioning his sense of divine direction.

"I hope it works out," she said doubtfully. "I guess you'll never know unless you try."

An hour later, a message from the clerk's office appeared on David's computer screen. The complaint was filed and a summons issued. David felt a mixture of excitement and fear. He paused to offer up a prayer for supernatural favor and success.

Brigham-Neal had a registered agent for service of process on file with the North Carolina Secretary of State. That designee would receive official notice of the lawsuit and then pass it along to the company. Instead of asking Katelyn about the procedure for service, David researched the issue himself. He was at Meredith's desk providing instructions when Katelyn walked up and overheard him.

"Do you want me to take a look and make sure everything is in order?" she asked.

"Yes," Meredith replied before David could say anything. "I've not done this in years and would hate to mess something up."

Katelyn flipped through the documents. "You're good to go," she said.

"I was going to send their general counsel a courtesy copy so the drug company knows it's coming," David said.

"That's fine," Katelyn responded. "And it makes sense given your litigation strategy. But I predict the outside law firm hired to represent Brigham-Neal will request at least one extension of time to answer the complaint, maybe two. *Quick justice* isn't in their vocabulary."

"I won't agree to an extension."

"Futile," Katelyn said and shook her head. "The lawyer will file a motion with the judge, who will automatically grant the request. You'll look silly."

David didn't respond.

"We sure don't want to look silly," Meredith said with an upward glance at David.

"I'm off to a meeting with Dr. Newberry, the dentist, about the noncompete agreement with his new partner," Katelyn said. "Any suggestions?"

"No," David muttered.

Returning to his office, David spent the next hour writing and rewriting a letter to Russell Detar, the drug company's in-house lawyer. In the end, he scrapped everything and decided to simply email the lawyer a copy of the complaint with a request that he call to discuss possible resolution of the case before engaging in a prolonged litigation. David believed he could express himself better on the phone than in writing. Before sending the email, he stopped to pray earnestly for favor and a speedy reply. He then quoted out loud several times, "Settle matters quickly with your adversary who is taking you to court." Satisfied that he'd done his part, he sent the email to Russell Detar. Now it was up to God to do his part.

David ate lunch alone at a local deli. While contentedly munching a potato chip, his cell phone vibrated. It was an unknown number.

"This is Russ Detar," a man said with a midwestern accent. "I received your email with a copy of the complaint you filed this morning."

David swallowed his food and cupped his hand around the phone to try to make the conversation more private.

"Thanks for calling so quickly," he said. "I'm at lunch right now. May I call you later this afternoon? My schedule is flexible if you want to set a specific time. I believe it makes sense for everyone if we have early, quick discussions and move toward a reasonable resolution of—"

"No need. Just wanted to let you know that once a suit is filed, my office doesn't communicate directly with the attorney on the other side. We work through our outside counsel."

David tried to keep from sounding desperate. "Please give me the opportunity to explain why a different approach makes sense in this matter," he managed.

"It's company policy never to settle a claim like this just because a complaint is filed. That's been the case during the twenty-two years I've been here. No exceptions. We have a duty to our share-holders to investigate every claim."

David searched for another reason or argument but came up with nothing. "Uh, thanks for letting me know."

The call ended. Devastated, David stared at a strand of sauer-kraut peeking out from the edge of his sandwich. He slowly picked up the sandwich, took a bite, and chewed without tasting it.

———

Katelyn left Dr. Newberry's office in a good mood. Once she knew David had filed the complaint in Zeke's case, she began the process of purging the patent infringement claim from her mind. The business meeting with the dentist helped her move on.

"Is David busy?" she asked Candy when she got back to the firm.

"I'm not sure. He hasn't left his office since he returned from lunch."

Katelyn knocked on David's door. She heard a verbal response inside but wasn't sure what he said. She entered. David was staring at his computer monitor.

"Are you in the middle of something?" she asked. "I wanted to give you a report of my meeting with the dentist."

"Sure, come in."

Katelyn sat down and summarized her conversation with the client. "There's something very satisfying about helping a small business navigate a challenging situation," she said. "And when the client expresses appreciation, it feels much more personal than with a big corporation that's matter-of-fact and soulless."

"You're right."

"In the end, the real issue had nothing to do with the

noncompete agreement. I'm so glad I'd studied the financial projections. When I suggested that Dr. Newberry guarantee the new dentist's salary, it brought everybody's focus back to center. I felt like a business counselor, not just an attorney."

"That's great."

Katelyn got up to leave. David spoke: "During lunch, I had a brief phone call with the corporate counsel for Brigham-Neal."

"Already?" Katelyn asked in surprise.

"He slammed the door in my face."

David's despondent look made Katelyn feel sorry for him.

"He told me they let outside counsel handle all discussions once a suit is filed."

"And that law firm will want to develop the case and bill the client for years."

"Years?"

"Probably. What are you going to do?"

"Pray that Russell Detar will change his mind. That's the key to success."

Katelyn remembered what Carter had told her about the key to success in the Caldwell case. Even a man recovering from a brain hemorrhage knew the correct legal strategy. She pressed her lips together tightly for several seconds as that thought and several other ideas cascaded through her recently purged mind. She returned to her office.

TWENTY-FIVE

EMERSON WAS GETTING READY FOR A DATE WITH
Roxanne, a woman he'd met a month earlier while she was walking
her dog near his new beach home. Roxanne lived three blocks away
and was awarded a beach house in the divorce settlement from her
ex-husband.

So far, Emerson hadn't acted on Lance's directive to spy on Zeke
Caldwell. But he'd increased his betting activity with Nick and was
currently up over $30,000 based on hitting a trifecta on Major League
Baseball games. He was trying to decide which shirt to wear when his
phone vibrated and Lance's name popped into view. He'd let two previous phone calls go to voice mail and knew he couldn't do so again.

"Well, thanks for deciding to take my call," Lance said in a sar-
castic voice. "Most of my business partners talk to me when I reach
out to them."

"Sorry about that, but I only have a few minutes to talk. I'm
getting ready for a date."

That comment led to a series of questions from Lance that Emerson
always found uncomfortable. It seemed like the gambling boss kept
adding personal information about Emerson to a dossier. Within a few
minutes, he knew almost everything Emerson knew about Roxanne.

"When you go on your Vegas trip, I'll hook you up with a guy who can get you backstage for any show you want."

Emerson perked up. That would be the perfect way to close the deal with Roxanne.

"That would be awesome," he replied.

"How are you coming along with your research about the other person in Wilmington that we're interested in?" Lance asked.

"Still working on it," he answered evasively.

"It's gone way up in importance on my radar," Lance said. "The lawyer for Caldwell filed suit in federal court against Brigham-Neal. My attorney is getting a copy of the paperwork. Do you want to read it?"

"Yeah," Emerson replied, as thoughts of Roxanne, Las Vegas, and backstage passes rapidly retreated.

"Even though you've assured me there's nothing to the claim, I always like to protect my assets. And the success of our little deal has made it important to me."

"It's been profitable. And there will be more checks coming. A recent peer-reviewed article in a medical journal in California praised Relacan. The doctors who wrote the article didn't call it a 'wonder drug,' but they came close."

"Well, I don't want to wonder if the money I'm receiving is going to be cut off. And to protect our investment, I'm not going to ask you to be an amateur private detective. This situation requires a professional."

"I totally agree," Emerson said with relief. "I checked the other day and there are several private detective firms in the Wilmington area. I can start calling around."

"I don't need a referral, and the fees are going to be your responsibility."

Emerson grunted. "How much do you think it will be?"

"It depends on what they have to do. Addressing the problem caused by the old man would be one price. If it has to go beyond that, the cost goes up considerably."

"What do you mean by 'addressing the problem'?"

"I'll let you work everything out with them," Lance answered cryptically. "Expect a call within the next few days."

"Who will be calling?"

"Nick will be the middleman. All initial communication will be through him. By the way, you're not recording this call, are you?"

"Of course not."

"That's good. If you did, it would be a very serious mistake."

Emerson's mind was now in turmoil. "I really need a cost estimate so I can be prepared," he said.

"To be determined, but it will be a lot more than the thirty grand you have in your account with us. Like I said, the services performed dictate the price."

Emerson swallowed. He couldn't believe what he was hearing. The innuendos were chilling.

"Lance. I'm just a chemist who—"

The call ended. Emerson leaned back against the wall and closed his eyes. In that moment, he didn't want to go to Las Vegas with Roxanne. He didn't want to go anywhere. All he wanted to do was disappear and hide someplace where no one could find him.

For the remainder of the day, the multiple demands on David's time helped keep his mind off the Caldwell case. He was putting the finishing touches on a commercial lease agreement for a client who owned a couple of car washes when Candy buzzed him.

"Annalisa Brighton would like to talk to you," the receptionist said.

"Put her through."

"How are you doing?" he asked.

"Our baby girl was born last Thursday."

"Congratulations! Is everyone healthy and okay?"

"Yes, I'm tired but happy. Adeline is nocturnal, which means I
have two children for one twelve-hour shift followed by an infant for
a second twelve-hour shift. But Ray's mom is here, and she's a world
of help. She's taking care of the older kids. I called Katelyn to let her
know about Adeline and asked about the patent infringement case.
She'd kept me in the loop about her conversations with possible
experts, but then I didn't hear from her. She tells me you've taken
over primary responsibility for the claim."

"For now. I filed suit this morning."

"Who did you find to help you?"

David glanced up at the ceiling in supplication before answering. "No one."

Annalisa was silent for a moment. "I didn't think that's how it
worked," she said.

"It's part of my strategy."

"Okay. I don't know the technicalities of the law, of course, but
during one of my long night shifts when the baby was awake, I came
up with an idea that might help. It may not fly because my brain is
only functioning at fifty percent capacity. Would you like to hear it?"

David sat up straighter in his chair. "I'm listening."

"Originally, I thought it'd be necessary to completely decon-
struct the two drugs into their component parts in order to support
an opinion that they are chemically the same and then prove identical pharmacological function, which would require analysis with

the equipment I mentioned when we first talked. But what if you went a different direction and instead of breaking them down went directly to the way they interact with the body?"

"How?"

"You gather together a group of people, give one group Emerson Chappelle's medication, the other group Zeke Caldwell's remedy, and then check for the presence of the active ingredients in their blood."

"It might vary from person to person."

"But there is a therapeutic range. And that's what makes the medication effective. If they both produce a therapeutic result based on the same active components, they're the same drug. One of the other things I did during my sleep-deprived state was check updated information about Relacan. A recent medical journal article discusses in detail the desired therapeutic range. There is also technical data that the drug companies provide to physicians as a routine practice, although I suspect few doctors remember enough from organic chemistry to reach their own independent opinion. They're more concerned about negative interactions with other meds and potential adverse side effects of the drug they're considering for their patients. Anyway, some of that might be helpful too."

David was intrigued. "Would the people given the two meds have to be sick?"

"If the drugs are safe for anyone, I believe you could use asymptomatic people as long as they're willing to undergo a blood test. The lab would be notified of what to look for."

"How many people would you need to include?"

"I don't know, but if you offer to pay them to participate in a brief drug study, it shouldn't be hard to get some volunteers. Do you know any doctors who might do this for you? They would have to be okay with Zeke Caldwell's remedies."

Dr. Mark Sparrow immediately came to David's mind. "I think so. What do you think about a group of twenty?"

"That should tell you something."

Annalisa's suggestion struck David as the type of easy-to-understand evidence that might appeal to a jury of ordinary people. You'd simply explain that if two medicines show up the same way in the blood, they're the same medicine.

"I could put together a memo for you," Annalisa offered.

"Forward me a link to the article you mentioned, and I'll take it from there. And prepare a bill for the time you spent thinking about this in the middle of the night and this phone call. Third-shift pay is time and a half."

Annalisa laughed. "Maybe three or four hours total. Most of that was reading the article. Based on the researchers' positive findings, the revenue generated by sales of Relacan should increase as it becomes more and more popular, which will likely make the drug company fight that much harder."

"Not necessarily," David replied hopefully. "It could also make them willing to pay to get rid of our claim before it becomes a serious threat."

After hanging up, David immediately called Dr. Sparrow and left a detailed message explaining what he had in mind.

―――――――――

The next morning, David had an hour-long meeting with Dr. Sparrow. The family practice physician with white hair, distinguished features, and a baritone Southern drawl had been by to see Carter in the hospital and knew a lot about Zeke's remedies.

"I think your father will make an outstanding recovery. And I'm glad Dr. Spies was fine with Zeke's remedy. How is Carter doing at home?"

"Better and better. Zeke took a leave of absence from his pharmacy job to help us take care of him."

"I knew they were longtime friends."

David told the doctor what he had in mind.

"Zeke never told me he'd patented one of his remedies, but it doesn't surprise me. I consider him an unsophisticated genius."

"Me too. I thought we could recruit twenty people. Give ten of them Relacan and the other ten Zeke's remedy."

Dr. Sparrow nodded. "I'd be very interested in setting up a clinical comparison trial. What I've seen over the years about the benefits of Zeke's products has been anecdotal. This would be more scientific. But I suggest you expand the pool to fifty people. A hundred dollars per person should attract plenty of candidates if we get the word out to college students and use them to populate the pool. A big advantage of using students would be the ability to administer the drugs to people who aren't taking any other medications that might skew the results of a blood test."

"As long as their blood is drawn early in the week, not after a weekend of partying."

"We'll make that clear."

"I'll initiate contact with the students and prepare the consent forms for those who are old enough to participate."

"I'd also want to send them a general health questionnaire," the doctor added. "We'll do two sets of twenty-five. The volunteers would come to my clinic on a Monday evening, give blood for a baseline, then receive one of the drugs to take every day for the next week and have a second round of blood drawn the following Monday. The research article you mentioned could serve as a template for therapeutic levels of the active ingredients."

"Would it be worth finding a smaller group of people who suffer from severe nausea and doing the same thing? Maybe through one of the local oncologists."

"That would be trickier. Not everyone is as open-minded about alternative therapies as Dr. Spies and myself."

"Okay, let's stick with this plan."

David was encouraged. However, he couldn't get too excited. Dr. Sparrow's academic and medical education credentials were fine for the patients who had filled his waiting room for the past thirty-six years, but they would appear thin in a federal courtroom filled with Ivy League–educated expert witnesses.

TWENTY-SIX

KATELYN AND ROBBIE ARRIVED AT THEIR TOWNHOME in DC where, for the next two days, they would pack up fragile and personal items and take them back to Wilmington in either her car or his truck. Everything else would be boxed by the professional movers and delivered directly to a local storage unit. During the drive, Katelyn had checked in with Annalisa Brighton to see how she and the baby were doing.

"I don't want to get too personal, but for obvious reasons I'm interested in every detail you want to share," Katelyn said.

As a scientist, Annalisa was the kind of resource most suited to Katelyn's analytical personality.

"I can't wait to meet her," Katelyn said after several informative miles passed on the highway.

"Oh, and to prove that I'm able to multitask beyond caring for an infant and two toddlers, I also spent time one night thinking about your case."

"My case?"

"The patent infringement case."

"Oh, sure."

Annalisa told her about the suggestion she'd passed along to David. Katelyn listened skeptically.

"That's creative," Katelyn said, searching for a nonnegative term for the sketchy theory of proving the claim.

"David was excited about it."

"I'm sure we'll discuss it when Robbie and I return from Washington."

"Have a good trip. And don't forget to come by and see me. I'll be at home."

———

The first day in DC, Katelyn and Robbie made excellent progress organizing their belongings. Katelyn created a spreadsheet to track everything.

"Should you include this toothbrush?" Robbie asked. "I found it behind the sink in the master bathroom."

The bristles were bent and frayed on the ends.

"That's one of your old ones that saw secondary duty as a cleaning tool."

"Correct."

"Landfill," Katelyn said.

Late that afternoon, she phoned Phoebe Jacobs.

"Where have you been?" the lawyer asked. "Your name dropped off anything having to do with our case, and you disappeared from the face of the earth."

"I resigned from Morgan and Monroe. My husband and I are moving to Wilmington, North Carolina. He's accepted a job as director for a boys' camp. Tell me about your little boy."

Listening to Phoebe brought a smile to Katelyn's face.

"I have news of my own," she said when Phoebe finished. "I'm pregnant."

Phoebe's enthusiasm, when added to the personal information Katelyn had received from Annalisa, was water to Katelyn's soul.

"Promise me pictures," Phoebe said. "Are you going to find another job?"

"Already have one with a small practice in Wilmington. Forty hours a week."

"Stop," Phoebe quipped. "You're making me jealous, but I'm so happy for you."

That evening Katelyn and Robbie returned to the seafood restaurant where she'd told him about the job offer at Morgan and Monroe, and he'd kept quiet about his interest in the Camp Seacrest job. Katelyn noticed that Robbie had brought his journal to dinner.

"This time, I understand why you're not going to order sushi," he said. "Would it bother you if I did?"

"No, go ahead."

Katelyn ordered a seafood casserole that arrived with melted cheese bubbling on top. During the meal, she stopped eating.

"Is something wrong with your food?" Robbie asked.

"Delicious. I just realized something that's different from the time we were here a few weeks ago."

"I think you ordered shrimp."

"No, different in me."

Robbie gave her a puzzled look. "There are so many differences in both our lives, you'd have to create another spreadsheet to keep track of them."

"I am so much more relaxed. That's what I just realized. Before, I was wound tight by all my responsibilities at the law firm and the immediate need to make a decision about the job offer in Chicago. All of that is gone. A huge weight has lifted."

Robbie smiled. "I'm glad."

"And there's no comparison between the frustration I feel toward David and the constant pressure I lived under at Morgan and Monroe."

Robbie ate a piece of sushi. "I wouldn't always want to admit it to him, but David means well."

"And I'm not responsible for what happens because of his decisions."

"Correct. Please try to keep it that way."

Toward the end of the meal, Robbie placed his journal on the table.

"Is this dessert?" Katelyn asked.

"I'd like to think so."

Robbie opened the book and slid it across to her. He'd created three sketches of the house he'd like to build on the marsh property. There was the front elevation, a side perspective, and a view from the rear. The house looked like it almost grew out of the sand. There were plenty of windows, and a complex roofline that would be expensive to build but gave the house great personality. Katelyn tried to imagine the interior.

"This is stunning," she said. "Especially looking at it from the marsh side."

"I'm glad you like it."

"And it makes me think about what I'd like on the inside."

"That's what I wanted to ask you."

They spent the next forty-five minutes listing interior features they would like to include.

"This is fun to dream about," Katelyn said. "But every idea is going to cost money."

"We'll deal with that later. Our job now is to dream."

Later than night, Katelyn lay awake after Robbie went to sleep. Slipping out of bed, she went into the living room and sat on the sofa. Robbie's journal was on the coffee table, and she opened it so she could revisit the house sketches and what they'd come up with at supper about the interior. Katelyn was practical enough not to let her expectations run wild, but she appreciated Robbie's prompting to dream. He made her life vibrant and rich. And adventurous.

She turned to the page on which Robbie had drawn the campfire scene. A lot had happened since she first admired the picture and read his prayer. Maybe he was right. She should create a spreadsheet to document everything, both internal and external, that had happened to them. But she didn't reach for her laptop to do so. Another thought grabbed her attention. Katelyn lightly placed her hand on the sketch and hoped that the musical notes drifting in the air above Carter's head might return to her father-in-law's life. A few moments later she turned her hope into a simple prayer.

David sat in the den with his father, who seemed the most clearminded he'd been since the brain hemorrhage. Andy and Courtney were playing with Charlie in the backyard. Nan was in the kitchen unpacking the food she'd brought for supper. David was going to be spending the night while Robbie and Katelyn were out of town. He'd told Nan about his disappointing interaction with Russell Detar but didn't want to bring it up with his father.

"How are things at the office?" Carter asked.

"It's a process, but we're adjusting."

"What about Katelyn?"

"That's part of the adjustment."

"Maybe when I get back to the office, I can help."

"You're doing much better, but going back to work is a whole different discussion," David said.

"I'm not old enough to retire," Carter replied. "Let's see how it goes. I have an appointment with Dr. Spies next week. I'll ask him what he thinks about the prognosis for my long-term recovery."

"Last week you were struggling to walk from the house to the mailbox and forgetting words you should know. You'd need a comprehensive neuropsychological exam to determine your level of functioning before considering a return to work."

"I agree. Do you want me to spell neuropsychological?"

"No," David said. "And don't ask me to either. I'm sorry. You know I miss you and would love to have you back."

"No need to apologize," Carter replied. "When you've felt as bad as I have, once the world starts looking more normal, it becomes possible to dream again. There are a lot of lawyers with limitations who are able to function. Maxine Carpenter has been in a wheelchair for years following her stroke. She quit going to court, but she still meets with clients at the office. She's the one I've been thinking about."

"She also brings in Chris Payne to handle complex matters."

"And I'll have both you and Katelyn to handle anything complicated. We know how smart she is."

"Yes," David replied slowly. "Very smart."

Later, while the kids were with their Pops, David mentioned to Nan what his father said.

"Even if he didn't practice law, it might be good at some point for him to hang out at the firm a few hours a day," she said. "His friends could drop by to see him, and the two of you could go to lunch."

"Yeah, I'd not thought about it that way. I'd just have to make sure he didn't give advice when he's not capable of doing so." David paused. "Which is exactly what Katelyn is accusing me of doing in Zeke's case."

"That's different."

"Maybe not in her mind."

"Keep believing. That's what I'm doing along with you."

Sleep had been a stranger since Emerson's most recent phone call with Lance. The chemist's relationship with Roxanne crashed and burned, even with the promise of backstage passes to a Las Vegas show. Dejected, Emerson nibbled a sandwich while sitting in the living room of his beach house. Through the front picture window, he had a postage-stamp-sized glimpse of the ocean squeezed between two palmetto trees. A tiny flash of white indicated a cresting wave. The phone on the coffee table in front of him vibrated. It was Nick, who had already called three times that day.

"Hello," he said.

"I thought you might be dead. I was about to call the cops to break down the door but realized you're alive."

"What are you talking about?"

"You've been sitting in your living room for the past thirty minutes doing nothing. You're wearing a yellow golf shirt, white shorts, and a black cap."

Emerson looked out the window but couldn't see anyone. The only vehicle in sight was the SUV owned by a man who lived in the house across the street.

"Where are you?"

"Close enough. Walk down to the beach. Be there in five

minutes. There's somebody you need to meet. And don't bring your phone."

Emerson hesitated.

"My friend doesn't like to be kept waiting."

"Okay, I'll be there."

It was a hot, humid day without a breeze. As soon as he stepped outside, Emerson immediately began to sweat. A family of four with two small children were taking the same sandy path. The presence of the family was a good sign. Better to be in a public place when encountering someone like Nick and his associate. They reached a wooden walkway that spanned the beachfront dunes. Up ahead, he could see people looking for shells at the edge of the water. Several beach umbrellas dotted the sand.

Emerson stopped at the top of some stairs that led down to the beach. The family reached the bottom of the steps, and the two children raced across the sand toward the water. As Emerson walked down the steps, he saw a man beneath a multicolored umbrella stand up and motion him over. It was Nick. Beside Nick was a deeply tanned man about the same height as Emerson. He was wearing blue swim trunks, a red cap, and dark sunglasses.

Emerson's deck shoes began to fill with sand, and he took them off. Continuing barefoot, he walked about a hundred feet to the umbrella.

"How long has it been?" Nick said, extending his hand. "Six months since you stood me up in Chapel Hill."

"I've been talking directly to Lance," Emerson replied.

"Dr. Chappelle, this is Jerry."

The man in the chair turned his head slightly and nodded to Emerson.

"I was only here to help you connect," Nick said. "My job is done. I'll leave you guys to discuss business."

Nick headed across the sand. Even though Emerson didn't like Nick, he found himself wishing the bookie would stay.

"Sit down," Jerry said. "The bottle of water is for you."

There was a plastic bottle of water in a pocket attached to the chair. Emerson unscrewed the top and took a drink.

"Tell me everything you know about Zeke Caldwell and this lawsuit," Jerry said. "I've read the complaint filed in court."

"I've not seen it yet."

"You should check it out."

Emerson repositioned his hat. "I don't know where to start," he said.

"Anywhere is fine, then we'll fill in the blanks."

In the pressure of the moment, Emerson resisted a crazy urge to confess that he'd pirated Zeke Caldwell's formula by deconstructing it in the lab and then filed his own drug patent. He took a longer drink of water before speaking. Then he fumbled and stumbled through a disconnected summary. Jerry listened without interrupting.

"Sorry if I keep backtracking," he said at one point.

Jerry didn't respond. Even beneath the shade of the umbrella, sweat poured off Emerson.

"I believe this whole thing can be handled quickly through the court system," he said, trying to sound upbeat. "Companies like Brigham-Neal know how to deal with these bogus claims and get them kicked out of court."

"Is that all?"

"I guess so."

Jerry took off his sunglasses and turned toward him. A deep two-inch scar creased the man's left cheek.

"For us to take care of the problem it's going to cost $250,000," he said.

They sat in silence for several moments as Emerson tried to absorb what he'd just heard.

"I don't have that kind of money," he managed, his voice trembling.

"Then get busy finding a way to get it. In the meantime, I have a few things for you to do."

TWENTY-SEVEN

KATELYN SLEPT LATE. SHE AND ROBBIE HAD ARRIVED back in Wilmington after midnight. She'd collapsed into bed while he stayed up to unload both her car and his truck. Then he was up early to interview candidates for jobs during the upcoming summer camp sessions. She heard him slip out of bed and mumbled good-bye before falling back to sleep. When she finally got out of bed, she could hear Zeke cleaning the dishes from breakfast. After getting dressed, Katelyn went into the kitchen. She added water to the teapot and set it on the stove to heat. While she waited, she checked on Carter. A book in his hand, her father-in-law was sitting in a chair a few feet from Zeke, who was also reading.

"Good morning," Katelyn said. "Is this a book club?"

"I'm reading a book about naval warfare during World War Two," Carter responded.

"And I'm studying about coastal plants," Zeke said.

"You could write that book," Katelyn replied to Zeke.

"I'm always picking up a bit of helpful information."

"Did you know there was significant submarine activity off the North Carolina coast?" Carter asked.

"No. World War Two history isn't one of my strongest categories in trivia games," Katelyn replied with a smile.

"Carter is staging a strong comeback," Zeke said. "There's been a lot of improvement while you and Robbie were gone."

"That's true," Carter confirmed with a nod.

"Wonderful. Dr. Spies needs to know."

Katelyn finished her tea and nibbled a piece of dry toast. Her appetite had been fluctuating dramatically. Sometimes she was hungry all day. Other days she had to force herself to eat. After she finished, she checked the spare bedroom where Robbie had stacked the boxes they'd brought from the townhome. He'd carefully separated her things from his. She began sorting through her belongings. It was close to noon when she finished and drove to the office. David was out at lunch. Candy greeted her with a smile.

"How was your trip?" the receptionist asked.

"Fine. It's good to be back."

The phone buzzed. Candy answered and put the call on hold.

"It's for you. A woman named Suzanne Nixon. I know you just walked through the door. Do you want me to send it to voice mail?"

"No, I'll take it," Katelyn replied quickly.

Katelyn went into her office as Candy transferred the call.

"Good afternoon," Suzanne said. "I saw that your firm filed suit against Brigham-Neal Pharmaceutical, although your name wasn't on the complaint."

"What?" Katelyn's eyes widened in shock.

"It came across in a conflict-of-interest notice from the New York office. There is a niche group there that dabbles in biotech litigation. Brigham-Neal is usually represented by Crowell and Moring, but like a lot of big companies, it occasionally hires other law firms, most likely to compare litigation processes."

Katelyn's mind was spinning. "Is Morgan and Monroe going to take the case?"

"What do you think? I advised you about potential expert witnesses to hire for your client. Do you believe that would disqualify us from representing the drug company under ethics rule 1.7?"

For a split second, Katelyn felt like a first-year associate summoned into a senior partner's office and asked the type of question that might appear on a law school exam.

"I'm not sure I should answer that question," she replied.

"Correct, but I can assure you that it's hypothetical."

Katelyn thought for a moment. "Our discussion took place before Brigham Neal contacted Morgan and Monroe. The potential client could waive any potential conflict if it chose to do so upon notification of the nature of your communication with me."

"Quick on your feet and technically right as always." Suzanne chuckled. "We turned it down without trying to jump through the necessary hoops."

"I'm sorry if I cost the firm business," Katelyn said.

"Don't be. It was easier to pass on the case than go through the process of obtaining a waiver of conflict from the company. Also, the New York group is more interested in merger and acquisition disputes."

"Okay."

"But I'm curious. How would you have felt litigating against us so soon after leaving the firm?"

It was Katelyn's turn to chuckle. "With the right law and facts, I think I would enjoy it."

"It would be interesting. Did one of the experts I recommended work out for you?"

"They were helpful," Katelyn replied evasively.

"Good. Take care and stay in touch."

"Yes, and if there's a case I can help you with, please keep me in mind."

"I will," Suzanne replied. "I certainly will."

A few minutes later, David came into her office and she told him about the conversation with her former boss. His eyes widened when she mentioned the possibility that Morgan and Monroe could have ended up on the other side in Zeke's case.

"If Morgan and Monroe had taken the case, do you believe you could have talked to them about an early settlement?" he asked.

"No. Whether it's Crowell and Moring, King and Spalding, or Morgan and Monroe, settlement won't be discussed with the other side until considerable discovery is complete and the plaintiff survives a motion for summary judgment."

The phone on Katelyn's desk buzzed.

"Is David in there?" Candy asked.

"Yes."

"Tell him Dr. Emerson Chappelle is on the phone. He says it's urgent."

"We'll take it in here," David called out.

"Are you sure?" Katelyn asked.

"If you're okay with it."

Katelyn nodded.

David stood beside Katelyn's desk as Candy transferred the call. He wanted Katelyn present in case he needed her advice.

"This is David Cobb," he said.

"Emerson Chappelle. I'd like to set up a meeting with you and Zeke Caldwell."

"What sort of meeting?"

"To discuss the lawsuit before the attorneys for Brigham-Neal prohibit me from having any contact with you directly."

"What is there to discuss?"

"The case! And we need to do it now! I'll come to Wilmington."

"We can meet here at our law office."

"No, what about the PinPoint on Market Street?"

The PinPoint was a fancy restaurant near the river. David had taken Nan there on a recent wedding anniversary.

"When?"

"This Saturday evening at six thirty. And bring Ms. Martin-Cobb too. I want her there as well."

"Why?" David asked, giving Katelyn a questioning look.

"Just do it. Believe me. It's important."

The call ended.

"Chappelle sounded even more agitated than the first time we talked," David said. "We know he's scared that what he did is going to be exposed, even with the power of the drug company and their lawyers fighting on his behalf. What do you think he has in mind?"

"I don't know, but I recommend you do a lot more talking than listening. And don't let Zeke say anything at all."

"Are you willing to go? For some reason he wants you there."

"Do you want me there?"

"Of course."

Katelyn hesitated. "Let me think about it."

"The appetizers are the best in town."

"No." She shook her head. "That's not going to be what makes up my mind."

Late Saturday afternoon, Katelyn put on one of her courtroom outfits, a black skirt with a white top. She ran her fingers down the front
of the skirt. Robbie was fixing a sandwich for supper before joining
his father in the sunroom.

"Whoa," Robbie said when he saw her. "You look dangerous."

"I am dangerous. You know that more than anyone."

"I've never faced you in the courtroom. The mere thought of it
makes me lose my appetite for ham and Swiss on rye."

"I doubt that. Has your dad already eaten?"

"Yes, all he wanted was yogurt. He said Zeke fixed a big lunch."

"Do you really think I'm overdressed?" she asked. "I have time
to change."

"Go with your first impression. You've met this Chappelle guy
once. Seeing you like this will send the message that you're taking
the battle to another level."

Katelyn paused. "And you still agree I should be there with
David and Zeke?"

"Yes." Robbie nodded. "They both need you."

"My job is to be a verbal bodyguard. I'll sit close enough to
David to kick him under the table if he starts down a wrong path.
How will he respond to that?"

"Better coming from you than me. Work out the details beforehand. One kick is a warning; two kicks is stop immediately; three
kicks is we just crashed and burned."

Katelyn laughed.

"Come into the sunroom so Dad can see you before you leave,"
Robbie said.

Entering the peaceful setting, Katelyn was again tempted to
cancel with David and stay home to enjoy the calm. Carter looked
up when she appeared.

"Let me pinch myself to make sure I'm alive," he said. "You look ready to attend a funeral."

"It's that bad?" Katelyn asked.

"He means it's somber and serious, appropriate for the gravity of the meeting," Robbie said. "And you make black a vivid color."

Carter smiled. "Good job, son."

Robbie sat down next to his father and took a bite of sandwich.

"Where are you going?" Carter asked.

"The PinPoint Restaurant to meet the chemist who pirated Zeke's antinausea remedy," she replied.

"That's a man who needs to repent," Carter said, shaking his head. "I'd love to see Zeke blessed financially for all the hard work he's put in to help people."

Katelyn leaned over and gave Robbie a quick kiss on the lips.

"See you when we're finished," she said.

"What time should I call the police if you don't show up?" he asked.

"Eight forty-five."

"Can I have a bite of that sandwich?" Carter asked Robbie. "Watching you eat makes me hungry."

Robbie was cutting off a piece of the sandwich as Katelyn left.

It was a ten-minute drive to the restaurant followed by a short walk. Katelyn hadn't been in high heels for a while. She reached the restaurant and went inside. It took a few seconds to spot David and Zeke at the back corner. No one else was with them. David was wearing a coat and tie, and Zeke had on a white shirt and black pants. He smiled at Katelyn when she approached.

"If Dr. Chappelle doesn't show up, we can look for a church service to attend," he said. "It would be a shame not to show off these fancy clothes."

A few moments later, Katelyn saw Emerson Chappelle enter and look around.

"There he is," she said.

The chemist looked like he'd come straight from the beach. He was wearing a T-shirt, shorts, and sunglasses with a white cap pulled down low. He removed his glasses, and his eyes met Katelyn's. He made his way to them.

"Sorry I'm late," he said.

Katelyn introduced everyone, and they shook hands. The chemist didn't look Zeke in the face. Meetings with the opposing party in a lawsuit were often cordial, at least in the beginning.

"Have we met before?" Zeke asked.

"No," Chappelle replied.

"I meet a lot of people, but your face looks familiar. Have you ever been to Hester's Pharmacy or stopped by my booth?" Zeke persisted.

"I rarely come to Wilmington," Chappelle answered.

The waiter came over to the table. "Is everyone here now?" he asked.

"Yes," David replied.

"What would you like to drink besides water? And perhaps an appetizer?"

"Nothing except water for me," Chappelle said. "And I'm not eating."

"I'll take something," Zeke said. "I haven't been here before. Do you have sweet tea?"

"Yes, sir."

"And tell me about this butter bean hummus. I've eaten enough butter beans to fill this room, but I've never heard of that before."

Katelyn listened as Zeke talked with the waiter. The herbalist claimed butter beans offered cardiac benefits.

"Wouldn't you agree, Dr. Chappelle?" Zeke turned to the chemist. "There's a lot that God has hidden in nature just waiting for us to discover. Beans are powerhouse plants."

"No comment," Chappelle replied, shifting in his chair.

By the time the waiter left, they'd ordered the hummus along with pimento cheese on toast and blue-crab fritters.

"I know where we met!" Zeke exclaimed. "You stopped by when I was set up at the craft fair near Washington Avenue and bought me out of my new remedy that treats both nausea and headaches."

"Mr. Caldwell, it must have been someone who looks like me. Can we discuss why we're here?"

"Sure, go ahead." Zeke shrugged.

Chappelle turned to David and Katelyn. "Did one of you assist Mr. Caldwell with his patent application?"

"My father did," David answered.

"Do you realize the significance of the extra carbon chain on the end of the trioxide in my patent for Relacan? And if the trioxide is combined incorrectly, the result can cause differentiation syndrome."

"None of that was mentioned in the letter we received from Russell Detar, the in-house lawyer for the drug company," David replied.

"Because he's a lawyer, not a chemist."

"What is differentiation syndrome?" Katelyn asked.

"A situation in which an arsenic trioxide affects the blood cells and can be fatal. There's nothing in your client's patent that would prevent that from happening."

"Nobody has ever gotten sick from my remedies," Zeke protested. "They make people better!"

The waiter arrived with the appetizers and placed them in the middle of the table. Nobody moved to touch them.

Chappelle continued. "My point is that the differences between the percentages of the compounds in the two patents are critical. When Ms. Martin-Cobb came to Raleigh requesting my assistance, it was clear that you didn't really know what you were dealing with. And from what I read in the complaint you filed in court, you still don't know the answers to the most important questions. This is just one of them. I'm not going to tell you the rest, but when you find out, you're not going to like the answers. I'm here to try to help you avoid a tremendous waste of time and money. If you're smart, you'll dismiss the lawsuit."

"That's not going to happen," David replied tersely.

"Hear me out," Chappelle said. "I believe Mr. Caldwell is sincerely trying to help people, and I'm willing to make a contribution to his efforts in return for a conclusion to the litigation."

"A contribution?" David asked. "How much?"

"Twenty-five thousand dollars. But only if you file a dismissal of the lawsuit within the next seven days."

"That's a—" Zeke started.

"We'll get back to you," David cut in. "After we discuss your offer among ourselves."

Katelyn sensed the meeting was about to end and decided to squeeze what she could out of it.

"One more thing," Katelyn said. "How much have you received so far in royalty payments for Relacan under the license to Brigham-Neal? We need to know in order to properly evaluate your proposal."

"New medications take a while to gain market share. Medical providers have to be educated and gain a level of trust to prescribe them for their patients."

"Has it been more than twenty-five thousand dollars? We'll be able to find out through the discovery process in the litigation, so you may as well tell us now."

Chappelle stood.

Katelyn continued. "And if you want to try to settle this case, it's going to cost a lot more to do so."

Chappelle hesitated. "How much?" he asked.

Katelyn turned to Zeke. "Would you accept a million dollars if that's what David and I recommend?" she asked.

"Yep." Zeke nodded.

"That's our number," Katelyn said.

The chemist's face was ashen. "Seven days. Then my offer is withdrawn."

TWENTY-EIGHT

ONCE HE WAS ON THE SIDEWALK IN FRONT OF THE restaurant, Emerson stopped to take a few deep breaths. He unclipped the microphone that had been hidden on the front pocket of his shorts. His phone vibrated. It was from an unknown caller. He took it out and answered.

"Walk to the river. I'll be on the boardwalk."

The voice sounded familiar, but Emerson wasn't sure who it was. He made his way down Market Street and stopped. Sitting on a bench with a view of the USS *North Carolina*, a World War II battleship anchored across the river, was a man he'd not seen in over a year. Emerson approached tentatively. Tinted glasses partially shielded Lance's eyes. He was wearing gray exercise pants, and his well-developed biceps bulged from a short-sleeved golf shirt.

"Hey, Lance," Emerson said.

"Good to see you. Have a seat."

Emerson positioned himself as far away from Lance on the bench as he could.

"This evening was a success," Lance said. "I heard every word."

"A success how? They didn't agree to anything."

"It wasn't about that. Having them in the same location gave our people an opportunity to install what we need to keep track of them and know what they're saying to one another."

Emerson didn't want to know any more details.

"And what was this about a meeting with you in Raleigh?" Lance asked. "You didn't tell me or Jerry about that."

"I guess it slipped my mind."

"No, you're too smart to let something important slip your mind. And it's a good thing I already knew about Ms. Martin-Cobb and Annalisa Brighton, your former student, coming to see you. What else have you forgotten to tell me?"

"Uh, nothing. How did you know about that meeting?"

Lance looked directly into Emerson's eyes. "Doc, we've been keeping tabs on you for a while, and it would be good for you to remember that."

Emerson swallowed.

"Did you recently buy a new product from Caldwell?" Lance asked. "The one designed to treat nausea and headaches? That was interesting too."

"Yes."

"Have you taken it to the lab and figured out what's in it?"

Emerson sighed. "It's Relacan plus an additional component derived from marsh grass."

"Are you going to file a patent application?"

"Not if it causes me as much trouble as this one has."

Lance turned sideways on the bench so that he faced Emerson. "You stole Caldwell's formula, didn't you?"

"No!" Emerson shot back. "This is a totally bogus claim!"

Lance shrugged. "You're lying, but I don't care. Just remember to be smarter in how you go about it with the new drug you're working on."

Emerson didn't trust himself to speak. Lance tapped the back of the bench with the fingers on his right hand.

"One last thing," Lance said. "Why didn't you let me know that you were going to try to settle the case? Don't you think that's important?"

"Yes."

"And you saw how effective you were. The woman attorney saw through your weakness."

"I just want this to be over."

Lance leaned closer to Emerson. "Given what you've done, that's understandable. Don't worry. It's going to be over soon, with or without your cooperation."

―――――――

Zeke picked up a crab fritter and dipped it into an orange-colored sauce. He popped it in his mouth and began to chew.

"This is tasty," he said. "I'll pass on my share of the butter bean hummus if I can have more of these fritters."

"I don't understand how you can focus on food," David said.

Zeke swallowed before he spoke. "Well, I'm not going to focus on the $25,000 tip that guy threw on the table to try to convince us to go away. He knows what he did was wrong, and he wasn't willing to answer Katelyn's question about how much he's already been paid by the drug company. That tells me he's pocketed a lot more than that."

"Were you okay with the way I sprang our counteroffer on you?" Katelyn asked. "Normally, we would have had a long discussion about that sort of thing, but I wanted to communicate with Chappelle while we could."

"Perfectly okay," Zeke replied. "I'm not greedy."

David picked up the pimento cheese toast and took a small bite. He couldn't shake his belief that the case was supposed to settle and wished Katelyn had proposed a lesser amount. But he didn't want to criticize her in front of Zeke.

"Something is better than nothing," he said.

"Twenty-five thousand dollars?" Zeke asked. "Are you serious?"

"No," David sighed. "I don't think you should accept Dr. Chappelle's offer."

When he spoke the words, David felt a burden lift off his shoulders. It was the right decision.

"That's what my gut tells me," Zeke said as he patted his ample stomach. "And that pimento cheese toast agrees."

"Chappelle may call us back and increase his offer," Katelyn said. "Then we'll discuss it."

"I like the sound of a million dollars," Zeke replied. "I'd rather stick to that amount."

David's heart sank. He paid for dinner. They said good-bye to Zeke on the sidewalk outside the restaurant.

"Thanks for the meal," Zeke said.

"You've done so much for my father that this is the least I can do to show my appreciation," David replied.

"Where are you parked?" David asked Katelyn.

"Around the corner and down the street a block or so."

"I'll walk you to your car."

They passed a bar with the doors open and loud music blaring from a live band.

"What did you think about the trioxide argument?" David asked.

"Until we can talk to someone who knows the difference between rat poison and a miracle drug, we won't have an answer. I think we should run it by Annalisa."

"Yeah."

"Would you like me to do that? I'd be glad to."

"Thanks." David ran his fingers through his hair. "How did you come up with the million-dollar figure?"

"Not through legal analysis. We don't have the data for that. But my best guess is that Chappelle stands to make millions in license fees and desperately wants to be left alone to do so. And there's the possibility he would have to indemnify Brigham-Neal for the litigation. That would be way more than what I proposed."

"Okay," David agreed. "I guess a million dollars makes sense."

"But do I think he'll pay it?" Katelyn asked. "Never, no way."

When Katelyn arrived home, Robbie was sitting alone in the sunroom with only a small lamp for light.

"Where's your dad?" she asked.

"Asleep. How was the meeting?"

"Not much happened."

"Can you provide any details?"

"Zeke really liked the crab fritter appetizer."

"I could have predicted that," Robbie said with a smile.

"And the chemist made a lowball offer out of his own pocket to settle that Zeke didn't want to accept. I suggested a more reasonable amount with no response. David was discouraged."

Katelyn saw a flash of light at the rear of the yard.

Pointing, she asked, "Did you see that? I saw a light over there."

Robbie sat up in his chair and peered out. "No."

"Let's go inside," Katelyn said.

The following Monday morning, Katelyn didn't feel well and delayed going into the office until almost eleven o'clock. When Candy saw her, the receptionist's face lit up.

"I did it!" Candy announced. "I took the test and completed an online certification for the new software."

"I didn't know they offered any certification."

"Yes, and the test wasn't a pushover. I've been studying for the past three days and took two practice tests before I logged on for the real one. I scored over ninety-five percent."

"That's good."

Candy lowered her voice. "And I think it justifies asking David for a raise. I know there's a ceiling for what I can earn as a receptionist, but when you add online bookkeeping skills it totally changes my job description. I'm not trying to be greedy, but I know what Meredith makes."

"She's been with the firm a long time."

"And he should take that into consideration. But I researched the salary range for what I can do and came up with a number on the low end of the scale. The increase would be around twenty percent, which isn't that much when you look at what I'm making now."

Candy told Katelyn the dollar amount she had in mind. It was still a lot less than what even the lowest-paid staff members earned at Morgan and Monroe. But Katelyn was concerned because she'd been the one to encourage Candy to enhance her skills. Also, an increase for Candy would have to be handled delicately with Meredith. There were no secrets at Cobb and Cobb.

"You have to be careful about the timing for this sort of thing," she said.

"This is the perfect time. David and his father always do a midyear performance and salary review. This is when we get a raise."

"I didn't know that. Let me bring it up with David first."

"Thanks, that would be great."

Katelyn was logging on to the computer when David entered.

"Had a rough morning?" he asked.

"I'm better now."

Katelyn entered her password and faced David as he sat down.

"What did Zeke have to say this morning?" he asked.

"Nothing, except he enjoyed telling your dad about the appetizers. We've avoided talking about the details of the case in front of him."

"Okay."

Katelyn's computer finished booting up. "Did you know Candy passed some sort of certification for the new financial software we're using?" she asked.

"Meredith asked if she should approve the charge for the testing, and I gave the okay. With increased capability, Candy will need to earn more money. Meredith ran some numbers and believes that Candy can organize financial data so as to justify a fifteen to twenty percent raise and generate a little bit of revenue for the firm. We've not been effectively billing that sort of paralegal-type activity up till now, so it makes sense."

"Good," Katelyn replied with relief.

"Did Candy ask you to lobby for her?"

"No, I volunteered because I was the one who encouraged her to do it."

David shifted in the chair. "Do you have time to call Annalisa?"

"Sure. Let's hope she has time to talk."

Katelyn placed the call on speaker and quickly explained the question.

"You talked to Dr. Chappelle?" Annalisa asked. "That's surprising."

"Yes, he requested the meeting."

"The presence of an extra carbon chain and its impact on the overall compound isn't something I could answer without researching it. There can be vestigial components to carbon chains. How soon do you need an answer?"

Katelyn looked at David.

"Within a week or so," he said. "For now, our focus is on Dr. Sparrow's comparative study. Once we have the results in hand, that's what I'm going to emphasize because it will be facts, not theory."

"Carbon chains are facts too," Annalisa said. "The right person can read them like a book. I'll see what I can find out."

"I have a present for Adeline," Katelyn said. "When would be a good time to come by and give it to you?"

"That's roulette. My mother-in-law is here for two more days, so before she leaves would be best."

Instead of going to lunch, David decided to fast and pray. He drove to a wildlife refuge where the Cape Fear River emptied into the Atlantic. On weekends the location was always crowded with fishermen who targeted freshwater species when the tide was going out and saltwater fish when the tide flowed in. Benches provided a panoramic view of the mouth of the river.

David found a deserted spot. It was cooler than normal, and an ocean breeze acted as a natural air conditioner. He stared across the expanse of water and silently petitioned heaven for help on earth: he asked for divine favor on Dr. Sparrow's testing protocol; the right words to speak to Zeke, Katelyn, and Emerson Chappelle; and that the claim would settle quickly for the right amount. His prayer was sincere. His confidence in an answer shallow. Then a different thought drifted into his consciousness on a soft breeze. He needed to pray for Emerson Chappelle.

David hesitated. The chemist had wrongfully licensed a drug patent to Brigham-Neal. But more pawn than powerful player, he would take a back row to the big-time experts hired by the drug company. Praying for enemies was an undebatable command from the mouth of Jesus himself. Regardless of what he'd done, Chappelle was a man in need, a man afraid. And anyone who would steal or defraud Zeke Caldwell was in very serious trouble when he eventually appeared in the courts of heaven, a day with much more serious consequences than any judgment handed down by a federal judge or jury.

David's thoughts spun in circles for a few moments until a direction in prayer came into focus. He asked God to forgive Chappelle for what he'd done to Zeke and set the chemist free from the sin that bound him. When he stood up from the bench, David was no longer burdened by his efforts to make something happen through the force of his will.

Turning around, he saw a black truck with deeply tinted windows parked across the roadway. Guessing whoever was in the truck wanted to claim the fishing spot, David raised his hand to signal that he was leaving. There was no response from anyone inside. At that moment a park ranger in a green truck pulled off the road. The black truck left. The ranger got out and came over to David.

"I was going to check your fishing license," the ranger said, glancing around. "But I don't see a rod and reel."

David took out his wallet. "I've not been fishing, but here's my license. It's current."

"Put it away," the ranger replied. "And have a good day."

Driving back to the office, David called Zeke and told him what he'd prayed.

"You're right," Zeke responded. "I need to do the same thing.

Unforgiveness binds our hearts to evil. Life is hard enough. I don't want to drag a heavy weight along behind me."

———

Late that afternoon, Katelyn was watching Zeke and Carter play checkers in the den. The two men had asked her to create a spreadsheet to keep up with their competition. Zeke had a commanding lead, but Carter was beginning to win a few more games.

"If I get one more king, you're going to be in real trouble," Carter said.

"Maybe, but even if you do, I think I can run from you until it's time for me to go home."

Katelyn went into the bedroom to rest until Robbie came home. She closed her eyes for several minutes but couldn't take a nap. When she rolled onto her side, she saw Robbie's journal on the nightstand. Scooting over, she took another look at the pages where he'd sketched his vision for their new house. Flipping forward, she stopped at a drawing he made after the recent dinner when Carter prayed for every member of the family. Robbie had re-created the entire scene. Katelyn chuckled at his portrayal of David. He'd added at least twenty pounds to his brother. The sketch of Katelyn's face was very good, but Robbie had completely forgotten what she was wearing. Beneath the sketch he'd written:

> I had trouble keeping it together when Dad prayed for us around the table, especially when he reached Katelyn. My heart ached for her but in a good way.

"What do you think?" Robbie asked from the doorway.

Katelyn glanced up, then read the prayer again. "Why did your heart ache for me in a good way? What does that mean?"

Robbie approached the bed, and Katelyn handed him the book.

"First, I need to show you something else," he said.

He found the entry where he'd drawn the picture of his childhood camping trip with Carter and David. In the upper right-hand corner was a small, bright red smudge.

"When I saw this, it made me laugh."

"Oops," she said. "I'm sorry I messed up your picture. It was right after I found out about the job offer in Chicago and had painted my nails."

"You didn't mess it up. You put yourself in the scene, which gets back to what I wrote the other night." Robbie took her hand in his. "I so want us to share every part of life with each other that it almost hurts."

Katelyn's heart started to beat faster.

"Including what God is doing in me," he continued. "I'd never try to pressure you against your will—"

"No, I want that too," Katelyn said. "I really do."

"Are you sure? This is not just believing in what I'm experiencing."

"I know. Every time I've read one of the prayers in your journal, it's been growing. Just as our baby is growing, something else new and fresh is stirring in me. It will be months before we meet our child. I don't want to wait on this."

Robbie's eyes shone.

"You've always loved me," Katelyn continued. "But it's getting deeper in a way I didn't imagine possible. I realize that your faith is the reason."

"Yeah," Robbie agreed with a gentle smile. "It's surprised me."

Katelyn took Robbie's left hand in hers and placed her fingers on his wedding ring.

"Just like you said, I want us to be united in everything that's important. Find the page where you prayed for me to know God's love and drew the sketch of the park bench."

Katelyn released his hands so Robbie could turn to the page.

"Lay it open on the bedspread," she said. "Will you pray now what you wrote then?"

Robbie took a deep breath. "'Lord, thank you for hearing and answering my prayer. What I've been feeling and experiencing is so real, I can't deny it. Even if I wanted to. Which I don't. Sitting on the park bench today during my lunch hour was amazing. And then during the drive home thinking about my love. Will you talk to her? Not sure that's how it works. Anyway, I place her in your hands. If you only answer one prayer, let this be the one. You love her even more than I do.'"

As Robbie read and Katelyn heard him describe her as "my love," joy welled up inside her. With her heart touched and her spirit called to life, she placed herself in God's hands.

"Yes, yes, yes," she said.

TWENTY-NINE

ALCOHOL HAD NEVER BEEN EMERSON'S WEAKNESS.
He preferred the natural rush of a big wager to the numbing effects of
whiskey. But numbness was what he craved. The previous night, he'd
passed out on the couch only to wake up and drink some more. Now
he stared at the empty bottle. Beside it was an unopened one. Thoughts
of ending his life had increased. To be free from torment would be
bliss. He owned a gun but had never fired it. Currently, it was in the
sock drawer of the dresser. Leaving the living room, he retrieved it and
removed the bullets. He held one in his hand. It was heavier than he
expected. Emerson reviewed the notes and numbers he'd scribbled on
the back of an envelope, picked up his cell phone, and placed the call.

"Jerry, this is Emerson Chappelle. If I take care of the lawsuit
myself, how much will I owe you?"

"What's your plan? Are you going to pay them a million dollars?"

"No. I'm still working out the details."

Jerry was silent for a moment. "One hundred thousand dollars."

"How long do I have?"

"No later than Saturday."

It was three days away.

"How would I pay you the money?"

"Bitcoins. But we don't accept payment without our friend's approval. Is that clear?"

"Yes."

"And in the meantime, we're not going to sit around. That's not an option if the right opportunity arises to take care of this situation."

"Give me a chance."

"No promises."

Emerson returned the phone to the coffee table. He couldn't give up. There were several numbers written on the envelope he'd received from the bank approving a line of credit secured by the beach house. He'd also written down the amount of his retirement funds rolled into a new brokerage account after paying his ex-wife the percentage awarded in the divorce decree. And he had recent gambling winnings in his regular bank account. To settle the lawsuit and get rid of Jerry would take more than he had. But if he pooled most of his resources, a successful bet at 3-to-1 odds would take care of his problems without wiping him out. Pushing aside the gun and ignoring the bottle of whiskey, he phoned Nick.

"What do you have on a twenty-four-hour turnaround at three to one?" Emerson asked.

"Why the rush? My best stuff isn't until the weekend."

"I'm feeling lucky."

"How much are you wanting to put down?"

Emerson hesitated. He took a deep breath. This would be the largest bet of his life.

"Four hundred thousand."

"For that amount, I can make something happen."

"I'll need you to advance part of it until I can cash out my retirement funds."

"No problem. Your credit is good with us."

The following morning, David was meeting with Dr. Sparrow about the drug study.

"It's amazing how quickly a college student will agree to do something in return for $100," David said. "We have twice the number of volunteers we need."

"Unless you want to make the sample larger," the doctor replied. "That always increases the credibility of the overall test."

"No," David said and shook his head. "If the results are good, we can always schedule another round to bolster the findings."

"True." Dr. Sparrow handed David a sheet of paper. "Here are the ones I selected. It's an equal number of men and women."

David glanced over the list. "Set it up for next week. I'll have my bookkeeper send over a check to cover the costs."

At the office, David gave Meredith instructions about issuing the check.

"Let's hope this works," she said. "I told one of my nephews at the college about it, and he signed up. He was going to get a bunch of his friends to do it too."

"I saw a student with your last name on the list."

"Is this safe?" she asked. "Kids never consider risks."

"Yeah. Zeke's remedies are all-natural, and Relacan has been approved by the FDA."

"Okay. His fraternity is doing it as a fund-raiser for a nonprofit organization fighting childhood leukemia."

"Let me know the name of the group, and I'll contribute as well."

David put aside the Caldwell case and spent the rest of the afternoon on other business. Late in the day, he took a break and checked the weather report for the weekend. He called Robbie.

"Looks like Saturday would be a good day to take Andy and Dad fishing," he said. "What do you think?"

"I was checking the forecast earlier, and there's a twenty percent chance of rain."

"Which is true almost every day."

"Yeah, I'd be willing to take the chance, and I think Zeke would like to go."

"Of course, and Andy wanted to make sure I invited Katelyn to join us."

"Ask her yourself. Isn't she at the office?"

"No, she's meeting with a new client at his place of business and then going straight home."

"I'll check with her this evening."

"Is anything else going on with the piece of property owned by the guy who's on the board of directors for the camp?"

"I've been out there several times, and I'm ready to pull an RV onto the site to live in while we build a house."

"I want to see it sometime."

"I'd like that." Robbie waited to continue. "Has Katelyn told you what's been going on with her personally?"

"No, we've gone our separate ways all day. Is there a problem?"

"It's good news."

Later that evening at home, David announced to an excited Andy the possibility of a fishing trip with Robbie and his Pops.

"I'm going to make sure my fly line is clean," Andy said as he headed up to his room.

David then told Nan about the rest of his conversation with Robbie.

"I'd like to see the property," she said. "I hadn't considered the possibility of them living out in the country."

"It's halfway between town and the camp, across the marsh from the fancy development at East End Country Club."

"Would you like to sell this place and build a house out there?"

"No, and don't give up hope for your new kitchen and master bath. Oh, and Robbie mentioned that Katelyn has some positive personal news to share but didn't want to tell me himself."

"Good news is always better than bad news."

Katelyn prepared a fruit-and-yogurt smoothie for supper. Zeke had left for the day, and Carter was taking a nap. Evening naps were becoming increasingly common. Her father-in-law would eat an early supper, then sleep from 5:00 p.m. to 7:00 p.m. and stay awake until 11:00 p.m. Katelyn turned on the ceiling fan in the sunroom and curled her feet beneath her as she sat on the wicker couch. Charlie joined her.

On her phone were the images from the ultrasound performed earlier in the day at the office of her obstetrician. As the technician prepped her for the test, Katelyn wondered if the excited thumping of her own heart would drown out the sound of the heartbeat of the tiny child growing inside her. Any hint of fear was banished when the tech told Katelyn and Robbie that everything was normal.

"I think he's way beyond normal," Robbie replied.

"Yes, she is," the tech responded. "We've caught her when she's wide awake and ready to play. Wait a second. Where were you hiding?"

"Who?" Katelyn and Robbie asked at the same time.

"Brother or sister," the tech replied, her eyes wide. "Looks like you're carrying twins."

At that moment, Katelyn saw a shape shoot across the screen. She couldn't make any distinction.

"Are you sure?" she asked.

"I've been counting to two for a long time," the tech answered as she continued to move the wand.

Katelyn looked up at Robbie, who was staring in shock at the screen.

"What do you think?" she asked.

Before he answered, the tech spoke.

"There they go," she said, moving her wand across Katelyn's abdomen. "They're racing from one side of the uterus to the other."

"I see them!" Robbie exclaimed. "Who won? If one of them is a sprinter, he might be able to get a track scholarship that will pay for college."

Katelyn smiled, but her emotions welled up so strongly that she didn't trust herself to speak. Robbie reached over and squeezed her hand.

"You always do everything better than anyone else," he said. "Most women have one baby at a time. You're so talented that you're going to have two."

Katelyn returned her gaze to the screen.

"There they are," the tech said. "That's the best image of both of them."

Sure enough, there were two tiny human beings living inside her. Love for them filled her heart.

"They're cute, aren't they?" Robbie asked in amazement.

"And appear perfectly normal," the tech replied.

Since leaving the appointment, she'd lost track of the number of times she'd scrolled through the black-and-white images. Her favorite was the first image in which she clearly saw that there were two babies. Absorbing the magnitude of that reality was going to take a while. In another image, she could clearly see one baby's tiny nose. She touched her own nose and thought about how soon after conception it appeared on her face. Taking another drink of her smoothie, Katelyn laid her hand on her stomach and prayed a simple prayer that God would bless not just her child, but her children. For several minutes, she sat peacefully in the quiet stillness. She realized that would soon be a rare commodity.

Going into their bedroom, she picked up the leather-bound book from the nightstand and returned to the sunroom. Once again, she was drawn to Robbie's rendering of the house on the marsh. Now the house seemed a bit small.

Early Saturday morning, Emerson stared at the results of the bet he'd discussed with Nick. To win at 3–1 odds didn't require picking the exact score of a game or correctly predicting which four teams would cover the point spread differential. It was a much simpler formula. All he had to do was pick the winner in four specific baseball games. The ones to include were at his discretion, so he could bet on heavy favorites playing against significant underdogs. After several hours of study, he'd identified the games to include. He'd been right about three out of four. But in the fourth game, the underdog team mounted an incredible rally in the bottom of the ninth inning and came back from five runs down to win. Emerson would have lost everything if he'd placed the bet. But he hadn't.

At the last minute, he'd sent Nick a text and told him he was going to pass on the wager. It was an uncharacteristic move. Once Emerson's adrenaline kicked in, he always rode it to a spectacular high or a catastrophic low. To bail on a bet wasn't in his thrill-seeking DNA. Avoiding the loss was a relief, but it didn't solve the problems he faced.

Sober for the past forty-eight hours, Emerson wasn't in the mood to start a fresh binge. He'd finished the paperwork giving him immediate access to his retirement funds, and all it would take to trigger the transfer of money from the home equity line was a request via his banking app. The time had come to end his torment, not his own life. He picked up his cell phone.

"Is Katelyn going to join you?" Nan asked as David and Andy ate an early morning breakfast of eggs and sausage.

"Robbie sent a text late last night that she was on board."

"Maybe she'll fish this time," Andy said. "I think it would be neat if she catches a fish. If she does, she'll be hooked."

Andy smiled and waited. David realized his son wanted acknowledgment of his play on words.

"That's the way it works," he said with a smile. "But don't put any pressure on your Pops to fish. He shouldn't be standing up, especially when the boat is moving."

"He's going today to watch you fish, not the other way around," Nan said.

"But I'm going to give it a shot," David said.

"With both Pops and Uncle Robbie with us, we're going to catch some for sure," Andy said.

"And as soon as you're gone, I'm going to catch a few more minutes of sleep," Nan replied with a yawn.

"Thanks for cooking breakfast," David said.

"It was worth getting up to see how excited you are."

David gave Nan a kiss as they walked out of the house.

"Be safe," she said.

"Don't worry," Andy replied. "Most of the time, the water in the marsh isn't over my head, even at high tide."

"Except in the channels," David said. "And that's where we're going to spend most of our time."

The boat and trailer were hooked to Robbie's truck. Inside the house, Robbie, Katelyn, and Zeke were waiting in the kitchen.

"Where's Dad?"

"Taking a shower," Robbie replied.

"Who takes a shower before he goes fishing?" David asked.

"I tried to talk him out of it, but he did it anyway." Zeke shrugged. "If it helps him feel better about the trip, then there's no harm. The only thing is that some claim my bug repellent has a stout smell. I don't think Carter will want the stink on him when he gets home later."

"I want some bug stuff," Andy said. "The bugs were all over us the other day when Noah Voss and I were playing in the creek near his house."

"Let's wait until we're about to launch the boat to smear it on," Robbie said.

His hair still damp, Carter came into the room. He'd put on a pair of brown pants with a light green shirt. He wore dock shoes on his feet.

"Good morning, Pops," Andy said cheerily.

"Hey, my best fishing boy," Carter replied. "Ready?"

"Yes, sir."

David watched his father as they left the house. Walking carefully, he seemed reasonably steady on his feet.

"Do you want to ride with Andy and me?" David asked.

"Yes."

David followed Robbie's truck to the spot near the store where they'd put the boat into the water. His father sat in the backseat with Andy and talked fishing strategy. Andy had brought a box with several different patterns, all tied by his Pops before the brain hemorrhage. They discussed the merits of each one.

"It's hard to believe I could do that," Carter said.

David glanced in the rearview mirror as his father held up a tiny shrimp. David could see the presence of a tremor in his father's hand.

"You're getting better all the time," Andy said.

"Yes, but being able to tie flies in my future may be too much to hope for."

Andy was silent for a moment. "What am I going to do when I run out?"

"I could start teaching you to do it yourself."

They reached the boat launch area.

While they'd been standing in the kitchen waiting for Carter, Katelyn almost pulled out of the trip. She'd not felt well when she woke up, and after a piece of dry toast her stomach was still mounting a protest. But the weather was going to be nice, and she was touched by Andy's insistence that she join them. By the time they reached the primitive boat launch, she was feeling better. The salt air was therapeutic. She took in a deep breath as Robbie came up beside her.

"You could enjoy this air every morning if we buy that piece of property on the marsh," he said.

"I'm thinking about it," she replied. "A lot."

She followed Robbie to the trailer and watched him smoothly put the boat in the water.

"This will be the most people we've ever had on this boat," Robbie said.

"It can easily handle six," Katelyn replied.

"I'm counting eight," Robbie answered with a grin.

"Keep quiet," Katelyn whispered with a glance over her shoulder.

Zeke came over to them and asked, "Who needs bug repellent?"

"Sign me up," Robbie replied, taking the bottle from Zeke.

"I'll pass for now," Katelyn said.

"You won't need any," Robbie said to her. "The smell from the rest of us will create an insect-free zone that surrounds the entire boat."

"This can be like the experiment David is putting together to test my nausea remedy," Zeke said. "Whoever doesn't use the repellent can be the control group."

Katelyn stood to the side while everyone rubbed the bug repellent on their arms and necks.

"All aboard!" Robbie called out.

As they came together, Katelyn caught a whiff that reminded her of road tar on a hot day.

"There's a little bit of a fragrance to it at first," Zeke said to David.

"'Fragrance'?" David raised his eyebrows.

"In fifteen minutes, you won't notice," Zeke replied. "Only the bugs will pick up on it."

"Can you smell it?" Zeke asked Katelyn.

"Yes, and it reminds me of asphalt or road tar."

"That's because there's pure petroleum in it," Zeke said. "But it's clear with all the color taken out of it."

"I like it," Andy said.

It took both David and Robbie to assist Carter onto the boat and position him in a chair in the bow. Katelyn placed her chair beside his.

"Is this spot taken?" she asked.

"Reserved for you," Carter answered.

Andy came up and began talking to his Pops about which fly to start with.

"Wait!" David called out to Robbie. "I left my cell phone in my car."

"I'm about to shove off. You don't need it."

David jumped from the boat to the bank. "Yes, I do. For pictures."

Katelyn had her phone, but she suspected David would want to use his. When he returned, Robbie started the boat's reluctant motor, and they puttered away into a channel. Katelyn glanced over her shoulder as their vehicles slipped out of sight. Through a scrubby clump of bushes, she caught a glimpse of another vehicle, a dark-colored truck pulling a boat into the area they'd just left.

"Looks like someone else is going fishing," Robbie said. "I just saw a truck at the launch area."

"We're ahead of them," Carter replied. "And Zeke and Robbie know where to find the fish."

Zeke was standing next to Robbie in the stern. He pointed to the right, and Robbie turned the boat. Andy and David finished setting up their gear. They sat in the bow with their feet hanging off the edge of the slow-moving boat. If she and Robbie ended up building a house on the marsh, she knew many hours spent drifting through the reeds awaited her. It wasn't a bad prospect.

The sun was creeping up in the sky, but so far there hadn't been any sign of an insect attack. The odor from Zeke's bug repellent wafted over her when the breeze blew in her direction.

"Over there!" Robbie yelled out. "Two of them are tailing!"

The call caused everyone to spring into action. Carter started to try to stand up from the chair. Instinctively, Katelyn reached out to restrain him. He gave her a look of defiance that quickly evaporated. He plopped back into the chair.

"It's hard to keep an old dog away from the hunt," he said. "But you're right. My job today is to stay put and bark encouragement. They don't need to have to stop the boat to pull me out of the water."

Robbie revved the motor and spun the boat to the right, then killed the engine to let it drift.

"Why did he do that?" Katelyn asked Carter. "He could have kept going slow."

"We needed the jolt to get us in position and then go silent as we drift up to the fish and try not to spook them."

Robbie pointed again and spoke in a much softer voice.

"Twenty yards off the bow at two o'clock," he said. "Andy, do you see it?"

Andy turned and gave a thumbs-up. He positioned the fly line in his hand and began the choreographed motion of moving the rod back and forth as he loaded up power. The line looped over his head as he released more and more. Even while being watched by all the men in his life whom he wanted to please, the boy appeared cool and confident. He released the line, which floated forward across the water. Katelyn still hadn't seen the fish.

"Nice," Carter muttered.

"Set!" Robbie barked.

Andy pulled up on the line. It seemed taut but just as quickly went limp.

"Missed him," he said.

"No," Zeke said. "She missed the lure, and now she's going to brag about how lucky she was this morning. Let's move on to another one."

Over the next hour, Andy cast to four more fish without hooking any of them. The cool confidence Katelyn had seen earlier in her nephew was beginning to wear thin. David had his arm around his son, talking to him. The boat motor was off, and Zeke was standing next to Carter. Katelyn heard the familiar ringtone of her brother-in-law's cell. He pulled the phone from his pocket and looked over his shoulder at Katelyn and Zeke.

"It's Emerson Chappelle," he said to them.

THIRTY

PHONE IN HAND, DAVID MADE HIS WAY TO WHERE
Katelyn was sitting.

"Zeke, come closer so you can hear," he said.

"Good morning, Dr. Chappelle," David began. "Your timing is perfect. I'm here with Mr. Caldwell and Ms. Martin-Cobb."

"Can they hear me?" the chemist asked.

"Yes, you're on speaker."

Chappelle was silent for a moment before continuing. "I'm prepared to make a counteroffer to settle the case once and for all. As part of the deal, Mr. Caldwell will transfer his patent to me. There will also be—"

"No." Zeke shook his head. "Why does he want my patent? I paid for that with my inheritance money!"

"What?" Chappelle asked.

"Just a minute," David said, then hit the mute button. "He's concerned that you'll sell it to another pharmaceutical company."

"That's right," Katelyn said.

"Go ahead," David said to Chappelle.

"And agreement to confidentiality of every aspect of the settlement."

A confidentiality clause was a common provision, but by this point everyone on the boat except Andy, who was putting on a new fly, was listening to the conversation.

"I'm taking you off speaker," David said.

"Why? Who else is there?"

"I'm on a fishing boat with my family," David replied. "Maybe we should talk later. This is too complicated to take care of now."

"No!" Chappelle replied, his voice rising in volume. "Listen, I'll pay $400,000 if you agree to all my terms."

David sucked in a quick breath. He again muted the call and told Katelyn and Zeke what the chemist said.

"I'm shocked," Katelyn said, her eyes wide. "That's a hefty proposal. To move from $25,000 to $400,000 is a big jump. Let's counter."

"Okay—$750,000?" David asked.

He looked at Zeke. He could tell the client was struggling.

"It's not the amount of money as much as I feel like I'm letting him get away with something wrong," Zeke said, shaking his head. "And does this mean I can't give my remedy to people who are suffering?"

"I'll get clarification on that," David said. "What about the figure Katelyn mentioned? You'd clear half a million."

"Sure." Zeke nodded.

David closed his eyes for a couple of seconds. "We can settle for $750,000 provided Mr. Caldwell retains the right to sell his remedy directly to his customers."

"He can sell to his customers," Chappelle replied. "But I'm not paying a penny more! I know you lawyers like to play your games, but we don't have time for that. I'm completely tapped out at $400,000. The funds are currently available, but I can't promise they will be in a few days. I'm taking a huge risk on your behalf."

David didn't understand Chappelle's last comment, but it didn't matter. He muted the phone.

"Zeke, I would reduce my fee to twenty-five percent so that you would clear $300,000."

"I've reduced my fee a time or two," Carter said.

"Do you think I should accept his offer?" Zeke asked.

David's mind and heart were in agreement. "I think you should take it."

Katelyn was carefully watching Zeke's face. He turned to her.

"What do you recommend?" he asked her.

"You should settle. The chances of forcing the drug company to pay a big settlement or winning in front of a jury aren't good. That might change down the road, but there's no way to know for sure."

"Carter?"

"Yes, and move forward," Carter said. "Remember when you told me about forgiving this guy? Settling this case is consistent with what you said then."

"Okay," Zeke said with a purposeful nod. "Do it."

David unmuted the phone. "We have a deal," he said.

"I'll get the bank to issue a cashier's check payable to your firm and Mr. Caldwell and deliver it to your firm on Monday."

David was stunned by how fast Chappelle wanted to act.

"Uh, do you want us to draft the settlement documents?" he asked.

"Yes."

Chappelle hung up. David lowered the phone.

"What else did he say?" Katelyn asked.

"He's going to deliver a cashier's check to the law firm on Monday and wants us to draw up the settlement documents."

"He could wire the money," Katelyn said. "That saves steps."

"I know, but I was caught off guard by the timing."

"There's something else going on that we don't know about," Katelyn said thoughtfully.

"I agree," Carter added.

"Are you practicing law?" David asked his father. "You've offered several opinions over the past few minutes."

Carter glanced up from his chair with a grin that was still slightly crooked. "Put me down for a quarter hour for 'advice regarding settlement' and pay me accordingly. But we're fishing and don't have time for any more chitchat about the office."

David returned to his place beside Andy. The momentous news began to sink in. God's direction had been right. The case had settled quickly.

"I'm ready," Andy said. "I'm going to catch one if I keep believing that I can."

By the time the tide started flowing out, Andy had caught two nice fish. David and Zeke brought one each to the boat. Robbie got a fish on the line, then handed the rod to Katelyn, who was standing beside him.

"Want it?" he asked.

"Of course I do," she responded as the rod tip bent sharply toward the water.

Andy let out a whoop. "Don't try to muscle it in, Aunt Kate!" he yelled. "You have to tire him out!"

"I've heard that advice before." Katelyn gritted her teeth as she took a step away from the edge of the boat. "This fish is heavy."

Fifteen minutes passed before the redfish came close enough to the boat that Robbie could capture it by lying on his stomach and reaching out into the water with the long-handled net.

"That's the fish of the day," Carter said when Robbie held up the net.

"Let's see how long it is and weigh it," Andy said excitedly.

Katelyn's arms were limp. She laid the rod on the boat deck and shook them out. Andy helped Robbie measure the fish. It was twenty-four and a half inches long.

"See how fat it is?" Zeke observed. "It's a mature female who's had lots of babies."

"Multiple births," Robbie said with a glance at Katelyn.

"Six pounds, eight ounces!" Andy announced.

"Let's get some photos so I can release this old girl," Robbie said.

Katelyn held the fish with both hands while Zeke took the photos. She posed individually and then with Robbie, David, Andy, and Carter.

"Get in there," Robbie said to Zeke.

"No, I'm not family."

"I insist," Katelyn replied.

After Robbie released the fish, Katelyn reviewed the photos and decided the one with Zeke was her favorite.

"That's what I'm going to post on social media," she said as she showed it to him.

"What are you going to say about me?"

"Nothing about your age or weight."

Zeke grinned. "Thank you."

The bugs were out in force by the time they returned to where they'd put the boat in the water. Once everyone was on dry ground, Robbie attached a cable to the front of the boat so he could winch it out of the water and onto the trailer. Katelyn was standing close to him behind the truck. Everyone else had moved away from the water to break down the fishing gear. Suddenly, there was a loud explosion and a flash of light.

THIRTY-ONE

DAVID AND ANDY WERE SPOOLING UP LINE ON THEIR
reels. Carter was standing on the other side of the car. Zeke leaned
over to untie the boots he'd worn on the boat. The blast caused
David to jump to the side, knocking down Andy. There was an
acrid smell of gasoline in the air. Andy looked up at him with a
dazed expression.

"Are you hurt?" David asked.

"What happened?" Andy mumbled.

David quickly inspected his son. There was no sign of blood.
He felt his own face and head. Nothing. He stumbled to his feet.
Zeke was sitting on the ground rubbing his ears and didn't seem to
be visibly hurt. Rushing around the car, David saw his father lying
on the ground.

"Dad!"

Carter didn't move. There were several cuts on his father's head,
and blood was beginning to run down his face. David gently lifted
his father's chin.

"Dad, can you hear me?"

Carter mumbled and groaned.

"What . . . ," he managed as he raised his head slightly.

Zeke joined him. "How bad is it?"

"Cut up, but he's conscious."

"Katelyn's hurt," Zeke said. "And it looks bad."

David stood and looked in the direction of the boat and trailer. All that remained of the boat was a twisted frame and one pontoon that was half submerged in the water. Bits of varnished wood from the seats were scattered about. Robbie was on the ground next to Katelyn.

"Call an ambulance!" he yelled at David.

David called 911. While he gave the operator their location, he stepped closer to Robbie, who was applying pressure to the side of Katelyn's neck with the bandanna he'd been wearing on the boat. When his brother repositioned his hand, there was a quick squirt of blood. David finished the call.

"They're on their way," he said. "Is it her carotid artery?"

Robbie didn't look up. "No, but it's close. I have to keep applying pressure."

Katelyn's eyes were closed. Not far from her head was a larger piece of metal that looked like it came from the motor.

"What caused the explosion?" David asked, all the while praying silently that Katelyn and Robbie's unborn child was unharmed.

"There must have been a gas leak that hit a hot pipe and ignited the extra gas can," Robbie said.

"Daddy!" Andy called out.

David rushed back to his son, who was leaning against the car. He was beginning to quiver and shake. David put his arms around him.

"What's wrong with me?" Andy asked in a trembling voice.

"I'm here," David replied.

Zeke joined them. "I put your dad in the car, and he is sitting up."

David guided Andy to the car and held him in his lap in the passenger seat until the ambulances arrived. The boy alternated between shivering and sobbing for several minutes before calming down to a few sniffles. Carter seemed to have fallen asleep but roused when Zeke touched his shoulder.

"Dad, are you hurting?" David asked.

"No, but I'm having trouble keeping my eyes open."

The small cuts on Carter's head had stopped bleeding, but he nodded off again.

"I don't know what's going on," Zeke said. "I can't see anything seriously wrong with him."

"They'll check him out at the hospital," David said.

From where he was sitting in the car, David couldn't see Robbie and Katelyn. Zeke shuttled back and forth with news.

"She's conscious and asking about everyone else," Zeke said when the sirens from the ambulances could be heard in the distance. "I told her Carter was shaken up but okay."

One set of EMTs went to Katelyn, and another pair came over to the car.

"My son and I are okay," David said to a young woman. "But please check my father. He's recovering from a brain hemorrhage."

The ambulances left with Katelyn and Carter. Everyone else piled into David's car.

"Did the EMTs say anything to you about Katelyn?" David asked Robbie.

"No. They continued to apply pressure to the gash on her neck. There was also a knot forming on the side of her head, but she's conscious. She was able to tell them her name and birthday. I told them that she's pregnant."

David drove as fast as he dared. He called Nan, told her what happened, and reassured her that he and Andy were shaken up but okay.

"Katelyn and Dad are in ambulances on the way to the hospital."

"Oh no!" she gasped. "How badly are they hurt?"

David told her what he could.

"I want to talk to Andy," Nan said.

David handed the phone to his son, who was sitting in the passenger seat with his legs curled beneath him.

"Hi, Mom," he said in a quivering voice.

David couldn't hear what Nan was saying, but Andy kept nodding his head until he handed the phone back to David.

"I'll drop Courtney off at Emmaline's house and meet you at the hospital," Nan said.

The thirty-minute drive to New Hanover Medical Center seemed to take twice as long. David spent the time praying. Nan was waiting for them at the emergency entrance to the hospital. She grabbed Andy and wrapped her arms around him.

———

Katelyn was groggy but became more alert as the IV fluids flowed into her body. She started to raise her hand toward her neck.

"No," said an EMT with closely cropped hair who was sitting beside her. "Try not to touch it."

"How bad is it?" she asked.

"It's a nasty cut. Your husband did a good job of stanching the wound."

"He's good at everything."

The EMT adjusted the IV bag. "Just relax and lie still until we get you to the hospital."

Katelyn closed her eyes, then immediately opened them. "I'm pregnant," she said.

"Your perfect husband told us that as well," the EMT said with a smile. "And he made sure we knew you have a knot on your head that's going to be sore in the morning."

"I'm glad to be alive," she sighed.

"You're lucky," the man at her feet said. "That boat was blown to bits. It was hard to tell much about it from what was left."

Katelyn was fully awake when they rolled her into the hospital. A woman doctor examined her and removed the bandage applied by the EMTs.

"It's going to take twelve to fifteen stitches to close the laceration," the doctor said. "Do you want me to do it or wait until we can bring in a plastic surgeon?"

"How technical is it going to be?" Katelyn asked.

"It's a clean opening," the doctor answered.

The young woman seemed confident.

"You do it," Katelyn said. "I'm pregnant. Should I have an ultrasound to check on the babies?"

"Where do you hurt?"

"Only my head and neck."

The doctor examined Katelyn's abdominal area. "Every place else appears fine. There's no sign of trauma to your abdomen, but you should follow up with your obstetrician as soon as you can."

Robbie arrived as the doctor was administering a local anesthetic to Katelyn's neck. She winced at the stinging pain. Robbie introduced himself to the ER physician.

"How is she doing?" he asked.

"I'm about to stitch her up. It's a deep laceration but not life-threatening."

Katelyn couldn't see Robbie while the physician worked, but it was reassuring to know he was close by. Once she finished, the doctor probed the right side of Katelyn's skull. Her hand came away with a sliver of wood between her fingers.

"Whatever hit you left a calling card," she said. "It's my guess you were struck in the neck by a piece of wood."

Robbie leaned over for a look.

"We were on the marsh in our old skiff," he said. "That looks like it came from one of the seats."

The doctor handed the sliver of wood to Robbie and patted Katelyn on the hand.

"There's no treatment needed for the knot on your head, and as young and healthy as you are, I don't recommend a blood transfusion. Your body will bounce back quickly. Is there anyplace else that hurts now?"

Katelyn's neck was numb. She had a headache.

"No, I don't think so."

"If something changes, don't hesitate to come back in," the doctor said. "I'll prepare your discharge papers."

"Thanks."

Once the doctor left, Katelyn looked up at Robbie. "We could have been killed," she said. "And you were closer to the boat than I was."

"I know. My ears were ringing for a few minutes, but there's not a scratch on me."

"How's your dad?"

"They're checking him out. David is with him. Nan took Andy home. He's physically okay but really shaken up."

"I hate that. This was such a good day for him."

"Except you caught the biggest fish."

Katelyn managed a slight smile. "Only a fisherman would think about that."

Robbie was silent for a moment. "I wonder if we ought to contact the sheriff's department and ask them to take a look at the boat."

"Why?"

"That old motor doesn't run much gas through it, and we couldn't have had more than ten gallons on board in the extra tank. I'd like to know how it happened."

———

Because of Carter's recent health issues, he received a close inspection by the doctor assigned to him. The middle-aged physician removed a few tiny shards of metal and cleaned the wounds. No stiches needed. Mentally, Carter bounced back and was as alert as he'd been when they began the day.

"We're going to send you home, Mr. Cobb," the doctor said.

"That's good news. I didn't want to kick anyone out of my old room."

"Will someone be with him for the next twenty-four to forty-eight hours?" the physician asked David.

"He has a caregiver, and my brother and sister-in-law are staying in the house as well."

One of Zeke's relatives was in the waiting area. She agreed to take Zeke and Carter home while David waited to check on Katelyn and Robbie.

"Don't worry about coming by the house later," Zeke said to David. "Robbie and I will be taking care of everything. You need to be with Andy."

"Thanks. I'll call you."

David was sitting in a chair in the waiting area when a deputy sheriff came over to him.

"Mr. David Cobb?" the deputy asked.

"Yes."

"We got a call about the boating accident. Because it took place on a public waterway, I need to fill out a report."

"Sure."

David was answering questions when Robbie appeared with Katelyn, who had a bandage on her neck. David motioned them over and introduced them to the deputy.

"Your brother says you were closest to the boat when the explosion happened," the deputy said to Robbie. "What did you see?"

"I didn't see anything. I was bent over and about to start turning the winch that pulls the boat onto the trailer when there was a loud boom. The next thing I saw was my wife on the ground near the back of my truck. After that I was focused on giving her first aid."

"Any problems with the boat earlier in the day?"

"No. It was an aluminum pontoon at least fifty years old with a motor that had to be over twenty years old. The motor can be hard to start, but this morning it fired right up."

"And it was fifty horsepower?"

"Yes, with a fifteen-gallon gas tank that was probably about half full. We also kept a ten-gallon can of gas on the boat as reserve fuel."

"Your brother said your truck was damaged. Do you think it's operational?"

"I don't know, but I'd like to unhook the trailer and see if I can drive it home," Robbie said. "I guess we'll need to put what's left of the boat and trailer on a flatbed and haul them off later."

"You might not want to leave the truck out there overnight. That's a very remote area."

"I'll drive you after we take Katelyn home and I make sure Andy is fine," David volunteered.

The deputy gave Robbie his card. "Call me if you need help or have any other questions."

Robbie stared at the card for a moment. "Would it make sense to have someone take a look at the damage to the boat and try to figure out what happened?" he asked.

"Not unless you suspect it wasn't an accident."

"We don't have a reason to suspect anything except an accident and don't want to waste anyone's time," David said.

"I don't know." Robbie shook his head. "It was a very big explosion for such a small motor and that amount of gas."

"You'd be surprised what gas can do if it's under pressure when it goes off," the deputy replied. "My grandpa's metal outbuilding blew up when the starter on his tractor malfunctioned. There was stuff scattered across an acre of ground."

The deputy left. Katelyn sat up front in the passenger seat for the short ride to Carter's house.

"Is the baby all right?" David asked her.

"The ER doctor thinks so, but I'm going to follow up with my obstetrician to make sure."

"That's a relief."

"The whole situation could have been so much worse. Imagine if we'd all been on the boat when it blew up. It could have—" Katelyn stopped.

"Yes, there's a lot to be thankful for."

They rode in silence.

"Let us know how Andy is doing," Katelyn said when they pulled into the driveway.

"And if you don't want to get my truck this afternoon, we can wait until tomorrow," Robbie said. "I mean, only a very evil person would steal or vandalize my truck after seeing what happened to the boat."

When David arrived home, Nan was in her study. He gave her a quick update about Katelyn and the baby and Carter.

"Thank God," she said.

"Amen. Where's Andy?"

"Playing a video game in his room. Once he got home, he bounced back quickly. He even used my phone to call Noah and tell him what happened. It's already moving from an event to a story."

David went upstairs. Andy paused the game.

"Hey, Dad," he said. "How are Pops and Aunt Kate?"

"They're okay. It took a few stitches to close the cut on her neck. They checked Pops over and sent both of them home."

Andy placed the controller near the monitor.

"Why was I shaking and crying so much?" he asked. "I couldn't stop."

"You were in shock and not in control of your mind and body."

"I was glad when it ended."

"Me too."

Andy looked down in thought for a bit before he spoke. "Is Pops going to buy a new boat?"

"If he doesn't, then either Uncle Robbie or I will."

"Okay," Andy said, the relief in his voice easy to read. "Just because the old one blew up doesn't mean we shouldn't go fishing again."

"You're right."

"May I go with you when you pick it out? I'd like to go to the boat store and see what they have."

"Absolutely."

Downstairs, David relayed his conversation with Andy to Nan.

"Andy is resilient," she said. "But we're going to have to keep a close eye on him and make sure he talks about what he's feeling and be ready to help."

David checked his phone. There was a text message from Robbie asking about Andy. He told Nan about returning to the marsh to retrieve Robbie's truck.

"Are you sure you should do that now?" she asked.

"I'd rather stay here with you, but Robbie is concerned about his truck."

David sent Robbie a message that he'd be there in fifteen minutes. He went to the refrigerator and took out a bottle of water. Nan followed him.

"One other piece of big news," he said. "While we were on the boat, I settled Zeke's case."

"What? How?"

"Directly with the chemist who stole the formula. The drug manufacturer isn't involved. Dr. Chappelle is going to pay $400,000 to resolve the claim. He's coming in Monday with a check and will sign the paperwork. I believe he was serious, but we won't know for sure until the check clears the bank."

"Is Zeke satisfied?"

"Yes. He's ready to put it behind him."

"You were right," Nan said, nodding her head.

"Even though I was wrong about how it was going to happen."

Nan touched him on the arm. "Your job was to believe. That's the important part. The rest was up to the Lord."

David picked up Robbie in Nan's minivan. Zeke's vehicle was parked in the driveway.

"I asked Zeke to watch Dad while we're gone," Robbie said.

"How is he?"

"Watching a fishing show with Zeke. After what just happened, I would have thought they'd choose something else, but that's what they wanted to do."

They got in the minivan.

"Decided not to drive your car?" Robbie asked.

"Yeah, its next destination is the body shop. There were some dents and nicks caused by debris from the explosion. How's Katelyn?"

"Asleep. Physically, she's stable, but her emotional tank is completely drained."

David retraced the route they'd taken that morning. That drive seemed like it had happened days earlier, not hours. He told Robbie about Andy.

"That's good to hear. I was worried this might turn him off from fishing."

"No, he wants to go with us when you buy a new boat."

"Me? I think you need a boat more than I do."

They discussed the right type of craft to buy.

"We won't find anything with those classy wooden seats," David said.

"But we can buy something that's not only suitable for the marsh but also has the capacity to go offshore for short distances on calm days."

They reached the launch site.

"What?" Robbie blurted out.

Once she woke up, Katelyn told Zeke he could go home and rest. She was sitting in the sunroom when she heard the door open.

"I'm out here!" she called out.

When Robbie appeared, the cap on his head was pushed back. He plopped down on the short couch across from her.

"The boat and trailer are gone," he said.

"And your truck?"

"Just like we left it. The back glass was cracked, the right rear tire was flat, and there were a bunch of dents and scratches caused by flying debris. We changed the tire, and it was drivable. It's sitting in the driveway."

"That's good. But what about the boat and trailer?"

"Between the time the ambulances arrived and when we returned, someone unhooked the trailer and hauled it off, along with what was left of the boat. There were a few small pieces of aluminum lying around. We couldn't figure out why someone would want the boat and a messed-up trailer, except to sell for scrap. I would have given them away."

"Somebody saved you the trouble."

"I guess. But I would have liked a closer look at the motor."

"You heard what the deputy said about his grandfather's tractor."

"I know, but now I can't satisfy my curiosity." Robbie leaned back against the blue-striped cushion. "I'm going to take a shower and wash off this day."

"Along with the bug repellent. Did anyone mention the smell when you were with me at the hospital?"

"No, I guess they thought I'd worked on a road crew all week."

While Robbie was cleaning up, Katelyn stepped outside to take a look at his truck. Already old, it now looked like it had escaped from a junkyard. There were a few pieces of metal in the bed, including a small rounded piece of one of the pontoons. Katelyn picked it up and caught a faint whiff of road tar. She held it closer to her nose. Zeke's bug repellent was so potent it stuck to anything someone touched.

THIRTY-TWO

DAVID ARRIVED AT THE OFFICE EARLY ON MONDAY morning. There had been a short article in the local paper on Sunday about a "Boating Incident" near Randolph Creek. Everyone's name was spelled correctly except Katelyn's, who was listed as Katherine Martin-Cobb. The reporter hadn't contacted David but used the sheriff department's report to write the article. The cause of the damage to the boat was listed as a "gasoline explosion," with only "minor injuries" to bystanders. The mysterious disappearance of the debris was omitted.

David called Zeke.

"Robbie is staying with Carter, so I'll be here at home waiting for your call," Zeke replied. "When I talked to Robbie, he told me about the boat and trailer."

"Yeah."

"I'm going to call a couple of guys I know who deal in scrap and give them a heads-up in case someone comes in to sell it."

"Keep your phone close by."

"Sure thing."

As soon as the call ended, Candy stuck her head through the door. "I don't read the paper, but my daddy told me Carter's boat was damaged in a fire this weekend. Then I saw your car. Are you okay?"

"Yes, but Katelyn suffered a nasty cut to her neck that took fifteen stitches to close. She probably won't be in today."

Meredith joined them, and David provided the details.

"I'm so glad Katelyn and the baby are okay," Candy said.

"And the last thing Carter needed was something bad on top of the brain hemorrhage," Meredith said.

"It could have been a lot worse. The good news is that while we were out on the boat, we settled Zeke Caldwell's case. Dr. Chappelle, the chemist who stole Zeke's formula, is coming in today to sign the paperwork. That's my first order of business. Then I'm calling my insurance company and taking my car to the body shop."

Ten minutes after nine o'clock, David's cell phone vibrated. It was Emerson Chappelle.

"I'm leaving the bank and on my way to your office," the chemist said. "Do you have the settlement papers ready?"

"Not quite yet," David replied. "Can you come around eleven o'clock?"

"Okay."

In the midst of throwing something together the best he could, David told Candy to hold all his calls.

"Okay, and Katelyn called and said she's on her way. She should be here any minute."

David was surprised and didn't want to put too much on his sister-in-law, but she could at least check what he'd done for obvious errors. As soon as he heard the sound of her voice in the reception area, he went out to see her. She was talking to Candy and Meredith. There was a large white bandage on the left side of her neck.

"Emerson Chappelle is going to be here around eleven," he said.

"That's why I'm here. Have you started drafting the settlement documents?"

"Yes."

"Forward what you've done and let me check it."

Relieved, David sent her the current version of the paperwork. An hour later a reply popped up in his in-box. Not surprisingly, the modified version was cleaner and more comprehensive. He called Zeke and told him to come to the office. A few minutes later, Candy buzzed him.

"Dr. Chappelle is here."

David went to the reception area. Chappelle was wearing dark pants and a light blue shirt. He jumped up from the chair when David appeared.

"Is everything ready?" he asked. "I want to get this over with as quickly as possible."

"Yes. Come to our conference room where you can read the proposed settlement documents."

"Where is Mr. Caldwell?"

"On his way."

David left Chappelle with the papers and stepped into Katelyn's office.

"Chappelle is reading the settlement papers. Zeke should be here shortly."

"Did you see the check?"

"Not yet."

"Ask him for it."

Katelyn and David entered the conference room. Dr. Chappelle had the settlement documents in his hand. When he saw them, the papers slipped from his fingers onto the table.

"What happened to you?" he asked.

Katelyn didn't want to share information with the chemist. "I had an accident this weekend," she replied stiffly.

"It was in the local newspaper," David said. "Remember, I told you our family was fishing on the marsh when we settled the case. As we were taking the boat out of the water, the engine blew up, and a piece of wood or metal sliced open Katelyn's neck. We ended up at the emergency room—"

"It's not necessary to go into all those details," Katelyn cut in.

"No, I want to know," Chappelle said. "That's terrible. Was anyone else injured?"

"My father had a few superficial cuts on his head from flying glass. My eleven-year-old son was in shock but bounced back. Everyone else was okay."

Chappelle shook his head. "I'm sorry that happened and appreciate both of you coming in today to take care of our business."

"Ms. Martin-Cobb prepared the settlement documents," David said. "Ask her any questions while I check to see if Mr. Caldwell has arrived."

David left the conference room. Instead of looking at the settlement papers, Chappelle continued to stare at Katelyn's neck.

"How many stitches did it take?"

"Fifteen."

"And it missed the carotid artery."

"If it hadn't, I wouldn't be here," she said. "I'd be dead."

She could see Chappelle swallow.

"May I see the settlement check?" she asked.

"Certainly."

Chappelle reached into the front pocket of his shirt, took out a cashier's check, and placed it on the table. It was made payable to "Cobb and Cobb, Attorneys, and Zeke Caldwell" in the amount of

$400,000. Katelyn had seen many checks for significantly greater amounts, but given the circumstances, this one seemed extraordinarily large. Chappelle returned it to his pocket.

"Please finish looking over the settlement papers, and let me know if you have any questions," she said.

Chappelle flipped through the sheets to the signature page. "Once this is signed, you'll dismiss the lawsuit?" he asked.

"Yes. With prejudice, which means Mr. Caldwell can't refile."

"I saw that."

"But I can't give you legal advice about the settlement papers. You'd need your own attorney to do that."

"I understand."

"Which is why there's a paragraph toward the end confirming your opportunity to do so and waiving that right."

"That's fine."

Chappelle checked his phone. "I need to leave for another appointment in a few minutes. Can I give you the check and sign? You can provide me with a completed copy of the paperwork after Mr. Caldwell signs too."

"Let's wait as long as possible," she said.

The door opened, and David entered with Zeke.

"Does Mr. Caldwell need to read this paperwork?" Chappelle asked in a harried voice.

"That would be my recommendation," Katelyn said.

"But you prepared it as his attorney," Chappelle noted, taking a pen from his pocket. "I'll sign so we can wrap this up. Forward one to me. I'll send you the correct email address. That's where you can send the paperwork dismissing the lawsuit. I assume you'll let Brigham-Neal know as well."

"Yes, by the end of the day."

Chappelle signed the settlement, reached in his pocket, and handed the check to David. Then, without another word, he left. Katelyn looked at David and Zeke.

"That was the oddest settlement meeting of my career," Katelyn said. "Not that we should have circled up for a group hug, but he couldn't wait to get out of here."

"Do you want to read the settlement?" David asked Zeke.

"Not if you and Katelyn say everything is okay."

"We do."

Zeke signed on his signature line. There was a place for David to sign as Zeke's attorney.

"I'll make copies for everyone," David said as he picked up the papers and left the room.

Zeke examined the check. "Is this real?"

"Yes," Katelyn replied. "We'll deposit it in our trust account and issue a check for your portion—$300,000."

Zeke didn't say anything. David returned with the copies.

"Are you sure a hundred thousand dollars is enough for your fee?" Zeke asked. "Nothing would have happened if you hadn't helped me. I feel like I should pay you more."

"That would only be fair if we'd helped develop the remedy," David replied with a smile. "I need to pay Dr. Sparrow for his time, but you'll also receive a partial refund for the expense money you deposited with the firm. Meredith will run the numbers and let me know."

"I thank both of you from the bottom of my heart," Zeke said.

He reached in his pocket, took out a vial, and handed it to Katelyn. "I brought this for you. I was going to give it to you later at the house but wanted you to have it first thing so you can start using it immediately. Put a few drops on your cut three times a day, and you'll be amazed. You won't be able to see any scar."

Katelyn unscrewed the top. It was odorless.

"Will it sting?"

"Maybe a touch, but that's just to let you know it's working. David and Robbie would brag about a scar on their neck and how close they came to dying, but as a woman, I'm sure you have a different perspective."

"You're right about that."

After Zeke left, David and Katelyn stayed in the conference room.

"Are you ready for my apology?" Katelyn asked, sitting up straighter in the chair.

David held up his hands. "No, I'm just glad it worked out."

"Here it is anyway. You were right and I was wrong about the case settling quickly on the way to court. I'm still not comfortable with your process, but I can't argue with the result. That's what ultimately matters. The client is satisfied and justice was done."

David picked up the check. "Katelyn, I couldn't have done any of this without you. I'm going to split the fee fifty-fifty with you."

Katelyn's mouth dropped open. "That's not necessary or justified. I bailed on you and refused to take responsibility for the case."

"Only in words. Without you, I wouldn't have considered taking it in the first place. You drafted the complaint and offered advice and input from beginning to end that really helped."

"You're talking about fifty thousand dollars."

David smiled. "I'm capable of correctly dividing one hundred by two. You and Robbie have a lot of expenses coming up. New baby, new house. I think it would be perfect if your new job could start with a big blessing."

Tears appeared in Katelyn's eyes. "But Robbie owes you money—"

"He and I will take care of that," David said. "I have a plan."

Emerson nervously shifted in place as he sat on the bench overlooking the river. He was six minutes late. His phone vibrated with an unknown caller.

"Hello," he said.

"You're late," Jerry said.

"I'm here. I had to wrap everything up at the lawyer's office. Are you coming?"

"No, but I see you. Is it done?"

"Yes."

"Who was at the meeting?"

"The two lawyers and Zeke Caldwell. The woman attorney was injured yesterday and had a bandage on her neck due to an explosion on their boat."

"And you should thank me because there's no evidence that could be traced to you. We had to be ready for all contingencies."

"That was unnecessary. I called you in plenty of time."

"When will you send confirmation of the settlement to our friend in Texas?"

"By the end of the day he'll receive a copy of the documents and dismissal of the lawsuit."

"And our payment?"

"I've purchased the bitcoins, and I'm ready to make the transfer upon your instructions."

The phone was silent for a few seconds. Emerson licked his lips.

"I'm texting you the account number now."

The message popped up.

"And after the transfer I won't hear from you again?" Emerson asked.

"Unless we're needed in the future. Thanks for the business."

The call ended. Emerson executed the transfer. He had less money in the bank than when he'd graduated from college. But he wasn't an accessory to murder.

He stayed on the bench watching the ships navigate up the river for thirty minutes. Then, reaching into the front pocket of his pants, he took out a burner phone he'd purchased over the weekend and placed a call. A woman answered.

"Detective Jenkins," she said.

"This is Emerson Chappelle. I made the transfer and have the account number. When I was at the lawyer's office, I saw that Katelyn Martin-Cobb was injured in the neck when their family boat blew up on Saturday. I'm sure the people I told you about last week were behind it. The local contact basically admitted it when I talked to him."

"I'd flagged the report of the incident when it came into our office because of the names of the people and the report you filed last week. Forensics will examine any debris for evidence of explosives."

"What do I do now?"

"Did you record the most recent conversation?"

"Yes."

"Come to the office and we'll archive it with the others you provided. We've been in touch with the FBI and local law enforcement agencies in Texas. Because there is interstate activity, the federal authorities will likely be involved."

Hearing that made Emerson feel better. When he decided to contact the police, he was terrified about repercussions. But until Lance Tompkins was removed from his life, he'd never feel safe.

"I'm on my way."

THIRTY-THREE

THEY HELD THE CELEBRATION AT CARTER'S HOUSE.
Everyone was present. After dinner, Zeke took Andy and Courtney
into the backyard to play with Charlie. David ate a final bite of coconut cream pie and sighed with contentment.

"Thanks again," Katelyn said to him.

"You're welcome," he replied.

"And I approved the fee split after he already did it," Carter
added. "Because I would have suggested it anyway."

"Credit given, Dad," David said with a smile.

"Yes, big brother," Robbie said. "It was a classy, generous move.
One that Katelyn might deserve but I don't, based on the boat business fiasco. We need to make arrangements to—"

"David and I talked about that weeks ago," Nan cut in. "We've
forgiven that debt and moved on. Everyone at this table has a clean
slate."

"Especially me," Katelyn said with a glance at Robbie. "Please get
your journal. I want all of you to hear what God is doing in my life."

David heard Nan sniffling as Katelyn described how Robbie
and the Lord lovingly pursued her soul.

"That is so beautiful," Nan managed when Katelyn showed

them the sketch of Robbie on the wooden bench and read his prayer. "And I love your drawings. Please show them to Courtney."

"Sure," Robbie replied. "But she's already passed me."

"It's your heart I want her to see," Nan said.

"And Nan spoke too quickly when she said your debt was forgiven," David said to Robbie. "I told Katelyn the other day that I had a plan to deal with it."

"What's that?" Robbie asked, raising his eyebrows.

"You're going to work it off spending time with Andy and Courtney. I'm not sure about the hourly rate, but we can negotiate that later. You'll receive overtime if you include Dad in the mix."

"I also approve that decision even though I didn't have any input into it," Carter piped up.

"Done," Robbie said.

David held up his right index finger. "One other condition. You have to agree that we'll go in together on a new boat. I know it's risky to have a partner on a boat deal, but I think it will help us work through some of the remaining issues in our relationship."

Robbie looked at Katelyn and shrugged.

"I don't think I have a choice," he said to her.

"Obviously not," she answered.

"And all God's people said, 'Amen!'" Carter added.

David and Katelyn were in the conference room. Now seven months pregnant with twins and her abdomen growing rapidly in size, Katelyn scrolled through her laptop. Zeke's treatment had proven effective, and there was virtually no sign of a scar on her neck. Carter, who was coming into the office a couple of days a week, not to practice law but to assist with client development, joined them.

"A friend at the police department called," Carter said. "The FBI has made multiple arrests based on grand jury charges in North Carolina and Texas."

"What about Emerson Chappelle?" Katelyn asked.

"I don't know, but apparently this ended up going way beyond blowing up my old boat and trailer. The detective said there were all kinds of racketeering and other crimes that occurred all over the country."

Katelyn and David had learned of the criminal investigation about a month after the explosion. A local detective sat down with David and told him an informant had come forward but didn't identify him. Katelyn immediately suspected it was Chappelle, but no one at the police department would confirm it.

"Maybe now we can thank Chappelle," David said. "By settling Zeke's case, he saved our lives."

"After putting us in danger by stealing Zeke's formula," Katelyn responded. "It looks like he went into business with an organized crime syndicate."

"And regretted it."

"I'm just grateful we're alive and well," Carter said.

"Yes," Katelyn said. "That's the main thing. And if David's right, maybe there's a reason to thank Chappelle down the road."

The conference room phone buzzed. David pressed the receive button.

"Annalisa Brighton is on the phone," Candy said. "She wants to talk to both of you."

"We'll take it," David said.

"I came across something a couple of days ago that will interest you," Annalisa said. "Brigham-Neal has pulled Relacan off the market."

"What?" Katelyn asked.

"Turns out in some patients it triggers an adverse kidney reaction and multiple people ended up on dialysis. A class-action lawsuit has been filed against the drug company."

"I wonder if Zeke should stop selling his remedy," David said.

"Possibly," Annalisa replied. "But there's always been the chance of a material difference given how they manufactured Relacan and Zeke's reliance on all-natural ingredients. I suggest he complete the sort of comparative chemical analysis we discussed when we first met."

"He can afford the testing," David said. "Do you know where it should be done?"

"No, but I'll help him find a place. Since it's not going to be for purposes of litigation, that will make it easier to set up and will cost less. Tell him to call me."

"Oh, and thanks again for putting me in touch with your sister," Katelyn said. "She's been a great resource on twins."

"You're welcome. Delana is the expert witness when it comes to that subject."

The call ended.

"No more money for Dr. Chappelle from Brigham-Neal," David said.

"And another reason you were right to settle the case when we did. Chappelle's patent turned out to be worthless and not worth defending," Katelyn added.

For the first time in months, Emerson sat on the deck of his beach house without fear. He rested his arms on the Adirondack chair and stared at his narrow view of the ocean. It was a calm, cool day. He was wearing a light sweatshirt and shorts. When he received the call that Lance was in federal custody in Texas, he wasn't sure how to respond. Part of him wanted to shout, but mostly he was numb. Maintaining the charade that everything was fine between them while the investigation unfolded had resulted in many sleepless nights.

They'd received one more decent royalty payment from Brigham-Neal before concerns about Relacan and its effect on the kidneys started to surface. When the drug company suspended further payments, it prompted a scary phone call with Lance. Not knowing what to do or say, Emerson began to sob so violently from all the sources of pressure that he couldn't talk. After listening for a few seconds, Lance hung up and sent him a text directing him to keep his lawyer informed about the situation.

The FBI agent who called about the arrests of Lance, Nick, Jerry, and their associates had further good news. There was a strong likelihood the government would be able to recoup the bitcoin payment Emerson had made to Jerry. Federal law enforcement authorities had made considerable progress in penetrating the veil surrounding cryptocurrency. Money was tight, and Emerson needed an infusion of cash.

His phone, which was resting on an arm of the chair, vibrated. It was David Cobb. Per instructions from his law enforcement handlers, Emerson hadn't communicated with anyone about the investigation. But he was curious and answered the call.

"We know the grand juries in North Carolina and Texas have issued charges and arrests have been made," the lawyer said. "And by answering the phone, I know you're not in jail."

"Correct, but I can't say anything else."

"Understood. May I tell you something?"

"Uh, sure."

"We've put together the pieces of the puzzle, and I wanted to thank you."

Emerson didn't know what to say. He was silent for several moments.

"Are you still there?" the lawyer asked.

"Yes."

"And if you get to the point that you want or need to talk to someone, I'm available. Not as a lawyer, but as a person who won't require an explanation of what's gone on."

Emerson bit his lower lip. He had no friends, no confidants, no one he could trust.

"Are you serious?" he managed.

"I am. And you have my promise that I will take your call anytime, day or night."

Emerson took a deep breath before he spoke. "Mr. Cobb, I'm sorry."

"To hear you say that isn't why I called, but it's a good start to the future."

"I hope so."

"Good-bye."

When Emerson looked again at the waves, he was able to feel a tiny bit of enjoyment at the beautiful scene.

———

A month later, Katelyn left the office and drove to the building site on the marsh property. The construction crew had finished the foundation and were framing up the walls on the first floor. A few minutes later, Robbie joined her. They held hands as they slowly walked to the front elevation and faced the house. Katelyn was seeing the doctor on a weekly basis. She was ready for the pregnancy to end and motherhood to begin.

"Does it look like the sketch in my journal?" Robbie asked.

"Better," Katelyn answered. "Your sketch and our notes didn't include the Jack and Jill bathroom for the children's bedrooms."

"Or the hot tub on the side deck. Are you still good with Spencer and Sarah as names for the babies?"

"Unless you want to go with Jedidiah and Joanna."

Katelyn smiled. They'd turned Carter's house into a newborn nursery. The process both excited and energized her father-in-law. A cool breeze from the marsh enveloped them.

"Are we ready for this?" she asked.

"The house?"

"No, being parents."

Robbie released her hand, put his right arm around her shoulders, and pulled her closer. "We're not the same people we were a year ago, and we have love to give from a place we didn't know existed."

Katelyn looked up at him with shining eyes. "Will you draw a sketch in your journal of this moment?"

"Are you sure?"

"Yeah, just be kind to the mother of your children."

Robbie gave her shoulders another gentle squeeze. "Always and forever."

ACKNOWLEDGMENTS

WRITING *RELATIVE JUSTICE* WAS A COLLABORATIVE effort. Those who contributed include my wife, Kathy, and my son, Jacob, from my actual family, along with Becky Monds and Deborah Wiseman, members of my fictional family.

DISCUSSION QUESTIONS

1. "Letting go" is an ongoing theme with several characters. They must each loosen their grip on something they want and accept the reality of the present. Letting go requires trust. What are some things the characters needed to let go of? How did it impact their lives? What areas of your life might require you to let go and have faith?

2. Robbie is much like the prodigal son. He borrowed and squandered large sums of money from his dad and David. Eventually he wanted to repay his debts but was told they were forgiven. What "debts" have you incurred that someone else has absolved? Have you forgiven someone of their debt to you?

3. David suggests he and Katelyn "put out a fleece" to determine what to do when making a business decision. This is a biblical term used in Judges 6:40 to intuit the will of God. What did you think of David's decision to implement this practice with his business? How do you seek God's will in your own life?

4. Nan's passion for healthy relationships and her passion for God is evident. Having a spouse, family member, or friend

carry you through times of complacency or doubt is a beautiful act of grace. Who in your circle has helped carry you through hard times or encouraged you to seek a higher level of faith?

5. In the Sermon on the Mount, Jesus said, "Settle matters quickly with your adversary who is taking you to court" (Matthew 5:25 niv). How did this verse come into play in the novel? How can it relate to your life when you come into conflict with people who want to ruin your reputation, ruin your finances, or wrongfully point a finger? Discuss what it means to settle first instead of seek litigation.

6. Accountability is a strong theme throughout this book. Do you think Emerson was ultimately made accountable for his actions? Why or why not? In what ways do you shy away from accountability?

7. Robbie's journal entries began as a private time with God. Eventually Katelyn was allowed to read the entries, and her relationships with Robbie and God strengthened. Has journaling helped you or served as a bridge back to God in your life? Have you shared a collaborative journal experience with a spouse or loved one?

8. Zeke says, "Unforgiveness binds our hearts to evil ... I don't want to drag a heavy weight along behind me." Have you been weighed down with resentment or unforgiveness? Can you consider letting it go, even a little at a time?

ABOUT THE AUTHOR

Photo by David Whitlow, Two Cents Photography

ROBERT WHITLOW IS THE BESTSELLING AUTHOR OF legal novels set in the South and winner of the Christy Award for Contemporary Fiction for *The Trial*. He received his JD with honors from the University of Georgia School of Law where he served on the staff of the *Georgia Law Review*.

Website: robertwhitlow.com
Twitter: @whitlowwriter
Facebook: @robertwhitlowbooks